RIVALS

RIVALS

SAM MICHAELS

An Aria Book

First published in the United Kingdom in 2019 by Aria,
an imprint of Head of Zeus Ltd

This paperback edition first published in 2020
by Head of Zeus Ltd

A CIP catalogue record for this book is available from the British Library.

ISBN (PB) 9781838930622
ISBN (E) 9781789542189

Printed and bound in Great Britain by
CPI Group (UK) Ltd, Croydon CRO 4YY

Aria
c/o Head of Zeus
First Floor East
5–8 Hardwick Street
London ECIR 4RG

WWW.ARIAFICTION.COM

To my dearest and beautiful daughter-in-law,
Lauren Eyles.

You are such a special lady – kind, hard-working,
loyal and an absolute stunner!

Thank you for giving me a wonderful gift –
the adorable Finley, my latest grandchild.

It's an honour to have you as a part of my small family.
Love you xxx

Battersea, London, 1934

'Come off it, what the bleedin' hell do I know about running a brothel?' Fanny Mipple said and rolled her eyes.

'How difficult can it be? You see the punters in, send them to a woman and collect the money,' Georgina answered abruptly.

'It ain't as straightforward as that, love,' Georgina's gran, Dulcie, interrupted. 'What if a bloke won't cough up or roughs up one of the women? You can't expect Fanny to deal with that sort of thing.'

Georgina Garrett drew in a long breath and, feeling exasperated, momentarily closed her eyes before opening them again to glance around at the four women sat in her gran's front room. These women, The Maids of Battersea, were supposed to be strong, warrior women. They were meant to aspire to Joan of Arc, the inspiration behind their club name. Yet all Georgina could hear from them were protests, and it seemed to her they were putting obstacles in the way of her plans.

Georgina's eyes set on Fanny. She wasn't surprised by the woman's objections about running the brothels. Georgina thought Fanny had always been feeble. She'd allowed her husband to abuse her and because of his tyrannical ways, Fanny had raised her children in dire poverty.

Dulcie, her beloved gran, slowly pushed herself up from her armchair. The way she hobbled towards the fire showed how much pain her hips were causing. Georgina had noticed they seemed to be getting worse lately, though her gran tried not to show her discomfort. Bending awkwardly, Dulcie stoked the burning coals. The room felt warm and cosy, safe too, but outside a fierce February gale blew and a thin layer of snow made the dirty, tatty street of terraced houses look fresh and white.

As Dulcie settled back in her chair, she broke the tense silence and said, 'I can understand where you're coming from, Georgina, but it's a big ask.'

'It's no more than we deserve,' she replied, her violet eyes steely cold. 'I'm fed up with thieving to put food in the cupboards. We should all be benefiting from the Wilcox business, but instead we're scrimping and scraping to get by.'

She looked at Jane Wilcox, who stared into space with a pained expression. After Jane had put a bullet in her son's head, the poor woman had become a shadow of her former self. Ridding the world of Billy Wilcox had been the most courageous thing Jane had ever done, but it'd affected her badly. She functioned and cared for her two daughters, but it was clear her mind was tormented. Georgina didn't expect any input from her, which she thought was a shame as Jane probably understood better than anyone about how the Wilcox business functioned. After all, it had been Jane's husband who'd been the proprietor of the small empire and been the most feared man in Battersea. That was until the day their son had cruelly killed him. Jane had exacted her own justice on Billy but she hadn't been the same since his death.

Georgina began to pace the small room. As she did, she twisted her mother's wedding ring that she wore on her right hand. An unconscious habit she'd developed whenever she was deep in thought. Her mother had died shortly after birthing Georgina and the ring was the only thing she had that had belonged to her, though her gran told her she'd inherited her mum's striking eyes along with her brains too.

She stopped pacing and stood directly in front of her best friend, Molly, and spoke firmly. 'Billy's business rightfully belongs to you.'

Molly looked up at her with wide eyes but didn't reply.

Georgina continued, 'As Billy's widow, you're entitled. Instead, we're all struggling to make ends meet whilst that weasel, Mickey the bloody Matchstick, is reaping all the benefits!'

'I never married Billy for his money, I had no choice, you know that,' Molly whispered, as if trying to conceal her words from her baby son. Edward gurgled softly in Molly's arms and she looked down, smiling warmly at him.

Edward Wilcox, Georgina thought, the three-month-old baby of Billy Wilcox. The child would never know his father; Jane had seen to that, and it was a blessing. After all, Billy had been a madman, an evil bully who'd left dead bodies, pain and destruction in his wake. Georgina shuddered at the memory of nearly burning to death at the hands of Billy Wilcox and being beaten unconscious on his orders. She pursed her lips and silently hoped that Edward wouldn't take after his father.

Molly looked back up and as if sensing Georgina's thoughts, she said quietly, 'He won't be anything like Billy.'

'No, of course he won't, and yes, I know you didn't marry Billy for his money, Molly, but that's not the point. You're still entitled and I can't understand why we, as The Maids of Battersea, can't take over running it all.'

''Cos none of us know the first thing about operating brothels, loans and protection rackets,' Dulcie snapped and tutted. 'And neither do you.'

'Well, Mickey the fucking Matchstick ain't exactly a genius and he's doing all right!' Georgina hissed.

'Don't take that tone with me, young lady,' Dulcie warned and wagged her finger.

Georgina immediately regretted snapping at her gran and hung her head. 'I'm sorry,' she muttered. 'I'm just frustrated. After everything that Billy put us through, it don't seem right that we ain't getting a penny from what he left, especially his widow and mother. Mickey the Matchstick is never gonna pay out so we need to take over.'

'All right, and I must admit, I'm fed up with thruppence worth of scrag end of mutton. But I don't understand how Mickey came to take charge in the first place?'

'It was my fault, Dul,' Molly said, her voice barely more than a whisper. 'When Billy died, Mickey came to see me and offered to keep things running for me. I told him to do what he had to do. Next thing I know, I got a visit from a couple of blokes warning me to stay away.'

'See, Gran, he just muscled his way in and it's about time we showed him that we won't be intimidated.'

'Huh, the audacity of him! All right, I can see how determined you are, Georgina, so let's hear it then. How exactly do you suppose we do this?' Dulcie asked.

Fanny, Molly and even Jane now looked at her. At last, she thought, she finally had their attention and they were taking her seriously. 'Well, first things first, I need information about Mickey.'

Molly spoke next. 'But shouldn't you be worried about his henchmen?'

'Not Malc and Sid, they're nothing without Billy. As for Knuckles, he's a big bloke but he ain't the sharpest knife in the block.'

'Leave Knuckles to me,' Jane said. The sound of her voice took everyone by surprise and all heads swung around to look at her. 'Knuckles is easily bought. I used to pay him for information and updates on what Billy was up to. Of course, he never divulged that Billy had killed my husband or anything about what Billy had done to you, Georgina, but I know the man won't have any loyalties to Mickey.'

'Let's get Knuckles on our side then. Do you think you can persuade him to meet with me?'

'Yes, no problem,' Jane replied, and for the first time in months, Georgina could see a spark of the woman Jane used to be before she shot her son.

'Great, now we're getting somewhere,' Georgina said and smiled, but she noticed a worried look on her gran's face, and asked, 'What's wrong?'

'I don't know this Mickey bloke and I'm worried about you dealing with him,' Dulcie answered.

'Honestly, Gran, you don't have anything to fear as far as Mickey is concerned. He's nothing but a weedy little arse-licker. You should see him – his face is all scarred on one side and he tries to claim he got injured in the trenches, but truth is, Billy burnt him for back-chatting. What sort of bloke would still be *yes sir, no sir* to the bloke who torched his face, eh? But that's Mickey for you.'

'Is that why you call him a matchstick?' Dulcie asked.

'Yes, and on account of his red hair.'

Dulcie chuckled, but then looking serious again, said, 'I still don't like the idea of you confronting him.'

'I can look after myself. Them boxing lessons me dad gave me when I was young have come in handy over the years. I've already seen that Mickey off once, when him and the others were getting at Molly.'

'Yeah, she did, Dulcie. You should have seen them scarper with their tails between their legs. She knocked Mickey on his arse,' Molly chirped and chortled at the memory.

'Maybe so, but that was a while back and before he got his boots under the table of Billy's business. He'll have ideas of grandeur now and I bet the power has gone to his head. He ain't gonna go quietly,' Dulcie said and shook her head.

'I ain't planning on marching in there and making demands. Don't get me wrong, as a last resort if I have to do that, I will, and if he won't listen to me, perhaps he'll take more notice of this,' Georgina said and smiled wryly as she pulled a pistol from her dress pocket.

She immediately regretted showing the small handgun when she saw Jane baulk and look in horror. It was the gun Lash had given her when he'd promised to come back from travelling with the fair and take her as his wife. Jane had killed Billy with that gun, and now Georgina quickly hid it back in her pocket.

'All right, I feel better knowing you've got that, but we still don't know anything about running the business,' Dulcie said.

Georgina walked over to the window and peered through the net curtains. The street was unusually quiet with just a couple of young boys throwing snowballs at each other. They were the lucky ones who had shoes and coats. She guessed the rest of the kids with bare feet and without warmer clothes would be sheltering indoors. 'I've thought long and hard about this and I believe we can do it. I know it would be unusual for women to be in charge, but we've all shown what we're capable of and we've proved we're stronger together. Come on, ladies, get a bit of fire in your bellies! Let's take back what is ours. Are you with me on this?'

The women glanced at one another then back at her and slowly nodded their heads. It wasn't exactly the reaction Georgina had hoped for but at least they were willing to back her.

'Why you, Georgina? Let's just say we do manage to get rid of Mickey, then surely it should be Molly who runs things,' Fanny said.

Molly was quick to answer. 'Oh, no thanks. I've got my hands full with Edward and I'm more than happy for Georgina to be in control. The thought of running the business scares the life out of me. I'd be bloody useless.'

'Well, what about Jane?' Fanny asked.

Georgina looked at Jane for a response but nothing was forthcoming. 'There's your answer, Fanny. Look, if you don't think I'm the right person for the job, just say so, or perhaps you'd like to have a stab at it yourself?'

'No, I'm sure you could handle it better than me. I'm just

7

saying that it's not rightfully yours. You're not a Wilcox.'

'You're right, but I'd be doing it for all of us. I won't do it if any of you object?'

This time, the women shook their heads and Fanny said, 'I suppose if the only way we're gonna get our hands on the business is by getting rid of Mickey, then you're the woman to do it.'

Dulcie rested her hands across her stomach and began to twiddle her thumbs. 'Looks like you've got our support, Georgina. All I can say is, Gawd help anyone who dares to stand in your way.'

2

Molly had been deep in thought as she'd left Georgina's and was relieved to be home, back indoors and protected from the bitingly cold wind outside. Though home wasn't really home. It was Jane's house, but for now it would have to do. At least her mum and her sisters, Ethel and Charlotte, lived on the same street and they'd been a great help with the new baby. It seemed silly really, her and Edward crammed into the house with Jane and her two daughters, but Molly couldn't face returning to Clapham. The house Billy had bought for them, so grand and luxurious, had become her prison and the thought of Billy's brains splattered up the walls gave her nightmares. She'd never seen a ghost, but what if Billy's soul wandered their house seeking retribution? She hoped he'd got what he deserved and was burning in the depths of hell, but the devil looks after his own. Billy was evil enough to have made a pact with Satan and she wasn't prepared to put herself or her son in harm's way. Molly shivered and though she was now standing in Jane's lounge, she pulled the collar of her coat up around her neck.

'It's cold in here. The fire has gone out,' Jane said as she walked into the room.

Yes, it was cold, but the thought of Billy Wilcox always sent a shiver down Molly's spine.

'The kettle's heating on the stove and it won't be long before I've got this fire roaring. Norman always used to see to the fire but it's another thing I've learnt to do for myself now. Maybe Georgina is right, you know. Maybe we could run the whole thing ourselves.'

Molly had no doubt in Georgina's abilities but she questioned her own. She had a baby to care for and knew nothing about Billy's shady world of prostitutes and violence. She didn't see how she'd be in a position to offer any help, but it was quite ironic really, as in theory, as Billy's widow, it now belonged to her. What Georgina said had made Molly think – she had Edward's future to consider. She didn't want her child growing up with nothing, with hunger in his belly instead of food, the way Fanny had raised her. No, he'd had a bad enough start as it was – being born in a dark, small attic, all alone with Molly fearing she would die. He deserved more, better, and drawing on Georgina's strength, Molly felt ready to fight for what was theirs.

'There you go, the embers are glowing again,' Jane said, and looked from the fire to Molly. 'I can see it in your eyes – you believe we can take on the business, don't you?'

'Yes, Jane, I think we can. I wouldn't attempt it without Georgina, but she's right, it's ours.'

'I'm not sure that Norman would want me having anything to do with the brothels. He never liked me even talking to the women, and if he had a proper grave instead of the cellar in Queenstown Road, he'd be turning in it now. To see me and his daughters living hand to mouth like we are would have broken his heart. He worked hard for us, and now I suppose it's down to me to step up and do the right thing.'

Molly was astounded at the turnaround in Jane. She'd hardly spoken since she'd shot Billy, but Georgina must have provoked something in the woman and she appeared to be more like her old self.

'Don't look so surprised, Molly. I've spent months wallowing in self-pity and guilt, but that's not going to change anything. I'll always feel awful about killing Billy, but we all know it was the right thing to do. No mother wants to take the life of their own flesh and blood, but he killed my husband, and I've no doubt that he would have killed my girls too. Now, it's time to move on. I don't want Norman's death to have been in vain. Norman built the Wilcox name. I'm still Mrs Wilcox, Mrs Norman Wilcox, and you and your son have the Wilcox name too. I refuse to let it be taken away from us.'

Molly gulped. Jane spoke so proudly of her family name, but if the truth was known, Molly hated it. She'd felt so ashamed at marrying Billy but had been too scared to refuse him. The Wilcox name was like a noose around her neck, choking her, suffocating her, snuffing the life out of her. But Billy was dead. Edward would always have his father's name, and for the sake of her son, so would she. Could she come to take pride in it as Jane did? Would she ever be able to hold her head high as Mrs Billy Wilcox? No, never, but it was her name regardless.

Edward cried out from his pram in the hallway. 'I'll see to my grandson; you pour the tea,' Jane said and went to the crying child.

Molly's eyes followed Jane as she left the room. The woman was even walking taller now and her shoulders were pushed back defiantly. It would be the first time Jane had held Edward. She'd always shied away from him, probably because looking at him reminded her of Billy.

Molly quietly walked to the door and peeked through to see Jane rocking the baby in her arms and gazing at him lovingly.

'He looks just like Billy, doesn't he?' Jane said without taking her eyes from the child.

'Yes, I suppose he does.'

'He must never know that I killed his father.'

Something in Jane's eyes made Molly nervous and she reached out for her baby. She didn't want to think that Jane would hurt Edward, but at times the woman seemed unhinged. It made her nervous of sharing the same house and the sooner they reclaimed the business the better. She'd then be in a position to put a safe roof over their heads, away from the madness of Billy's family and their tainted bloodline.

Georgina left her gran to doze in the chair next to the fire and went to her bedroom to think clearly. Now she had the backing of Molly, Jane and Fanny, she could make her move, but she had to do it correctly. There'd be no room for error as even the smallest of mistakes could cost lives. She was under no illusion as to what she was about to embark on, though she'd played it down to her gran. Mickey the Matchstick wouldn't roll over quietly. He'd fight, kill if he had to, but Georgina was prepared to hit back harder.

She walked over to the window and stared out at the white film of snow covering the backyard. It was strange, but the snow never settled over the spot next to the coal bunker where her gran had buried a barrel with her dead husband inside it. She was still shocked at discovering that, after a fierce argument, Dulcie had caved Percy's head in with a pan and then concealed his body. Georgina had grown up never knowing that her window overlooked his unmarked grave. She didn't like the thought of it, but if things didn't go as planned with Mickey the Matchstick, Percy's corpse may end up with some company.

Georgina turned away from the window at the sound of her dad piling through the front door. She could tell by the commotion that he was plastered again. It wasn't unusual these days. The man had been drunk since the day Billy Wilcox had organised for her to be viciously attacked. At the time, they'd thought she wouldn't pull through, but she had, albeit with a few scars and a couple of teeth missing from the back of her mouth. Georgina was well healed now, but her father's drinking had spiralled out of control. Her one hope was Lash. He'd told her he'd lock her dad in one of the caravans until his body was free from the alcohol. It sounded cruel, but Jack needed it and Georgina knew it would be the only way to save him from drinking himself to death.

The thought of Lash brought an uncontrollable smile to her face. She missed him more than she thought she would and, though she kept it to herself, she couldn't wait for him to return. Her bare-knuckle fighter, the brawny gypsy who'd unexpectedly won her heart and promised to take her as his wife. Her stomach flipped and her groin clenched. She remembered his touch, so gentle yet firm, stroking her skin as she tingled in response. His kiss, his lips full and soft, caressing her own and teasing her mouth open with his tongue. His masculine scent, of pine needles and tobacco, of hard graft, and his rippling muscles, broad shoulders and strong arms. She'd felt safe there in his embrace.

It would be weeks, maybe months before Lash would be back in Battersea, and in the meantime, she had business to do. It wasn't easy, but Georgina dismissed all thoughts of him and focused on the task at hand – Knuckles.

Jane said she'd arrange a meeting with the giant of a man. It was the first step and Georgina had to ensure she gained his trust. She couldn't risk Knuckles double bluffing her and running back to Mickey with valuable information that would put them all at risk. It wasn't as if they could offer Knuckles money and pay him for his loyalty. They didn't have much between them, and all the paperwork for the Wilcox assets were in Billy's office, even for the house in Clapham. Jane had never mentioned the house and Molly refused to move back into it, not that Georgina could blame her. It held nothing but bad memories and Billy's blood still stained the sofas. Anyway, Georgina doubted it would still be empty. She assumed Mickey was probably running a brothel or a gambling den from it now.

With little available cash, Georgina wasn't sure how she'd be able to persuade Knuckles to jump Mickey's ship and join forces with her, but one way or another, she had to do it. And if her powers of persuasion failed, she had one last option, she thought, and patted the small handgun in her pocket.

'Georgina, are you coming down for your dinner?' her gran called up the stairs.

Georgina's guts were churning. Nerves, she supposed. She couldn't stomach the thought of food. Instead, she went downstairs and put her coat on.

Her gran came from the kitchen. 'I'm just dishing up. Where are you going?'

'I'm not hungry, Gran. I'll be back in a while. I'm popping out to get a newspaper.'

'You and your newspapers. I don't know what sparked this sudden interest in world affairs. You've got enough to be worrying about here, let alone who's invading who abroad. Go on, bugger off. I'll keep your dinner in the oven. Stay out of trouble.'

Georgina closed the door behind her as her mind raced. *Stay out of trouble,* huh, that was a laugh. She'd be making trouble soon, more trouble than the likes of Mickey the Matchstick had ever seen.

As she turned the corner heading towards Mrs Peterson's shop, her heart thumped harder when she saw Malc and Sid's car parked outside. What were Mickey's men doing there other than robbing the place?

Georgina picked up her pace. Mrs Peterson was a widow thanks to Billy Wilcox and she wouldn't allow his gang to terrorise the woman.

Outside now, she paused and thought about brandishing her gun. But there were two of them and she'd likely get shot. Either that or arrested and she couldn't face being in a police cell again, not after what had happened last time. She dismissed that vile memory and peeked through the glass in the door but Sid blocked her view. She hadn't seen him and Malc since they'd bundled her into a car and beat her half to death. She intended on getting her revenge but now wasn't the right time. They were part of her plan in getting rid of Mickey but she couldn't turn her back on poor Mrs Peterson.

Gulping hard, she heard the bell above the door chime as she opened it.

Sid, still with his back to her, growled, 'The shop is closed. Fuck off.'

'It looks open to me,' she said, undeterred.

Sid turned to look at her, a wicked leer spread across his face. 'Ha, George Garrett, as mouthy as fucking ever.'

Georgina looked past Sid and was surprised when she saw Mickey's flame red hair, his face snarling, and Malc next to him.

'Get her out of here,' Mickey ordered.

Sid went to manhandle Georgina backwards, but she brought her knee up sharply and caught him in the groin. He gasped, doubled over and seethed profanities. She quickly brought her knee up again and grabbed the back of his head and yanked it down at the same time. As she kneed him in the face, the crunch of his nose bone was unmistakable and Georgina smiled.

Malc pulled a gun and pointed it at her, saying, 'You're only alive 'cos Billy told me not to kill you but Billy ain't here now.'

'No, put it away, Malc,' Mickey said. 'The street's busy. There'd be too many witnesses. Anyhow, she ain't worth wasting a bullet on.'

'I'll fucking kill her,' Sid barked, blood running from his nose.

'I'd like to see you try,' Georgina said to him.

Sid went to grab her but Mickey intervened. 'Leave her, let's just collect the money and go.'

'But I ain't letting her get away with this,' Sid said.

'Don't worry, I'll see to it that she doesn't. Right, Mrs Peterson, pay up and we'll leave you in peace.'

The woman rooted in the till and with shaking hands, she handed over some cash.

Mickey stepped towards Georgina. 'Don't get in my way, George, ever, or I'll let Malc put that bullet in you.'

Georgina stepped to one side, her pulse racing. Even though she was armed, she knew it would be suicidal to try and take on all three of them at once.

'I'll be seeing you, George, you can count on it.' Mickey smirked as he passed, Malc and Sid behind him, their eyes blazing at her.

The door closed and she watched as they drove off. Mrs Peterson looked unsteady and grabbed the counter for support.

'Have they done this before?'

'Yes, it's the third time. You're brave, Georgina, seeing to that bloke like that, but there's no way of stopping them. I'll have to shut up shop, sell it or something. With them taking all my money, it's not worth staying open.'

'No, don't do that. I'll make sure this doesn't happen again.'

'You can't, dear, but thanks for trying. I heard him – he threatened you. They won't let you get away with roughing up that man like you did. I don't know about you but I could do with a stiff drink. I've a bottle out the back if you care to join me?'

'No, thank you. If you're all right, I'll get off.'

Georgina paused in the shop doorway, more determined than ever to bring Mickey down now. And she knew she had to get to him before he got to her.

3

It had been a week since Georgina had talked Molly, Fanny and Jane into an attempted takeover of the Wilcox business, and now, as her granddaughter walked into the kitchen, Dulcie thought how magnificent she looked. For most of Georgina's life, in a misguided attempt to protect her from men, Jack had raised his daughter as a boy. She'd been made to wear boys' clothes, been taught to steal like a boy and to fight like one too. It had been less than a year since George had transformed herself into Georgina, and still the sight of her would take Dulcie's breath away. She looked a lot like her mother, only taller and broader, with dark hair that made her stunning eyes stand out. It was a blessing that she took after Sissy in the looks department rather than Jack. Though he was her son and she loved Jack dearly, she was under no illusion. He even said himself that with his sticky-out ears and wonky nose, he'd fallen out of the ugly tree and had hit every branch on the way down.

The long, dark-blue skirt Georgina wore, cut a few inches over her slender ankles, elongated her shape further and, teamed with a structured matching jacket, it gave her a powerful look. She was already a tall woman and the small-heeled shoes added another couple of inches to her impressive stature. She was dressed to make an impact.

'So today's the day?' Dulcie asked, knowing that Jane had arranged for Knuckles to visit her house.

'Yes, and I'm ready for this.'

'Good. You're a strong woman, Georgina, but don't let him fool you.'

'Don't worry, Gran. If Knuckles had half a brain, I might be worried.'

'I take it you've got a plan?'

Before Georgina could answer, they heard Ethel let herself in through the front door and she came bounding into the kitchen.

'I is here now,' the young woman announced with childlike gusto.

'I *am* here now,' Dulcie corrected her.

'Yes, me too,' Ethel said, oblivious to her grammatical mistake.

Dulcie concealed a smile. Ethel was twenty-five, Molly's older sister, and though sweet-natured, she had the mind of a seven-year-old.

'Right, Ethel will sit with you until I get back,' Georgina said as she quickly opened her clutch bag, looked inside and snapped it closed again.

Dulcie knew Georgina was carrying the gun in her bag. It offered some peace of mind but she hoped Georgina wouldn't have to use it.

'You take care, love,' Dulcie called as Georgina marched up the hallway. It was clear her granddaughter was set on a mission. She leaned back in her chair and watched in awe as Georgina took her coat from the newel post and threw it on before wrapping a fur cuff over her shoulders. Dulcie thought Georgina looked as if she'd just stepped out of the page of one of those fancy fashion magazines, rather than being on her way to confront one of the borough's hard men!

Georgina threw a wicked smile over her shoulder before leaving and Dulcie's heart began to race. She had every confidence in her and it wasn't the first time Dulcie had been sat at home waiting for Georgina to return from sorting out a bloke, but this was different. When Georgina had gone to cut out Mike Mipple's tongue, Dulcie had known it would be one on one and wasn't too worried, but this – Georgina could be walking into a trap! She could be taking on the whole gang! When Billy was at the helm, the gang had already made two attempts at destroying Georgina. Granted, Billy was dead now, but what if Mickey wanted to finish what Billy had started?

'Shall I makes us a cup of tea?' Ethel asked.

'Yes, love, that would be nice,' Dulcie answered and plastered on a fake smile, hoping to hide her nerves from Ethel.

Georgina had to come home safely, she just had to! Jack was too pickled to pay the rent, and she wasn't in a fit state to work the streets anymore. She relied on Georgina and she loved the girl dearly.

As Ethel filled the kettle, Dulcie took a long breath and tried to calm herself. She glanced through the back door towards the coal bunker, and though it was ludicrous considering that she'd killed him, she silently prayed. 'Please, Percy, keep my Georgie safe. You never did much for me when you was alive, but please, do this one thing for me. Watch over my girl.'

Georgina strode purposely through the streets of run-down terraced houses and up the small garden path towards Jane's house; but before she had a chance to knock, Jane pulled the door open.

'He's here,' she whispered as Georgina passed her on the step.

'Has he said anything?'

'No, but he looks worried.'

'Good,' Georgina answered. She didn't feel in the least bit nervous as she felt she had the upper hand.

Jane helped her off with her coat and followed her through to the lounge. Knuckles rose to his feet as she walked in and removed his flat cap, then nodded a greeting before throwing his huge frame back onto the sofa.

'Thanks for coming,' Georgina said and smiled charmingly.

'Yeah, well, I suppose I should have come round sooner, you know, checked on Mrs Wilcox and that. Billy would have wanted me to.'

'Yes, I'm sure he would. He loved his mother,' Georgina said, trying her best to sound sincere. She sat on an armchair opposite the large man and kept her clutch bag on her lap. She noticed Jane bite on her lower lip and look at the floor. 'It's been a difficult time for Mrs Wilcox and her daughters. She lost Billy in such tragic circumstances and so soon after the untimely death of her husband, Norman.'

Knuckles fidgeted uncomfortably and looked nervously from side to side. It was no secret that he'd helped Billy hide Norman's body in the basement of the brothel in Queenstown Road. Of course, he couldn't be sure if Mrs Wilcox knew the truth about her husband and the man had no idea that Jane had been the one who'd then killed Billy. The police had put his death down to a bungled burglary.

'It's been very good of you and Billy's friends to keep the business running smoothly, but Mrs Wilcox is ready to take over the reins now. You'll be generously compensated for your time over the past three months and if you'd like to continue working for the Wilcox name, a suitable position would be found for you.'

Knuckles pushed his massive bulk forwards and pointed his chubby finger at Georgina. His brow furrowed as he asked, 'I beg your pardon? Are you suggesting you're taking over?'

'No, I'm not suggesting… I *am* taking over.'

'Look, George—'

'Miss Garrett,' she interrupted.

'Miss Garrett, I ain't running nothing, I'm on Mickey's payroll, that's all. It's him you need to be having this conversation with, but he'll laugh in your face. I ain't being funny, pet, but a woman can't run the business. I know you can handle yourself, but even so, this ain't no place for a lady.'

'I appreciate your concern, Knuckles, and to be honest, I agree with you somewhat. That's why I'd like to make you an offer. Be on my payroll instead of Mickey's.'

'Thanks, but I don't think so. You ain't got a hope in hell of taking over from Mickey. Look, a word of advice – stay clear. He's already talking about getting you done over for what you did to Sid.'

'Jane, would you mind fetching us some coffee?' Georgina asked in a pre-planned ploy to get her to leave the room.

Jane agreed, and once she was alone with Knuckles, Georgina leaned in closer towards him and lowered her voice as she said, 'See this.' She opened her bag and showed Knuckles the contents. 'This is the gun that killed Billy. I fired two bullets. The first one left him breathing, so I fired again and blew his fucking brains out,' she lied. 'I've got four bullets left. Do you still think I need to be worried about Mickey?'

Knuckles rubbed his hand over his sweaty forehead. 'No way, you didn't do it... you didn't kill Billy... did you?'

'Yes, you know there was no love lost between me and him. I'm not going to threaten you to keep your mouth shut, but I am asking you to, for Mrs Wilcox's sake.'

'More like you're worried I'm gonna go back and tell Mickey what you're up to.'

'Worried is a bit too strong a word, but I would prefer to take him with the element of surprise. Either way he's going, and that'll be the end of your income.'

'I'm paid to protect him, even if that means taking a bullet for him.'

'You could do so much better, Knuckles, and let's face it, you're not very good at protecting your bosses, are you? I mean, look what happened to Billy. Wasn't you supposed to be protecting him?'

'I... erm...' Knuckles stuttered.

'And who's protecting Mickey now, whilst you're sat here with me?'

Knuckles jumped to his feet. 'You haven't, have ya? You ain't had him done in?'

Georgina threw her head back and laughed. 'No, Knuckles, calm down, your boss is still alive... for now. My point is, Mickey can be taken out at any time, and he will be. I don't think you want to stand in my way, do you?'

'No, but...'

'Billy's house at Clapham. I've got plans for it. Big plans. I need someone there, someone I can trust. Could you be that person, Knuckles? You wouldn't be having to take a bullet for anyone and I'd ensure you get paid more than you do now.'

'I don't know, I'm not sure...'

'You don't have to do anything for now. Just give me a bit of information and carry on as normal. I promise you, Knuckles, you'll get a good handshake.'

Knuckles scratched the side of his bald head and screwed his face up on one side. The sight reminded Georgina of the comic strip character, Popeye.

'I dunno about this, Miss Garrett, but I'm interested. Mickey's making a lot of bad decisions lately and he won't listen to sense.'

'What sort of bad decisions?'

'He's setting up a meet with that Liverpool gang, the Portland Pounders. Once he gets in with them, he'll be untouchable, but you must have heard what they're like... They'll kill anyone just for looking at 'em funny. I don't like the idea of it, I really don't.'

Jane came back into the room carrying a tray with a coffee pot. Knuckles sat back down on the sofa and smiled politely, exposing his rotten teeth.

'They're a nasty bunch, even my Norman was careful around them,' Jane said as she placed the tray on a small marble table next to the chair where Georgina was sat.

'What's the meet about, Knuckles?' Georgina asked.

'I dunno the full details but it's happening next week. The guv'nor and a couple of his blokes are coming to Queenstown Road on Friday. I think they're gonna exchange a couple of girls and the Pounders have got some cash needs cleaning.'

'I see, and you're telling me this because you're now working for me?'

'Looks that way, don't it. Mickey's a fucking liability. I've never been able to stomach him. 'Scuse me language, missus,' Knuckles said to Jane, then added, 'He'll have us all fucking killed. He's even on about going up against the Maynards. He reckons he can take on all of fucking London.'

'Does he, indeed, well, I'll see to it that he doesn't get far. Trust me, Knuckles, you've made the right decision.'

'I hope so, but I still ain't sure you're up to it, you know, with you being a woman and all.'

'You let me worry about that. Now, what can you tell me about where Mickey keeps the takings?'

'Ha, this'll make you laugh! None of us know where the key is for Billy's safe so Mickey can't use it. He has all the money stored in a dog's kennel in the corner of Billy's office.'

'A dog's kennel? Does the dog guard it?'

'He ain't got a dog,' Knuckles said and laughed. His shoulders jigged and his large belly wobbled. 'No-one guards it. Mickey sleeps upstairs with one of the tarts and the place ain't belled up or nothing. He thinks he's so fucking hard that no-one would have the balls to do him over.'

Georgina glanced at Jane who had raised her eyebrows as she poured the coffee into fine bone china cups.

'That's very useful to know, thank you, Knuckles. Is there anything else you can tell me?'

'Like what?'

'Malc and Sid collect the protection money—'

'Insurance,' Jane cut in. 'Norman preferred to call it insurance.'

Georgina continued, 'Malc and Sid collect the insurance, then I assume they bring the money to Mickey. Do they take their own cut first?'

'No, Mickey likes to have full control over everything. The money comes in by Saturday afternoon, then on Monday morning, Mickey has us all in the office and he does the ledgers. He counts the money out like a little Jew boy while his brother keeps the books. Then he dishes out what we're all due. Credit where credit's due, he don't keep none of us short.'

'Mickey has a brother?' Georgina asked. She hadn't reckoned on any family support for him.

'Yeah, but he's a streak of piss, scared of his own fucking shadow. He lives at home with his mum and does whatever Mickey tells him to do.'

'Great, I think I know all I need to for now. Just one more thing, Knuckles. At night, there's only Mickey and the prostitutes in the house? Are they open for business?'

'No, the doors close at midnight so there's just the three Russian whores and Mickey.'

Jane handed Knuckles a coffee and Georgina thought his giant hands looked as though they might crush the cup. It was almost surreal to see this rough, massive man daintily holding Jane's best china.

'What shall I do now?' Knuckles asked.

Georgina almost felt sorry for him. He looked like a little boy who'd lost his mummy in the market. Then she remembered how Knuckles had taken orders from Billy and had probably been involved in torching her Maids of Battersea club premises with her inside. 'Either keep your mouth shut about our conversation or get yourself away for a couple of weeks until this is all sorted.'

'I ain't got nowhere to go.'

'Then you'll have to go back to Mickey, but do you think you can act as if nothing has happened?'

'Yeah, I can do that. He hardly talks to me unless he has to. How will I know when you're coming for him?'

'You won't,' Georgina answered and her hackles rose.

'I know how that sounded, Miss Garrett, but I ain't gonna say a word, I swear. Like I said, it's bad enough about the Liverpool Pounders but if he starts taking on the Maynards, that's it, we'll all end up six feet under.'

'All right, Knuckles, you go back to him now and carry on as normal. I'll be seeing you... soon.'

Knuckles quickly finished his coffee and Jane showed the big man out. When she came back into the lounge, she had a face like thunder and drew the curtains before she spoke. 'What on earth was you thinking of?'

'What? And why are we sitting in darkness?' Georgina asked.

'Because I don't want anyone hearing us! You've revealed everything to that... that... that thug. Do you really believe for one minute that he's not going to tell Mickey exactly what we're up to? Have you gone totally mad?'

Georgina had a job not to giggle at Jane. How drawing the curtains would keep their secrets was beyond her. As far as she was concerned, there was only one mad person in the room and it was Jane. 'You heard him. He's worried for his life working with Mickey. For Christ's sake, who'd be stupid enough to go up against the Maynards? Not even Norman or Billy would have done that! No, Mickey's pushing his luck and Knuckles knows it.'

'And what if it's all lies?'

'Knuckles ain't bright enough. He's telling the truth. I've got until next Friday to get to Mickey before he meets the Pounders. That's just seven days.'

'Couldn't you go to the Maynards and tell them what Mickey's intentions are? Surely they wouldn't stand for it?'

'No, why would they believe me? Anyway, this is mine for the taking, for us, Jane, for The Maids of Battersea.'

The door opened and Molly popped her head around. 'Has he gone?' she asked.

'Yes, it's all clear. Is Edward all right?' Jane asked.

'Sound asleep. Well, how did it go?'

'According to Georgina, very well, but I hope she's not being naïve.'

Georgina gave her friend a *knowing* look. 'Take no notice, Molly, I think Jane is getting a little paranoid. Knuckles is on side and also spilled the beans about Mickey's plans for expansion, including taking over the Maynards' turf.'

'You've got to be kidding? South East London? Blimey, Georgina, if you don't get him first, the Maynards will definitely take him out.'

'Exactly and I've only got one week before he meets with the Liverpool Pounders. If Knuckles is right, Mickey is planning on working in some sort of cahoots with them so I need to shut him down before any deals are done. It's one thing getting rid of Mickey but I wouldn't want to face the Pounders.'

'This sounds like it's getting very complicated,' Molly said.

'It is, who wants one of these?' Jane answered as she poured herself a large brandy.

'No, not for me, I need to keep a clear head,' Georgina said and opened the curtains on the darkened room.

'Are you sure about this?' Molly asked.

Georgina looked into her eyes and saw the genuine concern. They'd been best friends since childhood and had shared so much together. Georgina had always protected Molly and always would. Molly was her one confidante, though Georgina never confessed that she'd been the person who'd accidentally killed her father, Mike Mipple. Granted, the man had subjected his family to a reign of terror, but still, some things were best left unsaid.

'Yes, Molly, I'm very sure. And I'm going to do this before Mickey completely destroys the Wilcox name and all that Norman and Billy built up.'

Jane looked petrified as she knocked back her brandy and Molly appeared equally worried as she sat on the sofa and wrung her hands.

'Don't worry, Mickey won't know what's hit him,' Georgina said trying to sound reassuring, though really, she was just as scared as her friend.

4

Fanny Mipple trudged home, her weary body aching from being on her knees and scrubbing floors. It was late on Sunday afternoon but Fanny worked seven days a week as a cleaner in Bolingbroke hospital. She didn't mind hard work, especially since Mike, her foul husband, had mysteriously passed away, so now she could keep her own wages.

The hospital catered for the middle classes who couldn't afford nursing care at home but didn't want to go into the infirmaries with the riff-raff working class. She rarely interacted with the patients, but when she did, Fanny knew they were looking down their snooty noses at her. Maybe that's why she preferred to work in the mortuary. She'd found it a bit creepy at first but had become accustomed to being surrounded by stiffs, and at least it was quiet and peaceful.

Thankfully, the wickedly cold wind that had ripped through the streets earlier in the week had dropped and the snow that had settled had turned to slush. Still, Fanny's toes felt numb and her cheeks burned. She knew it wouldn't be much warmer at home but at least she could crawl under her blankets.

Her thoughts went to Georgina and the plans to take over the Wilcox empire. The young woman's ideas were bold and Fanny had gone along with them, but she wished her daughter was stronger. After all, if Molly had the guts to claim what she should have inherited, Fanny would be sitting pretty now in that big house in Clapham. Instead, she was still stuck in the same shithole she'd lived in for years.

'Oh, Molly,' she mumbled under her breath, disappointed that it had been Georgina who'd come up with the plan. Now it would be the Garretts who would have everything and she and her daughters would be left accepting handouts and would be expected to show gratitude. She hoped Georgina would be generous. The thought of going cap in hand to ask for anything really grated on her. When Molly had married Billy Wilcox, she'd thought her days of begging for a living were well behind her. No, she'd never beg Georgina, especially as anything from the business should be Molly's earnings. Georgina was the right person to attempt the takeover, Fanny had no doubt about that. But Molly should have put her foot down and insisted that Georgina work for her, for a wage. If it went well tonight, Georgina would soon be lining her own pockets with money that rightfully belonged to Molly.

She wasn't too far from home now and as she passed Mrs Peterson's shop, she spotted a woman dressed in layers of rags huddled in the shop doorway. Fanny eyed the woman and gave her a smile. With her purse almost empty, friendliness was all she could offer the woman.

'Can you spare any pennies, please?' the woman asked.

Fanny could tell from her pronunciation that she wasn't from round here – she'd never heard an accent like it before.

'Sorry, I'm skint,' Fanny replied and felt sorry for the woman. She understood what it was like to have to beg for a living. After all, she'd spent years on the steps outside the railway station pleading for any small offering from strangers.

'It's hard times,' the woman said.

'You can say that again. You're not from these parts, are you?'

'No. Me and my husband moved here from Wales. There's no work there so we hoped to find something in London. Trouble is, we spent every last penny we had just getting here.'

'Where's your husband now?' Fanny asked.

'I wish I knew! I woke up the other morning and he'd gone. He probably thought it would be easier to look after himself without me.'

'Yeah, well, maybe you're better off without him. Bloody men are more trouble than they're worth. How did you end up in Battersea?'

'I'm not sure. I walked over a bridge and here I am. We were sleeping rough on the Embankment. There's loads of us there. Mostly Welsh and Northerners who'd travelled here hoping for a better life and jobs in the construction that's going on. But I think I would have been better off staying in Wales.'

'There's not much work here, I'm afraid. They're doing some slum clearance on the other side of Battersea but all the jobs would have been taken up by the local men. They could do with clearing these bleedin' houses too. I dunno about up in town but I doubt you'll find anything here.'

'Yes, I've realised that.'

'Tell you what. I can't give you any money but you're welcome to come to mine for a hot drink. You won't find my place much warmer than these streets, mind.'

'Really? Thank you. Thank you so much. I've not had anything to eat or drink since yesterday.'

'Come on, then. Me name's Fanny. Fanny Mipple.'

'Nice to meet you, Fanny. I'm Clarice Jones. I'm ever so grateful – you're so kind.'

'I know what it's like to have nothing.'

As Fanny turned onto her street, she saw Molly walking towards her, pushing a pram. She always enjoyed visits from her daughter and though Edward looked the spit of his father, Fanny was smitten with the little chap.

'Here come's my daughter, Molly.'

'Hello, Mum, me and Edward thought we'd pop in to see you. I know Ethel is staying with Dulcie tonight so thought you might want a bit of company but looks like you already have some?'

'That's thoughtful of you. Molly, this is Clarice. Come on, let's get inside and get that little mite out of the cold,' Fanny answered, feeling a stab of guilt knowing that she couldn't offer the child any more warmth than her own children had ever had.

Fanny opened the door and helped Molly lift the pram over the front step and into the decrepit hallway. 'Hello, my little man,' she cooed as she lifted Edward from his cosy pram and carried him through to her one room in the shared house. She invited Clarice in and told her, 'Come through to the scullery. I'll put a penny in the gas meter and you can warm your hands on the stove.'

She pulled out a wooden stool for the woman to sit on and showed her where to find the tea leaves.

'You get yourself warmed through. I'll be in my room.'

Nothing much had changed in the room since her husband had died. It was where she'd raised seven girls, though five of them had left home. Pallet wood still covered the window and allowed in a terrible draught. There had been a curtain separating her and her husband's bed from the girls' but Fanny had taken it down. Now, there was just her, Ethel and Charlotte and it was warmer for all three of them to share the same bed.

'Who's that?' Molly whispered.

'I don't really know. I just met her. She was sheltering in Mrs Peterson's shop doorway. I felt sorry for her so invited her in for a cuppa.'

'Ah, the poor woman.'

'I know. I'm gonna feel terrible getting rid of her but she can't stay.'

'Unfortunately, Mum, with this Depression, there's so many people on their uppers, you can't help all of them. Anyway, I've brought something for you and Charlotte,' Molly said as she rummaged in a cloth bag that had been over her shoulder. 'Where is she?'

'Gawd knows. She's a wild child, that one. I can't keep tabs on her. She does as she pleases and she takes no notice of anything I say.'

Molly frowned and asked, 'Do you want me to have a word with her?'

'No, you'd be wasting your time. The only person that girl would have listened to was your father, God rest his soul.'

'But she's only ten, Mum, she shouldn't be coming and going as she pleases.'

'I know, but what do you expect me to do if the girl won't do as she's told?' Fanny snapped. She felt tired and cold and the last thing she needed was any sort of righteous lecture from Molly.

'Give her a good bloody hiding, that'll make her pull her socks up!'

'Don't you think you girls saw enough *good bloody hidings* when your father was alive? I'll have no more violence in my house, ever. Do you hear me? No more!' Fanny spoke through gritted teeth. She would have shouted if she hadn't been holding Edward.

'Yes, I'm sorry, Mum, I didn't mean to upset you.'

'It's not your fault, love, I'm just bleedin' knackered. So come on then, what's this you've brought for us?' she asked and smiled, feeling awful for taking her mood out on Molly.

'Here ya go, a little treat,' Molly answered and taking her son, she handed Fanny a small paper bag.

Fanny peeped inside and asked, 'What are these?'

'Fizzy cola bottle sweets. Try them, they're delicious.'

She popped one in her mouth and relished the sugary coating and sour taste. 'These are… different. Thanks, Molly, I'll save them for Ethel and Charlotte.'

Edward began to softly whimper and Fanny outstretched her arms. 'Give him back 'ere to his grandma,' she said, 'and you can make us a hot drink.'

Molly handed over her child and disappeared to the scullery for a few minutes, soon returning with two steaming cups of weak, black tea. 'Clarice has got a bit of colour in her cheeks now. She seems happy enough sat in front of the stove. Aw, look at Edward. He settles well with you,' she said as she placed the cups on the bare floorboards next to the bed.

'Well, I've had plenty of experience with keeping little ones quiet.' Fanny remembered the times she'd fruitlessly rocked Molly back and forth as a baby, trying to quieten the child to save herself getting another beating from her husband.

'He never seems as comfortable with Jane,' Molly said and sat next to Fanny on the edge of the bed.

'She can be a bit uptight at times and babies sense that sort of thing,' Fanny answered.

'Maybe, but there's something else. I don't know what, but something ain't right.'

'Of course it ain't, she killed...'

'Don't say it, Mum, please,' Molly quickly interrupted before Fanny could finish the sentence.

'Sorry, but you know what I was going to say.'

'Yes, I do, but I don't want it spoken about around Edward,' Molly whispered.

Fanny thought her daughter was being a little oversensitive; after all, it wasn't as if Edward could understand what was being said. Still, she respected Molly's wishes and changed the subject. 'Am I allowed to talk about what Georgina is doing tonight?' she asked.

'Shush, no, not with these thin walls,' Molly answered and looked around her as if someone might be in the room and was eavesdropping.

'I don't know, all this cloak and daggers. I just hope that woman knows what she's doing.'

'She does and if it pans out how she's hoping, we might all be living somewhere better soon.'

'That would be nice. I've wanted to get out of this dump for years. You know I hate using that privy out the back, especially when it's so cold. I traipsed down there the other morning in the pitch blackness and had to wait ten minutes before that Arthur from two doors up came out. I really didn't want to follow him in but I was desperate by then.'

'Oh, Mum, you should have gone behind a bush or something.'

'I'd do no such thing! I might be living below standard but I'll keep up me own, thank you very much.'

'Hopefully, you won't have to share with all the neighbours for much longer.'

'I do hope you're right, Molly. Ethel's coughing a good 'un, which I'm sure the cold and damp in here makes worse. As for Charlotte, she's never home but let's face it, who'd want to spend any time cooped up in these rotten walls.'

'It'll happen, Mum, I know it will. And when it does, me and Edward can live with you too. I can't wait to get out of Jane's.'

'But I thought you was happy there. She's got a lovely house.'

'Yes, the house is lovely and I'm grateful to her for putting us up, but like I said, she's a bit… strange.'

'In what way?'

'I dunno, little things, she's so moody and keeps calling Edward *Billy*. She walks round the house at night, I can hear her, mumbling to herself for hours on end.'

'No wonder she's forgetful and irritated if she's not sleeping,' Fanny said.

'It's more than that, Mum. She gives me the creeps so can you see why I'm keen to move out?'

'I suppose so, but be patient with her. She done us all a favour when she… you know.'

'Yes, I'm trying to be but I'll be happier when I've put some distance between me and the Wilcox family.'

Fanny wasn't overly concerned about her daughter's situation. She'd rather have to put up with Jane losing her marbles than the filthy toilet she had to share with several families. And at least Molly could keep herself and Edward warm. Even with four coats on the bed and the extra blanket she'd bought, she, Ethel and Charlotte still felt the cold and slept with knitted hats on. At least Ethel had stopped wetting the bed so that was one blessing. She could move them all out but on her meagre salary, she doubted she'd find anything much better than what they had.

All their hopes rested on Georgina now, and though Fanny didn't divulge her fears to Molly, she hoped Georgina's plan didn't backfire. If it did, the shared privy and Jane's peculiar behaviour would be the very least of their worries.

It was the middle of the night and so cold that Georgina's teeth chattered as she carefully opened her front door. She didn't want to disturb her gran or Ethel. She wasn't worried about her dad – he was probably passed out on the sofa in a drunken stupor and even a bomb explosion was unlikely to stir him.

She tiptoed up the hallway and into the kitchen and was then surprised when she heard her gran whisper, 'Thank Gawd you're home.'

'What are you doing up?' she asked, straining her eyes to see her gran's shadowy figure sat at the table.

'Waiting for you to get home. I couldn't sleep, I was too worried.'

Dulcie lit a candle and Georgina could see the strain on her gran's face.

'I told you not to worry; anyway, I'm back now so you should get yourself off to bed.'

'No, Ethel's in it and snoring her head off. Boil some water, love, we'll have a cuppa and you can tell me what happened.'

Georgina stood at the sink and filled the kettle. As she did, she saw her reflection in the window. It was odd to see herself in men's clothes again, though she felt very comfortable in them. It had been a while since she'd worn trousers and a shirt with braces and a flat cap. Her face was stripped of any make-up and her small breasts were flattened with a tight vest. 'Hello again, George,' she whispered at herself.

'Eh? Who you talking to?'

'No-one, Gran, just meself. I was just thinking how different I look.'

'Funnily enough, I was and all. It's weird to see you as George again. I know you spent most of your life as him but I've got used to you being Georgina now.'

'Yes, but I could hardly go breaking into houses in me high heels and skirts.'

'No, I suppose not. So come on then, what happened?'

'It all went according to plan,' Georgina answered and smiled proudly.

'And no-one saw you?'

'No, I don't think so, and if they did, they would have thought I was a bloke.'

'Good. You're such a clever girl, just like your mother. I'd have never come up with the idea.'

'It's a good one, ain't it?'

'Yes, love, it's bloody genius! So tomorrow morning, Mickey the Matchstick will discover his takings are gone then all hell will break loose.'

'Yep, and hopefully he'll find Malc's driving glove that I planted under his desk. He should put two and two together then and discover his stolen cash in Malc's car. That should put the cat amongst the pigeons.'

'I'll say! But what if they don't end up destroying each other?'

Georgina poured the boiling water from the kettle into a teapot and chewed the inside of her mouth for a moment before she spoke. 'They will, I'm sure of it. I can't see Mickey letting this go, not having one of his own blokes robbing him. Hopefully, Malc will stick up for himself and Mickey will end up with a bullet in him.'

'And if he doesn't?'

'He will, one way or another, he will,' Georgina answered and thought about the pistol in her coat pocket as she carried two cups of tea to the table.

'I hope this all works out as you'd like. I suppose we won't be none the wiser until this afternoon.'

'No, not until Jane has been to see Knuckles again. She can get away with calling into Queenstown Road but I don't think I'd be very welcome,' Georgina said. She didn't like to send Jane there but had no other options. At least as Billy's mother, the woman commanded respect from her deceased son's gang.

'Cor, I'd love to be a fly on the wall when Mickey realises he's been turned over.'

'Yeah, me too,' Georgina said, but she'd have to rely on Knuckles for an account of events instead.

Her eyelids were beginning to feel heavy and she yawned, parroted by her gran.

'Do you think you can get some sleep?' Dulcie asked.

'I doubt it, but I'll finish my tea and try. Is my dad on the sofa?'

'Yeah, he rolled in after the pubs closed, in his usual bleedin' state. The sooner your Lash gets back and sorts him out, the better.'

Georgina rolled her eyes. She had enough to be worrying about at the moment and could do without the extra concern her father was causing. She hated seeing him like this. He'd always been a strong man, someone she'd looked up to and respected. He'd taught her how to steal and fight and given her all the skills she'd needed to survive on the tough Battersea streets. But this – she despised seeing him weak and controlled by the alcohol. She wanted her dad back.

'What's all this?' Georgina asked as she looked at the mixed items on the kitchen table – a doll's head, three shells, two cigarette cards, a marble, a cotton reel and a few scraps of wool.

'It's Ethel's. You should have seen her, pleased as punch. She got one of them farthing bundles down at Charlotte's school today. They've been doing them for years over the East End and now some good Samaritan has started it up here.'

'A farthing bundle?'

'Yeah. I gave Ethel the farthing and she came back with this lot wrapped in newspaper.'

'Looks like a load of junk.'

'It is, but it kept her amused for hours.'

'Simple things please simple minds, bless her. I'm gonna try and get some kip now, Gran.'

'All right, love. I'll come up wiv ya. If Ethel's still snoring, I'll give her a good bloody dig in the ribs. In future, if you're planning on being out at night and having Ethel sit with me, she can have your bed.'

'You can get into mine now – I'll sleep with Ethel,' Georgina offered.

'No, thanks, I'll sleep in my own bed. Night, love.'

Georgina slipped into her room and sat on the edge of her bed. Her mind was racing and she knew sleep would evade her. She twisted her mother's wedding ring and bit her bottom lip. Molly, Jane and Fanny, The Maids of Battersea – they'd all put their faith in her. Now it was time to deliver and she hoped she wouldn't let them down.

5

The next day, Molly looked out of Jane's lounge window, aware that behind her Georgina was anxiously pacing the room.

'Any sign of them?' her friend asked.

'No, nothing,' Molly answered.

'Something's not right. She's been gone too long.'

'It's not been an hour yet. I'm sure she'll be back soon.'

'I should never have let her go alone. Christ, Molly, what was I thinking?'

'Jane will be perfectly fine. She's Billy's mum so they're not gonna bat an eyelid at her calling in to see Knuckles.'

'We don't know that. They could suspect that she had something to do with the robbery last night. Shit, Molly, if anything happens to her it'll be my fault and I'll never forgive myself.'

'Here she is, and Knuckles is with her. See, panic over so calm down.' Molly offered a reassuring smile. For all of Georgina's hard-faced bravado, Molly knew her friend cared deeply for those around her.

'Do you want to go upstairs with Edward?'

'No,' Molly answered, 'I'll stay. I'm as much a part of this as you and Jane. It's about time I toughened up a bit and stopped hiding away.'

Molly stood next to Georgina in the bay window, waiting for Jane and Knuckles to enter the lounge. Her heart pounded and the room was so quiet that she was sure Georgina would hear it. Her friend was several inches taller than her and it was all Molly could do to stop herself from hiding behind her.

They heard the front door close and then Jane walked in, looking as glamorous and self-assured as she had before Billy's death. Knuckles followed and when he saw Georgina, his ruddy face broke into a broad grin.

He shook his head in disbelief as he spoke. 'I can't believe you pulled that off, Miss Garrett. I don't know how you did it, but they're gone. I take my hat off to you.' He removed his flat cap and offered his large hand for Georgina to shake.

She ignored his gesture but gave him a friendly smile. 'Sit down, Knuckles, and Mrs Wilcox will get you a drink. You can fill me in on what happened.'

Molly went to step forward but Jane left the room.

Knuckles threw himself down on the sofa. He was such a large man, Molly thought the sofa might break under his weight. Then he gabbled, 'Well, it's all over. Mickey shot Malc and then Sid did Mickey in. I told Sid to do a runner, and he didn't need telling twice.'

Georgina crossed one long leg over the other, then said to Knuckles, 'Slow down and give me the details. Start from the beginning and don't leave anything out.'

As Knuckles began to relay the events of the morning at the brothel in Queenstown Road, Molly took the armchair opposite Georgina's and listened, intrigued at Knuckles' every word.

'Mickey had us all in the office as usual and I saw him pick up a glove. He must have recognised it as Malc's and asked him what it was doing under his desk. Malc just shrugged. He weren't taking any notice 'cos he was busy talking to Sid. I didn't give it a second thought 'til Mickey's brother went for the cash and said it was gone.'

Knuckles paused, smiling, and impatiently Georgina said, 'Go on.'

'Yeah, well, that's when I knew. I thought to meself, Miss Garrett's got something to do with this. Anyway, Mickey went mental and started tearing the room apart. He couldn't believe someone had nicked his money. He kept saying nobody would have the bollocks to rob him, but I knew you would. I knew you'd done it.'

'So then what happened?' Georgina asked.

'Mickey got the tarts downstairs and slapped 'em about a bit. They were snivelling and saying they didn't know nothing about it. He had me search their rooms but I knew I wouldn't find nothing. When I told him the rooms were clean, he went quiet. Then he started screaming at Malc, accusing him. Malc laughed in his face and Mickey had me look in Malc's car. That's when I found the money.'

Jane came back into the room and Knuckles paused whilst she handed round cups of coffee. Molly had been hanging on Knuckles' every word and was silently willing the man to continue.

'I took the money to Mickey and by now him and Malc were having a full-blown row. When Mickey saw the cash, he asked me if it had been in Malc's car, so I told him yes. That was it, he didn't ask no more questions. Malc was denying knowing anything about it but then Mickey just shot him. I couldn't fucking believe it! He and Malc go back years; they've been mates since they were nippers.'

Georgina sipped on the hot drink, then asked, 'You said Mickey's dead too. How did that happen?'

'The next thing I knew, Sid started doing his nut. He went for Mickey and the gun went off but Mickey missed and Sid managed to get him on the floor. Mickey tried to fight him off but Sid grabbed this big, onyx ashtray from Mickey's desk and whacked him over the head with it. There was blood everywhere and Mickey weren't moving. Next thing I know, Mickey's on all fours trying to get up but Sid had the gun and fired it. He shot Mickey in the back.'

'What did you do then?'

'If you must know, I panicked. I thought how the fuck am I gonna explain away two dead bodies. Nobody would have called the Old Bill, but Cunningham calls in every day. He's the local bobby on Mickey's pay, but now Mickey's laid on the floor with his skull caved in and a hole in his back. Someone's going to the gallows, so I told Sid to help me carry Malc to the car. I said he had to get rid of Malc's body then have it away on his toes. I told him I'd cover for him... that I'd lie to Cunningham and say I found Mickey like that.'

'So Sid has gone for good?'

'Yeah, he couldn't get away quick enough. I reckon he was shitting himself without Malc to back him up. He'll be long gone now.'

'What about Mickey's brother?'

'He disappeared. I didn't see him leave but I know him – he'll be hiding behind his mother's apron.'

'So, Mickey – where's his body?'

Molly glanced at Jane and held her breath. She hoped Knuckles wouldn't say that Mickey was in the cellar. She wasn't sure how Jane would react to knowing Mickey was with her husband.

'He ain't dead. I went to drag him to the stairs and he made a strange noise. Frightened the fucking life out of me at first,' Knuckles said and laughed. 'I got the girls to clean up a bit then sent one of them for an ambulance. They carted Mickey off just as Cunningham turned up.'

'Mickey's alive?'

'Only just. Judging by the state of him, he ain't gonna be back.'

'What did Cunningham say, is he investigating?'

'Nah. He seemed more bothered about getting to the hospital to check on Mickey. He won't do nothing about it and said he'll put it down to Mickey having an accident.'

'Good. You did well, Knuckles.'

'Looks like you're the guv now, Miss Garrett, so what do you want me to do next?'

'I'd like you to return to Queenstown Road and carry on as normal for now. I'll be there to take over soon. Do you think you can do that?'

'Yes, Miss Garrett. I'll keep an eye on things for you.'

'Off you go then,' Georgina told him.

Jane saw Knuckles out, and once the front door was closed behind him, Molly felt she could finally breathe again. 'Is that it, Georgina? Is the business ours now?'

'Yes, and rightly so. Mickey had no right to take it over. It's always belonged to the Wilcox family.'

'You're not a Wilcox,' Jane snapped at Georgina, which shocked Molly.

'No, I'm not, thank goodness.'

'So really, Molly should be running it and you should be working for her,' Jane added haughtily.

'Oh, no... no... I couldn't... I don't want to be running it,' Molly said as she shook her head fervently in protest.

'What's your problem, Jane?' Georgina asked and stood up. She looked like she was ready to fight Jane, and Molly could feel herself cowering.

'I'm just pointing out the facts,' Jane answered.

'You heard Molly. She doesn't want to run it and someone has to or there'll be another Mickey the Matchstick waiting to jump in and take over. Is that what you want? Or perhaps you'd like to be in charge yourself?'

Molly sucked in her breath again and held it whilst she waited for Jane to answer.

'I was merely saying that as Billy's widow, the business is Molly's.'

Molly didn't like the atmosphere that was building between Georgina and Jane and they were referring to her as if she wasn't in the room. 'I don't want the business,' she blurted, and hoped that would be an end to the heated discussion. 'I – don't – want – the – business,' she repeated slowly. 'In fact, I'm handing over all rights to Georgina. There, job done. I'll be happy to sign any paperwork but as far as I'm concerned, any interests in the Wilcox business that belonged to me now officially belong to Georgina.'

'You can't do that!' Jane said and glared at her.

'I can do what I like. I had enough of Billy telling me what I could and couldn't do and I won't stand by and allow you to do the same.' Molly sounded firm but inside, she was trembling.

'Norman made the business what it is today, and if Billy hadn't killed him it would be mine. You've no right to be giving it away.'

'If it wasn't for Georgina, I'd have nothing to give away,' Molly answered swiftly.

'Fine, have it your way, but you'll come to regret this. Do you really believe that Georgina is going to look after us? What makes you think she won't take everything for herself?'

'Whoa, let's calm down, shall we,' Georgina said and came to stand in between Jane and Molly. She then addressed Jane: 'As I am to take charge, I'll make sure that you and Molly get a cut of the profits, twenty-five per cent each. Ten per cent to Fanny and forty to me. Is that fair?'

'I'm happy with that,' Molly said, thinking how money really brought out the ugliness in people.

'I suppose I'll have to be too,' Jane answered but Molly thought the woman looked like she had a bad smell under her nose.

'Good. I'll have papers drawn up but in the meantime, I've got work to do. If you'll excuse me, I'm off to my office. Molly, would you mind popping to mine and letting my gran know what's happened?'

'I'd be happy to,' Molly answered and smiled at her friend.

Georgina left and Molly was suddenly filled with dread. She didn't want to be alone with Jane. The woman was obviously in a foul mood and the Wilcox temper unnerved her. 'I'd better wrap Edward up nice and warm,' she said as an excuse to leave the room.

As she walked into the hallway, she heard Jane mutter, 'Yes, you do that. And while you're there, you can tell him how you willy-nilly handed over his father's business.'

Molly chose to ignore Jane's snide remark. She didn't understand why Jane was suddenly being difficult. After all, Jane had arranged the meetings with Knuckles and she'd been happy for Georgina to take control from Mickey. Mind you, Jane's moods were becoming more erratic lately and her strange behaviour seemed to be escalating. Molly was becoming increasingly concerned that Jane was delusional and believed Edward was *her* son. She'd referred to the baby as Billy on more than one occasion.

Molly lifted him from his cot. 'Don't worry, little one,' she cooed in a hushed voice as she held him protectively to her chest, 'we'll soon be out of here and away from your demented grandma.'

Georgina's mind raced. She felt hugely relieved that her audacious plan had worked, because if the truth had been known, she didn't have a back-up one. Now there was so much to do and she knew exactly where to start – Ezzy, her old friend who owned a jewellery shop near Clapham Junction railway station.

Her father had worked for Ezzy's father; the two families went back years. Ezzy was a good man, one she knew she could trust and he wasn't averse to being on the wrong side of the law. He was a fence of top quality jewellery and paid fairly for the things she and her dad nicked. Ezzy also had a group of young lads, dippers, working for him. They would bring him their stolen goods and he would exchange the merchandise with his cousin, Seth, who owned a jewellery shop in Manchester. In fact, she and her father had often done the London to Manchester runs on the steam trains. The income had kept the rent man happy on many occasions.

Ezzy let Georgina in through his new-fangled security system and greeted her with genuine affection. 'My goodness, is that really you, George?' he asked, holding her at arm's length and eyeing her up and down.

'Yes, Ezzy, it's *really* me, only I'm Georgina now. George is in a trunk under my bed. Anyway, you've seen me dressed like this before.'

Ezzy beckoned her out towards the back of his shop. 'Yes, but I forgot how beautiful you are. You look incredible – your father must be a proud man.'

'Thank you,' Georgina answered, and could feel herself blush. She wasn't used to receiving compliments.

'How have you been? I haven't seen you in such a very long time. Can I get you some tea?'

'Yes, thanks. I'm all right and I'm sorry it's been so long but I've had a lot of stuff going on,' she answered.

'It's fine, it's fine, I know how busy you young people are. How is your father? I heard he's, erm... not very well?'

'He's drunk, all the time. It's not good but my friend is going to make him better.'

'I'm sorry, George, I mean Georgina. It's a shame. You know I think highly of your father. I hope your friend can help him. Now, what can I do for you? Have you brought me some quality pocket watches?'

'No, don't be daft, Ezzy. It's been yonks since I did any pickpocketing,' Georgina replied with a small chuckle.

'You was the best dipper I've known. Your father taught you well. So to what do I owe this pleasure?'

'Actually, can you shut up shop for the afternoon? I've got a proposition for you.'

Ezzy raised his dark bushy eyebrows as he spoke. 'Shut up shop? But, Georgina, you know I'm a Jewish man. We never close for business unless we have to. My father used to tell me: *Money will buy you everything but good sense.*'

'Trust me, Ezzy, you won't lose any money.'

Ezzy wobbled his head from side to side as if weighing up his options, then went to the front door and locked it before returning to the back of the shop to sit in a worn leather chair. He offered Georgina a wooden slatted seat opposite his, and once she was sat, he said, 'I'd like to hear your proposal.'

'I've taken over the Wilcox business,' Georgina replied and paused, waiting to gauge his reaction.

'How? Mickey took over after Billy's death.'

'It doesn't matter how, but it's done. Malc and Sid won't be visiting you again. You won't have to give them any more money.'

'You know about that?'

'Yes, Dad let it slip to my gran and she told me. Malc's dead and you won't be seeing anything of Sid.'

'Dead? Are you sure?'

'Yep, it's true.'

'But what about Mickey? He'll soon have another of his ruffians round here and smashing up my shop if I refuse to pay.'

'No, Ezzy, he won't. Mickey's out of action. You've seen the last of him.'

'How do you know all this, Georgina?'

'Because I orchestrated it. I told you, I'm in charge now.'

'You're just a girl, you couldn't possibly...'

Georgina politely cut in, 'With respect, I think you're underestimating me.'

'Um, I think you might be right,' Ezzy said thoughtfully, then added, 'and that would be a mistake for anyone to do. Now then, what do you want from me?'

'I'm glad you've asked. I need someone who understands the books. I don't know the first thing about accounts but you do.'

'I'm not an accountant, Georgina.'

'I know but you run this place. I just need you to come to the office with me and look at the accounts. I need to know what sort of financial situation the business is in.'

'I'm not the right person for this,' Ezzy said and then snapped his fingers. 'But I know a man who is.'

'I'm not sure about asking anyone else. How do I know I can trust him?'

'Because I trust him. He's my son, Benjamin.'

'You have a son? I didn't realise.'

'That's because I never spoke of him. His mother died when he was very young. I couldn't care for him so he went to live with my sister. Now, he is a young man and has moved back with me.'

'Oh, great, but can he do the job?'

'Yes, of course, it would be easy for him. He's an accountant. He was working for a shipping company in Victoria, but against his advice they put a lot of money into a mining project and for whatever reasons, lost their investment. The company went bust and Benjamin lost his job. I think he would be happy for any work right now.'

'I need him today, right now, is that possible?'

'Yes, I'll call him,' Ezzy answered and went to the telephone.

Georgina wouldn't normally have trusted someone she didn't know, but she had every faith in Ezzy.

'He's coming immediately,' Ezzy told her when he returned to the back room.

'Good, thanks. Does he understand the sensitivity of what he'll be doing?'

'Yes, I briefly explained. He said it's exciting for him, a change from his usual boring jobs.'

'I can guarantee there won't be anything boring about this.'

'He'll be here in ten minutes. Now, if it is agreeable with you, I'll open my shop again,' Ezzy said and laughed as he went to the front door. Then he sounded more serious when he added, 'I'm very impressed with you, Georgina. I don't think I know of any woman who could have taken control of the Wilcox business. I hope you won't be expecting me to continue paying extortion money?'

Georgina followed Ezzy into the shop. 'No, of course I won't,' she answered, 'and it's not extortion, it's insurance.'

'Call it what you like but it's still taking money from people under duress.'

'Well, things are going to be different from now on.'

'I hope so, young lady. You can do better than the likes of Billy Wilcox or Mickey whatever his name is.'

Ezzy had a point that Georgina hadn't considered before now. Extortion or protection rackets or insurance as Jane preferred to call it – it wasn't a very nice business. Did she really want to be involved in using threats and violence to extract money from hard-working, innocent people?

It was something she'd have to give some serious thought to.

6

Varvara had scrubbed the office floor as best she could but Mickey's blood had stained the floorboards. She was glad he was almost dead. Billy Wilcox had been vile and when he'd been killed she'd hoped her new boss would be an improvement. Unfortunately, it hadn't taken long for her to discover that Mickey was just as cruel. Granted, he'd never mutilated her like Billy had done, but he'd still made her work as a whore, against her will, and for no money. His threats were enough to keep her from attempting to escape. She'd already lost one finger under Billy's rule and wasn't prepared to have any more of her anatomy cut off.

Varvara now sat on her bed and anxiously waited to find out what was going to happen next. She wanted to go to Dina, her sister, in the room next door but Knuckles had locked them in. All she could do was wait and pray.

Hours later, her body tensed when she heard the key in the lock turning. This was it – she was about to learn of her fate. Knuckles walked in and she leapt to her feet.

'Come with me,' he told her.

Varvara nervously licked her lips and followed the giant. He opened Dina's door and instructed her to come too.

When Dina cautiously walked from her room, Varvara could see she'd been pulling bits of her hair out again. Mind you, it wasn't any wonder, not after the way Knuckles had attacked her when they'd been cleaning up the mess from this morning's shooting. It wasn't as if Dina had asked for trouble – she'd accidentally dropped the bucket of bloodied water.

Varvara had tried to come between Dina and Knuckles. She'd have readily taken the beating for her sister but Knuckles had thrown her to one side and pointed a pistol at her. So, she'd watched, disgusted, as Knuckles had kicked Dina up the backside and when Dina had fallen to the floor, he'd put the boot in again, this time to her ribs. It should have hurt Varvara – the sight of Dina lying helplessly on the floor as the blood-stained spilt water seeped into her clothes – but Varvara had experienced so much pain in her life that she was numb to it now.

They followed Knuckles down the stairs. Varvara walked behind and hoped Dina would look over her shoulder. She didn't, probably she was too afraid.

When they entered the office, Varvara was astounded to see a strikingly beautiful, tall, slender woman standing in front of the desk. The woman had the deepest, bluest eyes she'd ever seen. They were almost purple in colour and, immediately, Varvara was mesmerised. She was sure she'd seen her before, in this same office when Billy had been alive. This woman's face wasn't one to be easily forgotten.

'Close the door, Knuckles,' the woman instructed.

Varvara briefly pulled her eyes away to see Knuckles stand in front of the door. His huge body filling the doorframe.

Whatever was going to happen, there was no getting past him.

Varvara looked back to the woman who now seemed to be studying her and her sister.

'So, you are the Russian ladies. What are your names?'

'Varvara and this is my sister, Dina,' she replied, speaking for them both, her Russian accent apparent.

'I'm Georgina Garrett, Miss Garrett. I'll be running things around here from now on.'

Varvara wasn't sure she'd heard correctly. Surely a woman couldn't be taking charge? She must be the wife of someone powerful; it was the only explanation.

There was a short pause then Miss Garrett said, 'I thought there were three of you?'

Varvara felt a little more confident talking to a woman, and answered, 'Yes, there is. Tattie is upstairs. She'll be tied to her bed.'

'I beg your pardon?' Miss Garrett said and turned her head to look at Knuckles.

He cleared his throat before answering. 'We, erm, I have to tie her up. She's always trying to run off. It's for her own good.'

'What do you mean, *for her own good*?' Miss Garrett asked, clearly angered at what she'd been told.

'Every time she did a bunk and we'd find her, Billy chopped a finger off. She's already lost three. I think Mickey would've done the same, so I thought I was looking out for her by tying her down.'

Miss Garrett's eyes widened and she spoke through gritted teeth when she growled at Knuckles, 'Get up those stairs and untie that woman, NOW!'

Varvara had to bite her lip to stop herself from grinning. She found it amusing to see the massive lump of a man jump to a woman's command.

Then Miss Garrett asked, 'Is this true? Is this how you've been treated?'

Varvara held out her hand and Miss Garrett appeared genuinely shocked to see that her little finger was nothing more than an ugly stump.

'Billy Wilcox did this to you?'

'Yes,' Varvara answered solemnly.

'I see,' Miss Garrett said and then the door opened again and Knuckles dragged in Tattie. At the same time, Varvara heard a man's voice from the corner of the room.

'Damn,' he said, looking embarrassed as he glanced round the room, then jumped up and grabbed a handkerchief from his trouser pocket.

Varvara had been so taken with Miss Garrett that she hadn't noticed the man at the desk in the corner who'd just knocked a drink over his paperwork and was now furiously dabbing it.

Miss Garrett ignored him and introduced herself to Tattie who appeared less than impressed at having a woman for a boss.

Varvara couldn't take her eyes off Miss Garrett as she walked behind her desk and sat down before addressing them again.

'From what I can understand, it sounds like you've been forced to work here against your will. This is not how things will operate anymore. If you choose to leave, you may. Get your things together and go – simple. However, should you choose to remain, I want you to know that you'll be looked after, paid for the work you do and nobody, and I mean nobody, will hurt you. You will be respected as working women and, in return, you will respect me as your boss.'

Varvara exchanged a glance with Dina. Tattie was already walking towards the door.

'Let her pass,' Miss Garrett said, and Knuckles stepped to one side. Tattie didn't look back and they heard the front door slam. She'd left, without collecting her belongings; she'd just walked out of the door. Varvara was stunned that Tattie had been allowed to leave and began to believe she could trust Miss Garrett.

'What about you? Are you staying or are you going too?' Miss Garrett asked.

Varvara could feel the woman's eyes boring into her and her heart began to race. She felt a knot in her stomach and though her head was screaming at her to walk out the door, she felt strangely compelled to stay. It was Miss Garrett. There was something about the woman that made Varvara feel she wanted to be near her. She'd craved her freedom all her life and here she was, being offered it, yet she heard herself say, 'I'm staying.'

She knew Dina must be staring at her in abhorrence but she couldn't bring herself to look. Her sister would be so disappointed – Dina had probably expected them to be running for the hills by now. But Varvara knew Dina wouldn't leave without her.

'Good, and what about you?' Miss Garrett asked, and looked at Dina.

'She's staying too,' Varvara answered.

'Right then. Thank you for clearing up the mess from earlier. You can have the rest of the day off though I'd prefer you to stay in the house for now. I'll speak to you both later about money. You can go now.'

Her dismissal left Varvara feeling deflated. She didn't want to go. She wanted to stay and gaze at this incredible creature. 'But, can I ask…'

'You can ask me later,' Miss Garrett cut in, sounding irritated.

That was it – Varvara quite clearly wasn't wanted in Miss Garrett's presence. She reluctantly turned to walk towards the door and noticed Dina was already in the hallway. As the door closed behind her, Dina was halfway up the stairs. 'Wait,' she called after her sister. But Dina threw her a filthy look and dashed to her room.

Varvara tapped lightly on Dina's door. There was no response. 'Please, can we talk?' she asked, but Dina didn't answer.

She'll come round, Varvara thought as she went to her own room. After all, they had no money and if they left the brothel where could they go? They knew nothing except prostitution. They'd been whored out since they were children, passed from one man to another. At least now, things were going to change. They would have their own money and they didn't have to live in fear of a man terrorising them.

Varvara threw herself back onto her bed and stared at the ceiling. All her life, she'd wanted to make her own decisions and choose her own fate. For once, she'd done that and it felt so good.

She closed her eyes and thought about the *real* reason for why she'd chosen to stay at the brothel. She'd been impressed with the way Miss Garrett had stood up for Tattie. The graceful manner in which the woman held herself. The strong, toned shape of her striking body and the sharp intensity of her eyes. How she commanded the room had thrilled Varvara. Yes, it was unnatural to feel this way about a woman, and she'd never before been attracted to one. But she found Miss Georgina Garrett exciting and it was clear the woman had compassion, something Varvara had never been shown.

'You can go too, Knuckles. I want you to visit Livingstone Road and tell them that I'm in charge now and I'll be in to see them soon. Then I expect every man working for the Wilcox business to be in this office on Wednesday morning.'

'Shouldn't I stay here to look after you?'

'I can look after myself and, in future, don't question my orders,' Georgina said harshly. She'd never been keen on the man and now she'd witnessed how he treated the Russian ladies, she liked him even less.

The door closed behind Knuckles and Georgina turned her attention to Benjamin. 'Well, tell me I'm a very wealthy woman.'

Benjamin looked flustered as he answered. 'I… I… I wish I could, Miss Garrett, but these books are a mess. They only go back a couple of months and, to be frank, a child could have done better.'

'So, what can you tell me?'

He pushed his round spectacles up his nose and placed his pen neatly on the desk. 'Erm… er… Not very much. There's no record of assets, monies owed, goods acquired – nothing.'

They weren't the words Georgina had wanted to hear but then she remembered what Knuckles had told her. The safe hadn't been opened since Billy's death because no-one knew where the key was hidden. She was sure that's where Billy's books would be stashed. She marched across the office and moved the dog kennel to one side. The safe was behind it, probably bolted to the floor. 'All the records will be in here,' she told Benjamin.

'Oh, right, good, yes, erm… do you have the key?'

'No, but that won't be a problem. Come back tomorrow, the books will be available to you then.'

'Yes, fine. I'll, erm, see you tomorrow then, Miss Garrett,' Benjamin answered gawkily and began to clumsily pack his pens away into a brown leather briefcase.

Georgina thought he was an odd man. He was probably only a few years older than her – she guessed about twenty-six. He had a nice enough clean-shaven face behind his glasses, and his father's dark hair and eyes, but none of Ezzy's self-assurance. She didn't know if it was the situation that was making him nervous or if that was just his character. Either way, she had a job not to smile mockingly at his awkwardness.

Benjamin gave her a final flimsy wave as he left the office and at last, Georgina was alone. It was quite an eerie feeling, especially as she knew Norman Wilcox was buried in cement in the cellar under her feet. She sucked in a long breath and momentarily closed her eyes to gather her thoughts. It had been quite a day so far and she knew there were going to be many challenges over the coming months. She was in a man's world now and it wouldn't do to show any weakness. She needed to be strong in order to gain the respect of the men who'd once worked for Billy. She hadn't yet met them but already she knew she hated them.

'It's only me,' Molly called as she let herself into Dulcie's house. She'd been to visit her mum and had got the key from Ethel. Now she hoped to find Georgina at home. It was late evening and she should have been settling Edward down to bed but she had to get out of Jane's house – the woman was mad, she was sure of it.

'In here, love,' she heard Dulcie shout from the front room through the closed door.

Molly gathered her son from his pram and opened the door. As she walked in, the warmth from the coal fire felt welcoming, as did Dulcie's friendly smile.

'Georgina is upstairs getting changed. She'll be down in a minute. Take a seat – you look shattered,' Dulcie said as she folded empty potato sacks.

'I'm all right, just sleepless nights. You know how it is. What are you doing with those sacks?'

'Oppo dropped them in. They're for Mary next door. She'll use them to make rag rugs. Her old man still can't find no work. They ain't got a pot to piss in.'

'Them and plenty of others. You should have seen the queue outside the soup kitchen today. Pitiful, it was. All men, looking so sad. So much for the country on the up!'

'I know, love. It's a bloody travesty. I bet most of them men fought for King and country but it didn't get them nowhere.'

'Anyway, how did Georgina get on today? Did that bloke manage to open the safe?' Molly asked.

'Yes, and I can't believe that Mickey didn't try to have it opened. Anyway, it's all good, better than expected. The books were in there and the business is worth a few bob. She'll tell you all about it herself,' Dulcie said, then cocking her head to one side she asked, 'What brings you out at this time of night? Shouldn't that little chap be in bed by now?'

'Yes, probably, but he... erm... I think he must be teething,' she lied.

Dulcie strained her neck to try and get a glimpse of the child. 'He looks fine to me. He ain't got red cheeks or nothing.'

Molly felt awful for telling fibs and looked down at the floor. There was no getting anything past Dulcie – she was a wise woman.

'Come on, out with it. What's bothering you?'

'I don't know, maybe I've got it all wrong, but I don't think Jane is quite right,' Molly answered as the door opened and Georgina came into the room.

She was stripped of any make-up and was in her nightclothes but she had a new regal air about her. 'Hello, Molly, I thought I heard you arrive. What's all this about Jane?' she queried as she sat next to Molly on the sofa.

'I don't like to talk about her behind her back, but I'm getting worried. My mum said to take no notice and she's a bit funny in the head 'cos of what she did... you know...'

'Your mum is probably right,' Dulcie answered.

'No, I don't think she is. Maybe, at first, but Jane's behaviour is getting more peculiar by the day. To tell you the truth, I don't want me and my son living there for any longer than we have to.'

'Is she *that* bad?' Georgina asked.

'Yes! I'm not exaggerating,' Molly answered emphatically.

'All right, I believe you. You'd better tell me what's been going on.'

'Well, it started with silly little things at first, just being forgetful. Then I noticed she wasn't sleeping. I hear her walking round talking to herself. But it became more sinister when she called Edward *Billy*. That gives me the creeps and she's done it a few times now. Today was the last straw, though. It was bad. Really bad,' Molly said and dashed a tear away.

'I'm not liking the sound of this and I don't like seeing you upset. What happened, Molly?'

'I was on the sofa and I must have nodded off, just for a few minutes. Edward's been restless at night. I'm tired.'

'That's normal, love,' Dulcie said, reassuringly.

'When I opened my eyes, Edward was gone. I guessed Jane had taken him but I had a terrible feeling that something was wrong. Anyway, I walked into the kitchen and saw she was just about to put Edward in the sink. I could see steam; I knew the water was too hot. I screamed at her, told her to stop. She did, thank God, just in time. She almost scalded my baby. She could have boiled him alive!' Molly instinctively pulled Edward closer to her. 'I ran across the room and took Edward from her, but you should have seen the weird look in her eyes. They looked blank… empty. It's like she wasn't there. She didn't seem to have any idea what she was doing. I'm telling you, it was very, very strange.'

'I don't like the sound of that,' Dulcie said and shook her head.

'I told her to go and have a lie-down. I thought maybe she needed a rest. She asked me why so I told her she'd nearly burnt Edward, that the water was too hot. It still didn't seem to register with her and then she walked off, but I heard her mumbling something about how she'd never meant to hurt her son.'

'Eh? What exactly did you hear?' Georgina asked, looking concerned.

'I'm not sure, but I think she said something like: *I never would have hurt my son. I'd never hurt Billy.* She ain't right in the head, is she?'

Molly saw Georgina and Dulcie exchange a look with each other, then Dulcie spoke. 'No, love, she's not, and you and Edward can't go back there.'

'But we've got nowhere else to go,' Molly cried and caught a sob in her throat.

'Don't worry, you're staying here with us,' Georgina said. 'I'll go to Jane's and collect what you need.'

'We can't stay here – you don't have room for us,' Molly protested, though she couldn't think of anywhere else she'd rather be. It felt safe.

'We'll make the room,' Dulcie said firmly. 'Georgina, go and get changed and leave your nightclothes in my room.

You can kip in with me so Molly and Edward can have your room.'

'Don't worry, Molly. I found out today that the business is in a reasonably strong financial position. We'll soon have a nice place for you and Edward to live.'

Molly had managed to stop herself from bawling her eyes out, but now Georgina's and Dulcie's kindness made her feel emotional again.

Dulcie reached her arms out for Edward. 'Give him here. His aunty Dul wants a cuddle.'

Molly handed Edward over and as she did, Dulcie said softly, 'It's all right, see, Georgina will look after you.'

Dulcie had warned Georgina to keep a cool head and reminded her that it was very likely Jane was ill. She knocked on her door, unsure of the reception she'd receive.

It was Sally who answered and Georgina could see the girl was distressed. Tears streaked down her young face, and she cried, 'Georgina, I'm so glad you're here. It's my mother, I don't know what to do.'

'Where is she?' Georgina asked as Sally pulled the door open wider.

'She's in my room... sitting on the window ledge. I'm afraid she might jump!'

Georgina, in her haste, took the stairs two at a time. When she reached the top, she could see Jane's back, at the window, with the curtains billowing around her in the breeze. Georgina paused. It looked like the woman was teetering on the edge of the window frame. She didn't want to go charging in and startle her.

Sally had followed her up the stairs and was now standing by her side as she said, 'I've tried to get her to come inside but she won't. Do something, Georgina, please, don't let her jump.'

'It's all right, Sally. She'll be fine. I want you to take your sister and wait in the front room.'

'No, please, let me help.'

'Do as you're told, Sally, and close the door,' Georgina spat. She hadn't wanted to sound aggressive but she didn't have time to argue with the girl.

Sally reacted to Georgina's tone, and once Georgina felt they must be downstairs in the front room, she cautiously stepped towards Jane. 'Hey, it's me,' she said casually. 'What on earth are you doing sitting in the window? It's bloody freezing and you're letting all the cold air in.'

There was nothing from Jane.

'Come inside, I've got some good news to tell you.'

Still nothing.

Georgina was just a couple of feet away from her now, but she knew, if Jane slipped, she'd be out of Georgina's reach. She stepped closer.

'Stop,' Jane snapped.

'Right, whatever you say. Do you want to tell me what this is all about?'

'Go away, George. I have nothing to say to you.'

'Come on, Jane, don't be like that. We're friends, good friends. You can tell me anything.'

Jane turned her head to the side. George could see her profile and her black eye make-up smudged down her cheek.

'We're not friends. We never have been. Billy hates you and he'd be so annoyed if he thought we were friends.

Anyway, what are you doing in my house?'

'I came to see you, Jane, to tell you the good news.'

'You'd better get out before he comes home and finds you here. You know what he's like.'

'Who?' Georgina asked.

'Billy. He won't like it. Go on, go... piss off, George Garrett.'

Georgina gulped. Jane was far worse than she'd imagined and she wasn't sure what to do next. Should she play along with Jane's fantasy or jolt the woman back into reality. She decided the latter probably wasn't a good idea, not considering Jane's precarious position on the window ledge. 'I'll be off then. Are you gonna come in and see me out?'

'You know where the door is,' Jane answered.

'Fine. I'll take Sally and Penny with me. They're all alone, downstairs.'

'Don't you touch my girls!'

Ah, thank goodness, Georgina had touched upon a raw nerve. 'Best you come and get them then,' she said and began to slowly back away, hoping that Jane would follow.

'I'm not mad, George. I know you think I am, but I'm not.'

'I don't think you are, Jane. But I do think you should come indoors.'

'He's here, you know. He's always here. He'll never leave me.'

'Who, Billy?'

'Yes. I know you can't see him, but I can. He speaks to me too. He's forgiven me – he says he understands. Actually, he blames you. Says it was all your fault.'

'Yes, yes, Jane. It was. I'm sure he wouldn't want you to hurt yourself, though; you really should come in.'

'Billy loves me! Of course he doesn't want to see me come to any harm.'

'So why are you still sat on the bloody window ledge?'

'Don't you understand, George? He'll never leave me. This is the only way.'

'No... No, Jane. Think about your girls. They need you.'

'They need a good mother and I'm not one. I killed my own son.'

'You did it for them, to protect them. That makes you the best mother. You've proved you'll do *anything* for them, whatever it takes. Think about how they'd feel if you threw yourself off that ledge. Your pain will end but theirs will begin. A lifetime of pain because of you. I know you and that's not what you want to do to your girls.'

Jane didn't say anything but Georgina heard her sobbing and slowly, she eased herself around until her legs were inside the room. Georgina ran towards her and as Jane went to stand, her legs gave way. Georgina grabbed her and managed to stumble across the room with her and laid her on Sally's bed.

'Oh, Georgina, what have I done?'

'It's all right. I'm going to get you help, Jane. We'll make you better, I promise.'

Sally appeared in the doorway. 'Is my mum OK?'

'No, but she will be. Come and sit with her, I think she'd like that.'

Georgina stood back and looked at Jane. She was broken but hopefully not beyond repair.

'What's wrong with her?' Sally asked.

'She needs lots of rest and special doctors. Your mum is going to go away for a while, just until she's well again.'

Jane looked aged beyond her years and exhausted. Thankfully, she'd fallen into a fretful slumber.

'Is she going to the asylum?'

'No, Sally. I'll make sure that doesn't happen but she will be going to hospital.'

'Who's going to look after me and Penny?'

'I don't know yet.'

Sally pulled a blanket up from the end of her bed and over her mother. 'This was Billy's room. I'm not stupid, I know my mum killed him. And I know Billy killed my dad. I can look after Penny. You're not sending us away.'

Georgina stared at Sally in disbelief. The girl sounded a lot older than her thirteen years. All this time, Sally had known the truth. The way she'd dealt with it impressed Georgina. She thought Sally would be very capable of looking after herself and her younger sister. She was obviously a strong little character, stronger than her mother. Maybe one day when she's older, Georgina thought, she could join the family business. But for now, until Jane was well enough to care for her girls, Georgina would arrange for them to stay with Jane's sister in Surrey.

8

The next morning, Georgina stifled a yawn and instructed Knuckles to fetch her a cup of coffee.

'Did you have a late night?' Benjamin asked, then quickly said, 'Sorry, it's none of my business.'

Georgina looked across to his desk. Benjamin had done a good job at making sense of the books. When he'd informed her of the very positive shape of the business, she'd offered him a permanent position. She hadn't really thought he'd accept so had been pleasantly surprised when he had.

'As it happens, yes, a very late night but it wasn't much fun.'

'Oh,' Benjamin answered, seemingly unsure of what to say.

'Jane Wilcox isn't very well. I had to call a doctor to her last night. She'll be away for a while, in hospital. In her absence, I'd like you to take care of her finances and ensure her medical costs are paid.'

'Yes, no problem. It's nothing serious, I hope.'

Georgina didn't answer. She had no idea how long it would take Jane to recover, or if she ever would. The doctor had arranged for Jane's transportation to a private medical facility and had told Georgina under no circumstances was anyone to visit. The woman required complete rest and isolation. Georgina didn't like to think of the treatment she would be receiving. The doctor had said Jane would likely be put into an insulin-induced coma. It was a horrific thought. At least Molly had been able to take Edward home and she'd arranged for Jane's sister to collect the girls.

Knuckles came back with coffee, which Georgina gratefully sipped. She would have liked to go home and climb into bed but she had to stay alert – in an hour, she'd be introducing herself to the men who worked for the business. She knew they were going to be in for a shock and the news wasn't going to go down well.

Georgina cricked her neck. She was tense and her shoulders ached. She twisted her mother's wedding ring and checked the time again. The minutes seemed to be passing so slowly. A light tap on the office door distracted her. Knuckles opened it and Varvara walked in.

'Yes, Varvara, what do you want?' Georgina asked as the woman approached her desk. She was pleased to see that Varvara looked less distressed than she had before and now walked with more confidence.

'I wondered if you would like Dina and myself to offer any services to the men today?' she asked with her strong Russian accent.

'No, not on my time and not unless they're paying.'

Knuckles sucked in his breath as he shook his head. 'The blokes won't like that, Miss Garrett,' he said.

'Why not?' Georgina asked.

'Billy and Mickey always made sure the blokes got looked after.'

'They will be, in their pay packets.'

'Yeah, but they'll be expecting their *extras*.'

'You mean sex with the girls?' Georgina asked bluntly.

'Erm... err... yes,' Knuckles replied and looked embarrassed.

'Like I said, if that's what they want, they can pay the going rate and it won't be during their working hours. The same goes for you, Knuckles. Is that clear?'

'As crystal.'

'Anything else, Varvara?' Georgina asked.

The woman smiled. 'No, thank you, Miss Garrett,' she answered and waltzed away.

It was the first time Georgina had seen Varvara looking somewhat happy and it was nice. As the woman now passed Knuckles she eyed him with disdain, and for a moment Georgina thought she was going to spit in his face. Not that she could blame her; though if Varvara had, Georgina would have reprimanded her. She couldn't allow that sort of behaviour in the ranks.

The door closed and she told Knuckles, 'You can wait outside.' She couldn't stand to look at the man. He had his uses, for now, but she wasn't intending on keeping him close. After all, Knuckles was easily bought and she didn't trust he wouldn't sell her up the river to the highest bidder. She was under no illusions. Yes, she had control at the moment but had no doubt that there'd be someone waiting in the shadows, ready to take over her position.

'I'd like you to stay for this meeting,' Georgina said to Benjamin. 'I think it's important that the men know you work for me too.'

'Oh, yes, of course, fine,' Benjamin answered in his usual jumpy manner.

'Be warned, it may get a bit heated.'

Georgina saw his Adam's apple move up and down as he swallowed hard. She didn't think this was really the sort of job that Benjamin was cut out for. It was his choice though – she wasn't forcing him to be on her payroll.

'I'd like to discuss with you where income can be optimised. Perhaps you'll have some time later?' he asked, and as was habit for him, Benjamin pushed his glasses up his nose.

'It's definitely a matter we need to look at but it'll have to wait for now,' Georgina answered. Before she could look at growing the business, she had to get her head round how it worked.

'Absolutely, sure,' Benjamin said and busied himself with his books.

Knuckles opened the door and stuck his big head through. 'A couple of the blokes are here already.'

'Send them through to the back room to wait,' Georgina answered calmly, though her stomach was doing somersaults. The door closed again and she turned to Benjamin. 'Between you and me, I'm shitting meself.'

'Me too,' Benjamin whispered and they both laughed.

Georgina thought Benjamin's laughter sounded very much like a girly giggle. He was different from most other men. She put it down to him being educated and raised in a posh part of London. He was quite a lean man and immaculately turned out. In his expensive suit and red and white spotted cravat, he'd have been just the sort of chap she would have dipped in her day. She smiled ironically to herself – she trusted Benjamin and thought the feeling was reciprocated, but really, he should be the cautious one.

After all, if things had been different, she'd have readily robbed him.

Georgina took a gulp of her now cold coffee and grimaced. She pulled a small mirror from her bag and checked her reflection.

'If you don't mind me saying, Miss Garrett, you look, erm, err, quite lovely,' Benjamin said.

'I don't mind you saying at all, thank you,' she answered, and hoped she wasn't blushing. She placed her mirror back in her bag, took a deep breath in through her nose, and said, 'Right, it sounds like there's more of them arriving. Are you ready for this?'

'I, erm, think so, yes.'

'Good,' she said, and stood up, straightened her jacket and pushed her shoulders back. 'Knuckles,' she called.

He popped his head through the door again.

'Are they all here?'

'Yes, Miss Garrett.'

'Send them in,' she instructed. She could feel her heart racing and hoped she looked more confident than she felt.

One by one, the men filed in and filled her office. Seventeen tough, streetwise blokes stood in silence and looked at her with suspicion. Georgina felt very uncomfortable but passed her eyes over each one of them, giving the impression she was summing them up. A few had shown some respect by removing their flat caps or fedoras but most wore scornful expressions.

Georgina kept a stern face and her voice in a deep tone as she addressed them. 'You all know the reason you're here. Mickey's not around anymore. I'm in charge now. I suggest if there's any of you who don't like that idea, you leave, right now.' She paused and waited to see what they would do.

A broad man with a large moustache and weather-beaten face spoke first. He was standing to the rear of the office and now headed towards the door. 'This is a fucking joke,' he shouted. 'If you think I'm taking orders from a woman, you've got another thing coming. You lot are fucking wankers if you wanna stay and listen to her.'

Georgina said nothing and watched as he walked out, slamming the door behind him.

'Anyone else?' she asked and looked around the room.

'I ain't sure about this, George,' another man said.

'You address your guv as Miss Garrett,' Knuckles piped up.

Georgina recognised the man as a friend of her father's. 'What are you unsure of?'

'Well, I don't mean no offence, but you're a woman.'

'That's right, I am. Very observant of you.'

'This ain't really on. Don't get me wrong, I know your old man and he brought you up good 'n' proper but you ain't George no more. I mean, look at ya.'

In a way, Georgina took his comments as a compliment. He was correct: she was a long way from looking like the child her father raised as a boy. Georgina smiled and spoke sweetly in an almost demure way. 'Regardless of my attire, and your thoughts on a woman's place in society, I'm now running the business. There will be some changes, I believe for the better, and I'd appreciate all of you working with me.' She waited a moment, then changed her voice to a growl and added, 'If you don't like it, then FUCK OFF!'

There were a few shocked faces, some murmurs and whispers, then another man said, 'You're taking the piss, love. What the fuck does a woman know about what we do, eh? I'll tell you what, just for a laugh I'll work for you, but I lay odds on you getting taken down by the end of the month.'

Georgina slowly nodded her head and pursed her lips. 'I see. And I'll tell you what… just for a laugh, you can go. Get out. You're sacked. You ain't working for me.'

The man looked her up and down but didn't budge.

'Knuckles, I think he needs some help to the door,' Georgina said.

'Don't worry, I'm going. You'll be finished soon enough and I'll have me job back.'

Once he'd left, Georgina asked, 'Any more objections or can we get down to business?' When she was met with silence, she continued. 'I want each of you to tell Mr Harel here your name, your role within the Wilcox company and your address.'

'Why do you need to know where we live?' an older man asked.

'Because if anything unfortunate happens to you in the line of your work, I can ensure your family are properly informed and taken care of.'

This seemed to win the approval of some, and several of the men began to form a queue in front of Benjamin's desk. She could see from the look of the others that she still had some work to do to earn their respect but hoped, once she'd made her mark, it would follow.

'For now, it's business as usual and I'll see you back here on Monday morning.'

Her father's friend spoke again. 'What about these changes you was on about?'

'All in good time,' Georgina answered. In truth, she couldn't tell them yet because she didn't know.

'Typical bloody woman,' another said, 'They all say one thing and mean another.'

There was some laughter but Georgina didn't like it. She couldn't allow them to joke at her expense. She walked round from behind her desk and straight up to the man who'd made the stupid comment. He saw her coming and snidely grinned. Georgina locked eyes with him. He had no idea what was coming. She clenched her fist, pulled her arm back and then punched him hard on his nose.

The whole room gasped as the man's head snapped back and for a moment he looked dazed. Blood began to pour from his nostrils and drip down the front of his trench coat. She thought he might come back at her and she was ready to knock him out this time. Instead, he smiled as he took a handkerchief from his pocket and held it to his face.

'Fuck me, you can pack a punch,' he said.

Her father's friend chuckled. 'I should 'ave told ya, Johnny. Miss Garrett's old man taught her how to box. As you can tell, she's bloody good at it and all.'

Johnny stepped closer to Georgina and said quietly, 'I don't know many blokes who can hit as hard as you. Well done, Miss Garrett. I'd be honoured to work for such a fine woman,' then he winked at her flirtatiously.

'Let's keep this professional. You ever look at me like that again and I'll put you on your arse.'

Once more, the men began to laugh but now Georgina didn't mind. She'd shown them she wouldn't take any of their crap. Johnny wasn't laughing though. She'd hurt his male pride.

'Cheer up, it could have been worse,' she said to him.

'Oh, yeah, how's that?'

'I could have shot you,' she answered, and this time, she winked at him. Her voice louder, she called to the room, 'One more thing. By a show of hands, who here has a gun?'

Every man in the room raised his hand.

'I have, Miss Garrett, but I've only got one bullet. Billy used to dish 'em out to us every now and then but Mickey never gave us none.'

Ned spoke now. 'You don't need any, you've had that shooter for ten years and never bleedin' fired it.'

'I heard he shot a rat once, blew the top of his own toe off,' from another.

'Yeah, well, I thought the thing was gonna run up me trouser leg.'

The men roared and Georgina smiled, though it masked the fact that she had no idea where she'd obtain bullets from. She could ask, but she wouldn't.

'All right, back to work,' she said. 'And save your bullets for the rats with two legs who walk upright.'

9

Molly stood on the front doorstep and pulled her cardigan around her as she waved Jane's daughters off with their aunt. Sally had protested but Penny seemed happy to skip off.

As they disappeared from sight, Molly was about to go back inside when she noticed a large, black car parked on the other side of the road. Apart from Norman and then Billy, nobody on the street owned a car. It looked very out of place. She could see two men sitting inside. They both wore dark trilby hats, and the one behind the steering wheel was looking at her. His face was blank, neither friendly nor threatening, but she didn't like it and quickly went back indoors.

Molly checked on Edward and found he was sound asleep. She went to the lounge window and sneakily peeked through the net curtains. The car remained outside. It unnerved her but she told herself she was being silly. After all, the men hadn't spoken to her or come to the door. They were probably visiting someone.

The morning went by quickly as Molly busied herself with domestic chores, but each time she looked through the window, she saw the car hadn't moved and the men were still inside. It was odd but she didn't give it too much thought. She was more concerned with thinking about what she'd cook for dinner later. She rifled through the larder and realised she'd have to do some shopping.

Edward was awake now and gurgled happily as she wrapped him up, ready to face the bleak weather outside. Ominous dark grey clouds had come across, threatening a downpour. If Molly was to avoid the rain, she'd have to dash.

With her son snug in his pram, she opened the front door and tried to avoid eye contact with the man in the car. He was looking directly at her and as she walked along the street, she could feel his eyes following. Then, to her dismay, she heard the car engine turn over and a moment later, it was creeping along beside her.

Molly looked straight ahead and picked up her pace. Her heart raced and she could feel tears pricking her eyes. As they came to the end of the street, she went to cross the road but the car pulled in front, blocking her pathway.

She knew it would be pointless to try and run away, and stood, paralysed with fear. The door opened and a very tall, slim man climbed out. He was smoking a cigarette, which he threw on the pavement and ground out with his highly polished shoes.

'What do you want?' Molly screamed, finding her voice and frantic now.

'Mrs Wilcox?' the man asked.

'Yes. Who are you?'

'Come with us, please.'

'I'll do no such thing,' Molly said, sounding much braver than she felt.

'It would be in your best interests to do as we ask... for the sake of your son.'

They'd threatened Edward! Molly wanted to scream her lungs out and shout for help but she knew no-one would come to her rescue.

The tall man opened the back door and gestured for her to climb inside. Fearing for her son's safety, she gathered him in her arms and slid onto the back seats. The car sped off, leaving Edward's pram abandoned on the pavement.

'Where are you taking me?' she asked, her voice cracking with emotion.

Neither man answered.

'Please, don't hurt my son,' she sobbed, 'he's just a baby.'

Her eyes were bleary with tears, but Molly could see she was being driven out of Battersea. As they sped through the streets, she prayed that whoever these sinister men were, they'd spare the life of her precious son.

The heavens had opened and it was pouring with rain as Georgina arrived with Knuckles at the Livingstone Road brothel. She was soaked through to the skin, not that it bothered her but she did decide she'd have to get a car and a driver.

Knuckles opened the door and they went inside. Georgina looked around. Nothing much had changed since she'd last been here. She'd been searching for Norman Wilcox to beg him to help get her dad out of the police cells. At the time, she hadn't realised her search had been in vain. Billy Wilcox had already murdered his father. She remembered Hefty, Norman's right-hand man. Just as big and ugly as Knuckles but with a kinder heart. And Joan, the prostitute who wore far too much make-up and looked old enough to be a great-grandmother. She'd heard they'd all fled Billy and run off to Hampshire somewhere. It was a pity as she could have done with their support now.

A young girl with wild, long brown hair came bounding down the stairs. 'Hello, Knuckles,' she said, sounding chipper as she then turned her attention to Georgina. 'You must be the new guv. I wondered when you'd show your face.'

Georgina was taken aback at the girl's outspokenness and assumed she must be the cleaner or something similar.

'Ivy, this is Miss Garrett. Don't you go giving her any lip. Where's the other girls?'

'They all did a bunk. Soon as we heard Mickey had copped it, they legged it. It's just me here now, all by me lonesome.'

'What do you do here, Ivy?' Georgina asked.

'What do ya fink I do? I'm a prossie, ain't I.'

'Oi, I said no lip,' Knuckles warned her.

Georgina couldn't believe this. Unless she was mistaken, the girl didn't look much older than fourteen or fifteen. 'How old are you, Ivy?' she asked.

She saw a look of panic flash in Ivy's eyes, then the girl answered, 'Nineteen.'

'I don't think so. Tell me the truth – you won't be in trouble.'

Ivy chewed her dirty thumbnail and her brow knitted.

'I promise you, Ivy, no trouble,' Georgina reassured her.

'I'm fourteen, but I'll be fifteen in a few months.'

'I see,' Georgina said and smiled at the girl, but she was fuming inside. It disgusted her that Billy and Mickey had allowed this and Knuckles must have known she was just a kid. 'Knuckles, lock the place up and, Ivy, you're coming with me.'

'But you said I wouldn't be in trouble.'

'You're not, but you're too young to be working here.'

'Please, Miss G… I ain't got nowhere to go and I don't wanna end up in one of them public institutions. I work hard, don't I, Knuckles? Go on, tell her… tell her I'm a grafter.'

'Ivy, calm down. I told you, you're coming with me. Don't worry, I'll find some work for you to do, but not this.'

'Really? I won't be a prossie anymore?'

The girl's eyes were wide with hope and Georgina couldn't help but feel sorry for the little mite. 'No, you won't. Now hurry up and get your stuff together.'

Ivy ran back upstairs and Georgina turned to look at Knuckles with disdain.

Ivy was soon back with a small cloth bag and a fur coat that was far too big, draped across her shoulders. She looked quite comical, just like a young girl dressing up in her mother's clothes.

'That's not your coat, Ivy,' Knuckles said.

'Emily left it behind. Finders, keepers,' Ivy answered and poked her tongue out at him. Then she sauntered towards Georgina and said, 'I like your hat, Miss G.'

'Thank you, Ivy.' She didn't know what it was, but there was something that Georgina liked about the girl. Ivy was cheeky. She was cute too, with her upturned button nose and big round blue eyes. Georgina dreaded to think how the girl had ended up being sold for sex or what horrid things Ivy had endured, but whatever had happened to her, it hadn't broken her spirit.

They stepped outside into the rain and as Knuckles locked the door, Ivy looked up and down the street. 'Where's your motor, Miss G?'

'I haven't got one.'

'What sort of guv are you? You gotta have a car, it's the rules.'

'Oh, do I indeed. Well, as it happens, I'm getting one.'

'Shame you ain't got one now. My coat is gonna end up stinking like a wet dog,' Ivy tutted.

'Knuckles, you can piss off. Go back to Queenstown Road. Tell Mr Harel he can finish for the day.'

'Yes, Miss Garrett. See you tomorrow,' he answered and waited for a response.

Georgina ignored him, which didn't go unnoticed by Ivy.

'I don't like him either,' she said as he walked away. 'And he's got the tiniest dick I've ever seen.'

Georgina tried to hold back but she couldn't help herself and burst out laughing.

'It's true.'

'I don't doubt you,' Georgina said and tried to shake off the image of Knuckles' private parts.

'Where we going?' Ivy asked.

'You're going to stay with Mrs Wilcox for now. She'll take care of you until I can work out what I'm going to do with you.'

'Mrs Wilcox... Billy's wife?'

'Yes, that's right.'

'Oh no! She ain't nuffink like him, is she?'

'No, Ivy, Mrs Wilcox is nothing like him at all.'

Twenty minutes later they were on Molly's road. The rain had stopped falling and a small glimmer of sun broke through the clouds.

'My feet are squelching,' Ivy moaned.

Georgina wasn't taking any notice. She was focused on something she could see ahead. It looked like Molly's pram. A black bassinet with shining silver wheels. She picked up her pace and as she drew closer, she began to worry. When she got to the pram, she looked inside with bated breath. Empty. Where was Molly? And Edward? And why was the pram left in the street?

'Quick,' Georgina shouted, and grabbed the pram before running towards Jane's house. Once there, she hammered on the front door, and called, 'Molly... Molly... Open up, it's me.'

When there was no answer, she ran to the lounge window and looked through. Nothing.

'What's going on, Miss G?' Ivy asked as she panted to catch her breath.

'I don't know. This is Molly's pram – Mrs Wilcox's. I don't know what the hell it was doing left in the street or where Molly and her baby are. Something's not right.'

'What should we do?'

'I don't know... Come on, let's try her mum's house. If she ain't there, we'll try mine.'

Georgina hurried to Fanny's but there was no answer there so she ran home with Ivy in tow. She flew through the door and found Dulcie in the kitchen.

'Whoa, girl, where's the fire?' her gran asked as Georgina burst in.

'Have you seen Molly?'

'No, not since she left here last night. What's wrong, love?'

'I dunno. I found Edward's pram at the end of her street but no sign of him or Molly. She ain't at home and there's no answer at Fanny's.'

'Oh, Christ, I don't like the sound of that.'

'I know, Gran, I'm worried sick and don't know where to look next.'

Dulcie looked past Georgina, then asked, 'Who's that?'

'Ivy. She'll be staying with Molly, when I find her.'

'You'll have to go back to Jane's. Leave Ivy here with me and if Molly turns up, I'll send Ivy to get you.'

'All right. Oh, Gran, what if something terrible has happened?'

'There's no point thinking the worst. I'm sure there'll be a simple explanation. There normally is. Go on, go and see if she's back home. And don't worry, she'll be fine.'

'Ivy, you heard. I'll see you later,' Georgina said as she passed her in the hallway.

She ran back to Jane's house as fast as her legs would move and wished she'd been wearing her old *George* clothes – it was much easier to run in boots and trousers compared to heels and skirts. Once back, she was filled with disappointment when she saw that Edward's pram was outside where she'd left it. She knocked on the door again. No-one answered but an elderly lady from next door came out onto her step.

'Have you seen Molly?' Georgina asked.

'I saw her go out earlier. Isn't that Edward's pram?'

'Yes. I found it in the street but I've no idea where Molly and Edward are. Did she say anything to you about where she was going?'

'No, but I did see a car outside.'

'What sort of car?'

'I'm not sure, a black one, I think.'

'Was it a bath or a gin tin?'

'I dunno. A gin tin, I think.'

'Did you see who was in the car?'

The old lady bit her bottom lip.

'Think, please, it's really important,' Georgina snapped.

'I'm trying... I think there was two men but I'd never seen 'em here before.'

'Did they say anything? Do anything? Talk to Molly?'

'I don't know. I wasn't paying them no heed and it ain't my business what goes on in that house.'

'You've been very helpful, thank you,' Georgina said but couldn't bring herself to smile.

If the men in the car had Molly, she had no idea who they were or why they wanted her. But she was sure it would have something to do with the Wilcox business.

Molly had been taken into the rear entrance of a small hotel. She wasn't sure where but knew they hadn't crossed the Thames, so they must be somewhere in South London. They'd passed Waterloo Bridge. She recognised it because it was being dismantled. Maybe she was in the South East on David Maynard's patch.

She was led through a maze of corridors. Any glimmer of hope that she had of running away had quickly diminished – she'd never find her way back through the corridors let alone through London.

They climbed several flights of stairs and then the men stopped outside of a white-painted door. There was no room number on display, no knocker, nothing. After five distinct thuds, the door opened a crack and one of the men nodded. It then opened wider and Molly was escorted into a narrow hallway. Edward began to fidget in her arms. He was becoming restless. Molly thought he was probably sensing her fear, and though she tried to remain calm, her heart hammered.

Another door opened and a bloke as large as Knuckles stood to one side. As she passed him, she saw another man, smartly dressed, sitting on a plush brown sofa. Two other huge men stood behind him, probably bodyguards. She guessed she'd been brought to see the man sat on the sofa as he looked like the boss.

'Mrs Wilcox, it's nice to meet you,' he said, and puffed on a fat cigar. 'I wondered what sort of woman would have been married to Billy. I must say, you're not at all like anything I'd imagined.'

She should have known this would have something to do with Billy. Anything bad normally did. Molly could feel tears streaming down her cheeks again and snot running from her nose. She didn't care how hideous she looked, she just wanted Edward to be safe.

'Now, now, Mrs Wilcox. Why are you so upset?'

'Are you going to hurt me or my son?'

'No, I can assure you I'm not. Please, calm down.'

Molly drew in a long, juddering breath.

'That's better. I trust you had a comfortable journey?'

Molly didn't answer him. He'd said he wasn't going to hurt them but she wasn't sure if she believed him.

'Take a seat. Would you like anything to drink?'

Molly didn't move, and asked, 'What do you want from me?'

'Of course, you must be curious. Let me introduce myself. I'm David Maynard.'

The man needed no further introduction. As she'd feared, Molly knew exactly who he was. His reputation preceded him. He was South East London's most feared gangster. He ruled over all the boroughs from Lewisham to Bexley and most of Croydon and Lambeth too. She knew Billy had always stayed well clear of the man and had been told that Norman had too.

'I've heard you've claimed back the Wilcox business,' David said. 'That's good, it should stay within the family.'

'I still don't understand why I'm here,' Molly said. Her hand shook as she wiped her nose with the cuff of her coat.

'I just want a little chat with you to make sure you understand your boundaries.'

'If you mean about the business, it's nothing to do with me.'

'Oh, I think it is, Mrs Wilcox. The thing is, your late husband and your father-in-law before him, they knew their limitations. I'm quite happy to turn a blind eye to what goes on in Battersea. It's not really worth my while. Small fry,' he said with a flick of his hand. 'I'd like to hear some reassurances from you that you don't have any plans for expansion. I don't care what goes on with you and the Vauxhall mob – that will be your fight, not mine. But I will care if you decide to step on my toes or come anywhere near the docks.'

'Honestly, Mr Maynard, I'm not running the business but I can tell you that there's no plans for doing anything more than we already are.'

'Good, as long as we're all singing from the same hymn sheet. Now, how about that drink?'

'No, thank you. I'd like to go home,' Molly answered.

'Fine. My men will drive you back. It's been nice talking to you, Mrs Wilcox.'

Molly spun round. She couldn't get out of the room fast enough. As she walked towards the door, she heard David Maynard say, 'And pass my best wishes on to Miss Garrett.'

The return journey to Battersea seemed to take twice as long and Edward was becoming more fretful. He was due a feed but he'd have to wait. As the car passed Clapham Common, Molly finally began to relax. She'd be home soon. Safe, away from David Maynard's heavies.

The man had clearly known about Georgina. He'd used Molly as a threat because she was an easy target. She needed the money but wished she could run away from it all. The trouble was, she was in too deep now and couldn't get out. God, she rued the day she'd ever become involved with Billy bloody Wilcox and his stinking business!

Georgina saw the black car pull up outside Jane's house and as she ran out towards it, it sped off, leaving Molly on the pavement looking exhausted.

'Molly, oh, Molly,' Georgina said and helped her friend indoors. 'Are you all right?'

'Yes, but Edward needs feeding,' she answered as she began to climb the stairs to her bedroom.

Georgina followed. 'Who were they? What did they want?'

'Georgina, please,' Molly snapped. 'Look, I'm sorry, but it's been a difficult day. Can you make me a cup of tea? I'll see to Edward and then I'll be down.'

Georgina was desperate to know the details of what had happened but she could tell Molly wanted to be alone for now. The main thing though, her friend appeared to be unharmed. That's all that really mattered.

Georgina stepped outside and called over a young lad in short trousers playing in the street. She held out a coin to him and said, 'You can have this if you run to my house with a message.'

The boy nodded enthusiastically.

'Tell my gran that Molly is home and bring Ivy back here. Have you got that?'

'Yes, miss, Molly is home and bring Ivy here,' the boy repeated and held out his hand for the coin.

Georgina's nerves were jangled and once she'd told the boy where to go, she went back inside and made a pot of tea, the cure-all remedy. She sat at the kitchen table, patiently waiting for Molly to come downstairs and drummed her fingers as her foot tapped. What was taking her so long? She hoped Molly hadn't fallen asleep.

Georgina was relieved when her friend finally came into the kitchen a while later and she poured her a drink.

'Are you sure you're all right? You haven't been hurt?'

'I'm fine. I was just so scared.'

'Who were they?'

'David Maynard's men. They took me to him, somewhere over Deptford way, I think.'

'What the hell did David Maynard want with you?'

'To give you a message. He sends his best wishes. It was a warning, Georgina. He obviously knows exactly what's been going on. He warned me not to step on his toes. He doesn't care what goes on in Battersea but he was basically saying to stay off his patch.'

'The bastard. Did they take you off the street?'

'Yep, and they made it quite clear I had no choice.'

'This ain't on, I ain't having this,' Georgina hissed.

'There's nothing you can do about it. Anyway, it's over now.'

Georgina scraped her seat back and began to pace the kitchen. 'No it bloody ain't! I'm not having him thinking he's got the right to turn up whenever he feels like it and scare the living daylights out of you or anyone else. If he's got something to say, he can bloody well tell me to my face!'

'Calm down, Georgina. What are you going to do? Go storming in there and shout the odds at him? Just leave it, you'll make matters worse.'

'No, Molly, I can't leave it. If I let him get away with it, what's to stop him doing it again?'

'If he does, he does. It's better than you starting an all-out war.'

They heard a knock on the front door and as Georgina went to answer it, she said to Molly, 'We'll talk about this later.'

'There's nothing to talk about,' Molly answered.

When Georgina walked back into the kitchen with Ivy behind her, she said, 'When I visited Livingstone Road today, I found this young lady working there. Ivy, this is Mrs Wilcox.'

'Hello,' Molly said with a warm smile.

'Ivy, you can sleep in the small back room for now. Go and make yourself at home.'

'Thanks, Miss G. I don't mind having a small room. It's better than having to sleep under me mum's bed like I did when I was little. Nice to meet you Mrs Wilcox.'

'Don't tell me she was working there as a prostitute?' Molly whispered after closing the door.

'I know, it doesn't bear thinking about. I had to take her out and bring her here. I hope you don't mind but I didn't know what else to do with her.'

'You did the right thing. My God, I can't believe they had young girls working there.'

Georgina sipped her tea and Molly's voice floated over her head as she thought about David Maynard. The man had some nerve. Just because he was a face in South East London, that didn't give him the right to intimidate Molly. No, she wouldn't allow it and she'd see to it that he didn't bother them again.

10

It was Thursday morning and Varvara was awake before sunrise. In fact, she'd hardly slept for most of the night. After making Miss Garrett a gift, she'd tossed and turned with her thoughts fixated on how fascinating she found her. The woman was inspiring, powerful and beautiful and Varvara couldn't stop wild fantasies from flooding her head. She didn't care if her feelings towards Georgina were unnatural. It felt good and exciting. She'd never experienced anything like this before. Not even Tom, who'd once promised to rescue her, had made her feel this way.

She glanced at the clock. Georgina would be arriving soon. As she walked towards the bedroom window, the idea of catching a glimpse of her caused butterflies to flutter in Varvara's stomach. She tried to tell herself to pull herself together but then she saw Georgina round the corner of the street. Varvara's jaw dropped at the sight. As always, the woman looked magnificent and left Varvara craving her attention.

She dashed out of her room and to the top of the stairs. There, she waited a few moments and timed it perfectly that she descended just as Georgina came through the front door.

'Good morning, Varvara,' Georgina said with a casual smile.

'Good morning, Miss Garrett. I was just getting myself a hot drink. Would you like one?'

'Yes, please. Coffee,' Georgina answered, and then entered her office and closed the door behind her.

Varvara's pulse quickened. She wished she could come up with a reason to be in the office for longer than it took to place a cup on a desk!

Once poured, as she carried Georgina's coffee along the hallway, she met Mr Harel as he arrived for work. She found him to be a strange man. There was something about him that set him apart from others. She wasn't sure what it was – maybe the way he looked at her? He didn't gawp with any sign of desire, neither did he seem to look down on her status.

'Good Morning, Varvara. Is that for Miss Garrett?'

'Yes.'

'Would you like me to take it?'

'No, thank you,' Varvara answered brusquely. She wished he didn't have such impeccable manners and a kind face. It was very frustrating. She wanted to hate him the same way she loathed all men, but Mr Harel made it difficult for her to dislike him.

He held the office door open and Varvara took in the coffee. As she placed the cup on the desk, she was left disappointed when there was no acknowledgement from Georgina. She didn't want gratitude but she did want to be noticed. She stood, waiting, though she had no idea what she was waiting for.

Georgina looked up from her desk. Once again, Varvara was struck by the woman's striking eyes.

'Yes, Varvara, what is it?'

'Is there anything else I can do for you?' she answered, hoping Georgina would say there was.

'No, thank you.'

'Perhaps you would like me to prepare you some food?'

'No.'

'I have this for you,' Varvara said and reached into her pocket for a lace doily. She'd spent until the early hours of the morning preparing it, unravelling the threads from the only shawl she owned and refashioning them to make the doily.

'Oh, erm, thank you.'

'You are welcome, Miss Garrett. It is for your cup and saucer.'

'Yes, I see, thanks. Now, I'm very busy so if you don't mind...'

That was it. Her cue for dismissal. Miss Garrett hadn't seemed impressed with the doily, but Varvara realised it wasn't much of a present. Unfortunately, she didn't have the means to lavish the woman with expensive jewels and French perfumes.

Varvara slowly left the office but as she pulled the door closed behind her, she left it slightly ajar. She stood outside and carefully listened.

She heard Georgina say, 'We have a problem at Livingstone Road. The place is empty.'

'Oh, erm, that's not ideal. There's no mortgage on the property but it needs to be operational.'

'Yes, Benjamin, I realise that, and I need another woman here too. I just don't know how to go about recruiting prostitutes. I'm not going to ask Knuckles for any help. He seems to have an eye for the very young ones.'

'Where is he?'

'I bumped into him on the way here and sent him on an errand.'

Good, thought Varvara, and with Knuckles out of the way, she tapped lightly on the door.

'I'm sorry,' she said as she entered, 'but I was passing the office and overheard your conversation.'

Georgina looked at her with narrowed eyes. The woman wasn't stupid and had probably worked out that Varvara had been eavesdropping.

'You need women, prostitutes.'

'Yes. Do you know any who'd work here?'

'No, I don't. Mickey and Mr Wilcox made it impossible for me to leave the brothel so I only saw the men who came to my room. I know what makes a good whore though and I know how to run an efficient brothel. I can manage here for you and Dina could look after Livingstone Road. It would be less for you to worry about.'

Georgina paused before answering. Varvara could tell she was mulling over the proposal, and behind her back she crossed her fingers.

At last, Georgina smiled and said, 'I suppose that arrangement could have benefits... I'll give you a trial period. You'll both still have to take customers.'

'Of course, Miss Garrett.'

'I'll arrange for Knuckles to take you and Dina out tonight. He'll know where to find the women but you are to vet them and have the final say.'

'Thank you, Miss Garrett. I won't let you down.'

'Good, and ensure the women you bring here *want* to work and are not forced to.'

Varvara felt as though she was walking on air as she ran up the stairs. This would bring her closer to Georgina, she was sure of it. She tapped on Dina's door but as was usual nowadays, Dina ignored her.

'Please, Dina, I have some good news. Can I come in?'

Dina unlocked her door and opened it but glared at Varvara with hatred in her eyes.

'Let me in, I have to talk to you.'

Dina stood to one side, and though reluctant, she allowed Varvara through.

'May I?' Varvara asked as she walked across the room and went to sit on a velvet-covered gold gilt seat.

Dina nodded but her face remained sour-looking.

'Miss Garrett would like us to run the brothels. I will control here and you will take care of Livingstone Road. This is a very good opportunity for us, no?'

'Our freedom was a good opportunity for us but you have made sure we are still whores,' Dina snapped in Russian, and pulled a cigarette and a strip of matches from her pocket.

'Dina, there was nothing else for us to do. If we had left, we would have starved on the streets. But life is better for us now, yes?'

Dina blew smoke rings into the air and gave Varvara a sideways glance.

It hurt to see the contempt her sister held towards her. 'Please don't hate me for making us stay. I did what was best for us,' Varvara said sincerely.

'No, Varvara, not what was best for us. I've seen the way you look at her... You did what was best for you!'

'That's not true. I've always cared for you. I've always tried to protect you. You're my sister, Dina.'

'No, I'm not though, am I? We don't share the same blood.'

'That doesn't matter. You are still my sister.'

'You are no sister of mine.'

Varvara sighed. 'You are angry – it is fine. You can hate me for now. But however much you deny me, I will *always* be your sister.'

Dina furiously stubbed out her cigarette. 'At least if I am to work at Livingstone Road, I won't have to see you and your ugly face.'

Varvara hid a small smile. Dina, though older than her, had always been like an impertinent child and now she was behaving like one again. 'No, you won't, but you'll miss me,' she teased.

Tears began to well in Dina's eyes, a rare sight, and then the reality hit Varvara. 'And I will miss you,' she said and realised it would be the first time they would ever have been apart.

Georgina heard a car engine outside and looked out of the office window. Johnny Dymond had pulled up and as he climbed out, Georgina could see he was sporting two black eyes – inflicted by her the day before.

She quickly smoothed her hair with her hands then clasped them in front of her and rested them on the desk.

'That was very sweet of Varvara,' Benjamin said.

'Was it?'

'Yes. The woman has nothing yet she gave you a gift.'

'I hadn't thought of it like that.'

'Good morning, Miss Garrett,' Johnny said as he came in and offered a genuine friendly smile.

'Hello, Johnny, this is a pleasant surprise. I wasn't expecting you,' she replied, and was glad he wasn't harbouring any ill feeling towards her.

He pulled a seat round and, uninvited, sat in front of her desk. 'That's very girly,' he said, pointing to the lace doily. 'You'll get used to the routines soon enough. I normally call in on Thursday mornings.'

'Any particular reason?'

'Yeah. It's a big poker night on Wednesday, which means big loans. Here's last night's tickets,' Johnny said and handed her three pieces of folded paper.

Georgina looked at him as she took the papers. Even with his purple bruises, he was still attractive and his bright blue eyes had a mischievous glint. He didn't look quite as roguish as most of the other men and dressed with more class, a waistcoat under his suit rather than a pullover.

She studied what he'd written – three separate names and amounts with repayment schedules.

'It was a good night. As you can see, Willy West copped it for a ton and his cousin, Gilbert, had a pony. Taff signed up for forty quid. Fucking mugs.'

'And you've every confidence they can meet the repayment terms?'

'Yes, and if they don't, they're fully aware of the consequences,' Johnny answered and rubbed his hand over his knuckles. Then he jokingly added, 'Though the way you can throw a punch, I reckon we oughta set you on 'em instead of me.'

She ignored that and instead, said, 'I've been looking at the poker games and the associated loans. You're doing a good job, Johnny. I'm impressed but I think we can do better.'

'What do you mean? I've been running this side of things for years and there ain't never been no complaints before.'

'Jump down off your high horse. I'm not complaining, I said you're doing a good job.'

'So what's your problem?'

'We should aim for a more discerning player, one with deeper pockets.'

'Come off it, Miss Garrett. You ain't gonna get the likes of the bowler hat brigade gracing the top room of the Queen's Head with their presence.'

'I know, but I'm sure they could be enticed to a very select residence in Clapham.'

'Are you on about Billy's house?' Johnny asked.

'Yes. What do you think?'

'I like it. The more money they've got, the more they've got to lose.'

'Precisely. Do you think you can pull in the right people?'

'Without a doubt. I know exactly who to talk to.'

'Great. Give me two weeks to sort a few things. The first game will be the last Saturday of the month.'

'I'll have the room filled by then. Now, if you can reimburse me for last night's expenses, I'll be on me way.'

'You can see Mr Harel for matters to do with money. Just one more thing, Johnny... the loans, you only operate with those playing the cards? You're not lending to anyone else?'

'No. Talk to Bruce about that. He's a bugger for taking on the mothers. I won't touch 'em, me. Not my game, Miss Garrett. I can't be doing with roughing up a woman.'

Georgina was glad to hear it. She didn't want to like Johnny Dymond but found she couldn't help herself. He reminded her of a younger and better-looking version of her dad – a cheeky chap, or as her gran would say, a lovable rogue.

The office door opened again and Knuckles lumbered in.

'See ya, Miss Garrett, and by the way, in case you was wondering, Mr Maynard is the man to see for bullets and guns,' Johnny said and doffed his fedora to her as he passed Knuckles and left the office.

Georgina smiled at Johnny, but not at Knuckles. 'Well?' she asked the giant man.

'Here you go, I've wrote it down,' Knuckles replied and gave Georgina what she wanted.

'You're sure this is correct?'

'Yep. What do you want it for?'

'That's none of your business, Knuckles,' Georgina said, then warned, 'and keep your mouth shut about this.'

She slipped the piece of paper into her clutch bag, alongside the pistol Lash had given her.

'Benjamin, fill Knuckles in on what he's to do later with Varvara and Dina. I'll be back in a while,' she said, and marched from the office, turning before she left to say to

Knuckles, 'And remember, you are not the boss of my women. Treat them with respect or you'll have me to deal with.'

Outside, the sun was shining but Georgina was chilly as she headed to the Junction to find a taxi cab. This was one of those times when she could really have done with a car and driver. It would have made her trip to South East London much easier.

As she walked, Georgina twisted her mother's wedding ring and hoped she'd soon be back in Battersea, and in one piece. She knew a visit to David Maynard was daring. Some would say stupid or even suicidal. Regardless of what she'd heard about the man, she reasoned he couldn't be as bad as Billy Wilcox and on more than one occasion, she'd managed to survive him.

This wasn't something she was looking forward to doing, but it had to be done. She had no choice but to stand her ground. Georgina had something to prove. She was a woman but that didn't give this Maynard bloke the right to walk all over her – and she was about to let him know.

'I'm here to see Mr Maynard,' Georgina said to the scarred-faced man who opened the door before she'd even knocked.

'Fuck off,' the man growled back.

'No. Tell Mr Maynard that Miss Garrett is here. He'll want to see me.'

The man turned his head and whispered but Georgina couldn't see who to. She guessed he was passing on the message. As they waited for instructions, Georgina fixed her eyes on him. He sneered back at her and grimaced but she refused to be intimidated.

A few moments later, another man appeared, equally disturbing-looking as the first. He beckoned her inside where she found she was greeted with three guns being pointed at her head.

'Well, this is a fine welcome,' she said boldly.

'Are you carrying?' the man with the scar asked.

'Yes, I never leave home without my powder puff and my pistol,' she answered and opened her bag.

She heard the guns cock and with wide eyes, she froze. 'You'll be wanting this,' she said and slowly held out her bag at arm's length.

The scarred-faced man took it, removed the gun, and handed back her bag. Then with a nod of his head, he indicated to the others and she was led through to another room, but all three guns remained pointing at her.

The room was long and filled with furniture that she thought must be French. It wasn't like anything she'd ever seen. Fine art adorned the flocked wallpapered walls and heavy drapes framed four tall windows. Directly in front, standing at the end, she could see a man with his back to her, peering out of a window and smoking a cigar. She knew by the cut of his fine suit and the way he carried himself that this was David Maynard.

'You're as brazen as I'd heard,' he said and slowly turned to face her.

Georgina was surprised at how young he looked. She'd been expecting to meet a man in his fifties or sixties but David didn't look a day past thirty. As his eyes set on her, he appeared to be just as surprised as she was.

'They told me you had some bottle but I wasn't told how beautiful you are.'

Georgina could feel her cheeks flush but she hadn't come here for compliments and kept her face expressionless.

'What can I do for you, Miss Garrett?'

'Firstly, you can call your apes off me... I rather like my head the way it is and don't particularly relish the thought of it being blown off.'

'You heard the lady.'

His men dropped their aim and held their guns at their sides.

Georgina glanced round and then looked back at David. 'Thank you,' she said. 'I'm here to discuss your methods of delivering messages to me.'

'I assume Mrs Wilcox passed on my best wishes?'

'Yes, she did, in a sort of traumatised way. Mr Maynard, I'd like to make it quite clear that any business should be conducted directly through me. I am in charge of all matters relating to the Wilcox company, and as such, please refrain from harassing any other persons.'

'Ha, you're a piece of work, Miss Garrett. What makes you think that it's acceptable to march in here off the street and tell *me* how to conduct myself? Do I need to remind you who you're dealing with?'

'No, that won't be necessary. I'm well aware of your influence and capabilities. That being said, I was hoping that we could hold a civilised conversation without resorting to the use of violence or threats.'

'Oh, I do apologise, Miss Garrett,' David said in a mocking theatrical voice. 'Where are my manners? Please, take a seat and let me get you a drink. After all, you're an uninvited, loud-mouthed, up your own arse WOMAN, clearly living in cloud fucking cuckoo land!'

'Well, if we're going to throw insults around, at least I don't need half a fucking dozen dicks with guns to make me look big and hard.'

She expected David to react with anger, but he looked somewhat taken aback.

'Do they? Do they make me look big and hard?' he asked.

'A bit,' Georgina answered, and they smiled at each other.

'All right, you've made your point. I'll leave Mrs Wilcox out of it. To be honest, she wasn't what I'd expected Billy to have married. She's nothing like you. I would have thought you'd have been more his sort. Anyway, as I told Mrs Wilcox, as long as you keep your operations in Battersea, you won't encounter any problems from me.'

'I can assure you, Mr Maynard, unlike Hitler, I have no intentions of expansion outside of the borough.'

'Hitler? Is he on your patch?'

'No, Adolf Hitler. I know Chamberlain says there won't be another war but I'm not so sure. Why else would Britain be re-arming the forces?'

'I don't get involved in politics, Miss Garrett, and as a woman, neither should you.'

'I like to know what's going on. If there is another Great War, it will affect us all.'

'Yes, but it'll be out of our control. It'll never happen. You should be concentrating on what's going on under your nose or someone will jump up and bite you on the ar— backside.'

'I'm well aware, thank you, and talking of which, did you know that Mickey the Matchstick planned on working with the Portland Pounders and taking over all of South London?'

'Yes, it was no secret. The Pounders were gonna take him out on my behalf but you got to him first. You did us all a favour, really.'

'The Pounders know about me?'

'Miss Garrett, *everyone* knows about you. You're a woman – it's going to cause a lot of talk.'

'What are they saying?'

'Most think you won't cut it. Meself, I wasn't sure but now I've had the pleasure of meeting you, I believe you can hold your own. You've got guts and to do what you're doing, you're going to need them.'

'Thank you,' Georgina answered. David Maynard was a revered gangster and having his stamp of approval really meant something within the criminal underworld of London.

'I like you, Miss Garrett, and I admire your grit. But a word of advice – watch your back. There's a few who think the Wilcox business is up for grabs. I wouldn't like to see it change hands again. It looks very attractive from where I'm standing.'

Again, Georgina could feel herself blushing but kept her composure. 'I appreciate the warning.'

'I've always done business with the Wilcox family and I see no reason why that should change. The Pounders bring in a lot of contraband from the Liverpool ports, which is good profit for me. Your lot normally get my dregs. My blokes usually deal with yours as I don't like to lower myself. I tend to think of the Wilcox men as the bottom feeders. But you, Miss Garrett, you've brought a bit of class to the operation. I'll be dealing with you directly in future.'

Georgina was pleased with this new arrangement. Her men hadn't yet gained her trust. This way, she had more control. 'Fine. Now that the communication channels are clear, I'd like to get back to the office. If you could arrange for a taxi cab.'

'My man will drive you. He will ensure you get back safely. And, Miss Garrett, I suggest you find yourself some protection... other than Knuckles.'

Minutes later, Georgina was feeling very smug in the back seat of David Maynard's very flash car, though she could have kicked herself for bringing up politics. She didn't really know what all the fuss was about the man. So much for him being a terrifying villain. Huh, she thought, he's a big pussycat and she sensed she'd had him wrapped round her little finger.

11

The evening scouting for prostitutes to work at the Wilcox brothels had been successful, though Varvara was still laughing to herself about what Miss Garrett had said. *'Make sure they want to work and are not forced to.'* What woman in her right mind would *want* to be a whore? But she understood what her boss had meant.

Now, on Friday morning, as she sat on the other side of Miss Garrett's desk and updated her on progress, she was hurt to see the doily wasn't on view.

'Right, fill me in,' Georgina said.

Varvara looked at her and hoped the woman wouldn't see the desire she had in her eyes. 'Jenny is twenty-two, no drug or alcohol problems, no children and no education. She is grateful to be off the streets. Hettie is young, just seventeen, but we took her from a man who was not happy to be letting her go. It was good for Knuckles – he likes to beat people.'

'Can we be expecting any unwanted visits from her pimp?'

'No, we won't be seeing him again and Hettie is pleased to be working in these conditions.'

'Fine, and is Dina now at Livingstone Road?' Miss Garrett asked.

'Yes. There is just one more space to fill but Kathy is hoping her friend will join them there tomorrow.'

'You've done good work, Varvara. I shall expect to see diaries full of clients from Monday. Knuckles will get word to your customers that we're back open for business. And by the way, I shall have a telephone line installed at Livingstone Road. Dina can call here if she encounters any problems.'

'Thank you, Miss Garrett,' Varvara replied and as she scraped her seat back, she gazed longingly at her boss and asked, 'Is there anything else?'

Before Miss Garrett could answer, they heard a kerfuffle outside and Knuckles shouting. 'You can't go in there,' he yelled, but then Varvara flinched as the office door flew open.

A man staggered through, and to her horror, she saw he was manically waving a gun in the air.

'You fucking bitch,' he spat as he stomped towards Georgina.

Varvara didn't know if he was mad or drunk, but he was unsteady on his feet, and lurched sideways towards her. She should have jumped out of his way and run for cover, but instead she hunched her head down and charged at him. She ran into him with enough force to knock him off his feet but the momentum carried her forward and she landed on the floor on top of the now winded and dazed man. In a blind panic, she looked for the gun. Thankfully, his hand was empty. He groaned, and then she saw Miss Garrett standing over them and pointing the gun at the man's head.

Varvara pushed herself off him and to her feet, then went to stand in a safer position behind her boss. Both women looked down at the man who now realised he had a pistol to his head and was holding his hands up.

'Who the fuck are you?' Miss Garrett asked.

'That's Willy West,' Knuckles said from the other side of the room. 'I tried to stop him but he whacked me over the head.'

Varvara noticed a small amount of blood just above Knuckles' ear, but she was surprised that Willy had managed to get past him. Knuckles was a huge man and, in comparison, there wasn't much to Willy.

'You owe me money from a poker game, Willy. A hundred pounds. Is that why you're here? Trying to wipe your slate clean by getting rid of me?'

'Yeah, that's right,' Willy slurred.

'Get up,' Miss Garrett told him. 'Benjamin, give up your chair for the man.'

Mr Harel had taken cover under his desk, and ashen-faced, he edged along the wall towards the door, clutching his briefcase to him.

'Sit down,' Georgina told Willy. 'Knuckles, tie him up.'

Willy West didn't protest and now looked as terrified as Mr Harel.

Varvara watched in awe at Miss Garrett's composure. She didn't shake with fear or show any sign of nerves. She kept the gun aimed at Willy, and Knuckles began to wind rope around him and the chair.

'Varvara, take this,' she ordered, 'hold your finger on the trigger and don't take your eyes off him.'

Varvara gulped hard as, with a trembling hand, she took the gun from Miss Garrett. Her palm felt sweaty and her heart raced. She barely blinked, keeping her focus firmly on Willy. Moments later, Miss Garrett was by her side again. Varvara watched with confusion as she saw the woman point another gun at Knuckles.

'You big, fat, fucking snake,' she hissed at him.

Knuckles spun around then held himself rigid when he saw the hand pistol.

'Do you think I'm stupid, Knuckles?'

'What? Why are you pointing that thing at me?'

'You're in it together. But someone else is pulling your strings.'

'Honest, Miss Garrett, I don't know what you're on about,' Knuckles pleaded.

'Varvara, bring my chair over and tie him to it.'

Varvara stumbled as she dashed to fetch the chair and reprimanded herself. She'd have to hold it together if she wanted to impress Miss Garrett. She grabbed some rope and Miss Garrett ordered Knuckles to sit down. As she secured him to the chair, she took great pleasure in seeing fear in his eyes.

Georgina sat on the edge of her desk, just a foot away from Knuckles. She placed her pistol to one side but kept it close, then she leaned towards him. 'Now, are you going to tell me what's going on or am I going to have to beat it out of you?'

'I don't know nothing. Willy barged in and I couldn't stop him.'

'You and I both know that's a load of bollocks. I'm going to give you one more opportunity to tell me the truth,' Georgina pressed.

'It is the truth, I swear.'

SAM MICHAELS

'What about you, Willy? Do you want to save yourself from a pasting and tell me who you're working for?'

'You was right the first time, Miss Garrett. I just wanted to clear me slate. A hundred quid is a lot of money and I'm skint.'

'I see, have it your way,' Georgina said with a shrug, then picked up the gun, turned it around and, with the butt, she swiped Willy hard across the head.

Varvara winced. She was sure she heard his skull crack. Georgina had knocked Willy out and his head lolloped to one side.

'Whoops, too hard. I can't get him to talk if he's unconscious. Now, what about you, Knuckles? Anything you'd like to say?'

'Please, Miss Garrett. I ain't been disloyal to you.'

Georgina rolled her eyes and pulled her arm back ready to hit him but Varvara quickly interrupted.

'Please, allow me,' she said.

'Fine,' Georgina answered, somewhat bemused.

Varvara clenched her jaw as she pistol-whipped Knuckles' face with Willy's gun. Knuckles hardly moved though Varvara knew she must have hurt him.

'You dirty, fucking slag. I'll have you for this,' he said, and then spat out a rotten tooth.

Georgina moved her face to inches away from his. 'Now, now, Knuckles. That's no way to talk to a lady,' she whispered. 'And for the record, you won't be touching Varvara for this. Unless you want to lose the few teeth you have left, I suggest you start talking.'

'And what if I tell you what you wanna hear? What happens then?'

118

'You'll be saving yourself from a whole lot of pain.'

'But then what? You'll kill me anyway.'

'Who said anything about killing you?'

'I know how it works. You can't let me walk 'cos you know I can talk.'

'I'm not Mickey or Billy. That might have been how they did things, but that's not my way. I'll make sure you live because I want you to talk. I want you to tell every fucker out there they can't try and get one over on me, not without consequences.'

'What consequences? See, I knew it... you ain't gonna let me get off with this.'

'Knuckles, I promise I'm not going to kill you, though I might, if you don't cough up. You're worth nothing to me unless you talk.'

'Please, Miss Garrett, can I hit him again?' Varvara asked.

'Yes, I suppose so,' Georgina answered, then quickly added, 'Oh, I forgot to tell you, Varvara. I met a young lady who told me Knuckles has the tiniest dick she's ever seen. We could take a look. You could cut it off. Have it stuffed and keep it on your windowsill to give you a laugh.'

Knuckles looked horrified. 'All right, all right... I'll tell you everything, but please, just leave me bits out of this.'

Georgina exchanged a quick smile with Varvara, then told Knuckles, 'Start talking then.'

'It's Bruce. He heard you're gonna shut down his operations. He's got wind that you ain't happy about his loans to the mothers. It's his livelihood, so he got Willy pissed and convinced him it'd be a good idea to get rid of you. Willy was desperate. He's already up to his neck in debt and knew he couldn't repay Johnny. Bruce told him his debt would be written off and he'd sack Johnny then Willy could have Johnny's job. Bruce is a sly fucker. He thought he'd take over here.'

'And how much was you paid to allow Willy access?'

Knuckles hung his head.

'How much?' Georgina shouted.

'Nothing. He didn't pay me nothing.'

'So why did you go against me if you weren't paid to?'

'I... erm... I didn't think you'd manage here. There ain't never been a woman in charge so I thought Bruce would be me next guv'nor. I'm sorry, Miss Garrett, I went along with what he told me to do 'cos I thought he'd soon be running everything.'

'Mr Harel, do you have any scissors in your desk drawer?' Georgina asked.

Benjamin was holding his briefcase up against his chest and seemed startled when Georgina spoke to him. 'Er, yes, err, top drawer,' he answered.

Georgina indicated to Varvara to fetch them. 'Hold him,' she told her next.

Knuckles began to violently shake his head as Varvara attempted to keep him still.

'Wait, please, Miss Garrett, what are you gonna do to me? I've told you everything... please,' he begged.

'You have indeed, Knuckles. I did consider removing your tongue but I'd like you to take a message to Bruce, so instead, you can give him your ears. Tell him if I ever hear of his name again, I'll kill him.' Then she looked over Knuckles' shoulder and said to Varvara, 'Both ears please and try not to make too much mess.'

'No,' Knuckles screamed and as he struggled, Varvara accidentally stabbed his cheek. 'Stay still, Knuckles, you're making it worse,' she said as his blood flicked across her blouse.

'Erm, err, Miss Garrett. Can I interrupt?' Benjamin asked nervously from near the door.

'Go ahead,' Georgina answered.

Knuckles stopped flaying his head and Varvara stood poised with the scissors in hand.

'I... I'm not sure that this is the best course of action.'

'Oh. What do you think would be best?' Georgina asked.

'Well, erm, firstly, Johnny Dymond should deal with Willy. The man owes the business money so we want to make sure it's repaid. Anyway, judging by the state of him, I doubt he'll remember much about this incident once he's sobered up. As for Knuckles...'

'Yes, go on,' Georgina urged.

'Sorry, I was just gathering my thoughts. As for Knuckles and Bruce, I think it would be prudent for Knuckles to bring Bruce to you. Bruce thinks he can take over here, so he needs a firm reminder of who is running this company.'

Varvara tightened her grip on the scissors and waited for Miss Garrett's reaction. She hoped she'd still be permitted to cut off Knuckles' ears.

'If you can be trusted to bring Bruce to me, you're temporarily pardoned.'

'Yeah, yeah, you can trust me. I give you my word.'

Varvara's shoulders slumped with disappointment. She wouldn't be relieving Knuckles of his ears today.

'Your word means nothing to me. You bring Bruce here, tomorrow morning. If you don't, it'll be more than your fucking ears that I'll have cut off!'

Knuckles was relieved of his gun and then untied and instructed to take Willy away. Varvara thought Miss Garrett was mad to have let them both go – Billy Wilcox would have killed them, that's for sure. She hoped her boss's methods didn't end up backfiring on them all.

Georgina straightened her desk and Varvara went to fetch some soapy water to clean up the spilt blood. When she came back into the office with a bucket, Miss Garrett was telling Mr Harel to take the rest of the day off. The man was grateful and couldn't leave fast enough.

The door closed and Varvara began to wipe up the mess. 'Thank you for today, Varvara. That was very brave of you, to run at a man with a gun. It was me he wanted though, so why did you risk your life?'

Varvara kept her head down and scrubbed the floor. She didn't want Miss Garrett to see her face, sure that the woman would read the truth. She'd risked her life for Georgina because she was in love with her and she'd readily risk it over and over again if she had to. 'It was instinct, I didn't have time to think,' she lied.

'You've proven yourself loyal to me and an asset to the business. I won't forget this, Varvara.'

'Thank you, Miss Garrett.'

Once she'd finished cleaning, as Varvara poured away the dirty water, the reality of what had happened struck her – Miss Garrett could have been killed today! The thought stabbed her heart like a knife. Georgina was tough but she was vulnerable. Varvara had no doubt that there'd be more men like Bruce ready to finish off Miss Garrett, but first, they'd have to get past Varvara. She'd protect her love, at any cost.

That evening, Georgina had never been so pleased to be at home and sat on the sofa with her feet tucked under her.

'That was one hell of a week,' she said to Dulcie.

'I'm sure things will settle down.'

'I hope so. It's made me realise that David Maynard was right. I need some proper protection around me. Norman had Hefty and Billy had Knuckles. I'll have to find myself a man.'

'You've got Lash.'

'Yes, but he's going to be my husband, not my bodyguard.' Georgina laughed.

'What about that Johnny Dymond? You seem to get on all right with him.'

'I did consider it but he does such a good job with the gambling and loans, I'm reluctant to pull him off it.'

They heard a tap on the front door and Dulcie said, 'That'll be Oppo. Let him in, love.'

Georgina opened the door to her very good friend. She'd grown up with Oppo always being around. 'Hello, I'm glad you're here,' she told him as he walked behind her with his permanent limp and followed her into the front room.

'Hello, missus,' Oppo greeted Dulcie in the way he'd addressed her since they'd first met when he'd been ten years old. 'I've got some pot-herbs here for you. If you don't want the veg, I'm sure Mary next door will appreciate it. So, Georgina, why are you so pleased to see me then? You must want something,' he said with a cheeky grin.

'Actually, I've got an offer for you.'

'Oh, yeah, one I can't refuse, I bet?'

'You'd be silly if you did,' she answered, 'it's a very lucrative offer.'

'Go on then, let's hear it,' he said as he took his coat off and threw it over the back of a chair.

'I need someone to run me from A to B. If I buy a car, how do you fancy being my driver?'

She'd hoped Oppo would have jumped at the chance, but he looked worriedly at her gran.

'What? You don't seem too keen?' she pressed, waiting for an answer.

'I dunno if I'm the right man for the job,' Oppo said.

'You drive Mr Kavanagh's fruit and veg van, don't you? I remember you telling me how much you enjoy it. You said it's better than being stuck in the shop. Go on, Oppo, I need someone I can trust and I'd pay you twice what Kavanagh does.'

'I don't think I'm cut out for that sort of work, not with me gammy leg, and all.'

'What, driving?'

Dulcie cut in. 'I think what Oppo's trying to say, love, is he ain't happy about working for the business. You can't blame him – you know yourself how dangerous it can be.'

Georgina stuck her bottom lip out and pretended to sulk like a little girl.

'That face ain't worked with me since you was nine years old and don't bother trying the fluttering your eyelash look at me either,' Oppo said.

'Is there anything that would change your mind?' she asked.

'If your life depended on it, I would.'

'Huh, don't joke about things like that. Tell him what happened today... some nutter burst in her office with a gun,' Dulcie said through pursed lips.

'Bloody hell, Georgina, are you all right?' Oppo asked, his eyes wide.

'Yes, you don't see any bullet holes in me, do you? Gran, please shut up. I'm never gonna be able to persuade Oppo to work for me if you blurt out stories like that.'

'I think Oppo's mind is made,' Dulcie said, then told her, 'Put the kettle on. Molly will be here in a minute.'

It didn't go unnoticed on either woman that Oppo checked his reflection in the mirror over the mantel. And now Georgina realised that he was more spruced up than usual.

'You're looking dapper this evening,' she teased. 'Going somewhere nice?'

'No, but a fella's gotta look his best. You never know who you might meet.'

'Come off it, Oppo, you've got your eye on Molly, haven't you?'

'Course he has. He's had a crush on Molly since you and her were kids,' Dulcie said and chuckled.

'Blinkin' 'eck, is it that obvious?' he asked.

'The penny didn't drop with me until tonight, but me gran seems to have known for ages. Are you going to ask her out?'

'Nah, she'd never say yes to someone like me.'

'Actually, she's always thought you were a bit of all right,' Georgina said, remembering a time when Molly had said so and Georgina had told her off for being silly.

'You're kidding me?' Oppo asked.

'No, straight up. You should ask her. I reckon she'd love to go out with you.'

Georgina went through to the kitchen with a warm feeling inside. It would be nice to see her two friends together and for Molly to be happy with a good man. She deserved it, especially after what she'd been through with Billy Wilcox.

She stood at the stove waiting for the water to boil, and her mind drifted back to more pressing matters. She needed a driver and more importantly, a man or two close by to look after her.

Her father stumbled in through the back door, and held out his arms. 'There she is, give your old man a cuddle.'

Even from the other side of the room, Georgina could smell the alcohol fumes on his breath. 'Sod off, Dad,' she said, disappointed at the sorry sight of him.

'Aw, don't be like that.'

'Like what? You're a bleedin' mess, Dad. Sort yourself out.'

'You begrudge your old man a drink, do ya?'

'No, but I can't remember the last time I saw you sober. What's happened to you?'

'I didn't come home early to listen to this crap. Who do you think you are? You should be showing me a bit more respect.'

'Huh, what do you expect?' Dulcie snapped when she came into the kitchen. 'You only get respect when you've earned it.'

'Ganging up on me now, are you?'

Dulcie folded her arms across her chest. 'It's about time someone told you a few home truths, Jack. You've left everything to Georgina. She's out grafting for us to pay the rent whilst you're spending what little we've got on getting pissed out of your head.'

'I had a couple of beers, big deal.'

'You've had a damn sight more than a couple. It's about time you started behaving like the man of the house, instead of leaving it to your daughter!'

'I've heard enough of this,' Jack yelled and almost fell out the back door, slamming it behind him.

'Sorry, love, but he needs telling.'

'I know, Gran. I hate seeing him like it.'

'Me and all. If your mother was here, she'd have his guts for garters. Has that kettle boiled yet?'

Georgina poured the boiling water, her mind on her father. He'd taught her to be wily and had armed her with the skills she needed to fight any man. Now she wished he'd sober up and be the father he once was.

Benjamin was glad the cold weather had kept most people inside tonight. He stood outside of The Penthouse Club and glanced over his shoulder before ringing the 'members only' bell. The dark streets were almost empty so he'd be able to slip inside unnoticed.

The door opened and he was shown into a dimly lit corridor then down a flight of stairs and into a brighter reception area. Here, a tall man dressed as a butler stood behind the counter of a cloakroom and asked Benjamin, 'May I take your coat, sir?'

'Do you know, Buckster, I'm quite tempted to keep it on. It's absolutely dreadful outside. Do you have my powder and rouge there?'

'Yes, of course, sir,' Buckster answered and reached to a shelf below the counter then handed Benjamin a satin pouch.

'Thank you. Are the usual crowd in tonight?'

'Yes, sir, and Aubrey has a special treat for you all this evening.'

'Oooo, I'm tingling in eager anticipation,' Benjamin said and fluttered his hands above his head.

Before entering into the main club area, Benjamin popped into the gentlemen's toilet, dabbed on some face powder and rouge on his cheeks. He pulled his red and white spotted cravat from his pocket and proudly wore it round his neck. For anyone in the know, the cravat was more than an item of fashion – it was a sign to other men of his sexual inclination. A secret code that only another queer chap would understand.

'Quite lovely,' Benjamin said to his reflection and blew his painted face a kiss. 'Now I'm ready for the ball!' he added, and flounced from the toilets and down a further set of stairs deeper into the basement. The irony of the club name wasn't lost on him – The Penthouse Club – yet it couldn't have been any further from the roof of the building.

A stocky man in a platinum-coloured wig and red lipstick pulled open the door to the club, saying, 'Welcome, Mr Harel.'

Immediately, Benjamin could hear the falsetto tones of Princess Miranda singing along to the notes being banged out on the jazz piano. The smoky atmosphere from inside hit him, and he breathed it in. This illicit club for homosexual men felt like home for him. It was the only place he could be himself and meet with like-minded friends.

As he minced in, Princess Miranda spotted Benjamin from the stage and gave him a little wave. He'd once spent the night with Miranda but had found him to be impotent. The man preferred to talk about sex rather than doing it. Benjamin waved back and admired his costume. The Princess had outdone himself tonight with sequins and ribbons.

'Dahling, at last, you're here!' Aubrey cried melodramatically and opened his arms to greet Benjamin.

'And what a relief it is to be. There have been several occasions this week when I feared for my life,' Benjamin replied and kissed his friend on each powdered cheek.

'Oh, Benny, baby, come and sit down and tell me all about it,' Aubrey said, and led Benjamin to a small round table. There, he clicked his finger at the barman and ordered a bottle of champagne. Benjamin knew it would be the finest French fizz and as Aubrey owned the club, it would be free.

The barman, dressed in a chiffon blouse and silk pantaloons, fetched the bottle and two glasses.

'I swear, you would not believe the week I've had,' Benjamin said as he sipped his drink.

'Do tell,' Aubrey replied, and rested his elbow on the table and his chin on his hand.

'I'm working for the most fabulous woman, Georgina Garrett, but her business is quite illegal. It's terribly exciting and terrifying all at the same time. Honestly, Aubrey, I've never felt so alive!'

'It sounds fascinating, dahling. What sort of business?'

'She's just taken over from a gangster family. They're running brothels, and protection rackets, amongst other things. As you can imagine, it comes with its dangers. I mean, today, this morning, a man brandishing a handgun came into the office. One of the tarts knocked him to the ground and then everything became quite brutal. Shocking. But I love it.'

'Gosh, Benny, you're so brave.'

'No, not really, I was terrified. But, Aubrey, you'd adore some of the men who work for Miss Garrett. They're so big and very brutish,' Benjamin said and raised his eyebrows to his friend.

'Oh, Benny, you're so naughty, dahling, but that's why I love you.'

A man on stilts shouted from the small stage and hushed the room.

'You're going to enjoy this, Benny. I've brought Raphael all the way from Paris. He's very special,' Aubrey whispered.

A stockinged leg appeared from behind the stage curtains and the men in the club cheered. Then the curtains flew back and the tune from the piano burst into the *cancan*.

'My favourite, Aubrey,' Benjamin squealed and clasped his hands together.

Raphael high kicked his way across the stage in time to the energetic music, ruffling his 1840s-style French cabaret dress.

'Isn't he amazing,' Aubrey purred.

Yes, he was, and Benjamin couldn't take his eyes off him.

The crowd cheered and clapped, and once the act had come to an end, Raphael gesticulated towards Aubrey, who in turn, stood up and did a small bow.

'You've pleased your customers, as always,' Benjamin said. 'Bottoms up,' and they clinked glasses.

'Actually, Benny, I also have some news though I'm afraid mine isn't as thrilling as yours and I fear you're not going to be a happy bunny.'

Benjamin poured them both another drink and waited for his friend to continue.

'I'm going to close The Penthouse. Unless someone is foolish enough to buy it from me.'

'No, Aubrey, why would you do such a thing?' Benjamin asked.

'I'm getting far too old to be worrying about police raids and imprisonment. Humphrey's place was raided last week and I feel it's only a matter of time before they turn up here. Don't get me wrong, dahling, you know I love a man in uniform, especially one with a large truncheon, but really, perturbing is no good for my health.'

'I do understand, Aubrey, and I think we're all far too delicate for prison. But I can't imagine how dismal my life will be without you, my friends and The Penthouse. Has there been any interest for purchasing?' Benjamin asked hopefully.

'No, not as yet, which is tragic. You know my books – the club is very profitable. But I think most men have the same concerns as me – the long arm of the law.'

Benjamin sipped more of the chilled champagne. Yes, most men probably were worried about the law, but he knew a woman who wasn't. But if he could persuade Miss Garrett to look at The Penthouse Club as an investment, it would mean revealing his secret identity. He wondered how she'd react and the more he thought about it, the more he realised she wouldn't be the least bit disconcerted.

12

It was late on Sunday afternoon and Georgina had gathered The Maids of Battersea into Dulcie's front room for a round-up of the week. She'd discovered a lot about the activities of the business, some of which she didn't like. She knew the others wouldn't be pleased about it either. She planned on making some small changes to start and hoped they'd listen to her reasoning and agree with her ideas.

'Did you see that picture in the *Daily Mail* yesterday?' Dulcie asked Molly.

'No, I ain't seen the papers in yonks.'

'Oooo, I'll show you. Pass me the paper on the sideboard. You won't believe your eyes.'

'Why? What is it, Dulcie?'

'It's a blinkin' monster! There's a real-life picture of it. The Loch Ness Monster, up in Scotland. Bloody ugly thing it is too.'

'No way!'

'Yes, it's true. Some surgeon bloke took the photograph and seeing as he's a professional man, he wouldn't be lying, would he?'

Georgina cleared her throat. 'Sorry to interrupt your fascinating conversation but can we look at photographs of monsters later, please, and get on with what we're supposed to be talking about.'

Molly, Fanny and Dulcie quietened down.

'Right, ladies, as you know, this week has been eventful,' Georgina began.

'Sorry, Georgina, but what happened with Bruce yesterday morning?' Fanny asked.

'I left him with Knuckles holding him down and allowed Varvara to deal with him. She was more than happy to oblige.'

'So you don't know where he is?'

'He'll be incapacitated so there's no need to worry about the little worm.'

'Have you heard any news about Jane?' Molly asked.

'I rang the hospital this morning. All they would say is that she's undergoing treatment but it's too early to expect results. Any more questions or can I tell you about our business plans?'

'Go on, love,' Dulcie urged.

'Right, but before that, there's something else... I think it would be for the best if each of you had a pistol. Just something small, but enough to protect yourself.'

'No way, I'm not carrying a gun,' Molly answered first.

'No, can't say I'm keen either,' Fanny said.

'And I don't need one, love,' from Dulcie.

'Fine, I thought that's what you'd say. Anyway, I've been through each aspect of the business. The good news is, it's all in profit.'

'What's the bad news?' Molly asked.

'Some of the ways the profits are made.'

'It's a Wilcox business. It's hardly going to be nice and fluffy,' Fanny said.

'Quite, so keep that in mind. Firstly, Johnny Dymond has been doing a smashing job with the poker and loans. We're aiming for a more exclusive clientele, you know the sort, so we're opening up in Clapham.'

'What, in mine and Billy's house?' Molly asked.

'Yes, and I knew you wouldn't mind. It's just sat there empty, so we might as well make use of it. There'll be two games a week and the bigger the stakes, the bigger the loans. I'm also renting out the upper rooms to a bloke who's setting up a photographic studio. He likes making them risqué postcards of naked women. We'll be doing his distribution so we'll be quids in on that too.'

'Great idea,' Dulcie said.

'Now, both brothels are up and running but we won't be earning as much from them as Billy did. That's because we're paying the women for their work.'

'Fair enough,' from Fanny.

So far, so good, thought Georgina, but she hadn't yet divulged everything. 'The protection racket, or as Jane says, the insurance… I don't like the idea of it but it's easy money. If we don't do it, someone else will.'

'Are you suggesting we carry on with it, even after knowing how it affected Ezzy?' Dulcie asked and didn't look happy at the prospect.

'Yes and no,' Georgina answered. 'I reckon we should reduce the payments and increase the numbers. I want the businesses to know that we are looking after *their* interests. We'll ensure no other gangs infiltrate the area and take over the protection. The emphasis will be on keeping our turf safe for the traders. They won't have to pay extortionate rates to anyone else, just smaller affordable payments to us. Doing it this way will make it like it really is insurance.'

'No skin off my nose,' Fanny said.

'The next thing is the drugs supply. Heroin is in big demand, especially round the slums. We've all seen what it does to people and I don't like it any more than you. The thing is, if we don't supply it, someone else will and I don't want another supplier coming in and taking over. It'll lead to trouble. So, I've instructed the Barker twins to not push their shit on anyone who's clean and no selling to kids. I'm afraid that's the best I can do.'

'If you think that's for the best, it's fine with me,' Molly said.

'Good. Now, the contraband. David Maynard wants to deal directly with me from now on but I'm going to keep Ned and Phil for selling it on.'

'Are you saying that the dodgy cigarettes and booze come from the Maynards?' Molly asked.

'Yes and I was surprised too. The Portland Pounders supply him and we get what he can't shift. Any black market stuff comes via South East London. Talking of which, the races – I really don't want to get involved with what's going on at the racecourses. I know the Maynards are having wars with some Birmingham lot and the papers are full of news about shoot-outs all over the place. At the moment, Old Cyril in the bike shop takes the bets but he's been instructed to send any big wagers to the Maynards. Can you believe the one legit part of the business and that old codger is running a bookies and selling potcheen out the back door? So much for the bike shop being a front.'

'I've known Cyril for donkey's years. He was a friend of your grandfather. Nice bloke, or so I thought until I heard he was working for Norman Wilcox. Talk about ironic, eh,' Dulcie said.

'I haven't got round to meeting him yet but I'll send him your regards, Gran.'

'Yes, you do that.'

'The one thing I really don't like and I'm changing, is the loans for mothers. Bruce looked after that side and now he's gone. I want you on it, Fanny.'

'Me?' Fanny exclaimed. 'But I can't rough up the women who can't keep up their repayments. Gawd, Georgina, I know all about how Bruce did things. There was many a time when I was tempted to go to him but then thought better of it. I took enough bleedin' hidings from my old man, let alone getting a clout or two from Bruce.'

'There won't be any roughing up of the mothers and the interest rates are going to be next to nothing. That should help to make repayments easier.'

'How are we gonna make money from it then?' Fanny asked.

'We won't, well, not much.'

'I see, so what are we now, a bloody charity?' Fanny snapped. 'More of Molly's money going down the drain.'

'No, Fanny, far from it. But I've been wrestling with my conscience and we either cut the loans to mothers altogether or we offer an affordable alternative.'

'You're going soft in the head. Once them women get wind of easy money available with no slaps for non-payment, they'll take the piss, you mark my words,' Dulcie warned.

'I'm sorry, Georgina, but I think your gran is right,' Fanny added. 'I know what it's like to be desperate and not to be able to feed your kids. You'll be dishing out money hand over fist.'

'All right, I'll have a think about it; see what else I can come up with. But in a nutshell, that's it all pretty much covered. There's the commission on the rent collections but that's something I want to look into.'

'How do you mean, love?' Dulcie asked.

'Well, we get Queenstown Road rent free in exchange for collecting rents from the landlord's other properties. I don't think it leaves us in a secure position. We need to own property, like Livingstone Road and the house in Clapham. But with me cutting the traders insurance, paying the prostitutes and stopping the mothers' loans, there's not as much profit as there once was. I need a cash injection for investment, but leave it with me 'cos I'm working on something.'

Molly smiled warmly at her friend. 'I think you're doing an amazing job, Georgina. Thanks to you, Mum's looking at a new place to rent tomorrow, ain't that right, Mum?'

'Yes, its only round the corner but I'd have my own front door and my own bedroom. Ethel and Charlotte will still share 'cos I'm keeping a room spare for Molly.'

'That's nice, but why the room for Molly? She's fine at Jane's and someone needs to be there to keep an eye on Ivy,' Georgina said.

'She'd be happier with me. And anyway, what are you gonna do with that Ivy girl?'

Before Georgina could answer Fanny, they heard hammering on the front door. Fanny was nearest to the window and jumped up from the sofa to look outside. 'It's a young lad,' she said.

Georgina went to open the door and immediately recognised the boy she'd sent on an errand before. He looked pale-faced and wide-eyed.

'You've gotta come quick, miss. It's Ivy. She's been smashed up real bad,' he cried hysterically and yanked on Georgina's sleeve.

'Hang on, slow down. Tell me what's happened.'

'I dunno, I just saw her come home... Come on, quick,' he urged again.

Georgina reached round for her coat from the newel post. Molly and Fanny were both in the hallway now.

'Ivy's been hurt. Stay here, I'll be back as soon as I can,' she told them and ran with the boy towards Jane's house.

She was soon running through Jane's front door and found Ivy semi-conscious on the sofa. She quickly glanced over her but it was obvious the worst of her injuries had been inflicted to her face. Ivy had a deep cut above her eyebrow, her nose looked broken and there were copious amounts of blood around her swollen mouth. Georgina bit on her bottom lip. Who could have done such a heinous thing to a young girl?

'Ivy, it's me, Georgina, Miss Garrett. Can you hear me?'

Ivy groaned and slowly opened her bruised eyes.

'Who did this to you?'

'A punter, Miss G.'

Ivy lisped as she spoke and Georgina could see at least two of her front teeth were missing. 'Do you know his name?' she asked.

'It hurts, miss, really hurts.'

'All right, you rest now. I'll get the doctor and we can talk later.'

'I'm sorry. Am I in trouble?'

'No, sweetheart, don't you worry about a thing,' Georgina answered and stroked the girls' blood-matted hair back from her face.

As Ivy slipped into unconsciousness, Georgina went to the telephone table and briefly paused. Her lips set in a grim line and her violet eyes narrowed. Was history repeating itself? She'd once been battered beyond recognition on Billy Wilcox's orders and had lain unconscious on their sofa at home. In the end Billy hadn't got away with it, and she was determined to ensure that neither would whoever did this to Ivy.

That same evening, on the other side of Battersea in a mid-terraced house, Jimmy Hewitt closed his eyes and tried to block out his wife's incessant whinging. Her squeaky, high-pitched tone grated on him and he knew if he looked at her sour face, he'd be tempted to slap it. He'd had a fascinating and fulfilling evening but now his wife's nagging was spoiling the exhilarating memory of it.

He was sat in an armchair, spent, close to the fire whilst his wife had walked across the dim room to peep through the net curtains and onto the street.

'I don't know why you had to drag us over here to this shithole. I was quite happy in Blackheath. It was like the countryside compared to this filthy pit. And the neighbours, well, don't get me started. Common, they are. Common as muck,' she said.

Jimmy had heard it all before, at least a dozen times since they'd moved into the two-up two-down. Granted, it was a step down from the semi-detached house opposite the green that they'd rented, but now that David Maynard had sacked him from the company, it was all he could afford. Anyway, Jimmy needed to be in Battersea. He'd heard about a woman running the Wilcox business and to him, this sounded like an opportunity for an easy takeover.

'Are you listening to me, Husband?' his wife asked.

Jimmy opened his eyes to see her standing in front of him with a scowl on her lined and podgy face and her arms folded. She was wearing her housecoat and her salt and pepper hair was in rollers under a garish scarf. He must have loved her once, maybe when they'd married twenty-five years earlier, but she'd been barren and being childless seemed to have left her bitter. But she was loyal to him and kept his sordid secrets. Like it or lump it, he couldn't leave her and risk her blabbing about his sadistic sexual ways.

He eyed her up and down. A short woman, she was as round as she was tall and for a moment, Jimmy wondered if he pushed her over, would she roll? 'Yes, *Wife*, I'm listening,' he answered.

'That David Maynard has got a lot to answer for. You've been good to him over the years, and his father before him. You've always done as they wanted. One silly mistake and this is how we end up paying for it!'

'It was a bit more than a silly mistake.'

'Aw, come off it. How was you supposed to know that she was married to a copper? The silly cow shouldn't have been on the hill at that time of night. No woman in her right mind would have been there unless she was an old tom. She should have known better, and you should have spoken up for yourself to Mr Maynard!'

Jimmy reached across for his pipe and sucked hard on it as he held a match to the tobacco. His wife was on one now and he knew she wasn't finished yet.

'That's your bloody problem: you never speak up for yourself. Did you try and explain to Mr Maynard? No, of course you didn't. You wouldn't want him knowing about your little collection, would you? No, that wouldn't do. Jimmy Hewitt, The Dentist. David Maynard's right-hand man who extracts the teeth of them who wrong Maynard's little empire. Oh dear, we couldn't have Mr Maynard knowing about the *other* teeth you take out, could we?' she sneered.

'Leave it,' Jimmy snapped, feeling she was going to belittle him again.

'No, I won't and why should I? It's me that has to pay the consequences for your sick perversion! It's me who has to put up with living in this shitting dump! It's all right for *me* to have to live with what you get up to but woe betide anyone else finding out about it! Oh no, we couldn't possibly let David Maynard know that you like to fuck whores and yanking out their teeth turns you on. You sick bastard. It's bad enough I turn a blind eye to it but to keep their teeth in that jar upstairs as souvenirs is just horrible. It turns my stomach, it really does.'

'All right, all right, I'm sorry I forgot to put it away in my drawer.'

'It doesn't matter. Whether that jar is on my dressing table or hidden in your drawer, I still know it's there. Can't you just get rid of it?'

Jimmy straightened his back and glared at his wife. 'No, and don't you dare think about slinging it out.'

'Huh,' Daisy grunted and threw her chubby bulk down in the seat opposite him. 'Don't worry, Husband, I'm not touching that jar, not even if my life depended on it. But my point is, if you'd explained to Mr Maynard about it being a genuine mistake and you thought that woman was a prostitute, I'm sure he would have turned a blind eye and we wouldn't be stuck here now.'

'It wouldn't have made a difference. He had to get rid of me or kill me, otherwise he would have had Scotland Yard on his back.'

'If you say so. Still, I suppose what's done is done, but you'd better start working on how you're going to get your hands on this Wilcox business. I don't want to be living in this squalor for any longer than I have to.'

'Don't worry, Wife, it's all in hand,' Jimmy answered as he savoured the mellow aroma of his tobacco and recalled the pleasure he'd had this evening. When he'd pulled the teeth on the young tart's face, her agonised expression had been delightful and he'd climaxed in his trousers. He'd been careful this time and kept his scarf pulled over his face. She could live, unlike some of the others. He hadn't enjoyed killing them. He took no pleasure in corpses. A dead face could bleed but it didn't express pain. Anyway, he needed her. The tart had been part of his carefully thought-out plan. He'd done his research well. He knew all about Georgina Garrett and the women in her so-called club. The Maids of Battersea – huh, he thought to himself. Once he had his way, they'd all be begging him for mercy.

13

The following morning, Georgina held the usual weekly meeting in the office with her men. This time, compared to last, she felt there was a little more respect in the room.

'Right, just a couple more things before we finish,' she said. 'You've probably all heard by now that Bruce is no longer working for the company.'

'Serves him bloody right,' one of the Barker twins said and the other added, 'We never liked the sly bastard.'

'Well, if any of you did and would like a memento of him, I'm pretty sure there's a few bits of him in the grate in the room next door.'

'Fuck me, Miss Garrett, that's a bit rough,' Johnny Dymond said, smirking.

'I don't muck about, Johnny. If anyone crosses me, that's what happens. Bruce ain't dead but he ain't quite all together, if you get my drift.'

'Fair enough and if Willy don't make his repayments this week, I'll remind him of what happened to Bruce,' Johnny said, which caused a few of the men to chuckle.

'On another note, a girl was hurt last night. I realise it ain't unusual for the prostitutes who aren't under our protection to get roughed up, but some of you may know Ivy. She's no longer working at Livingstone Road but she's still one of ours.'

'I know Ivy, mouthy little tart but sweet with it. Is she all right, Miss Garrett?' Ned asked.

'Yes, but this weren't someone giving her a backhander. It was a bit odd. The bloke took out her front teeth.'

'What, punched 'em out?'

'No, Ned, that's why I find this odd... He pulled them out, with pliers, and she reckons he enjoyed doing it. Do any of you know who might have done this?'

The men glanced around at each other and shook their heads, then Knuckles spoke. 'The Dentist. He works for the Maynards. He's the only geezer I know who takes out teeth.'

'What's he doing on my patch and why would he target Ivy?'

'I dunno, Miss Garrett. I ain't saying it was definitely him.'

'I want you all to keep your eyes and ears open. I ain't having this sort of thing going on in Battersea. If you get wind of who did it, come straight to me.'

Knuckles began to chortle. 'Are you gonna set Varvara on him?' he asked.

'No, this one's for me,' Georgina answered gravely.

The room cleared and Georgina sat back at her desk but she had a knot in her stomach, which was making her feel sick. The meeting with the men had gone well but she knew she'd have to meet Cunningham next. He was a policeman and Georgina had a deeply rooted hatred for all coppers, especially bent ones. This one had been on Billy's and then Mickey's payroll so now she'd inherited him. She could only hope that he wasn't one of the policemen who'd abused her so appallingly when she'd been arrested for a murder that she hadn't committed. The awful memory of what had happened in the police station cell would never leave her. She'd had some retribution when she'd blown up the station, and though her actions had caused the death of a few coppers, most of her abusers were still on the force. If Cunningham walked in and she recognised him as one of them, Georgina wasn't sure if she'd be able to control herself.

Benjamin's voice broke into her thoughts.

'Miss Garrett... Miss Garrett...'

'Yes. Sorry, Benjamin, I was miles away.'

'I, erm, err, I, I'd like to suggest an investment for you. A relatively small outlay for good returns. Due to the changes you are implementing and the split of profits, the income forecast for the business is taking a downward turn. To counteract this, I firmly recommend you...'

'Yes, thank you, Benjamin. Look, I'm sorry to cut in but can we have this discussion later?'

'Erm, yes, yes, certainly.'

Georgina was already fully aware that she needed an increase in revenue and had some ideas but right now, she couldn't think straight. Not when at any minute, Knuckles could be showing in one of the policemen who'd tried to sodomise her with a truncheon. Her hand rested on the handle of the drawer where she kept Willy's gun. If she were to shoot him, she wouldn't use the pistol Lash had given her. But murdering a policeman – it could be her downfall and she'd swing for his death. She knew it was a terrible idea but could she resist blowing out the copper's brain? The thought was so appealing and she was very tempted.

'It's perfect, Mum,' Molly said as she and Fanny headed back to Jane's house.

They'd just viewed a new property for Fanny to rent and the smile on the woman's face told Molly that her mother was pleased with what they'd seen.

'Are you sure you won't move in with me and the girls?' Fanny asked.

'No, thanks, Mum. Jane could be in hospital for ages and someone needs to keep an eye on Ivy, especially now she's been hurt.'

'Don't get me wrong, I feel sorry for the girl, but she ain't your responsibility, or Georgina's.'

'I know, but once she's recovered, Georgina will get her working for her keep.'

Fanny scowled. 'Yeah, then what? After this one, there's bound to be another and what about this business with the mothers' loans? What's happening to Georgina? Anyone would think she's taking over the National Relief Fund.'

Molly looked at her mother in disbelief. She couldn't understand why Fanny had become so mean-hearted. 'Why are you being like this, Mum?' she asked.

'Like what?'

'I dunno... horrid. You've not been very nice to Georgina lately. If it wasn't for her, you wouldn't be moving into the nice house we've just seen.'

'Oh, Molly, take your blinkers off. It's thanks to you that I'm moving home and can finally jack in me cleaning job at the hospital.'

'How do you work that out?' Molly asked.

'Well, you was the one that had to suffer Billy. It's your business, not Georgina's. She's in it for what she can get. She ain't doing you no favours. How come she gets the biggest cut of the profits, eh? It's your company, you should be getting the lion's share.'

'Leave it out, Mum. If Georgina hadn't taken it over, none of us would be getting anything. You should be a bit more bloody grateful. You ain't had to do nothing, yet you're still getting paid. She don't have to dish the money out to you, you know,' Molly snapped. She didn't like to use that tone to talk to her mother but Fanny's attitude wasn't very nice.

'I've got more rights than that Ivy who's getting housed, fed and watered.'

'After what that poor girl's been through, you're not telling me you resent a kind hand being offered to her?'

Fanny sucked in a deep breath. 'No, of course I don't. I'm just worried that Georgina's being over-generous in the wrong places and you'll lose out on what's rightfully yours.'

'Don't worry, Mum. Georgina knows what she's doing.'

As they arrived outside Jane's house, Fanny went to the front of Edward's pram to help lift it over the step. From out of nowhere, a short, smartly dressed man appeared.

'Please, let me help you with that,' he offered, and edged his way in front of Fanny.

After being taken off the street by David Maynard's gang, Molly was very suspicious of people now and quickly retorted, 'Thank you, but we can manage.'

The man stepped to the side and leaned over the pram. 'Such a bonny baby. A boy?'

'Yes, now if you'll excuse us,' Molly said.

He then looked at Fanny and smiled broadly as he lifted his bowler hat. 'You must be the boy's aunt? Such a young lady couldn't possibly be his grandmother.'

Fanny looked quite charmed by the out-of-place-looking stranger and replied, 'No, I'm his grandmother.'

'Really? Well, what a very lucky little boy. What's his name?'

'I'm sorry, but we don't have time for this,' Molly said brusquely and pushed the pram forward.

'Molly, don't be so rude to the gentleman,' Fanny hissed and frowned at her, then turned to the man and said, 'I'm sorry about my daughter. This little fella is called Edward.'

'Pleased to meet you, Master Edward. And may I enquire, what is the name of Edward's delightful grandmother?'

'Fanny. Fanny Mipple,' she answered coyly, much to Molly's annoyance.

'Well, I shan't keep you any longer. I'm new to the area and I must say, I'm grateful it's a friendly place and I hope to bump into you again. Good day.'

Both women watched as he clicked his heels together, doffed his hat again, then marched off with his elegant walking cane tucked under his arm.

'What a funny little man,' Fanny said and lifted the front of Edward's pram.

'I don't know about funny but there was something about him that I didn't like.'

'He seemed harmless enough to me. Anyway, I'll get the kettle on, I could do with a cuppa.'

Now in the hallway, Molly left Edward sleeping soundly in his pram and went upstairs. She tapped lightly on Ivy's door. The girl was in her bed, resting after her abysmal ordeal. 'How are you feeling?'

'Sore,' Ivy answered.

Her mouth was terribly swollen and Molly could see she was finding it difficult to talk. 'Can I get you anything?'

Ivy shook her head.

'I'll be back to check on you again later,' Molly said.

She went to close the door but heard Ivy say, 'Wait.'

'What is it?'

'I remembered something else... about the bloke who attacked me.'

'What? What have you remembered, Ivy?' Molly asked. She knew Georgina was desperate to find the man and would be grateful for any detail that could help.

'The knife he held to me throat... It weren't a normal sort of knife.'

'Can you explain?' Molly gently tried to coax.

'It was on the end of a long stick thing.'

'Like a makeshift blade, secured to a bit of wood?'

'No, it weren't no makeshift piece. It was proper,' Ivy answered and closed her eyes.

Molly could see the girl was trying to recall the details.

'It was polished wood, and the blade, it should have been the handle. I can see it now... it looked like one of them walking sticks.'

Molly could feel the blood draining from her face. 'You mean a cane? A gentleman's cane?'

'Yeah, yeah, that's it.'

Molly gulped but tried to remain calm in front of Ivy. 'Well done, you did good. Now, rest up and I'll be in again later.'

She closed the door behind her and dashed down the stairs and into the kitchen where Fanny was pouring the tea. 'Oh, blimey, Mum. That man, the funny little one outside... I think it was him who attacked Ivy!'

Fanny looked up but didn't seem concerned. 'Don't be daft. I know you didn't like him but you can't go round spouting accusations like that.'

'No, Mum, listen! Ivy just said that the knife was a cane.'

'Sounds like Ivy's delirious. That don't make no sense.'

'The handle of the cane... I dunno how but he's had it made into a concealed knife. Oh, Christ, Mum! He was here! He was looking at my Edward!'

'Hey, calm down, Molly. Go and check on Edward, then sit down and take a few deep breaths.'

Molly did as her mother told her but as she leaned over her son, her mind was in turmoil. What if the man came back? As she pulled the blanket back that half covered Edward's face, she noticed a small package lying beside him – a little ball of white paper. Molly picked it up and curiously opened it. When she saw a blooded tooth inside, bile rose in her throat. She managed to run back into the kitchen and dart across the room to the sink before violently vomiting.

Fanny handed her a glass of water. 'This all seems to have affected you pretty badly. What exactly did Ivy say?'

'She said she remembered the man had a blade on a long stick. Polished wood. A cane.'

'That's it? That's all she said?' Fanny asked.

'Yes.'

'And from that, you've deduced that the polite chap outside is the man who attacked her and now he's after us and the baby? Oh, Molly, honestly. I don't know where you get your imagination from. Do you realise how many men carry canes? Bloody thousands. Pull yourself together and stop being so silly.'

Molly glared at her mother. 'That's not all, Mother. Look,' she said and handed her the tooth in the piece of paper.

'Where did you get this from?'

'I found it, in Edward's pram.'

'Oh, Gawd, do you think it's Ivy's?'

'Yes, and that man put it in the pram for us to find.'

Molly had known, as soon as she'd seen him that there was something she hadn't liked. It was him; she'd known it in her gut. He'd been the man who'd taken Ivy's teeth and now he'd been on her doorstep and returned one of them! Thank goodness Jane had a telephone because Molly had to get word to Georgina and there was no way she was stepping outside the front door. No matter what it took, she had to protect her son.

Georgina crossed her arms in front of her and rested them on her desk. PC Cunningham was speaking but she wasn't really listening. Instead, she was looking at his smug, round face and refraining from the urge to smash it in. He was wittering on about his unblemished reputation and something about his arrest rate. From the bits that Georgina did take in, she thought it sounded like bullshit but guessed it was leading to him requesting more money. If that was his game, he could go and take a running jump.

'And seeing as you're a woman, you'll be needing extra protection from me,' he said and leaned forward in his seat with his narrow grey eyes boring into her.

Georgina thought he looked far too relaxed. His easy lumber and the way he leaned his elbow on her desk caused her great irritation. 'I beg your pardon?' she said.

'With you being a lady, you'll have all sorts trying to take advantage. But you don't need to worry your pretty little face about stuff like that. See, my name carries a lot of clout round here. One word from me and you'll be all right. I'll keep the scoundrels off your back.'

'Thank you, PC Cunningham, but I'm quite capable of looking after myself.'

'Hah, I'm sure you believe you are but you don't know what some of these criminals can be like. I could tell you stories that would make the devil cry but I wouldn't want to frighten you. No, Miss Garrett, it's a wicked world out there and not one that a woman of good standing should be dealing with.'

'PC Cunningham, I appreciate your good intentions but there'll be no requirement for you to do any more than you already do. We'll keep to the same arrangement you had with Mr Wilcox and with Mickey.'

'It was different. They were men, and you can't really think you can do the same as them.'

The telephone rang, which came as a welcome relief to Georgina. 'Mr Harel will arrange your payment. Now, if you'll excuse me,' she said indicating to the trilling phone. 'Good day, PC Cunningham.'

He looked a bit put out at being rebuffed but Georgina didn't care. Fortunately, he hadn't been one of the coppers who'd abused her and as it turned out, she thought he was a wet blanket. She'd keep him on the payroll but she couldn't envisage what use he'd be, except for turning a blind eye to her gang's activities.

PC Cunningham walked over to Benjamin's desk and Georgina picked up the telephone receiver. After being connected, she said hello and then heard Molly's desperate voice, begging her to come to Jane's. Molly hardly paused for breath as she explained about the man with the cane and what Ivy had said and then something about a tooth in Edward's pram. Georgina could tell her friend was terrified and promised to be there as soon as she could. Thankfully, this seemed to pacify her somewhat.

The policeman left with his pockets full of the Wilcox business money and Georgina said a hasty goodbye to Benjamin.

'We'll talk about that investment tomorrow,' she called as she dashed out of the door and checked her clutch bag for Lash's pistol. Molly had been rambling and Georgina wasn't entirely sure what was going on but she wasn't taking any chances. If the man who'd attacked Ivy had approached Molly and Fanny, then it was more than just coincidence. Something was amiss and this man needed stopping before he hurt anyone else.

By the time Georgina arrived at Jane's house, she found Molly almost hysterical.

'I've tried to calm her down but she's worked herself up into a right state,' Fanny said.

Molly was running from the back door to the front room window. Tears streamed down her face and her eyes were blazing with fear. Georgina stepped in her pathway and firmly grabbed her friend's shoulders.

'Listen to me, Molly. I'm here now. No-one is going to hurt you or Edward. I promise you, you're safe now.'

'But... but... he was here. He was so close to my baby. What if he'd stabbed him or something?'

'He didn't. Edward is perfectly well and needs his mum to pull herself together.'

At last, Molly drew in a long, juddering breath and appeared to compose herself.

'Does Ivy know what's going on?' Georgina asked.

'No, not unless she's heard Molly ranting,' Fanny answered.

'Good. Can you check on her please, Fanny?'

Fanny went upstairs and Georgina led Molly to the sofa. 'Tell me exactly what's happened. Slowly.'

Georgina listened as Molly explained about the cane, the man on the step and finally the tooth in the pram.

'Right, this is a clear message and I've no doubt it's aimed at me and the business. Whoever this character is, he's using scare tactics to get to us.'

'Well, it's working 'cos I'm bloody petrified!' Molly said.

'Knuckles mentioned a name – The Dentist. He's one of David Maynard's gang and if it is him, he'll know where I can find him.'

'You're going to see David Maynard? You can't, Georgina, please. You can't leave us.'

'It's all right, Molly. I'll leave you with this.' Georgina opened her handbag and showed Molly the pistol.

'No, no, no, please, George...'

'This is what you're going to do. Leave Edward with Ivy and arm her with a kitchen knife. Your mum will be in the kitchen and keep an eye on the back door. I want you to sit on the stairs with this pistol. If anyone tries to come through the front door, shoot them. Don't ask questions, don't hesitate. Just shoot.'

'I don't think I can do this.'

'You don't have any choice. Now, take this gun. It's loaded. I'll be back soon as I can.'

Fanny came through from the kitchen clutching the bread knife. 'What about Ethel and Charlotte?'

'Oh, Christ. Ethel is at my house. There's no way me gran will be able to walk here and I can't leave her alone.'

'I've no idea where Charlotte is. She's supposed to be at school but I doubt she bothered going in. The little madam is always bunking off.' Fanny paused then her eyes widened. 'She could be anywhere. You've got to find her, Georgina,' Fanny said and the despair in her voice was apparent.

'Hang on, calm down. If you don't know where Charlotte is, then neither will The Dentist.'

'The Dentist. That's what he's called? Oh my Gawd, this is getting worse. What if he does know where Charlotte is? What if he's been watching us all?' asked Fanny.

'That's unlikely. Remember, we are The Maids of Battersea and we're strong together. Fanny, I'll call a taxi cab to take me to fetch Ethel and me gran and then I'll telephone Knuckles, tell him to come. I'm sorry, but there's not much I can do about Charlotte other than leave a note at yours telling her to come here. I'll get word out to the blokes and tell them to keep an eye out but they don't know what she looks like.'

'Oh, dear Lord, I hope she's not hurt,' Fanny said as she wrung her hands.

'Don't worry, Fanny. I think it's me he's trying to get at. Charlotte will be fine.'

A little while later, Knuckles arrived at almost the same time as the taxi and Georgina quickly explained to him about the situation.

'I'll make sure no harm comes to 'em, Miss Garrett,' Knuckles said as she went to leave.

'You'd better,' Georgina warned but she knew Knuckles meant what he'd said.

Georgina didn't wait to hear any more protests from Molly and darted out the front door, keeping her wits about her and her eyes peeled. 'Come on, you fucker,' she whispered. 'Come for me now.'

Minutes later, the taxi cab pulled up outside her home. She told the driver to wait, but as she ran up the path, she saw the door was ajar and her heart began to race.

'Gran... Gran...' she shouted.

Georgina hurried into the front room and was relieved to see her gran stirring, obviously waking from a nap. 'Where's Ethel?' she asked.

'Hello, love. I don't know, she was in the kitchen when I dozed off.'

Georgina called to Ethel and ran from room to room looking for her but she was nowhere to be found.

'What's going on? Why the panic?' Dulcie queried as she pushed herself up from her armchair.

'I haven't got time to explain now, Gran, but I need you to come with me. Quickly, grab your coat and your bag.'

'I won't budge until you tell me what the hell this is all about!'

'Please, Gran, I'll explain in the taxi cab that's waiting outside for us. Are you sure you never heard anyone knock on the door or Ethel talking to anyone?'

'No, I told you. Last I knew, she was in the kitchen washing up.'

After helping her gran into the taxi, Georgina told her about The Dentist.

'Oh no, do you think he's got Ethel?' Dulcie asked.

'I hope not.'

'Fanny's gonna go out of her mind with worry.'

'I know, but I haven't got time to see to her. I'm going to drop you off and get straight over to David Maynard. If this Dentist bloke has got Ethel, the sooner we find him, the better.'

'Oh, Georgina, poor Ethel. She's like a child. She'll be so scared,' Dulcie said, her eyes brimming with tears.

'I know, Gran, but try not to think the worst. I know it's unlikely that she's just wandered off, but she may have done.'

'No, not Ethel. He's got her. You've got to find them and when you do, you make sure you kill the bastard!'

'Don't worry, Gran, I will, but I'll make him eat his own fucking teeth first.'

14

In a small disused concrete storage hut, once used during construction of Battersea Power Station, Jimmy Hewitt had thrown Ethel onto the dirt floor and bound her hands behind her back and her ankles together. She lay there, whimpering, whilst Jimmy took his pipe from his coat pocket and lit it.

As he smoked, he stood looking over Ethel with disgust. She'd wet herself and the strong stench of her foul-smelling urine twitched his nose. He wasn't going to gain any pleasure from this one. She wasn't his sort. She was too thickset for one and though she looked like a young woman, she seemed to have the mind of a child and he wasn't into kids. Though he still planned on taking her teeth. After all, he had to get his message to Miss Garrett and pulled teeth were his signature.

'Please, I want to go home,' Ethel cried.

'Shut your mouth. One more peep out of you and I'll gag you,' he said and gave her a sharp kick to her thigh.

Ethel yowled but quietened down. He guessed by now that they'd have discovered she was missing and must have found Ivy's tooth in the pram. He'd kept her other tooth for his collection. No doubt, they'd be looking for him and if that Garrett woman was as clever as he'd heard, then he was sure she'd pay his old boss a visit. Not that David Maynard would be able to tell her anything useful. No-one knew about this hideout, not even Daisy, his wife.

'I want my mum,' Ethel cried.

'What did I tell you? You stupid cow, you've brought this on yourself,' Jimmy sneered and pulled a handkerchief from his pocket. He scrunched it into a ball, knelt down and grabbed Ethel's head.

'Please, get orf me,' Ethel pleaded.

He was pleased to see her ordeal had left her weak and she didn't struggle very much as he stuffed the handkerchief in her mouth then removed his scarf and tied it around her head. 'Ah, that's better. Peace at last. Now I can hear myself think clearly.'

Ethel lay silent.

'You're going to be here for a while. I want those bitches to sweat, worrying about what I'm doing to you.'

Ethel made a small grunting noise.

'It's all right. I'm not going to kill you, not unless I have to. It's quite good fun this, don't you think?'

Jimmy stood up and pulled an envelope from his inside jacket pocket. 'Listen to this,' he said excitedly and took a letter from the envelope. 'It's addressed to Miss Garrett and it says:

As you will undoubtedly be aware, I have returned one of Ivy's teeth to you and now have Ethel Mipple with me. Unless you would like to see her endure the same fate as that other slut, I suggest you step down from your position within the Wilcox business. Failure to do so will result in death. Not yours, Miss Garrett. You can watch as I systematically kill the rest of the Mipple females. Not forgetting sweet Edward.

A word of warning – don't think that you can pretend to step down, only to finish me off as soon as you set eyes on me. Any such plan will fail because I will be keeping Ethel Mipple until I see fit. You have absolutely no chance of finding her, so if anything happens to me, she will die of starvation. However, she will be released back to your custody once I am assured of my position, though my threat will still stand if you make any future move against me.

'I've signed it off with *The Dentist*. It's good, isn't it? I'm self-taught, you know. I had hardly any schooling but you wouldn't know, would you?'

Jimmy carefully placed the letter back in the envelope and returned it to his pocket. Then, he clicked his heels together and picked up his cane, which was leaning against the wall. 'I'll get this to Miss Garrett this evening and then give her a day to think about it. If nothing happens, I need to show her I'm serious so I'll have to remove your teeth; but don't worry, Ethel, it doesn't hurt for very long.'

Georgina's taxi pulled up outside of David Maynard's well-appointed office. She didn't have her pistol to hand over to his heavies but they still frisked her before she was shown through to see him.

'Good afternoon, Miss Garrett. This is an unexpected but nice surprise,' he greeted her with genuine pleasure.

'I wish I could say the same,' she replied.

'Please, take a seat and allow me to get you a drink and then you can tell me what's troubling you. But I hope you haven't come to discuss politics. I've had a run-in with some Blackshirts today, fucking fascists. That Mosley has a lot of followers round here.'

'No, I'm not here to talk about politics and I don't have time for niceties. Would you like to explain to me what the hell your Dentist is doing in Battersea?' Georgina was direct in her approach and noticed Mr Maynard seemed somewhat staggered at her news.

'I'm sorry, I had no idea. Has he been causing you problems?'

'Yes, he bloody well has. He's attacked one of my girls but worse than that, he's kidnapped Molly Wilcox's sister. As you can imagine, I'm extremely concerned for her safety and it's imperative I find out where she and this Dentist bloke are.'

'Yes, yes, I understand. He's an evil piece of work. You have every right to be concerned.'

'That's not helping.'

'I'm sorry, Georgina. Do you mind if I address you as Georgina? And please, as we're friends, call me David.'

'Fine, *David*. So, can you tell me where I can find him?'

'I really wish I could. I had to let him go after a misunderstanding. I suppose you know why he's called The Dentist?'

'Yes. My girl is minus two front teeth now, though he returned one to me.'

SAM MICHAELS

'Jimmy Hewitt, aka The Dentist, worked for me for years and was good at what he did. Unfortunately, his dentistry skills go further than roughing up my enemies. He has this weird thing for prostitutes and, well, you can work out the rest. Kidnap is new behaviour for him. Sounds to me like he's upped his game and he wants to be top dog now.'

'Yes, I believe so. I can't predict his next move but at this moment in time, I just want Ethel Mipple back. Is there *anything* you can tell me about his whereabouts?'

'No, but I'll put the word out, though I don't reckon he'll show his face round here again. He's as sly as a fox, that one. However, Georgina, you have my assurance that if we find him first, it'll be the last anyone sees of him.'

'Thank you, but I'd rather you brought him to me.'

David smiled at her. 'As you wish.'

'And if you hear anything, you'll call?'

'You have my word.'

'Thank you. I must get back. Would you spare me a driver again please?'

'Don't tell me you still haven't got a man and a car? Especially now with this nutter on the loose.'

'I've been busy but I will get round to it.'

'You must. It's a priority, but in the meantime, you can have mine. Victor is the best and will take good care of you,' David said, then turned to the muscular man standing by the door. 'Victor, you heard all that. Stay with Miss Garrett and don't let anything happen to her. And what she says, goes.'

'Yes, Guv,' Victor answered.

Georgina was taken aback by Victor's voice. It was so deep that it almost sounded like rolling thunder. She wasn't going to be proud and decline David's generous offer. She needed Victor and if he was David's best man, she'd be able to trust him.

'Thank you, David. I owe you one.'

'It's the least I can do. And, Georgina, if you catch up with Jimmy Hewitt before I do, don't give him a quick death. Make the bastard suffer.'

Georgina had every intention of ensuring Jimmy's death was slow and torturous but first she had to find him and could only hope she did before he hurt Ethel.

'Queenstown Road,' she said to Victor as they set off in David's gin tin palace. 'There's something I need to collect,' she added, thinking of Willy's gun in her desk drawer.

Varvara wasn't sure what was going on but she knew something wasn't right. First, Georgina had rushed out of the house and a short time after, following a telephone call, Knuckles had too. There was trouble brewing. She could feel it and prayed Georgina was safe.

Varvara had already seen to three customers that day and now her fourth had just arrived. She looked the man up and down. Barney's blubbery stomach hung over the top of his trousers and the few strands of hair on his head looked greasy. He was one of her regulars and though she found him repulsive, she was relieved to see him. Barney was easily pleased and didn't take long to glean his pleasure. Easy money. All she had to do was bend over at the window and smoke a cigarette whilst he'd take her from behind.

'You're looking lovely,' Barney said and slavered from his lips as he rubbed his hand over his groin area.

Varvara couldn't be bothered to answer him. Instead, she positioned herself at the window and pulled her skirts up to her waist, revealing her pert bottom.

'Ah, that's it,' Barney said huskily. 'Light a fag.'

Varvara rested her elbows on the windowsill as she dragged on the cigarette and grimaced as she felt Barney enter her. He always started off slowly and rhythmically and as she faked her pleasure, he'd build into a crescendo.

As expected, Barney's pace was slow and she offered a slight moan of faked ecstasy every now and again, hoping it would spur him on.

'Oh, Barney, you're so big... Aw, I love it, Barney, love it,' she lied before drawing on her cigarette again.

As he pounded away, Varvara spotted a very smart car pull up outside. A large man with brown hair climbed out of the driver's seat and opened the back door. To her astonishment, she saw Georgina's long legs emerge followed by the rest of her slender body. She looked stunning in a burgundy wool coat and her black hair shone with almost a blue-black hue in the afternoon sun.

Varvara felt her vagina clench at the sight of Georgina and as Barney pulled in and out of her, she used her muscles to squeeze his penis. He groaned and she could feel his manhood becoming more engorged. She reached between her legs and stimulated herself. 'That's it... Oh, yes... yes...' she husked, imagining Georgina grinding against her.

Barney thrust harder and seconds later, they both climaxed. It was the first time Varvara had ever orgasmed, though she knew it was the thought of Georgina that had brought it on.

Barney pulled out of her and grabbed a tissue from the side to wipe himself. 'Bloomin' hell, you've never been like that before,' he said.

Varvara reached for a tissue too. 'It will cost you extra. Pay me and I will do that every time,' she said in her Russian slur.

'Fair enough. It was worth it,' Barney answered breathlessly and rummaged in his pockets for some coins. 'See you in two weeks,' he said and slapped the money next to the tissue box. As he went to walk out of the door, he turned and added, 'There's something I should tell you, only don't say it came from me.'

'What?'

'There was talk last night, down the Queen's Head, about Miss Garrett.'

'What about her?' Varvara asked defensively.

'There's a few of the landlords getting together. They ain't happy about paying for protection from a woman.'

'Pathetic. What do they intend to do about it?'

'I didn't hear the whole conversation but from what I could gather, they're gonna tell her blokes that she can sling her hook.'

'Thank you, Barney. I'll inform Miss Garrett but I won't mention your name.'

Once the door had closed behind him, Varvara didn't bother to douche herself and quickly ran to the stairs, desperate to see Georgina. As she trotted down, Georgina was coming out of her office and heading for the front door.

'Miss Garrett,' Varvara called.

Georgina spun around and once again, Varvara was struck by the woman's beauty. 'I have to speak to you.'

'It'll have to wait, Varvara.'

'It's important.'

'Not as important as what is going on right now. Listen, be aware of a dangerous man called Jimmy Hewitt. Only let regular customers in today. No, in fact, don't let anyone in. Mr Harel will be leaving in a minute. Once he's gone, lock the place down. I'll get Mr Harel to telephone Dina and tell her to do the same at Livingstone Road. Keep indoors, all of you. Is that clear?'

'Yes, but...'

Georgina cut in and as she opened the front door, Mr Harel came out of the office.

'I've got to go. Just do as I've said. Benjamin, call Livingstone Road before you leave. Tell them to shut down until further notice.'

The door closed and Varvara stood on the stairs not knowing if she had anything to fear or not.

'Has Miss Garrett spoken to you about what's going on?' he asked.

'Yes. What is the problem with this Jimmy Hewitt?'

'It's not for me to say, Varvara. Just do whatever Miss Garrett has told you to and be careful,' he said, pushing his glasses up his nose.

'Can I call Dina?'

'Yes, you can do it, but make sure she understands what she has to do. Goodbye,' he answered and then he left too.

Varvara didn't like the sound of this and after locking and bolting the door she ran through to the back room where she could telephone her sister. She relayed Miss Garrett's instructions to Dina who seemed less concerned. She then hurried upstairs to knock on the other girls' doors, but found herself filled with a feeling of foreboding. She should have insisted she went with Miss Garrett. She'd vowed to herself that she'd do anything to look after Georgina, but how could she do that if she wasn't by her side?

'Stay safe,' she muttered. 'Please, my beautiful one, stay safe.'

There'd been no consoling Fanny and much to Molly's dismay, her mum had taken out her angst on Georgina. She'd spat venom at her, telling Georgina it was all her fault and that if anything happened to Ethel, she'd never forgive her. Fanny was now rocking back and forth on the sofa and crying for her daughter.

In the kitchen, Molly said to Georgina, 'I'm sorry about my mum. She's beside herself with worry but that's not really an excuse to talk to you like that.'

'It's all right, Molly. If I was your mum, I'd be angry with me too. I suppose she feels like I've let you all down. I was supposed to protect you and I haven't.'

'You've done everything you can. You can't be with each one of us at every minute of every day.'

'I realise that, but it shouldn't have come to this. Nobody would have done this to Billy and do you know why? Because they were too scared of him. I'll get this sorted, I promise and then I'm gonna get really bloody nasty. I can't allow this to ever happen again. I need it to be known that if anyone comes near me or mine, they'll be fucking sorry. I obviously haven't made that clear enough.'

'Do you think Ethel will be all right?'

'I hope so, Molly, I really do. But I can't promise anything. Knuckles is out now looking for Charlotte and all my blokes are searching for Jimmy Hewitt. He's got to be in Battersea somewhere and when we find him, we'll find Ethel.'

Molly was trying not to cry again. She had to stay strong for her mum. 'I know you're doing everything you can. I wish we could help look for her. I feel so useless just sitting here.'

'Me too, but if Jimmy's got something to say to me, I reckon this is where he'll come for me.'

'Knuckles was really good with Mum. He managed to calm her down. I'm glad he's out looking but I wish he was here now. I don't know what to do with her, but he did.' Molly picked up the tea she'd poured for Fanny. Her hand shook, which made the cup rattle in the saucer.

'I know you're scared, Molly, but this is the safest place for you to be. Jimmy Hewitt is gonna be in for a shock when he meets me... and Victor.'

Molly smiled weakly at her friend and took the tea through to her mum.

'What's she doing, hiding here? She should be out there looking for my girls!' Fanny spat.

'Georgina's got everyone looking, Mum. She has to be here to take care of us in case Jimmy comes here.'

'So she says! Well, she ain't got everyone looking, has she? The Old Bill ain't looking. They don't know that a maniac has got my Ethel. I've got a good mind to get on that telephone contraption thing and call them.'

'No, Mum, you can't! You understand how this works. It's got nothing to do with the police. Anyway, off the record, they are looking. Georgina's got contacts with police and she's had a word.'

'Oh, Gawd, where's Charlotte? It's bad enough that he's got Ethel but what if he's got Charlotte too? How would we know?'

'Stop, Mum, you're upsetting yourself. Charlotte will be back soon as she gets hungry. You know what she's like.'

'Upsetting meself... Of course I'm bloody upsetting meself! Oh, Molly, I feel sick, I really do.'

Molly sat beside her mum and placed her arm over Fanny's shoulder. 'I know. I'm out of my mind too.'

Fanny rested her head on Molly and they cried together until Molly thought her heart would break. 'Oh, Mum,' she said. The thought of Ethel's frightened face. The pain was unbearable.

They'd been sobbing together for long enough for Fanny's tea to have turned cold. When she reached for it she pulled a face. Molly offered, 'I'll make you a fresh one.'

As she stood up from the sofa, the house fell into a tense silence when they heard a light tap on the front door. Molly ran to the window. 'It's a young lad,' she said to Georgina who had now walked into the room.

'He may be a ruse to get us to open the door,' Georgina said. 'Molly, Fanny, get upstairs... Quick.'

Molly dragged her mum to the stairs and pushed her upwards. As Fanny darted into the bedroom where Ivy was with Edward, Molly stopped at the top of the stairs and watched what was unfolding below. She saw Georgina nod to Victor, indicating for him to open the door. Victor had one hand on his holster and Georgina had her hand in her bag. She could feel her heart hammering and the sound of blood rushing in her ears. Molly thought her friend was the bravest person she knew and though she was desperate for news of Ethel, she wasn't sure if she would have had the courage to open the door.

Victor slowly opened it. The evening sun was low in the sky and flooded the hallway with an orange haze. Molly could see the silhouette of the lad and he was holding out an envelope.

'Who gave you this?' Victor asked.

'A man. He gave me tuppence to deliver it,' the lad answered proudly.

'Where is the man? Did you see where he went?' asked Victor.

Georgina pushed past Victor and ran out into the street.

The lad shook his head. 'No, mister, he's long gawn. He told me to count to one hundred. I said I could only count to ten so he said I had to count to ten for ten times.'

'What did the man look like?'

'A bit posh, I suppose. Short. Old. Bowler hat and cane, you know the sort.'

Molly knew from the description that if was definitely Jimmy Hewitt.

'Did he tell you to do anything else?'

'No, mister, that was it. Can I go now? I ain't done nuffink wrong, 'ave I?'

'No, lad, you did well. Off you go but if you see the man again, come straight here and tell me. I'll pay you twice as much as he did.'

'Cor, fanks, mister. I hope I sees him. See ya.'

Victor looked behind him and spotted Molly quivering at the top of the stairs. She knew he was going to chase after Georgina and desperately whispered, 'Please, stay here. She'll be back in a minute.'

Victor nodded but stood at the door with it wide open. Thankfully, Georgina soon returned.

'Nothing?' Victor asked.

Georgina shook her head. 'Give me the letter,' she said and held out her hand.

Molly tiptoed back down the stairs. She was desperate to know what news the letter held but didn't want her mother to find out about it yet. If it was bad news, she would have to prepare herself to tell Fanny. She followed Georgina through to the front room and quietly closed the door. 'What does it say?'

Georgina had read it and handed it to Molly. 'Oh. Dear God,' Molly gasped as her hand flew to her mouth.

'But she's alive, Molly, and he hasn't taken her teeth out.'

'What are you going to do?' Molly asked. She knew nothing less than giving in to this man would satisfy her mother but she also knew her friend well. Georgina wouldn't bow down to him and wouldn't believe that she could lose this battle. Even if Ethel could lose her life.

Jimmy Hewitt had clicked his heels together and tucked his cane under his arm as he bid the lad goodbye and darted into a maze of alleys. He'd liked to have seen the look on Miss Garrett's face as she digested the words of his very well-put-together letter. Of course, that wasn't possible but nonetheless, he relished in the thought of her horrified expression.

The sun was dipping behind the houses now. He had to get back to his hideout and leave some water and food for Ethel. The temperature was dropping as quickly as the sun was setting. It was going to be a cold night but he'd had the foresight to wear an extra coat. It would do to keep the chill off Ethel. After all, if she was going to be his bargaining tool, he had to keep her alive. But the thought of returning to that stinking hut turned his stomach. He contemplated the idea of just leaving her as she was. Surely she'd survive one night without any water? And yes, she'd get chilly but she was unlikely to freeze to death. He eventually reasoned she'd be fine for the night and he'd see to her in the morning.

Feeling very pleased with himself, Jimmy headed off to the other side of Battersea. Mind you, the thought of seeing Daisy's miserable face wasn't much more appealing than returning to the hut. At least she'd have a hearty meal cooked for him. He found her a revolting sight and her whinging and nagging drove him mad but she could turn out a good dinner. The woman had to have something positive going for her.

He was still a good twenty minutes' walk from home and now it was dark. Knowing that Miss Garrett would have people out looking for him, he'd been careful to keep an eye over his shoulder. But, being new in the area, he was confident no-one would recognise him. They soon would though, he thought, and pictured himself as the boss of the Wilcox business. Oh, yes, once he was running the show, everyone would recognise him. He'd be revered wherever he went and might even give David Maynard a run for his money. Jimmy was on a high and felt as if he was walking on air. He was sure Miss Garrett would comply. She was a woman and wouldn't have the spunk to fight him. She'd had her little go at playing boss but now it was time for a real man to head the realm. He'd be king in these streets and his reign would be a fierce one.

Jimmy was feeling very pleased with himself. He'd come a long way from the little boy with no schooling and raised in poverty who, up until the age of nine, had been forced to suckle on his mother's breasts for nourishment. The runt of the litter, that's what his father had called him. The man had been huge and did nothing to conceal his disappointment at Jimmy's small stature. Wimp, little shit, weasel – he'd heard it all from his father and the name-calling had always been accompanied by a clout round the ear.

But his mother had loved him. She'd displayed her affection in secret, away from the accusing eyes of his father. He realised now, as an adult, that some would have called their relationship incestuous, but Jimmy didn't like that word. It implied that what he shared with his mother was wrong. It wasn't, it was a deep love that no-one could understand. He missed his mother. She'd be so proud of him now, dressed as a gentleman and on the cusp of controlling Battersea.

Jimmy turned a corner and stepped out into the road to cross the street. His mind was filled with fantasies of power and just as he thought to himself that he'd need a bigger jar for his keepsakes, he heard a car horn and looked to his left only to be blinded by headlights. He didn't see who was driving the car but it screeched to a halt.

It was then that Jimmy recognised the car. He turned and ran but had only taken a few steps when he felt the force of strong arms grabbing at him.

'Get off me,' he yelled and struggled to pull away but he knew he was no match for one of Maynard's men. Defeated,

Jimmy, slumped and allowed himself to be dragged back to the car. Maynard's heavy threw him onto the back seat, and after straightening himself up, he looked to his side to see David Maynard sitting beside him.

'Evening, Jimmy,' David greeted, his mouth set in a grim line. 'I have a friend who'd like to meet you. Now, before I take you to her, would you like to save yourself a lot of grief and tell me where to find Ethel Mipple?'

'I don't know who you're talking about,' Jimmy answered but already knew his plan for domination had been scuppered.

'I had a feeling you'd say that. Not to worry, but a word of advice – tell Miss Garrett the truth otherwise I think you'll find yourself in a very unfortunate position.'

'Please, Mr Maynard, there's been a terrible mistake. I don't know anything about a Mipple woman. I'd just like to get home to my wife.'

'Shut it, Jimmy. I don't want to hear your pathetic little voice again. I should have gotten rid of you properly in the first place. But now I'll leave that to Miss Garrett.'

'I'll be straight there,' Georgina said and replaced the telephone receiver.

'Where are you going?' Molly asked, her voice full of concern.

Georgina lowered her voice to a whisper so that Fanny didn't hear and told Molly, 'That was Varvara. I have to go to the office but don't worry, Jimmy Hewitt won't be coming here.'

'How do you know?'

'Because David Maynard has him and they're waiting for me.'

'I'm coming with you. That man has my sister and I need to know where!'

'No, wait here. Trust me, Molly, you won't want to see this. I'll do whatever it takes to make him talk.'

Molly nodded and Georgina dashed out of the door with Victor.

'Get me to Queenstown Road, fast,' she told him as she jumped into the car.

When she walked into her office, David Maynard was sat at her desk smoking a fat cigar.

'Georgina, it's very nice to see you again. I've brought you a gift...'

Georgina looked to the corner of the room where Jimmy Hewitt was secured to a wooden seat. His hands were tied behind him and his ankles to the legs. The man was much smaller than Georgina had imagined and she was pleased to see he looked terrified.

'The Dentist, I presume?' she asked David.

'Yes. He's not talking, yet, but I'm sure you'll be able to persuade him to divulge Miss Mipple's whereabouts.'

Georgina marched towards Jimmy then slapped him hard across his face. 'Where is she?'

'I don't know... I've never even heard of her. Please, someone *has* to believe me. I'm being set up.'

Georgina turned to David and rolled her eyes. A cloud of smoke curled around his face as he spoke.

'I know, he said the same to me. They always do but denial is easily overcome.'

'Fetch Varvara for me,' Georgina told Victor. 'And tell her to bring the pliers from the toolbox.'

'No... no... please Miss Garrett... I'm telling the truth, I swear,' Jimmy pleaded.

Georgina ignored him, instead saying to David, 'I'm sorry, I haven't offered you a drink. Can I get you anything? Though you've already made yourself at home.'

'You don't mind?' he asked, gesturing to the fact that he was sat in her chair behind her desk.

'No, but don't get too comfortable.'

'Is that a threat, Georgina?'

'No, David, just a warning.'

'I must say, I like the view from here.'

Georgina knew he was referring to her but chose to ignore his coquettish remark and instead asked again if he'd like a drink.

'Yes, a large brandy would be nice whilst I watch this display unfold.'

As Georgina poured the drink, Varvara came into the room behind Victor.

'Are these what you are looking for?' she asked.

'Perfect,' Georgina answered as she handed David a glass, their eyes locking. For a brief moment, his finger touched hers and she was sure he'd done it deliberately.

She quickly pulled her hand back and broke the long stare between them but his wry smile wasn't lost on her.

Grabbing the pliers from Varvara, Georgina stood in front of Jimmy Hewitt, looking down at him with hatred.

'I'm only going to ask you one more time and then I'm going to give you a taste of your own medicine. Where is Ethel Mipple?'

When Jimmy refused to answer, she instructed Victor to hold the man's head back and his jaw open. 'Help Victor,' she told Varvara. 'Pull his chin down.'

Jimmy was powerless and Georgina clamped the pliers on his upper front tooth. She pulled and yanked, twisting the tool. She hadn't imagined it would take so much force to pull a tooth and the pain Jimmy felt was evident from his cries. The tooth came away and blood filled the man's mouth.

'Now do you want to tell me?' Georgina asked, stepping back and peering at the long root of the tooth she held in the pliers.

Jimmy spat blood from his mouth. 'Never,' he croaked.

'Varvara, here, pull another,' she said, discarding his tooth in the waste-paper bin before handing her the pliers. 'I think I'll join you in that brandy,' she said to David.

'He's wet himself,' Varvara sneered, the contempt in her voice clear.

'The dirty bastard,' David said.

Varvara began tugging at Jimmy's tooth whilst Georgina clinked glasses with David.

'Thank you for bringing me such a thoughtful gift,' she said.

'You're very welcome. I'm glad you like it.'

The screams from Jimmy fell quiet and as Varvara stepped back, a look of triumph on her face as she held the tooth in the air. Georgina saw that Jimmy's head had slumped to the side.

'I think the pain has knocked him out,' David said.

'I will keep this tooth and make it into a broach for Dina.' Varvara laughed.

Georgina walked across the room and studied Jimmy's still body. 'He's not breathing,' she said, panic rising in her.

'Are you sure?' David asked.

'Yes, I'm bloody sure! For Christ's sake, he can't die! Victor, untie him… quick.'

Once the ropes had been released, Jimmy Hewitt's body fell forwards and onto the floor. Victor bent over him and checked for signs of life.

'He's dead, Miss Garrett. His heart must have packed up.'

Georgina looked at the body sprawled face down. With The Dentist dead, so were her hopes of discovering where he'd hidden Ethel and in frustration, she kicked him hard in the ribs. 'Get rid of him,' she told Victor flatly.

'That didn't go according to plan. You scared him to death,' David said, rising to his feet.

Georgina didn't answer, her mind turning with fears for Ethel's life. How would they ever find her now?

15

It had been three days since Jimmy Hewitt had died. Benjamin looked across the office to Georgina. It was clear from the dark circles around her eyes that the woman had hardly slept. There'd been no news. Every man in the business was still searching for Ethel, as were PC Cunningham and his colleagues. Benjamin daren't say but he feared their search would be fruitless. He suspected Ethel was dead.

Varvara tapped on the door. He knew it was her because of her distinctive four raps. Benjamin was grateful to see she was bringing them coffee and thought Georgina probably needed it. As Varvara passed round the coffee cups, Benjamin covertly watched Victor with lust. He found the man far more pleasing on the eye than Knuckles and apart from his well-groomed good looks, Benjamin thought the man was an asset to the company. He'd have a word with Miss Garrett later and see if he couldn't persuade her to keep Victor on. With him in the office on a daily basis, it would make coming to work a most enjoyable experience.

Georgina didn't acknowledge Varvara. Benjamin noticed the woman's hurt expression and could tell she was loitering. Georgina was unlikely to notice but Benjamin had, and thought to himself that it was quite funny that he wasn't the only one in the office who was harbouring a secret crush.

'Miss Garrett,' Varvara said.

Georgina looked up, her brow knitted into a deep frown.

'It is very quiet today. I was thinking that maybe I could be of use elsewhere?'

'No. It's fine, Varvara.'

'I could stand alongside Victor and work in protection.'

'That won't be necessary.'

'But you remember how I knocked Willy to the ground? I am not scared of men or guns. I would risk my life to save yours,' she said, then quickly added, 'because it would be my job, of course.'

Benjamin hid a smile. Careful, Varvara, he thought, Georgina will cotton on soon.

'Thank you, Varvara, but I wouldn't like to see you get hurt. You're very good at running the brothel. I need you here for that, not in a hospital bed or worse.'

'Perhaps I could...'

Georgina cut in, 'Varvara, please. I have a lot on my mind at the moment. Go and do some cleaning or something.'

She left the office, obviously deflated.

Georgina turned to Benjamin. 'As callous as it sounds, I've got to get things running like normal again.'

'Yes, yes, you must. We can't afford to have all the men looking for Ethel instead of working.'

'I know and to be honest, I'm beginning to think that if we haven't found her by now, then we never will.'

Benjamin wasn't sure how to answer. He agreed but didn't have the courage to say. Instead, he remained silent.

'Right, talk to me about this investment proposal,' Georgina said.

'Oh, erm, right. It's a little club I know. I've been doing their books for years and it turns a good profit. The owner is looking to sell and I believe the price he's asking is below market value and will offer good returns. This is the ideal business for you to invest in – small outlay with high profits.'

'I like the sound of that. Why is the owner selling it cheap?'

'Ah, well, that's the thing,' Benjamin said, gathering his thoughts. Once she knew all the facts, Georgina was sure to put two and two together and realise the truth about him. 'It's a private members club and the members are, erm, all men.'

'I see. You want me to invest in an old boys' lunch club. I suppose they all sit around on their fat arses drinking port, smoking cigars and talking shit. I can't say I'm keen on the idea.'

'No, Miss Garrett, it's not that sort of members' club, far from it. It's for men who err, prefer the company of other men.'

'Oh, you mean homosexuals?'

'Yes,' he answered, surprised at her bluntness.

'Which is illegal. Hence, he needs a buyer and nobody wants to touch it.'

'Exactly, but I thought you might be interested. It needs someone like you, with influence, who could keep the police from snooping.'

'I'd like to see the place before I commit to anything.'

'Yes, I can take you, anytime you like.'

'Right then, arrange a visit, preferably when it's closed. I don't think the members would be too happy about seeing a woman in their club.'

'On the contrary, Miss Garrett, they would adore you.' As soon as Benjamin had said it, he cringed. If Miss Garrett hadn't already worked out about his sexuality, then she most certainly had now.

They all heard the sound of a car pull up outside. Benjamin looked out of the window to see Johnny Dymond rushing to the front door.

'Let him in, Victor,' Georgina instructed.

Moments later Johnny came bursting through and announced, 'I've found his wife. I know where the bastard lived.'

'Jimmy Hewitt's house?' Georgina asked, already getting out of her seat.

'Yeah, Jimmy fucking Hewitt. It's on the other side of town.'

'Take me there,' Georgina said firmly.

Benjamin watched as Georgina dashed out of the office behind Johnny and Victor followed. He hoped his fears about Ethel being dead had been unfounded and that they'd find her alive and well. And as for Jimmy Hewitt's wife, if she had anything to do with Ethel's disappearance, Benjamin knew the woman wouldn't have much longer to live on this earth.

*

'It's this road, about halfway down, number eighty-two, Miss Garrett,' Johnny said and turned his car into the street before pulling over.

'Johnny, you go round the back in case she tries to do a runner. Victor, don't bother knocking. Just kick the door in. We need the element of surprise,' she told them.

They climbed out of the car and Johnny darted down an alleyway. Georgina wasn't familiar with this part of Battersea, near Nine Elms, but she thought it looked just as deprived as where she lived. She was aware of a few curtains twitching and knew her fashionable puffed sleeve coat with fur cuffs made her stand out. It wasn't the sort of attire poor working-class women would wear. They didn't know who she was over here, but if anyone challenged her, they'd soon find out!

Victor pointed out the house. The door number had been painted on to the front gatepost but there wasn't a gate hanging. 'Ready?' he asked.

Georgina nodded. She was more than ready. Her mouth felt dry and though she hid it, tears pricked her eyes at the thought of possibly finding Ethel dead or mutilated.

It only took Victor two kicks to bash the door open. He stood to one side to allow Georgina to run in first. She went straight into the front room. It was empty. Victor was in the kitchen and when she walked in, she saw he had a plump, middle-aged woman against the wall with his hand clasped around her neck. 'Where is she?' Victor demanded.

The woman was pulling at Victor's hand and answered, 'I don't know.'

Georgina opened the back door and let Johnny in. 'Check upstairs,' she told him, then walked over to the woman and stood at Victor's side before growling, 'Where is Ethel Mipple?'

'I haven't got a clue, I swear. Jimmy's not been home. He's either dead or he's been nicked. I don't know what he's done with her.'

Georgina used her eyes to tell Victor to release the woman, then told Mrs Hewitt to sit at the kitchen table. She pulled out a chair and sat opposite her. 'I'm not going to waste time. You've got one more chance to tell me where your husband hid Ethel.'

'I'm telling you, I – don't – know.'

Johnny came back into the room. 'She ain't upstairs but I found this.'

Georgina scraped her chair back and walked over to look at the jar Johnny was holding. Her stomach lurched when she saw it was almost full to the top with human teeth. She turned back to Mrs Hewitt and picked up a cobbler's last off the worktop. 'You nasty, ugly fucking bitch. This proves you know what your husband does!'

'Yeah, but I'm not involved. It's got nothing to do with me.'

Georgina looked at the woman with utter disgust before she pulled her arm back and whacked her across her chubby cheek with the heavy metal last.

The side of Daisy Hewitt's face exploded open and she screeched as bits of flesh, blood and a tooth landed on the kitchen table.

'Now are you going to tell me where she is?' Georgina demanded.

The woman could barely speak, but with her head slumped, she managed a just about audible, 'Don't know.'

'I don't believe you. You're either very fucking loyal to him or just plain stupid. Tell me where she is and I'll leave you alone. If you don't...' She left the threat hanging in the air.

Daisy held her hand over the gaping wound in her cheek and looked at Georgina through hooded eyes. Blood seeped from her mouth, and she spluttered. 'I hate him. I want to tell where she is but I don't have a clue.'

This time, Georgina believed her. 'Come on, let's get out of this shithole,' she said to Victor. 'Johnny, I want you to go over the place with a fine-tooth comb and look for anything that could help us find Ethel. Victor can take me home and then come back for you.'

'What do you want me to do with her?' Johnny asked.

Georgina stared at Mrs Hewitt with repulsion. She had condoned what her husband did. Instead of doing something to stop him, she had done nothing. She had no sympathy for her and said, 'Finish her off. And you can leave her body here to rot for all I care.'

Johnny looked at her with shock and Victor raised his eyebrows.

'It's what she deserves. If you can't do it, I will,' Georgina said.

Johnny's shock turned to a look of admiration. 'Nah, you're all right. We can't have your fancy hat and clothes getting messed up,' he said and smiled.

Daisy Hewitt said nothing as it appeared she'd passed out.

'There you go, that should make it easier for you,' Georgina said before she and Victor left.

The journey back to Queenstown Road was a solemn one. For a while, Georgina had believed they might find Ethel and had been filled with hope. Now, those hopes had been dashed and they were back to square one – knowing nothing, fearing the worst and praying for the best.

16

Another two days past. The atmosphere in Jane's house was becoming more fraught and Georgina could see Dulcie had had enough. 'I want you to take me home,' she told Georgina.

They had visited after breakfast, though no-one really had the stomach for food.

'We've only been here ten minutes.'

'I don't care. I want to go home now. Don't get me wrong, I feel for Fanny, but I can't stand the way she talks to you. We're all upset about Ethel, but it ain't on that she blames you. I've bit me tongue 'til now but I'm on the verge of losing it.'

'Just let it go over the top of your head. I do.'

'No, I bloody won't and why should I? You've been good to her and her family and she needs reminding.'

'Just leave it, Gran, please. Now's not the right time.'

'I know, and that's why I want to go home. I'm sorry, love, I don't care if it looks rude. So, no arguments please, young lady, and get that Victor bloke to drive me.'

Molly came into the room with Edward in her arms. 'Sorry about that, but I had to give him a feed. Are you off already?' she asked.

'Yes, I've just remembered that I put a pie in the oven. Silly old bird, I'm getting forgetful,' Dulcie answered.

Georgina could see from Molly's red-rimmed eyes that the girl had been crying again and felt sorry for her. 'I'll pop back later,' she said, finding it difficult to find the words to comfort her friend.

Minutes later, Dulcie was sitting in the back of Victor's car and they were driving down her street.

Georgina, sat in the front, looked over her shoulder when she heard her gran tut.

'That Charlotte really is a right little madam. The way she speaks to Fanny is appalling.'

'I know. I'd never have spoken to you like that at her age, or any age.'

'No, you wouldn't dare. 'Ere, look... is that Lash sat on the garden wall?'

Georgina spun her head back to the front and gasped.

'It is, ain't it?' her gran asked.

'Yes! Yes, it's him all right!' Georgina answered and was opening the car door before it had stopped moving.

Georgina didn't see her gran smile, she was too busy running towards her man and melting into his arms.

'What are you doing here?' she whispered to Lash as he embraced her so hard that she almost couldn't breathe.

'I missed you, Georgina. I couldn't stay away any longer and my family were travelling North with the fair.'

'I missed you too,' Georgina said but reluctantly pulled away when she heard her gran call from inside the car.

'Oi, you two. Have some decorum in the street please, and give us a hand out of this motor vehicle thing.'

Georgina peered up into Lash's dark eyes and for a moment,

all her fears vanished. 'I'm so glad you're back,' she purred.

'Me too, and I plan on taking you as my wife as soon as possible.'

It pleased Georgina to hear Lash say those words but she hadn't yet told him about her new role in the Wilcox business and she worried he wouldn't be happy about it.

They helped Dulcie inside and over a hot drink, Georgina sat in the kitchen and explained to him all that had happened during his absence. 'I realise it's a lot to take in,' she said, hoping that he'd be supportive and not make any silly demands on her to step down from the company.

'It is, but nothing you do surprises me – though I must say I'm amazed. I know you to be a determined woman, Georgina, but this, well, it's incredible.'

'It hasn't been easy and there's still a lot of work to do, but my priority is finding Ethel.'

'I'll do anything I can to help,' he said and reached across the table to cup her hands.

'Thank you,' she answered but was feeling at a loss to know what to do or where to look next.

'I can see the burden you've been carrying. It's etched into your face. Don't worry, we will bring her home.'

'But what if it's a body we bring home?' Georgina said and a sob caught in her throat. She felt a tear slip from her eye. With Lash, she could show her vulnerability. She didn't have to be tough and could allow her true feelings to surface.

'I want to tell you that it won't be like that but you have to be realistic. Listen to your heart, Georgina. What does it tell you? Can you hear Ethel's voice talking to you? If there's silence, then her spirit has gone.'

'Oh, Lash, you know I love you but I don't believe in your superstitions. I can't hear Ethel's voice but that doesn't mean she's dead... does it?'

'I think you know the truth but you don't want to accept it.'

'I won't believe it until I see her for myself. If she is dead, it will be my fault and I don't know how I'm going to live with that.'

'Stop it, Georgina, you mustn't talk like that. You are not responsible for her death. Jimmy Hewitt will be held accountable, not you.'

'I don't think Fanny sees it that way.'

'Fanny is a mother with a mind warped by grief. She's looking for someone to blame and you're the obvious target. She'll see the truth, in time.'

'Maybe. It's so good to talk, Lash, and get things off my chest.'

'You don't have to bottle things up anymore and you're not doing this by yourself.'

'I know but I do have work to do this evening, and it's such a relief to know that my gran will be looked after.'

'What do you mean?'

'With my dad in the pub all the time, I worry about my gran being by herself so it's a weight off my mind knowing that you can sit with her.'

'You want me to sit with your gran whilst you go to work?'

'Yes. That's not a problem, is it? Victor will be with me and I'm not leaving Knuckles with her.'

'What work will you be undertaking that requires your attention in the evening?'

'Something and nothing really. Varvara gave me the heads-up that a few of the pub landlords are going to be difficult. Apparently, they're going to refuse to pay the insurance fees as they don't believe a woman can offer them protection. I thought I'd pop in to the Queen's Head and show them otherwise.'

Lash pulled his hands away from hers and frowned as he spoke. 'I don't know what sort of a man you think I am, Georgina, but I'm telling you, I'm not going to granny-sit with my hands under my arse whilst you're out fighting in public houses.'

'It's not like that, Lash.'

'It is. That's exactly how it is. No, Georgina, you can't think that I'd stay at home and turn a blind eye to you putting yourself in danger. I'm not going to lay down the law and tell you that you can't go out and do this, but I am firmly stipulating that I will be with you and you can find someone else to sit with your gran.'

That was fair, thought Georgina. If Lash had allowed her to carry out her plans without objection, she realised she probably would have come to think that he wasn't quite the man she thought he was. 'Fine, but you mustn't interfere. I have to make my point and if you jump in with your big fists flaying, it'll defeat the object. I suppose Oppo can sit with me gran.'

Lash chuckled. 'I can't believe you'd think that I'd let you walk into a pub and make your threats without me by your side.'

'I hadn't thought, Lash. But you really have to promise me that you'll stand back and let me get on with it.'

'I'll give you that promise, but it will be broken the moment anyone even so much as breathes on you.'

Georgina looked at her man with affection. He was everything she wanted – attractive, mysterious and most of all, he offered her security. Protection from other men hurting her again. Well, at least that's what she thought she'd wanted when they'd first met. But now things had changed. Billy Wilcox was dead and that had caused a power shift. She was no longer in danger from him. She was at the top now and about to embark on a mission to instil fear in anyone who had ideas of challenging her. She no longer felt she needed Lash like she once had. Nonetheless, it didn't stop her loving him and her passion for him was stronger than ever.

That evening, Benjamin had daubed on his face powder and rouge and was sitting at a small round table with Aubrey in The Penthouse Club.

'Yes, she's keen to view the place,' Benjamin told Aubrey and sipped chilled champagne.

'Oh, Benny baby, that's wonderful news though I'm afraid there's a bit of a complication.'

'Such as?'

'You remember that American chap, Dickie? Vile creature, the one who prefers them very young.'

'How could I forget him! He assaulted my ears in the gentlemen's when he told me about his boys and how he prefers them before they've sprouted any pubes. He put me off sex for months!'

'Yes, that's him. Disgusting. Well, he's been in again and is insisting that I sell the club to him.'

'He doesn't have the money. He lost it all when the New York stock market collapsed in twenty-nine.'

'He's not working alone, dahling. Apparently, he's associated with some thugs who own a few clubs up west. I've been making a few discreet enquiries and I've found out that these men aren't the sort that one would disagree with.'

'Sounds like they're more the sort that Miss Garrett would be comfortable dealing with.'

'Yes, quite,' Aubrey answered. 'My point is, if Miss Garrett is serious, then you'll need to get her to act quickly. Then I can get away and she can deal with Dickie and his friends.'

'I'm not sure that I'd like to advise her to complete the transaction without fully disclosing everything I know.'

'It's business, Benny, don't be so naïve! Anyway, if she's everything you tell me she is, a few heavies from the west end won't be a problem for her.'

'That's not the point, Aubrey. I'd feel like I was hoodwinking her.'

'You've known this woman for how long? Yet you're showing more loyalty to her than you are to me and I've known you forever. I'm hurt, Benny, devastated.'

'Stop being such a drama queen. Like you say, you've known me forever so you of all people should realise that I'm not the sort of person to be deceitful. I will inform Miss Garrett of the change of circumstances and hopefully she won't change her mind about investing.'

'Have it your way,' Aubrey said and flicked his head round and his nose in the air.

'Don't worry, Aubrey. I really don't think a few thugs will deter Miss Garrett. I don't know if she believes it herself, but I know she could crush them.'

Aubrey turned his head back to look at Benjamin. He wore a wicked smile and said, 'I cannot wait to meet this woman. I think I'm in love with her already!'

'You can join the queue.'

'Really? Are you holding a torch for her?'

'Don't be ridiculous, Aubrey, you know she's not my type. But I'm pretty sure one of the tarts has a crush on her and so does one of her men, Johnny Dymond. Don't you think that's a glorious name?'

'Johnny Dymond – it sounds like one of the acts I'd have on my stage.' Aubrey laughed.

'I suppose it does, I hadn't thought of it like that. Though if you saw him, I could guarantee you wouldn't want him performing up there.'

'Is he grotesque?'

'No, far from it. He's very sexy but a bit too cheeky-chappy and flash with it. I prefer the strong, quiet type… Like Miss Garrett's bodyguard.'

'Tell me more,' Aubrey said teasingly.

'There's nothing to tell. Victor is delectable but I'm sure he's another one who fancies Miss Garrett. Not that one could blame him. She has it all: beauty, wit, charm and a sharp mind. Of course, Victor's far too professional to reveal his feelings,' Benjamin sighed, then added, 'but I can gaze from afar at him and have my naughty thoughts in bed.'

Aubrey giggled. 'Can you imagine Victor's reaction if he knew what was going on in your head? You never know, he might swing both ways, dahling. There's many a man who thinks he's straight until he's met someone like us! I'm sure I've turned plenty over the years. That electrician for one. You remember, the man who came in to convert our lights from gas. He was married and still is but he enjoyed a fumble with me behind the stage.'

'Victor's not like that, I'm sure. But it doesn't stop a poof from dreaming.'

'Quite, dahling, quite.'

Benjamin drained the rest of his glass and Aubrey refilled it.

'Do you know what Dickie's planning next?'

'Not really. He said he'd give me a week to consider his offer. That was two days ago. I got the impression that something awful would happen if I declined.'

'Did he threaten you?' Benjamin asked, mortified.

'Yes, indirectly. He said that his was the best offer I would get and if I refused to accept it, he'd make sure my club was worthless. He told me it would be *hot property* and then he laughed.'

'Are you thinking the same as me, Aubrey?'

'Probably. He's going to burn the place down, isn't he?'

'Not if Miss Garrett has anything to do with it!'

'Oh, please, Benny, you *have* to get her to buy it. It's unbelievably distressing to think of this place razed to the ground. Don't get me wrong, the club is just bricks and mortar, but it's special to all the members. It's meant so much to so many people, you included.'

'Absolutely, Aubrey. And I don't like the idea of it being destroyed any more than you do. I also can't abide the thought of Dickie owning the place. Don't worry, I'll use all my powers of persuasion on Miss Garrett.'

'You must, Benny, you really must!'

Benjamin took another sip of his champagne. The bubbles were going to his head and making him feel slightly giddy. 'Don't worry, Aubrey. Miss Garrett will be our saviour,' he said, his mind swimming with thoughts of Dickie's demise.

Whilst Lash talked with Oppo in the front room, Georgina had a quiet word with Victor in the kitchen.

'Whatever happens tonight, if you have to, I want you to hold Lash back.'

'But, Miss Garrett, if he witnesses you coming to any harm, it's only natural that he's going to want to protect you.'

'Have you forgotten who you're working for? Mr Maynard gave you clear instructions. He told you what I say, goes, and I'm saying you are not to allow Lash to get involved. In fact, neither of you are to step in.'

'What's all this?' Lash asked as he walked into the room.

Georgina hung her head.

'We need to talk. Victor, give us a minute,' Lash said then closed the door behind the man and pulled out a seat at the table for Georgina. 'I thought we'd already discussed this and now I find you going behind my back and giving Victor orders to hold me back.'

'I'm sorry, Lash, but I don't think you'll be able to help yourself. You're a fighter, it's what you do for a living. I know you're going to get involved tonight and if you do, you'll undermine my work.'

'I gave you my word that I would stay back unless anyone tries to hurt you. Is my word not good enough for you?'

'Yes, of course it is, but if I'm honest, I'd rather you waited outside the pub.'

'You cannot be serious!'

'Yes, I am, deadly serious. You have to understand how important it is for me to earn a reputation. People *have* to know that they can't challenge me. I should have been firmer from the start then maybe Ethel would be here now, safe and alive.'

'Let me do this with you. I'm to be your husband – you don't have to fight the world alone anymore. *I'll* go in the pub and lay down the rules. We should work together.'

'No, you don't get it, Lash. This is a one-man show, or in this case, a one-woman show. I'm Georgina Garrett and my name is going to mean something. I'll put the fear of God in people if I have to but I swear, no-one will ever hurt my loved ones again. This is *my* job. Sure, you can work for the business if that's your choice, but you are not taking it away from me.'

'You're a fierce woman, Georgina, and believe me, I wouldn't want to take anything away from you. I just want to look after you because I love you.'

'If you love me, really love me, then you'll respect how I feel and give me the room to do things my way. Or it's not going to work with us.'

'God, you're so frustrating,' Lash said through gritted teeth.

'You wouldn't love me if I was any different,' Georgina replied with a sexy and teasing smirk.

He pulled her up from the seat and into his arms. 'I'd love you no matter what,' he said, and fervently kissed her.

She responded with equal ardour, then pulled away and breathlessly asked, 'You agree to do things my way?'

'It goes against everything I believe in, but I know how stubborn you can be. No talking to you will change your mind, will it?'

'No, Lash, it won't.'

'I don't want to lose you, Georgina, so I will concede to your wishes. I'll wait outside and you can do whatever you feel you need to. But if you come out hurt, don't try and stop me going in.'

Georgina nodded and smiled at her man. She had no intention of getting hurt tonight and once again, she'd charmed Lash into getting her own way. 'Lash, I'm going to need more bullets. Can you get me any?'

'No, my family are a long way from here. But why the need for more?'

'Just as a precaution really. I'll have to see David Maynard for them.'

'I'll see the man.'

'No, it's my job.'

'Do you even know what bullets to ask for?'

'What do you mean? Don't I just ask him for handgun bullets?'

'No, Georgina,' Lash answered with affection and a shake of his head. 'Different guns fire different bullets.'

'Oh, blimey, good job you told me that. I could have made myself look like a complete idiot. Let's go, and en route, you can tell me all about it,' she said, and picked up her bag.

They drove to the Queen's Head with Lash educating Georgina about ammunition. Lash sat in the back, and in the darkness, he held her hand. When they pulled up outside the pub, Victor opened the door for Georgina and she whispered to Lash, 'This won't take long. Wait here, and thank you.' She took the gun from her bag and put it in her coat pocket and then removed her felt hat and placed it on the seat. 'Don't be surprised if you hear shots. It'll be me. No running in with the heroics.'

She could tell Lash wasn't happy but he replied, 'Be careful and don't take any unnecessary risks. I can't believe I'm allowing this. I must need my head testing.'

'You're doing it for me because you love me. And I love you even more for standing back, especially as I understand how difficult this is for you to do.'

'Go on, do what you have to do,' Lash answered, then turned his anxious face away from her.

Victor walked into the pub first and held the door open for Georgina. She took a deep breath and marched in. One by one, heads turned and eyed her and all conversations ceased. She tried not to cough in the smoky atmosphere and confidently strode to the bar.

'I'm Georgina Garrett,' she said to the burly man who rested one of his thick arms on the ale pump. She saw he had tattoos on each of his fingers.

'I know who you are,' he replied in an unfriendly manner.

'Good, then no further introductions will be required. Do you want to talk here or in private?' she asked and looked around at the faces that were all now staring at her.

'You can say whatever you've got to say here. My customers are my mates and they know the score.'

'Fine. I understand you have a problem paying your dues?'

'No. No problem.'

'So you'll be paying up then?'

'No.'

'Would you care to explain why you don't think you need to pay them?'

'No. I wouldn't.'

Georgina cleared her throat. The landlord's response didn't come as a surprise to her. 'Right then, I'll remind you,' she said and walked to the end of the bar where she lifted the hatch.

'What do you think you're doing?' the landlord asked and stomped towards her.

By now, Georgina was behind the bar and in front of the cash register. 'I'm helping myself to all of your takings,' she said and opened the till.

'Ger orf,' the landlord snapped and grabbed her arm to pull her away.

Georgina yanked herself free and turned to him. 'I've tried the nice approach and my men have explained the terms of our arrangement with you. Your payments have been reduced because I don't believe in extortion. You pay me a fair and affordable price and in return, I ensure that no other unwelcome gangs infiltrate the area and demand stupid money from you, as Billy Wilcox did. You're not getting robbed blind like you was. This is the best insurance policy for your business.'

'Look at you.' The man grimaced at her. 'You're nothing but a fancy tart. What fucking protection could you offer me? Go on, clear off, you stupid slag.'

Without hesitation, Georgina reached for a bottle of spirits, smashed the end on the bar and jammed the jagged glass under the landlord's chin. She held it there, just piercing his skin. 'Do you want to call me that again?'

He glared at her but seemed too scared to move his head for fear of the broken bottle stabbing him.

Georgina dropped the bottle. 'Oh, I'm sorry, that was unfair. Go on, I don't have a weapon now, so would you like to repeat yourself?'

'Yeah, all right. I said you're a stupid slag,' he sneered as he dabbed at the blood where the bottle had been.

Georgina was quick to move. Before the man saw it coming, she jabbed him under his chin with her left fist followed by a heavy right hook to the side of his head.

The man staggered and looked dazed before flying back at her. Georgina could see his huge clenched hand coming towards her and expertly dodged the punch and at the same time, she threw another in his direction. This one caught him in the eye socket and his brow split open.

'Did I mention that I can box? Now, would you like to call me that again?' she asked. He didn't answer but several men were out of their seats.

Georgina was quick to react and pulled her gun from her coat pocket and fired a shot into the air. The noise was deafening and bits of debris from the ceiling fell to the floor. 'Sit back down, the lot of you,' she growled and pointed the firearm from one man to another. Everyone did as they were told, so Georgina refocused on the landlord. 'I think it would be in your best interests if I give you a taster of why it's important that you pay your insurance,' she said, then called over to an old man at the piano, 'Play me a tune, something cheerful.'

The old man took the roll-up hanging from his mouth and threw it to the floor and began banging out a lively piece that she'd never heard before. As the music played, Georgina walked along the bar and meticulously knocked bottle after bottle to the floor. The overwhelming smell of the spilt alcohol turned her stomach but she remained staunch until every bottle had been smashed. 'Stop,' she shouted above the sound of the piano. The old man immediately pulled his hands back from the keys. 'Anyone got a match?' she asked with a smirk.

'NO!' the landlord yelled, 'you'll set us all alight!'

'I know, but this is what will happen if you don't pay me. It won't be me who comes in here and demolishes your establishment. But someone will. Someone like Billy Wilcox. And once they've got a hold, they'll go through Battersea like a dose of salts. You don't want that, do you?'

'No, of course not.'

'Good. You've seen sense. My men will be in for collection on their usual day. You can pay them double this week, for the inconvenience you've caused me. Here's my contact details,' she said and laid a piece of paper on the sticky bar. 'Please feel free to call if you encounter any problems. Good evening.'

Georgina's heels clicked over the wooden floor as she walked towards the exit with her gun in her hand hanging by her side. Victor held open the door and before she left, she turned and said, 'I'd be obliged if you could let the other pubs know to expect my men. And let it be known – don't mess with Georgina Garrett.' She fired another shot. The bullet just missed the landlord's head and shattered the mirror behind him. She glanced around the bar. Everyone had ducked; some had dived for cover. The landlord stood motionless with his hands over his head. 'Take that as a warning.'

She left. Her work this evening was complete. She'd achieved what she'd set out to and no-one had been hurt, apart from a few bruises to the landlord's face and probably his pride.

Lash was directly outside. 'Are you all right?' he asked.

'Yes, but my feet are soaked with booze.' She laughed.

He took her hand but she pulled it away. When Georgina saw his hurt expression, she quickly explained. 'I had to throw a few punches. I'm a bit out of practice and bruised my knuckles on the landlord's face.'

Lash turned to Victor. 'Did anyone attempt to go for her?'

'No, she showed them who the guv is,' he answered.

'That's my girl,' Lash said and as they walked back to the car, he placed his arm over her shoulder. 'I'm proud of you.'

'Thanks. It means a lot to have your support.'

'You've got it, Georgina, always. But I think I already know who's going to be wearing the trousers in our marriage.'

'Probably not me,' she answered, smiling. 'I grew up wearing trousers and now I rather like my skirts. Anyway, I'm an old-fashioned girl at heart. I'll be a good wife at home, but in the office, I'm in charge.'

'Yes, sir,' Lash answered jokingly.

But it was no joke to Georgina. She meant every word. If Lash wanted to be a part of her life, he'd have to put aside his traditional views of a woman's role and accept her for who she now was – Georgina Garrett. The boss.

17

Varvara had taken coffee into the office and as she handed the cups around, she scowled first at PC Cunningham and then at Lash. She hated them both, especially Lash, and couldn't see what Miss Garrett saw in him. Granted, he was an attractive man, if you liked that sort of thing, but she believed Miss Garrett could do far better. A gentleman, perhaps, possibly a banker or a doctor. But this man, he was nothing but a gypsy, hardly a step up from a vagrant.

'And another thing, Miss Garrett,' PC Cunningham said. He slurped on his coffee then continued, 'Could you try and refrain from firing random shots in pubs, please.'

'There was nothing random about my firing,' Georgina answered haughtily. 'Why, has the landlord complained?'

'No, far from it. Even though I could see the damage your gun had caused, he denied anything had happened. But we did receive two complaints from customers. Fear not, I have had the paperwork swept under the mat, but you can't go round shooting at things like that.'

'Why can't I?'

'Because it's against the law!'

'You're paid well enough to turn a blind eye.'

'And I do, Miss Garrett, but in future, try not to draw so much attention to yourself.'

'I think we're done here now. Mr Harel will see to you. Good day, officer.'

Varvara tried not to smirk as PC Cunningham placed his unfinished coffee on Georgina's desk and huffily scraped his seat back.

'And by the way, there's a large group of people heading to London from up North. A hunger march by all accounts. A lot of us have been assigned extra duties to manage it. You'll find the streets barren of police over the next day or two. Could be a good opportunity to do whatever you need to do.'

Georgina acknowledged Cunningham's information with a small nod of her head but nothing more. Then she turned to Varvara and asked, 'Can I help you?'

'I'd like a word, in private,' she answered and threw Lash a filthy look.

He was standing behind Miss Garrett, as if watching over her. Huh, thought Varvara. Miss Garrett didn't need *him* for protection! She wished the woman could see her fiancé for what he was – scum. All gypsies were scum.

'Not now, Varvara. I'll be back later, we can speak then. And get rid of these weeds on my desk.'

Varvara had spent time scouring the backyard for wildflowers and had picked daisies, dandelions and buttercups. She'd carefully arranged the flowers in a small glass and hoped Miss Garrett would like them. She doubted that Lash ever brought the woman flowers. Now, the glass in her hand, she left the office disappointed though she'd enjoyed hearing Miss Garrett put that dirty policeman in his place. She loitered in the hallway for a while, hoping to get another glimpse of Miss Garrett as she left for wherever she was going.

The office door flew open and Victor came out followed by Miss Garrett. As always, the sight of her left Varvara in awe and she gazed at her longingly. Then her eyes snapped to Lash who looked at her with his eyebrows raised. He must have seen the way she'd been ogling Miss Garrett. Not that Varvara cared what he thought. She just hoped he wouldn't say anything about it to Georgina.

With the house empty and no customers, Varvara decided to telephone Dina. She knew it wouldn't be a long conversation – Dina never had much to say. She missed her sister but didn't think Dina seemed bothered. In fact, Dina didn't appear to care about anything. She rarely smiled and never cried. The only emotion she ever expressed was anger and even that was rare. Her sister needed to find love, as she had with Georgina. But Varvara doubted that would ever happen as Dina's heart was frozen.

'Miss Garrett, it's such a pleasure to meet you,' Aubrey gushed. 'I've heard so much about you from Benny.'

'All bad, I hope.' Georgina smiled.

'On the contrary, my dear. You're quite as delightful as he said you'd be. Please, come through and let me get you something to drink. Champagne?'

'No, thank you. If you don't mind, I'd like to get straight down to business.'

'Of course, I understand how terribly busy you must be. Do you mind if I partake? It's past twelve, a perfectly civilised time for bubbles,' Aubrey said and giggled.

Georgina got the impression that Aubrey was nervous. Good, she thought, that was the sort of reaction she now wanted from people.

'Benjamin has filled me in about everything, and I'm still willing to make you an offer.'

'Fabulous,' Aubrey squealed and clapped his hands together.

'However, considering the situation with this American chap and his association with the West End gang, the offer will be considerably less than you're asking for.'

'I find it awfully vulgar to discuss money but do tell, I'm dying to know.'

'Ten per cent lower than Dickie's offer and there's no room for negotiation.'

'Lower? But surely you'd at least match it?'

'Why would I? You want to sell the club but not to him. I'm not desperate to buy it. It makes no odds to me if you don't accept my offer. I'll just say good day to you and be on my way. Ten per cent lower, take it or leave it.'

Aubrey knocked back his glass of champagne whilst Georgina sat looking at him steely-faced. She'd never played poker but Johnny Dymond had given her some good bluffing tips. Truth was, she desperately wanted the club in her portfolio. It earned a very healthy income and the coffers would soon be low in the business. As Benjamin had pointed out, it was a good, sound investment and with a word and a few quid in the ear of PC Cunningham's colleague, she could guarantee it wouldn't be raided.

'I could accept Dickie's offer and run.'

'Do it then. You're the one who'll have to live with your choices.'

Aubrey let out a deep sigh. 'I can't, can I? How could I possibly sell it to that scoundrel and live happily ever after knowing that all my loyal customers and friends will have their club ruined by him. All right, Miss Garrett, you have a deal.'

Georgina shook the man's hand. 'I'll have Benjamin arrange the payment immediately after the paperwork has been signed. Congratulations on your retirement.'

Aubrey waved his empty glass in front of him. 'And congratulations to you, Miss Garrett, the new owner of The Penthouse Club. You will look after it for me, won't you, dahling?'

'Don't worry, Aubrey, the place will be in safe hands,' she assured him.

Once outside, Lash opened the car door for her.

'I got it,' she said, chuffed with herself, 'and at a silly price.'

'Well done, Georgina. I don't mind telling you that was one place I was happy to wait outside.'

She climbed in and Lash sat next to her on the back seat. 'Why?' she asked.

'I don't feel comfortable around them queer folk,' he answered and shuddered. 'It's not natural, is it?'

'So you don't want to be the manager there then? It comes with a room.'

'No, thank you. I'm quite happy in the Clapham house. I have a comfortable bed, though I'd rather be sharing it with you.'

Victor cleared his throat. 'Back to Queenstown Road?' he asked, somewhat uncomfortably.

'Yes,' Georgina answered and felt herself blush. She leaned over to Lash and whispered in his ear, 'Shush, don't say things like that in front of the men. And I'll soon be in your bed, once we're married. In the meantime, I hope you don't have eyes for the scantily clad women visiting the house to see the photographer.'

'Georgina, my love, I only have eyes for you.'

'Good answer,' she said with an affectionate smile and reached for his hand. Just the touch of his skin alone sent shockwaves through her body. She longed to share his bed too.

They were soon back at the office where Benjamin was eager to hear news of how the meeting had transpired. 'The Penthouse Club is now part of the business,' she told him and was delighted to see how pleased he was. But her delight was short-lived as she had the bothersome task of dealing with Dickie, and Ethel was never far from her mind.

Victor had proved his worth to her but he was another thing she'd have to deal with. 'I suppose I should think about sending you back to Mr Maynard,' she told him. 'I have Lash here with me now. He can drive and be by my side.'

Victor was stood in his usual spot guarding the office door. He looked to the floor and placed his hands in his trouser pockets before speaking. 'I'd rather stay here,' he said, and scuffed the floor with one of his big boots. She thought he seemed to be squirming, much to her amusement.

Georgina considered keeping him on and liked the idea, but wasn't sure how David would feel about it. She knew Lash was more than capable of looking after her but she didn't think it would be healthy for their relationship to be tied at the hip. 'I see. We can ask David. I must admit, I quite like his car too.'

'Georgina, a word,' Lash said, clearly unhappy with the arrangement.

She walked into the hallway with him. 'What's your problem?' she asked but already knew what he would say.

'I should be looking after you,' he answered.

'It's not practical. I need you for other things. If David allows me to keep Victor, how would you feel about taking over from Knuckles? I don't like the man and neither do I trust him. You'd be responsible for the safety of the girls in both brothels and for making sure the punters pay up. And elsewhere across the business, if someone needs roughing up, I'd send you.'

'You're basically asking me to be a pimp, Georgina.'

'But it's not really like that, is it? I'm asking you to take on a role that I need filling with someone I can rely on.' She knew how to play Lash and softened her approach: 'You'd be here a lot of the time, with me,' she said quietly and ran her fingers up his firm chest and over his broad shoulders.

'You're a bad woman, Georgina. You know I can't deny you anything you ask of me,' he answered and his mouth met hers.

As their passions rose, she could feel his bulging manhood pressing against her. 'Stop,' she said breathlessly and pulled back from him. 'Not here, Lash. Never here.'

Lash pulled up the collar of his jacket. 'I'll go and see Knuckles and tell him to move on.'

'Yes, but not yet. I have to speak to David first.'

She straightened her blouse and was wiping smudged lipstick from around her mouth when the office door flew open.

'It's Aubrey on the telephone,' Benjamin said urgently. 'Dickie is at the club. And he's not alone!'

'Lash, Victor, with me, quick. We'll pick up Johnny en route,' she said and ran into the office and grabbed her bag.

'He can never refuse a drink, Miss Garrett, never,' Benjamin called as she dashed out to the car.

Victor had already started the engine. She jumped in next to Lash and ignoring the newly introduced thirty mile an hour speed limit, they sped away.

'I don't like her, Mum,' Charlotte whined.

Fanny was busy scrubbing the white laundry over a board in a large copper pot that she'd boiled on the range stove. She'd scrubbed with such vigour that her knuckles were starting to bleed. But keeping busy kept her mind off Ethel. 'Yeah, well, we've got good reason not to like her, but at the end of the day, Georgina keeps a roof over our heads and food in our bellies, so no more giving her lip.'

'She thinks she can boss us all around.'

'I know, but we've got to put up with it for now. Go on, bugger off and find something to do with yourself, and stay out of trouble, for a change,' Fanny answered and added the blue rinse to the wash. The laundry was a much easier chore in Jane's kitchen than it was in her own scullery. She could never afford the blue rinse to make her whites gleam and would often have to use cold water instead of hot. And Jane had a proper iron to warm on the stove. Fanny had chucked hers out long ago for fear of her husband using it to whack her one.

She heard someone knock on the front door and Charlotte stomped off to answer it. Moments later, Knuckles walked into the kitchen. The sight of the big man and the softness in his eyes made Fanny want to run into his arms.

'Hello, Fanny. I hope you don't mind me calling in. I just wanted to see how you're bearing up?'

'Thanks, Knuckles. It's nice of you to care. Take a seat, I'll put the kettle on.'

'I can't stop long, I don't want Miss Garrett to think I'm skiving.'

'Sod what she thinks!'

'That's all right for you to say, you don't work for her.'

'No, and I wouldn't. It's her fault that my Ethel ain't home.'

'I dunno, Fanny, I mean, I can't say I like her much but she's doing everything she can to find your girl.'

'She killed the one person who could have told us! And if it weren't for her and her big ideas, Jimmy would never have taken Ethel in the first place.'

'I suppose. But I thought you and her were friends?'

'She's Molly's friend, not mine. I used to have a lot of time for her but since she's taken over the business, I reckon her head has got too big for her shoulders. And what gives her the bleedin' right to think she should be in charge, eh? That's my Molly's right, not hers. She should be working for Molly and getting a fraction of the money she takes. You've seen her, prancing around in her fancy clothes. They must have cost a few bob. As far as I'm concerned, she's to blame for Ethel and she's robbing my Molly.'

'Bloomin' 'eck, I didn't realise you felt like that, but you ain't wrong. The Wilcox business has got fuck all to do with her.'

'I'm glad you see it my way. I wish Molly would too but she's blinded by loyalty to her. I'm telling you, Knuckles, that woman needs bringing down a peg or two.'

'Yeah, but I don't know who'd do it. She's got the blokes doing her bidding for her and there ain't no-one else waiting to jump into her shoes.' He downed his tea in one gulp.

'There will be, you mark my words. And when there is, make sure you pick your side carefully.'

'I will, Fanny, I will. Thanks for the cuppa but I'd better get off. I'll pop in again soon, if that's all right?'

'Yes, I'd like that. It's been good to talk to someone who understands. You won't give up looking for Ethel, will you?'

'Never, I promise. See ya soon.'

Fanny watched the door close behind him, disappointed that he'd gone. Even though he looked intimidating, she thought he was a big softie really. Yes, he'd done bad things in the past but only on Billy Wilcox's orders. She was seeing a side to the man that he rarely showed, a gentle nature, caring too. She thought it a shame that Georgina treated him with such contempt. Regardless of how that bitch viewed him, Fanny decided she liked Knuckles.

*

As they hurtled towards the club, with Johnny Dymond sitting in the front next to Victor, Georgina told them, 'Check your guns. Make sure they're loaded.'

'Lash, you're gonna need this,' Johnny said and passed a pistol over the seat. 'Are we to expect a shoot-out, Miss Garrett?' he asked.

'It's likely. Be prepared,' she answered but kept quiet about only having one bullet left in her gun.

'Great. It's been a good year since I've fired this baby,' Johnny replied as he rubbed the shiny barrel of his revolver. 'I've heard this West End lot 'ave been throwing their weight about in loads of places where they shouldn't be. They're taking fucking liberties but no-one's had the front to call 'em out. Nasty bunch, they are, right fucking nasty.'

'Yes, I made it my business to find out about them. You know I can't promise that any of us are going to come out of this alive?'

Lash's head spun to look at her and he said quietly, 'This sounds very risky, Georgina. Why are we bothering with it? No money has been exchanged.'

'It's the principle. They're taking the piss out of me and I ain't having it. If I let them do this on my turf, who knows what they think they could get away with next.'

'Does it matter enough to you to put your life in danger?'

'Yes, Lash, it does. This *is* my life.' It irked her that Lash still didn't seem to comprehend what she was trying to achieve. He had at least accepted her terms but she couldn't have him questioning her every move, especially in front of the men. For now though, she had more pressing things on her mind and twisted her mother's wedding ring. Her nerves were starting to get to her but she tried not to show it.

They pulled up outside and Georgina looked around her before entering the dimly lit club. 'Follow my lead,' she instructed the others. Her confident stride masked her anxiety.

With trepidation and gripping tightly to her pistol, she took the stairs past the cloakroom and toilets until she came to the door of the club. A large man stood there with his hand resting on the belt of his high-waist trousers. She knew he was ready to pull his gun if necessary.

'They're expecting me,' she told him and without waiting for a response, she pulled open the door and marched in.

She saw Aubrey looking very pale and clearly shaken sat at a small round table where she'd been seated earlier. A trickle of blood had run from the corner of his mouth, down his chin and stained his pristine white collar. They'd obviously already started with the bully tactics.

The man she assumed was Dickie stood closely behind Aubrey. He was taller than she'd imagined but wiry. His lank, greasy hair, patchy beard and hooked nose gave him a sinister appearance. Knowing how he abused boys turned her stomach. She could barely bring herself to even look at him but there was business to be done.

In contrast to Dickie, a short, stocky man stood next to him. He wore an expensive suit and didn't have a hair out of place. She knew immediately that these were the men she'd be dealing with and hoped that Lash, Victor and Johnny had spotted the other four. One at the bar, one a few feet from Dickie, one on the inside of the door and another near the stage. Her rivals had the place covered and outnumbered them.

'Good afternoon, gentlemen,' she said, though she knew Dickie wasn't anything like a gentleman. 'You're welcome to visit my establishment but I'm afraid we're closed at the moment. Perhaps you'd like to come back on another occasion and sample the delights on offer?'

'Here she is,' Dickie said snidely with his American accent. 'Georgina Garrett. The woman who's trying to make a name for herself round here.'

'With respect, I'm not trying – I *am* a name round here. And who are you?'

'Folks call me Dickie but you can call me sir.'

'No, Dickie will suffice. Are you here to request membership?'

'Cut the bull, Garrett, you know full well what we're doing here so gather your chimps and piss off.'

'I don't think so, Dickie. Tell you what, let's have a drink and we can talk.'

'Talk… that's about right for a woman. You gals love a bit of chit-chat.'

'Aubrey, would you be so kind as to bring me a bottle of your special champagne. Dickie's quite right, we girls do love a chit-chat, especially over a glass of bubbly. Please, do join me, Dickie – I wouldn't want to be lonesome.'

Dickie laughed. 'You're quite charming, Miss Garrett, and it would be rude of me not to accept your invitation.'

'Aubrey, bring us two glasses, please,' Georgina said and walked to the table where the shorter man pulled out a seat for her.

'Make that three,' the man added, then introduced himself. 'Charles Brennan, better known as Charlie Chops. You've probably heard of me?'

'No, Charles, I can't say I have,' she lied. Georgina knew all about Charlie Chops and how he'd got his nickname by chopping off his adversaries' fingers. When she'd been told, she'd wondered if it was Charlie Chops who'd inspired Billy Wilcox to do the same to his prostitutes.

Charlie placed his large gun on the table in front of him. She thought it was a move designed to intimidate her. If it was, it hadn't worked. As he did so, Lash, Victor and Johnny moved closer. Now they were out of the shadows, Charlie looked across at them and asked, 'Is that Victor? David Maynard's bloke.'

'Yes,' Georgina answered.

'What's he doing here?'

'David and I work in collaboration. Sorry, do excuse me, that's rather a big word – you probably don't understand it. David Maynard and I work together.' She realised her cheekiness wasn't doing anything to defuse the fraught situation and, though the atmosphere felt explosive, she was enjoying toying with them. After all, she was fully aware that this could be the last conversation she'd ever have.

Charlie ignored her derogatory remark and asked, 'Does Mr Maynard know you're here?'

'Not yet, but he will.'

'Right. In that case, I'll give you a run-down. This is how it's working. Dickie is fronting the club but it's my money going into it. Well, it was but I didn't know the Maynards had an interest too.'

'Didn't you? That was rather short-sighted of you, not to have asked all the right questions. Oh, well, you know now so what are you going to do about it?'

Aubrey poured them all a drink but his hand shook and he spilt champagne meant for Dickie's glass onto the table. The liquid dripped down onto Dickie's trousers. He jumped up, sending his chair flying backwards, and backhanded Aubrey across his cheek. 'You stupid fucking queer!' he barked.

Aubrey cowed down with his hands held up in defence while Georgina jumped from her seat and shoved Dickie, scowling as she said, 'Don't you treat him like that, you piece of shit.'

Suddenly, there was the sound of guns being cocked and Georgina's eyes darted around the club. Everyone seemed to be aiming at each other, she at Dickie and Dickie at her. Everyone, that was, except Charlie. He'd remained seated. His gun was still on the table and he sipped the champagne. 'It ain't 'alf bad this, Aubrey. You'll have to give me the name of your supplier,' he said, and drained the rest from his glass. His comment immediately defused the situation.

Dickie didn't take his beady eyes or his gun off Georgina. 'Ladies first,' he said, inferring that she should lower her weapon before he did his.

'No, after you,' she replied.

'Come on, ladies, you're not going to let this fine champagne go to waste, are you?' Charlie said as he poured himself another.

Dickie took his aim off Georgina and they both sat back at the table where she was pleased to see that he quickly drank from his half-filled glass and she was grateful that she didn't have to use her last bullet.

'Bring us some more, please, Aubrey, and leave the bottle,' she said, intending to encourage Dickie to drink plenty.

'That was exciting,' Charlie said. 'I thought you two were gonna blow each other's brains out.'

'I'd have to be a good shot to have hit Dickie's tiny brain.' Georgina laughed and Charlie joined in but the look on Dickie's face told her that he hadn't found her quip quite as amusing. Instead, he drank greedily from his refilled glass.

Charlie turned to Dickie. 'The thing is, mate, this ain't as straightforward as we first thought, not with the Maynards involved. I respect the man too much to go stepping on his toes.'

Georgina tried not to splutter her mouthful of champagne and bit her tongue. Respect, my arse, she thought. It was more like Charlie Chops and his gang were scared shitless of the Maynards. She didn't know anyone who wasn't.

'I'm sure David would appreciate you stepping away from this investment,' she said to Charlie.

'Yes, I'm sure he would. To be honest, Miss Garrett, it was never really my cup of tea anyway. I've got half a dozen clubs up west and we cater for men but not in the way this gaff does. Dickie was keen so I went along with it, but you're welcome to it.'

Georgina raised her glass and clinked with Charlie's. 'Congratulations to me then,' she chirped, 'and I sincerely mean it this time when I say, welcome to The Penthouse Club.'

'Thank you, and yes, congrats. You'll do all right here with this. But I won't be one of your customers, no offence.'

'No offence taken, Charles.'

At last, the tension had dissipated and Georgina found she was quite enjoying Charlie's company. He had a lot to say and as they talked, she kept refilling Dickie's glass who thanked her each time with a forced smile.

An hour later, Georgina felt relaxed as she said, 'This has turned out to be a very pleasant afternoon. And yes, thanks, Charlie, I'd love to come up and spend an evening in one of your clubs. I haven't been up west for a while, so I'll have to dig out something fancy to wear.'

'You look lovely as you are, Miss Garrett.'

'Thanks, Charlie, and call me Georgina. Miss Garrett makes me feel like an old spinster.'

'You're not married though, are you?'

'No, but I'm not an old spinster either.'

By now, Dickie had slouched in his seat and he looked bleary-eyed. ''Scuse me,' he said, and stumbled as he got to his feet.

'Poor sod can't handle the booze,' Charlie whispered to her and laughed as Dickie crabbed his way through the club towards the gents' toilet.

'If you'll excuse me too,' Georgina said, 'whilst I powder my nose.'

As she headed for the door, Lash glared at her when she passed him. She guessed he wasn't happy about her not mentioning to Charlie that she was getting married. But Lash had to understand, this was business and she'd explain later at home.

For now, she followed Dickie as he unsteadily made his way to the toilet. Once he'd gone in she waited a few moments before slowly and quietly opening the door. She saw him standing at a urinal, leaning forward and resting an outstretched arm on the wall in front. As she walked towards him, he spotted her.

'Come to take a look, have you?' he asked and turned full frontal exposing his shrivelled manhood. 'Do you like what you see?' he slurred.

Georgina smiled seductively. 'Not bad, Dickie,' she said, 'but I think we can make this a bit happier to see me.'

She grabbed his flaccid penis and gently pulled it.

'You won't get that working. You're not my sort, Miss Garrett, but feel free to take your pleasure how you find it,' he said and undid his trousers so they fell around his ankles.

Georgina pulled his long johns down and rubbed her hand over his testicles. Dickie swayed and she looked up to see he'd closed his eyes. She felt sick at the thought of what the disgusting pervert was imagining. He lavishly licked his lips and at that point, she dug her long nails in hard and twisted his balls at the same time. Dickie gasped in a sharp intake of breath and was about to let out a scream, but Georgina was quick and punched him in the mouth. His teeth hurt her knuckles but she was pleased to see that the strength of her blow sent him falling. As he landed in a heap on the floor, his head flopped back and thudded on the tiled floor. She looked down at him and placed her heeled foot on his chest. Slowly, Dickie's eyes opened. 'I know all about you and the little boys. See how you enjoy this,' she said, and lifted her knee then stamped her foot down savagely between his legs.

Her heel squelched into his body and this time, Dickie let out an ear-piercing scream. She pulled her knee up again and stamped harder, hoping to destroy everything that made him physically a man. Again she stamped, and grunted with the force she used, showing no mercy. Blood began to pool on the white tiles and Dickie's screams faded as he fell into unconsciousness.

She was about to stamp again on what was left of his penis when the toilet door flew open and Charlie, Lash, Victor and another of Charlie's men jostled with each other to get through.

Georgina looked at them and then at Dickie. She was satisfied with the mangled mess she'd created. Her chest heaved up and down as she sucked in air. She'd exerted a lot of energy in annihilating Dickie's male parts. She saw the men all look down at him and then back at her. No-one spoke. They were clearly shocked.

She caught her breath then told them, 'He won't be bothering little boys again.'

'For fuck's sake, Georgina, look at the state of him,' Charlie muttered. 'You've done a right job on mashing up his bollocks.'

'He's a kiddy fiddler.'

'Yeah, I'd heard, but it ain't none of my business.'

'Well, it's up to you to run your patch as you see fit, but I don't allow that sort of thing on mine. He's all yours. I'd be obliged if you would get him out of my club.'

'No fucking wonder you ain't married,' Charlie said with a chuckle then told his man to fetch the others and get the place cleaned up. 'And, Georgina, you might wanna give your shoe a wipe.'

Back in the main part of the club, Charlie waited for his men to finish then said to Georgina, 'I know I invited you up for a VIP night at one of my places, but do me a favour and stay away. You're a bleedin' nutter, and I mean that as a compliment.'

'Thank you, that's the nicest compliment anyone has ever paid me,' she answered and they parted company.

Once they'd left, Georgina relaxed. She looked around and surveyed her new club. She was very pleased with the place and relieved that she'd gained ownership without the need for gunfire. But now, she had to go home and explain herself to Lash and judging by the look on his face, she thought she had an even bigger battle to come.

18

Dulcie had got used to having Victor around. Where Georgina went, Victor followed. He was sat bolt upright on her sofa whilst they listened to Georgina and Lash upstairs arguing again. It worried her. They seemed to be doing a lot of shouting at each other lately. She could understand Lash's frustrations but she knew how stubborn her granddaughter could be. If Lash wanted to take Georgina for his wife, Dulcie knew the man would be spending his life backing down to her demands. Still, she thought, if he loves her as much as he claims to, he'll let her have her way.

She heard the front door open and watched as Victor jumped to his feet to check who was coming in. Ivy appeared in the front room and offered a gummy smile.

'Hello, love. What are you doing here?' Dulcie asked.

'I've walked round with Molly,' Ivy answered and stepped to one side to allow Molly to pass.

'Hi, Dulcie. I can hear Georgina is home but she sounds a bit busy,' Molly said and grimaced.

'Yes, they're at it again. Gawd knows what Mary next door makes of all this blinkin' commotion. Be a sweetheart,

Ivy, and make us a cuppa. There's a sponge in me cake tin, help yourself.'

Ivy went through to the kitchen and Molly sat on the sofa. Victor, ever polite, remained in the passageway.

Dulcie noticed Molly's worried brow and asked, 'Is everything all right?'

'No, not really. It won't be until we know what's happened to Ethel.'

'I know, love. It's been two weeks now, your poor mother must be out of her mind.'

'She is, Dulcie, we all are. And it don't help that Charlotte hasn't been to school again. Knuckles went to meet her but Charlotte weren't there. He'd dropped her off in the morning but her teacher said she must have slipped out. Turns out her and a friend have been missing from school most afternoons. She'll turn up, at dinner time, like she always does, but me mum could do without the added worry.'

'I bet she could. But at least Knuckles is doing what he's been told to do. It was a good idea of Georgina's to show that there's protection around us all. Tell you what, bring Charlotte round here. I'll give her what for, the little madam. You know what they say, spare the rod, spoil the child. That girl needs a bloody good spank across the back of her legs.'

'Maybe, but my mum won't allow anyone to hit us. She reckons we saw enough of all that when my dad was alive.'

'Your father used to knock your mother around, not you kids. There's no talking to Charlotte. The only thing she'll listen to is a good bleedin' clout.'

'There's something else, Dulcie…'

'Go on, love, what's wrong?'

'Nothing, really, but...'

'Spit it out, girl.'

'It's Oppo.'

'What about him?'

'Well, you know we've been seeing each other?'

'Yes, though sitting in your kitchen ain't exactly romantic.'

'I know, but I couldn't enjoy meself, not while I'm worried sick about Ethel. But it's nice to have Oppo pop in. He's so easy to talk to.'

'He is, he's a lovely lad. You could do a lot worse, you know!'

'I have,' Molly answered, 'Billy Wilcox. Anyway, the thing is, Oppo's worried about me, and Edward. Especially after Ethel going missing.'

'I should think he is. But you've got Knuckles around a lot.'

'Yeah, but I mean in the future. He's concerned about my involvement with the business.'

'You don't really get involved though. Georgina sees to everything.'

'But it's my name, Dulcie. Everyone knows I'm Mrs Wilcox, Billy's widow.'

'What are you saying?'

'I don't want nothing more to do with it. I realise I've got Edward's future to think about, but this isn't the future I want for my boy. Ethel could be dead, Dulcie, and I can't even bring meself to think of anything terrible happening to Edward. Once Ethel has been found, Oppo wants to take me away from all of this. Away from Battersea. Somewhere where no-one knows who I am or that Billy

Wilcox is Edward's father. We just want to live a quiet and normal life.'

'Well, that's a lot to take in.'

'How do you think Georgina will react when I tell her?'

'I don't suppose she'll be happy but you've got to do what you believe is right for you and your son. Georgina's tough, but she'll miss you. You two have been best friends since you was knee high to a grasshopper. Are you sure this is what you want and you've not been talked into it by Oppo?'

'I'm sure, Dulcie. I've thought about it long and hard. What's happened to Ethel has been an eye-opener. I can't have my son at risk and as long as we stay in Battersea, he always will be.'

They heard a door slam upstairs and Georgina's footsteps stomping down the stairs.

'I shouldn't mention it just yet,' Dulcie whispered. 'Sounds like she's in a foul mood.'

The door swung open and Georgina marched in. 'He's driving me bloody bonkers!' she ground out through gritted teeth. 'Why do men have to be so bloody manly? If the boot was on the other foot, no-one would think twice about *him* being in charge. He wouldn't like it if I questioned everything he did! I love him but there's times I feel like throttling the man!'

Dulcie chuckled. 'You sound like every married woman I've ever known. You wait 'til you get his ring on your finger. If you think he's a pain now, I'm telling you, it doesn't get any better.'

Georgina rolled her eyes then smiled at her friend. 'Sorry, Molly. Hello. All right?'

'Yeah, I suppose.'

'I realise you're worried sick about Ethel but I've still got people out looking for her, including the Old Bill.'

'I know you have, Georgina, thank you.'

Ivy brought in the tea and then excused herself to go back to the kitchen.

'She's looking a lot better,' Georgina commented.

'She is. She was astounded at me feeding Edward. She said her mother fed them all on diluted Carnation milk so she could go out to work. From what I can gather, her mother left Ivy to bring up her brothers whilst she went to work in service.'

'What happened to her family?' Dulcie asked.

'I think her dad was in the Merchant Navy and died at sea. Her mother couldn't cope so Ivy and her brothers were sent to a council home. She was in the girls' dorm and separated from her brothers. She couldn't stand it there and ran away. She went back to her mother's house but the woman had moved away. From then on, Ivy had to do what she could to look after herself.'

'I suppose that's when Billy's gang got hold of her. I'll find her some work soon. Is Knuckles at home with your mum?'

'Yes. They get on like a house on fire. She likes his company, which is a bit of a surprise.'

'There's no accounting for taste but I suppose it's nice for your mum to have someone to talk to. As for Jane, the hospital have said she's going to be in for some time yet. They said they're going to send me written reports every month but she's far from ready to accept visitors.'

'Poor Jane,' Dulcie said and tutted.

The door opened again and Lash stuck his head around. 'Have you told them?' he asked Georgina sheepishly.

'No, give us a chance,' she replied, then added, 'Me and Lash are getting married.'

'Yes, we know that,' Dulcie said.

'What I mean is, we're going to do it as soon as possible. But it'll just be the two of us. No fuss or nothing. It doesn't seem right to be celebrating or having a do, not without Ethel.'

'Can't you wait?' Dulcie asked.

'We want to be husband and wife, sooner rather than later.'

'Fair enough. It's your decision and if that's how you want to do it, then it's up to you. I would have liked to see you all dolled up but given the circumstances, I think you're doing it the right and respectful way.'

'Congratulations,' Molly piped up. 'But it's such a shame Ethel won't be here to see it,' she said and sniffed as she began to cry. 'I'm sorry, ignore me. I'm really happy for you.'

'Thanks, Molly. Like I said, no fuss. We'll get it done and nothing much will change, except Lash will be moving in here. We was hoping to get me dad sobered up first but that's going to be harder than we thought.'

'Don't get me started about your bloody father!' Dulcie said. 'He's following in Percy's footsteps and if he carries on like he is, I've a good bloody mind to put him in the ground too!'

'Gran!' Georgina snapped.

Dulcie realised she'd said too much and now Molly and Lash were looking at her. 'You don't want to know, it's a long story,' she said and hoped they wouldn't push her. She thought Molly was far too nice a girl to understand and worried Lash might not feel comfortable living in the house if he knew the truth. After all, what man would want to sleep in a bedroom that overlooked the rotten corpse of her husband buried in the backyard.

'I've got to go and see David Maynard now, so I'll see you all later.'

'Why do you need to see him?' Molly asked.

'To find out if I can keep Victor. Oh, and I've got a little explaining to do. I sort of used David's name in securing the deal for The Penthouse Club. I hadn't meant to but it saved anyone from getting hurt, though I think Johnny was disappointed that he didn't get to shoot anyone.'

'What are you on about? Why would Johnny be shooting anyone?' Dulcie asked. There was clearly more to the deal for the club than Georgina had revealed. It sounded like it'd been dangerous and Dulcie realised her granddaughter was getting more deeply involved with the criminal underworld.

'I'll tell you about it later, Gran, or Lash can fill you in but I've really got to get going. Molly, do you want me to drop you and Ivy home?'

'No, thanks. We'll be fine,' Molly answered.

Lash saw Georgina out and Dulcie waited to hear the front door close. She leaned forward in her chair and whispered to Molly, 'You're right, love. Get out of this business. Get out as soon as you can.'

*

Varvara was positioned on all fours on her bed. She didn't mind her client taking her this way as it meant she didn't have to look at his ugly face and could instead picture Georgina's.

'You filthy whore,' Elmer said with venom.

His voice broke into Varvara's thoughts and irritated her. Then she felt a searing pain in her scalp as he grabbed a handful of her hair and yanked her head back. It gave him better leverage and he thrust himself inside her deeper.

Elmer spoke again. 'This is all you're good for, you slag.'

She wanted to scream at him to let go of her hair but she was sure he was close to finishing and didn't want to delay it.

'Slut... you love it inside you...'

Huh, thought Varvara, if only he knew the truth. She hated it. She hated him. She hated men.

Elmer pulled out of her. 'Turn around,' he ordered.

Varvara was disappointed he hadn't yet climaxed and rolled over onto her back. Before she had a chance to do it herself, Elmer roughly spread her legs. She expected him to climb on top of her and turned her head. She knew how badly his breath smelt and didn't want to get another stomach-turning whiff of it. But then Elmer grabbed her calves and pushed her legs to where they were almost over her head. She felt him enter her again and closed her eyes.

'Look at me, you dirty whore,' Elmer growled.

Varvara opened her eyes to see the hatred in Elmer's glaring back at her. She didn't know why the man seemed to dislike her so much yet seemed to enjoy using her body.

'That's it… tell me how much you want it… TELL ME!'

'Oh, I love it, it feels so good,' Varvara lied.

'Yeah… yeah… do you like this?' Elmer said and before Varvara could protest, he managed to slip out of her and roughly shoved his penis up her bottom.

Varvara yelled in pain, which made Elmer move faster.

'This will cost you extra,' she spat.

'Shut up, bitch,' Elmer spat back and pounded her until thankfully, just a few grunts later, he was done.

Elmer climbed off the bed and after wiping himself clean, he dressed. Varvara stood up and pulled a gown around herself. Her behind felt sore but she'd had customers before who preferred it that way, though normally she'd lubricate first.

'You'll pay for that,' she said, 'double the flat rate.'

'Fuck off. You're a whore. A hole's a hole,' Elmer answered and threw some coins on the floor. 'Get down on your knees and pick them up,' he said.

Varvara wasn't one to look as if she was grovelling to any man but there was something menacing in his voice that unnerved her. With her eyes fixed firmly on him, she knelt down and gathered the coins. Elmer smirked.

'This isn't enough,' she said as she rose to her feet.

Elmer moved closer to her. 'It's all you're getting,' he sneered.

'Fine, but don't bother coming back here again. You can take your stinking breath and your pathetic dick and fuck the street whores instead. I'm too good for the likes of you.'

She was about to walk away but Elmer suddenly clasped his calloused hand around her throat and pushed her back until she was up against the wall.

Varvara found herself struggling to breathe and then felt Elmer's stale breath on her cheek.

'I'll screw you whenever I want to screw you because that's what you're paid to do,' he said quietly and snidely.

Much to Varvara's relief, Elmer released his grip and she sucked in lungful's of air, which made her cough. Then, when she thought he'd had his say and was about to leave, he swiped her face with the back of his hand. His knuckle caught the corner of her mouth and she tasted the distinct metallic flavour of blood.

'I'll be back on pay day.'

Varvara remained silent. She didn't want to provoke another physical attack but in her mind, she cursed him. As he walked away and out of the door, she felt her legs go to jelly and she collapsed to the floor. She lifted the back of her hand to her mouth. Yes, as she thought, it was bleeding. She muttered, 'You won't get away with this,' and imagined straddling his naked body and sticking a knife in his fat chest. Oh, the thought was so satisfying.

The sound of a car engine pulling up outside distracted her from her murderous thoughts. She pulled herself back to her feet and walked shakily to the window, pleased to see Georgina climbing out of the back.

Varvara ran to the mirror on her dressing table and winced as she dabbed at her split lip. She had to get down the stairs quickly if she was to get a glimpse of her boss. She secured her gown around her as she dashed to the top of the stairs just at the moment Georgina was entering the office.

'Miss Garrett,' she called and ran down the stairs.

Georgina stopped and looked up. The woman's beauty was undeniable and once again, Varvara yearned for more of her.

'Miss Garrett, I have a problem with a customer but what am I to do if Knuckles is not here?'

'I can see. Are you all right?'

'Yes, but he did not pay me enough and as is apparent, he did not like me to point it out.'

'Your neck… did he strangle you?'

'A bit.'

'Come through and sit down. I want to know who did this to you.'

Varvara sat opposite Georgina and again dabbed at her bleeding lip, pleased that she was receiving the attention she craved from her.

'Benjamin, would you mind getting Varvara a drink, please? Brandy would be good.'

Benjamin didn't hesitate in responding and when he handed Varvara the glass, she couldn't help but notice the sympathy in his eyes. She thanked him and wanted to detest him for being a man, but there was something about Benjamin that she warmed to.

'Who did this to you?' Georgina asked.

'Elmer. Elmer Newman. It is not too much bother but without Knuckles in the house, we are all very vulnerable.'

'Don't worry, Varvara, from tomorrow, Lash will be here to look after you and the women at Livingstone Road. In fact, you can call Dina in a minute and let her know.'

'But what about Knuckles?'

'That's not your concern but you won't be seeing him again.'

'I see. So will Lash be here to stop Elmer from visiting next week?'

'I can promise you that Elmer will never be visiting any of my businesses again.'

'Thank you, Miss Garrett,' Varvara said and though it stung, she smiled.

'You can take the rest of the evening off. I don't care if you send any booked customers away. They'll come back. You must rest now.'

'Thank you, Miss Garrett,' Varvara repeated. She desperately wished she could think of something else to say. Anything at all that would keep her sitting at Miss Garrett's desk, but her mind was blank.

'That will be all,' Georgina said, dismissively.

Varvara went through to the back room to call her sister, not that she thought Dina would be bothered one way or the other about what bit of muscle looked out for them. She supposed Lash was better than Knuckles, but she didn't like him. No matter what, he would never be good enough for Miss Garrett and now that he was the paid pimp, he'd proved Varvara's point exactly.

Benjamin looked across at Victor standing in the office doorway, then asked Georgina, 'Did it go well with, erm, with Mr Maynard?'

'After a fashion. He'd already heard about The Penthouse and wasn't too pleased with me. I managed to smooth it over,' Georgina answered with one of her charming smiles.

'Do you mind me asking how?'

'Don't worry, Benjamin, it didn't cost the business any money, though this lot did,' she answered and placed several boxes of bullets on her desk.

'How much?'

'A lot less than David first demanded. The cheeky sod tried to stitch me up. I suppose he thought he could try and take advantage of me being a woman and assumed I wouldn't know about guns and the like. I think I left him suitably impressed and I know from the books that I paid less than Billy used to.'

'Good, because after the transaction for The Penthouse has cleared, there won't be a bulk of spare cash left.'

'Yes, I'm aware of the finances, thank you. I've swapped Victor and the car for Knuckles.'

'Seriously?'

'And I've agreed to help David with a matter.'

'Can I erm, ask what matter?'

'You can, but I'm not telling you. Well, not yet. The less anyone knows, the better. Now, about The Penthouse. I'll need a manager.'

'Yes, and a new barman. Betsy is Aubrey's plaything so I would assume they'll be running off to Paris together.'

'Oh bloody hell. I was hoping Betsy would at least temporarily run the place. I think they're mad going to Europe with all the unrest there at the moment but it's their lookout.'

He wasn't surprised to hear Georgina talking about an impending war. She wasn't the only one who believed Hitler had ambitions of world domination, though the government thought otherwise. Benjamin preferred to believe Chamberlain.

'Do you think you can help me find suitable replacements for the club?' she asked.

Now was his chance. 'I… I think so,' Benjamin answered. He'd always quite fancied running the place himself and as the club was only open in the evenings, he didn't see why he couldn't do that and remain as Miss Garrett's accountant.

'What are you smiling at?' she asked him.

'I'll do it... manage The Penthouse.'

'You?' Georgina exclaimed, sounding rather incredulous.

'I know I must seem like a blabbering fool, but I'm a different person when I'm there. Please, Miss Garrett, allow me to be your manager. I won't let you down.'

'Fine, if you think you're up to it. How do you suppose a woman would be received as bar staff?'

'It would, erm, depend on the woman. You're not thinking of yourself?'

'Don't be daft. She's very young, but I was thinking of Ivy. She needs to earn her keep, but as I'd prefer to keep her away from men it seems to me The Penthouse would be the perfect place. However, you're the manager so the decision is yours.'

'I don't see a problem, though I'd like to meet her first.'

'Of course. I'll bring her in with me tomorrow. I warn you, she's a cheeky madam so make sure you're firm with her.'

They heard a light tap on the front door and Georgina instructed Victor to turn away any of Varvara's clients.

Benjamin began to pack away his pens but looked up from his desk when he heard PC Cunningham's voice. It wasn't Monday and unusual for the officer to make unscheduled visits. And it was even more unusual for him to be carrying his policeman's helmet under his arm.

'Good afternoon, Miss Garrett.'

Georgina looked irritated at the intrusion but invited the man to take a seat.

'No, thank you, I won't, if you don't mind.'

'Is there a problem?' Georgina asked.

Benjamin saw PC Cunningham's Adam's apple rise and fall as the man swallowed hard. Immediately, he sensed the officer had come with bad news and by the look on Georgina's face, she thought the same.

'It's Ethel Mipple, isn't it?' Georgina asked.

PC Cunningham nodded. 'I'm so sorry, Miss Garrett, but her body has been found.'

Georgina lowered her head. 'Tell me,' she said firmly as she looked at the top of her desk.

'A couple of young lads were playing by the new power station. They found her in a disused builder's store. She was bound and gagged but there was no obvious sign of any injury. We believe she starved to death, Miss Garrett.'

'And Jimmy Hewitt?'

'No sign of him.'

'I see. And you're certain it's her?'

'Yes, though we will need a formal identification. I'd suggest someone with a strong stomach. The body is somewhat decomposed and not something her mother should have to see... or smell.

'I'll do it. In fact, I think it's best to keep this to ourselves until I've confirmed it's Ethel.'

'Yes, of course, Miss Garrett.'

The conversation continued but Benjamin was no longer listening. He didn't know poor Ethel and had never met her, but nonetheless, it was very upsetting news and his heart went out to the girl's mother. But he'd known what he was getting involved in when he'd signed up to work for Miss Garrett. He wasn't so stupid to believe that there wouldn't be violence and sometimes even death. Yes, it was incredibly sad about Ethel but he wasn't going to allow it to mar his good fortune – Manager of The Penthouse Club, fancy that! His mind was already whirling with super ideas for the place and he couldn't wait to get stuck in. If he'd had the money, he may have bought it for himself but that would have left him open to police scrutiny, something Miss Garrett could avoid. He wasn't the owner but he was the manager with free rein. Whilst Miss Garrett was queen in her world up here, he intended to be king in his world below ground.

19

It was Sunday morning, three weeks since Ethel's funeral and Fanny hadn't stopped crying.

'I'll never forgive her, Molly, never. It should have been Georgina! It should have been her six feet under, not my Ethel.'

Molly was desperate to offer her mother some comfort. 'Would it help if we moved away? Started a new life – me, Edward, you, Charlotte and Oppo.'

'Eh? What are you on about, girl?'

Molly stirred a large spoonful of sugar into her mother's teacup then sat at the kitchen table with her. 'It was Oppo's idea. He doesn't like the thought of me and Edward being at risk. And well, since Ethel's death, I think he's right.'

'What, move out of Battersea?'

'Yes, Mum. Maybe out of London altogether. I don't know that I would have been brave enough to do it by meself but Oppo will look after us.'

'I'm not sure, love. I ain't never been outside of Battersea before, let alone out of London. It would mean taking Charlotte away from all her friends.'

'Yeah, well, that ain't a bad thing.'

'I suppose it could work. I wouldn't have to look at that cow's face anymore. Honestly, Molly, every time I see Georgina, I'm reminded of my lovely Ethel, dying scared and all alone. It breaks my heart,' Fanny said and started sobbing again.

Molly gave her mother a few moments, then told her, 'Let's do it then. There's nothing to keep us here.'

Fanny blew her nose. 'I reckon with what we earn from the business, we could live more than comfortably,' she said and sniffed.

'Actually, Oppo suggested that I talk to Georgina and ask her to buy me out. We can't expect to live on handouts from her if we're not pulling our weight. If she paid me a lump sum for my share of the company, it would be enough to set us up.'

'Sounds like Oppo has thought of everything.'

'He has, Mum. I would have quite happily just walked away but he talked me into selling my shares.'

'Good on Oppo. That lad's got a sensible head screwed onto his shoulders.'

'So, you'll do it then?'

'Yes, if it makes you happy. Like you say, there's nothing to keep me here. Knuckles is the only person who ever bothers to see me and even he don't call in often.'

'He's working for David Maynard now. Anyway, I'm glad you're on board with us moving. Will you keep an eye on Edward for me? I'm going to pop round to Georgina's and have a word.'

A while later, Lash opened Dulcie's front door and invited Molly in. The house smelt of freshly cooked bread and Molly knew that Dulcie had been baking again.

'Hello, Molly. Are you all alone?' Georgina asked.

'Yes, I've left Edward with Mum. I thought he might be a good distraction for her. She's hardly stopped crying since...'

'Poor Fanny,' Dulcie said and shook her head. 'Such a tragic waste. Do you know, I've never cried at a funeral, not even when I buried my first husband. But Ethel's, Gawd, I couldn't help meself.'

'Please, Gran, can you stop going on about it. I feel terrible about what happened and don't need constantly reminding,' Georgina snapped.

'It wasn't your fault, love. Tell her, Molly. She keeps blaming herself,' Dulcie said.

'Your gran's right, Georgina. It wasn't your fault. But I do agree, I'd rather not keep going over it. If we talk about Ethel, it should be about her life and the good memories.'

'If you'll excuse me, ladies, I'll leave you to it,' Lash said and gently closed the door behind him.

'We're getting married next week,' Georgina said and a big grin spread across her face.

Molly hoped that what she was about to say wouldn't wipe away Georgina's smile. It was nice to see a bit of happiness amongst all the sadness of late. 'Are you sure you still want to do it with just the two of you?'

'Yes, we've made up our minds. Anyway, what brings you here today? I hope Ivy is behaving herself?'

'Yes, Ivy's in her element now she's working at the club. I think she likes being the only female there and she doesn't have to worry about any blokes trying it on. The customers seem to like her cheeky personality too.'

'Are your mum and Charlotte going to be moving into that new house soon, the one she looked at before?' Dulcie asked, her voice faltering towards the end of the question.

'Actually, that's what I wanted to talk to you about,' Molly said nervously. 'It's just that after what happened, you know, to Ethel, I feel I have to keep Edward safe and the best way to do that is to move far from here. He's always going to be known as Billy Wilcox's son, and let's face it, Billy must have made plenty of enemies. I don't want anyone seeking their revenge through my son.'

'Blimey, Molly, moving away seems a bit drastic. I'll look after you and Edward, you know that.'

'I'm sorry, Georgina, my mind is set. It won't be easy, but I'm taking my mum and Charlotte too... and Oppo is coming.'

'Oppo... I hadn't realised it'd grown serious between you.'

'It has. But I've known him for most of my life so it's not like we're rushing into things. Anyway, Oppo thought you might like to buy me out of the business. That way, you'll have more of the profits.' There, she'd said it and now Molly bit nervously on her lip as she waited for Georgina's response.

'I can see you've given this a lot of thought and I know you, Molly. You wouldn't have taken this decision lightly. If it's what you want and it makes you happy, then I'll do whatever I can to support you. But, and it's a big but... you have to stay in touch and expect regular visits from me and my new husband.'

Molly sighed with relief. She loved Georgina dearly but knew her friend could sometimes fly off the handle. Thankfully, she'd taken the news well. 'I wouldn't have it any other way,' Molly said and wiped away a tear. 'Oh, dear Lord, this is really happening! It didn't feel real 'til now, but

I'm off to start a new life with Oppo. Who'd have thought it, eh? Me and Oppo!'

Mickey was sick to death of staring at the white walls of the hospital and equally fed up with the apples his brother kept bringing him. If he could have, he would have discharged himself and gone straight to Queenstown Road. But he still had a bullet in his spine. The doctors had told him it would be too dangerous to remove it and they'd also said he'd never walk again. Fuck 'em, he thought, fuck 'em all. He would walk again and when he could, he'd march out of this hospital and claim back the Wilcox business.

The ward slowly began to fill up with visitors and through the flurry of activity, Mickey spotted PC Cunningham walking towards his bed. The man was out of uniform and greeted him with a friendly smile.

'You're looking a lot better, Mickey. How are you, mate?'

'Not bad, thanks, Frank. Bored shitless.'

Frank Cunningham looked over his shoulder as he pulled out a seat next to the bed. 'She's a bit of all right, that nurse. I wouldn't mind her giving me a bed bath.'

'Yeah, she ain't bad but I'm not sure if it's all working down there,' Mickey said and indicated to his groin area.

'Don't worry, mate. Once you're up and about, you'll be back to your old self.'

Mickey forced a smile. He and PC Frank Cunningham were cousins, their fathers brothers. They'd played together as kids, and shared most family Christmases together. When Mickey had taken over the Wilcox business from Billy, his policemen cousin had willingly remained on the payroll.

He'd offered his services as more of a partnership and had big ideas for expansion with Mickey. 'So, any updates?' Mickey asked.

'She keeps her cards close to her chest but Knuckles is now working for David Maynard.'

'You're fucking kidding me?'

'No, straight up. She's got Victor and Maynard's car in exchange for Knuckles. There's got to be more to it. There's no way that was a fair swap and Maynard isn't anyone's fool.'

'Do you reckon she's screwing him?' Mickey asked. If she was, it would make his life a lot more difficult. It was one thing to go up against Georgina Garrett but he didn't have the resources to destroy her and Maynard. At least, not yet.

'Who knows? She's got her gypsy bloke and he don't look the sort to allow her to sleep with other men.'

'Well, she must be doing him some sort of favour and I'm guessing it's a big one,' Mickey replied.

'I've heard Johnny Dymond is turning good profits at the Clapham house and that poofter club is doing well. When you get out of here, I reckon she's set up some nice little earners for you to take on.'

'Fucking club for bent blokes. I'll be changing that once I get my hands on it. I'll have them Russian whores dancing down there. That'll keep the pervs away.'

A man visiting a patient in the next bed turned around and politely requested, 'Mind your language, ladies present.'

'Piss off,' Mickey growled and pulled his lips back to bare his teeth at the man.

The well-dressed gentleman recoiled and quickly spun back the other way.

'Fucking cheek of it,' Mickey said and they both laughed.

'Your mum sends her love. She said she'll be up to see you in the week and your brother is coming next weekend.'

'Are they all right?'

'Yes, mate, don't worry about them. I'm checking on them regularly and me and Claire'll bung 'em a few bob.'

'Thanks, Frank. You and your missus are good sorts.'

'We're family, Mickey, blood bonds.'

'How the fuck you ever got into the police force is beyond me. Our family have never been on the right side of the law. They must have slipped up when they did their checks on you.'

'I know. My old man's been in and out of jail more times than a priest's dick has been in and out of a choirboy,' Frank said and chuckled.

'Is he staying out of trouble now?'

'Yeah, but only 'cos the old codger has got dodgy lungs and can't leg it anymore.'

'Ah, I've always had a soft spot for Uncle Ron. Tell him I said hello when you see him next.'

'Yeah, will do, Mickey. Have they said when you'll be getting out?'

'Nah, it'll be a while yet and they said I'll have to be wheeled out in one of them chair things. Sod that, I'll be walking, Frank. A poxy bullet lodged in my spine ain't gonna stop me. And when I walk out of here, I'm gonna fucking kill that Garrett bird. You'll see. It's her fault I'm in this mess and I'm gonna make sure she's sorry for crossing me.'

20

Varvara had been mulling over her thoughts all weekend. The incident with Elmer Newman was nothing new to her. In fact, over the years, she'd experienced a lot worse at the hands of depraved men. But since meeting Miss Garrett, Varvara had been inspired by the woman's strength and her confidence had grown. She no longer wanted to tolerate abuse handed out by men. And she most definitely didn't want to have sex with one again. She had a newfound passion, feelings that overwhelmed her yet felt exhilarating and warm. It was love, something she'd only heard of but had never known before meeting Georgina. But every time a man violated her body, it marred her love and enough was enough. She hoped she wasn't cutting off her nose to spite her face, and if things didn't go how she hoped, she'd have to leave, taking Dina with her.

Varvara waited patiently on Monday morning for Miss Garrett's associates to leave and then the policeman came and went. As Victor closed the front door behind the visitors, Varvara seized the opportunity and told him, 'I'd like to speak to Miss Garrett.'

Victor showed her through and before she sat at the desk, she glared at Lash.

'Yes, Varvara, what do you want?' Georgina asked.

'I am a free woman, this is correct?' Varvara replied.

'Yes, you are. You can come and go as you please.'

'And if I so choose, I can leave without any consequences to my health?'

'Yes, if that's what you want.'

'Fine. In that case, it is with regret that I have to inform you of my departure.'

'You're leaving? But I thought you were happy working for me?'

'I am, Miss Garrett, but I no longer want to be a prostitute. It is all I have done since I was a child. I do not like it but I do like working for you.'

'I see. What will you do, Varvara?'

'I do not know yet, Miss Garrett, but I will not sleep with men.'

'When are you planning on leaving us?'

'Tomorrow.'

'That's a bit quick. It's a shame. You're an asset to the business and very loyal. I'll be sorry to let you go.'

'Yes, it is sorry for me too. I would like it if you would offer me an alternative job, one in which I am not a whore. You know I am strong and am not afraid of men. I could help Victor, yes?'

It was a bold move for Varvara to have spoken so bluntly and she covertly crossed her fingers. Please, she thought, please agree. She wished now that she hadn't been so quick to say she was leaving. If Miss Garrett didn't offer her an alternative, she may not ever see the woman again and sudden panic surged through her veins.

Georgina sat back in her chair and chewed on the end of her pen. Varvara thought this was a good sign as Miss Garrett was obviously considering her proposition.

'I'm not sure, Varvara. As much as I like you, this is a business I'm running and if I'm to keep you on, I need you to be financially viable.'

'I would die for you, Miss Garrett, my life for yours,' she said with conviction. 'How much is that worth to you?'

'That's a very persuasive argument. I suppose I can probably find work for you. In fact, I'll be visiting a night club in the West End tonight. You will come with me and we will test your worth. It's business, Varvara, not pleasure and you will do exactly as I tell you. I'll have to find another woman to take your place here and you'll need accommodation elsewhere. You can take the attic room at the house in Clapham.'

'But I'd rather live here.'

'Where? I'll need your room and whoever is in it to earn money.'

'It is a very big room. Perhaps it could be divided? I want to be here, Miss Garrett. I can protect you from here.'

Georgina sighed. 'Fine, I suppose that could work. Lash will arrange that. Be ready at eight tonight. Oh, and you'll be needing this but only use it if absolutely necessary. Lash will show you how.' Georgina unlocked a drawer in her desk and handed Varvara a pistol. 'It belonged to Knuckles,' she said.

'Thank you, Miss Garrett. I promise you, I'll work hard,' Varvara said as she pushed her seat back.

She walked out of the office elated and could hardly believe what had just transpired. She was finally working with Miss Garrett. She'd be spending more time with her, and travelling with her too. She'd risked losing everything, but luckily, taking a chance had paid off and now her dream had come true.

'Where are you going tonight?' Lash asked Georgina once Varvara had closed the door.

'I have some business to sort out at Charlie Chops' club. In the meantime, I need you to find Elmer Newman, the bloke who roughed up Varvara.' She realised she probably should have mentioned it sooner but couldn't be doing with the onslaught of questions from Lash.

'But I've already seen to him,' Lash protested.

'I know, but I want you to see to him again. If not Elmer, someone else who's just as horrible.'

'Why do you want this done? Am I missing something here, Georgina?'

'No. I just want you to make sure whoever you find is unconscious and lying in the middle of the street on Battersea Bridge. Johnny will take you in his car, he knows what to do. I've instructed him to do a drive-by and push the body out, that way, no-one will see you.'

'Why? What's this all about, Georgina, and why are you going to Charlie Chops' club when I heard him specifically ask you to stay away?'

'I can't tell you yet, Lash, but I will. Please, just trust me and do as I ask.'

'As always, you'll expect to have your own way,' Lash muttered as he stomped across the office and left, slamming the door behind him.

'Victor, go after him. Make sure he's going to do what I've asked. Go, quick!'

Georgina glanced over at Benjamin who was peering at her over the top of his spectacles.

'What?' she snapped. 'Out with it. You're obviously thinking something.'

'It's erm, none of my business, Miss Garrett.'

'Just say it!'

'You're, erm, undermining Lash. I think he's finding it difficult, yet it's plain to see he adores you.'

'Yes, thank you, Benjamin. Tell me something I don't know!'

'If you don't mind me saying, perhaps you could try being a bit nicer to him? As an outside observer, I do think you're a little short of patience with him.'

Georgina sucked in a deep breath. She didn't like to admit it but Benjamin was correct. Lash's masculinity was what had first attracted her to him but now she found him irritating. He made it clear that he didn't like the way she did things. He thought he should be in charge, but it was purely based on the fact that he was a man – that it was his so-called right. She loved him, more than she cared to admit, yet was fully aware that her role in the Wilcox business was a bone of contention between them. Very soon there'd be another one – surnames. Lash would expect her to take on his name but he was going to be in for a shock.

Georgina Garrett, married or not, would always be Georgina Garrett.

Later that evening, Varvara sat next to Georgina as Victor drove them to Charlie Chops' club. Georgina had been impressed with how Varvara had dressed and thought she looked quite the part. Though her trouser suit was very masculine, it was smart and gave her an air of sophistication. It crossed her mind that she would make a very worthy Maid of Battersea. Thankfully, Lash had calmed down and had agreed to go along with her plans, though he'd made it clear that he didn't like being kept in the dark.

'You can drop us at the door, Victor.'

'But you'll need...'

'No, thank you, Victor. Pick me up at midnight. I'll see you later,' she said sternly.

Georgina ignored Victor's confused expression and walked up to the club entrance with Varvara at her side. Several people, mostly couples, were queuing at the entrance, but Georgina by-passed them and approached the doorman.

'Mr Brennan is expecting me,' she told him.

He stepped to one side and allowed her through where another man, the size of a mountain, took her to one side. 'Miss Garrett, I presume?'

'Yes.'

'Are you carrying?'

'Of course.'

'May I ask you to leave your gun in our secure locker?'

'No, you may not.'

He didn't argue with her. 'This way,' he said and led them along a corridor plastered with framed photographs of famous actors and singers, all of them personally autographed to Charlie.

'Grotesque,' Georgina whispered to Varvara. 'It's all for show.'

The upbeat music from the orchestra played out along the corridor and got louder as they approached the main club area. Double doors were opened wide and Georgina looked in, momentarily dazzled by the lights from the stage area. The man handed Georgina over to another, much smaller man dressed as a waiter.

'Miss Garrett, welcome. Mr Brennan has reserved a special table for you. He'll be joining you shortly. Can I get you a drink? Champagne or one of our specialty cocktails?'

'Champagne,' Georgina answered and as she took her seat she pulled off her long gloves to place on the table in front of her. Leaning forward she whispered to Varvara, 'Don't drink too much booze. You have work to do shortly.'

The waiter returned with the bottle in an ice bucket. 'Our finest, compliments of Mr Brennan.'

As the champagne was poured, Georgina looked around the club impressed with what she saw. This looked like the place where the rich and dandy liked to be seen.

'Georgina, I'm so glad you've graced us with your presence.'

'Charlie, hello,' she answered and extended her hand to shake his but he took hold and gently kissed above her knuckles.

'This isn't what you were expecting, is it?'

'No, Charlie, far from it.'

'I bet you thought it'd be a dingy little back-street place with strippers and dirty old men, didn't you?'

'I'm ashamed to say that's exactly what I was expecting.'

'I've got a few clubs like that, but this one is for my more refined customers. It's classy, ain't it?'

'Yes, though you manage to lower the tone,' Georgina said and laughed.

'I like a woman with a sense of humour. And who's this beauty you've brought with you?' Charlie asked as he eyed Varvara.

'Eyes off, she stays with me.'

'Fair enough. How's your champagne?'

'It's acceptable,' Georgina answered, knowing that Charlie now used the same supplier as The Penthouse Club.

'Excuse me, Mr Brennan, there's a matter that requires your attention,' the waiter interrupted awkwardly.

'I'm sorry, ladies, duty calls.'

'Not at all, Charlie. We're quite happy listening to the band. Take as long as you need.'

Once Charlie was out of earshot, Georgina snuck a large pouch under the table to Varvara. 'Quickly, put this in your bag. Now, I want you to go the toilets and wipe your lipstick off. Come back looking ill. You're going home. I'll get Charlie's man to take you. That bag I've just given you – make sure you hide it in the car but somewhere where it can be easily found. It's very important – do you think you can do that?'

'Yes, but I'm not a good actress.'

'Your acting is fine when you pretend to be enjoying sex with the customers. Varvara, can you manage this job or not?'

'Yes… pretend to be sick and sneak this bag into the car somewhere to be found.'

'Don't let me down. Go on, off you go.'

Varvara went to the ladies' toilets whilst Georgina sat alone and slowly sipped her drink. She could feel her heart hammering in time to the music and hoped she didn't look as nervous as she felt.

Charlie appeared again and sat down. 'Sorry about that. Where's your friend?'

'I don't think she's feeling very well. She's popped to the ladies'.'

'Are you enjoying yourself, Georgina?'

'Yes, Charlie, it's fabulous. I hope I don't have to cut the night short if my friend is poorly.'

Varvara returned and having cleaned her face of lipstick and rouge, with her blonde hair, she now looked pale, and swayed as Charlie jumped up and pulled out a seat for her.

'Oh, Varvara, you look awful. How are you feeling?' Georgina asked, feigning concern.

'Dreadful.'

'You should be in bed at home but how silly of me to have given Victor the evening off.'

'You're not with your driver?' Charlie asked, sounding surprised.

'No, I knew I'd be fine here with you to look after me,' she answered with a little flutter of her long dark lashes, knowing that playing to his ego would charm him. 'Would you be a sweetie, Charlie, and send Varvara home in your car? I don't think she's well enough to wait for a taxi cab. That way, I can stay and have some fun.'

'Yes, of course. She'll find my motor far more comfortable than one of them cabs. Take her out the back door. I'll get my driver.'

Georgina held an arm under Varvara's and helped her through the club. 'When you get to Battersea Bridge, there'll be a police roadblock. Get out of the car and don't let *anyone* get a picture of your face. The police won't ask you any questions so just walk away. Got it?'

'Yes,' Varvara answered.

Georgina was pleased that Varvara didn't bombard her with questions. The fewer who knew about what was going on, the better.

Once in the fresh air, Charlie held the back door of his car open for Varvara.

'I think she'll be better in the front,' Georgina told him.

Varvara climbed in and once again, Georgina was impressed with the woman's composure. If Varvara was feeling nervous, it didn't show.

'I'm glad you're staying,' Charlie told Georgina as the car sped off. 'It's nice to have the company of a woman who can hold a decent conversation, for a change.'

'I'm glad too,' Georgina lied, and hooked her arm through his to walk back into the club.

Georgina took her seat but had a job to stop her legs from jigging with nerves. She twisted her mother's wedding ring and plastered on a big smile though she was sure Charlie could see through her act and that her smile didn't reach her eyes.

She tried to sneak a glance at the watch on Charlie's wrist. Any minute now, it'll be happening any minute now, she thought, hoping everything would go according to her meticulous plan. If it didn't, there was a strong possibility that Varvara may already be dead and Charlie would drag her outside and put a gun to her head.

She wouldn't know until midnight when Victor returned to take her home – if she lived that long.

21

Two weeks later, Georgina sat in David Maynard's office and accepted a celebratory glass of champagne.

'We're all square now. You stuck to your side of the bargain so Victor and my car are officially yours,' David said and raised his glass. 'Well done, Georgina. The world will be a better place without the likes of Charlie Chops walking it.'

'You can be honest with me, David. You didn't believe I could pull it off, did you?' Georgina asked.

'I had my doubts but hoped you could. I should have had more faith in you. You've proved yourself time and again. Let me get it straight though. Firstly you arranged for a bloke to be battered and left on Battersea Bridge. You then paid off your copper to find him and put up a roadblock. Next you arranged for your Russian woman to be driven home in Charlie's car, giving her the opportunity to stash the diamonds, and of course your copper had been tipped to know exactly what car to stop and search. It was a stroke of bloody genius to have a news reporter there. He got a photo of the diamonds in the pouch and a good shot of Charlie's driver. Once the story ran on the front page, the

Portland Pounders saw it, assumed Charlie Chops had done them over so they gunned him down and his doormen with him. No-one to talk. No-one can put you at the scene. But what about his driver, the one who got nicked on the night?'

'That's where I got *really* lucky. I did a bit of digging and found out he's been seen in The Penthouse Club, but long before I owned it. With that bit of knowledge, Benjamin dropped by his police cell to cut him a deal. Of course as soon as the man saw Benjamin, he recognised him. His silence about Varvara and me was agreed in return for us keeping quiet about him liking men. Last I heard, he's buggered off to Bristol.'

'So now everyone's happy.'

'Yes, and by the way, David, those diamonds you stole from the Pounders' heist. Only the large ones were real. The rest of them were paste.'

'How do you know that?'

'Because I was brought up by a thief whose good friend has a jewellery shop and is a fence. You've got the real ones, haven't you?'

'Of course I have. I wasn't going to go to the bother of turning over the Pounders for no reward. Bloody hell, Georgina, nothing gets past you.'

'Why have Charlie set up for it?' Georgina asked.

'He's a wanker. Sorry to be so blunt but I can't think of any other word to describe him. He's stitched me up one too many times but always worms his way out of trouble.'

'I see. You don't know about him then? His thing for little boys?'

'Charlie Chops? No way, he reckons he's a right ladies' man.'

'It was all front, David. I thought it was a bit strange that he wanted to do business with that Dickie, the American child molester who wanted to buy my club. So I looked into it and found out they both have the same taste in boys. As it turns out, I agree with you – the world *is* a much better place without Charlie Chops.'

'Well, well, well, Dickie and Charlie Chops, the filthy gits. It seems birds of a feather really do flock together.'

'It seems they do.'

'You're good at what you do, Georgina, especially as you've only been at the top for a short while. I suppose you'd like to know why I turned over the Portland Pounders?'

Georgina sipped her champagne and inwardly smiled at the familiar taste. The same as the brand served in both her and Charlie's club. 'I was wondering,' she answered.

'It's been a long time coming. That heist, the diamonds. It was mine in the first place but I needed a good safe cracker, one who understood combination locks and didn't want to just blow the door open. I knew the Pounders had a bloke so approached them about it. Next thing I know, they swooped in and did the job behind my back. All I did was take from them what should have been mine in the first place.'

'You should have asked me.'

'You can crack safes?'

'No, silly, but I know a man who can.'

'Why doesn't that surprise me?' David said with a little chuckle to himself. 'Anyway, I hear congratulations are in order?'

'Are they?'

'Yes. You're getting married, aren't you?'

'Oh, I see. Yes, next week. Just a small affair. I don't want a fuss, not so soon after Ethel Mipple.'

'Well, he's a very lucky man, Georgina, and brave. I can't say I'm not a little bit jealous. I'd like to meet him, the man who charmed the hardest and smartest woman I've ever met. I've heard he's a fighter?'

'Yes, that's right,' she said, 'but I'm not the only one who's been doing some digging lately. You seem to know quite a bit about my personal life.'

'Just protecting my interests. Good job I did some checking up or I might have made myself look like a fool.'

'How's that?' Georgina asked.

'I was set on asking you to dinner and I don't like to be turned down. I won't be asking now. Anyway, tell me, how's Victor getting on?'

'Great, though I must say I was surprised when he said he wanted to stay on with me.'

'I wasn't. I think he needed a fresh start. I don't suppose he's told you about his wife and kids?'

'No, he never says much about anything.'

'Tragic, it was, absolutely bloody tragic.'

'What happened?' Georgina asked, more curious than ever now.

'I've known Victor since we were kids. We lived on the same street and were always good mates. But we chose different paths in life. I followed in my father's footsteps, whereas Victor set up a little company of his own. All legit. He had a mechanical spares shop. It was only small, and he used to ride about on his bicycle dropping parts off. He did all right. It would never make him a fortune but he earned enough to support Doris and their two lads. Then one day,

Doris went to see her sister. She was at the train station with their youngest in her arms and the other lad running on ahead. No-one really knows how it happened but the lad was at the end of the platform and fell in front of a train. Doris went to pull him back but she fell too. All three of them were killed.'

'Oh no, that's terrible.'

'Their bodies were caught under the wheels for quite a while,' David continued, 'long enough for Victor to have heard about the accident. They say he tried to push the train off them, and was eventually dragged away, screaming for them. No man should ever have to see his family killed like that.'

The atmosphere suddenly became very solemn and Georgina fought to hold back tears. She remembered hearing about the tragedy, years earlier, but hadn't realised Victor had been involved. 'The poor man, I had no idea,' she managed to say.

'He hardly ever talks about it. After the funerals, he went downhill. It was like he gave up on life. I was worried that he'd try to top himself, so I started dragging him around with me. It was the only way I could keep an eye on him. Anyway, he got through it but he's never been the same. I reckon a new start with you will do him good.'

'I hope so, but I doubt he'll ever get over losing his family. Thanks for telling me, David. It was good of you to take him under your wing.'

'I'd do the same for anyone I care about, just as I know you would.'

Georgina looked at David over the top of her champagne glass but quickly pulled her eyes away from his. She felt a pang of guilt at finding the man exciting and attractive. It was a betrayal to Lash and he would be sickened if he knew what had gone through her mind. It had only been a fleeting moment but there had been a definite spark. David had felt it too, she was sure. But she'd never act on any feelings she had towards him. She loved Lash too deeply and this was business. No matter what, for Lash's protection, she had to keep her desire for David to herself – if the head of South East London's biggest crime syndicate ever discovered there might be a chance for him, he could easily get Lash out of the way and that thought terrified her.

Mickey sat upright in his hospital bed and stared at his toes, willing them to move. His hands gripped the bed linen, turning his knuckles as white as the sheets. But no amount of willpower would encourage even the smallest amount of movement and his heart sank.

'Still nothing?' PC Frank Cunningham asked as he approached the bed.

'Nah, fuck all. All right, mate, how are you?'

'I'm fine, Mick. But you look pissed off?'

'I am. They've been talking about me being transferred to an institution. They're saying they can't do any more for me here, but I've heard about them places. I ain't going, Frank. I'd rather cut me fucking wrists.'

'It's all right, Mickey, you won't be going anywhere except home. You've got family and we'll look after you.'

'I don't want to be a burden, Frank. It would be too much for me mum. I can't expect her to do everything for me.'

'Stop worrying about that for now. I told you, we'll sort it. In the meantime, I've got some news that might cheer you up.'

'What? Is Georgina Garrett dead?' Mickey asked hopefully.

'No, but Charlie Chops is.'

'You're kidding? Who knocked him off?'

'The Portland Pounders but Garrett set it up. She got me involved and paid me well, so I've given my bonus to your mum.'

'Thanks, Frank, I really appreciate that. Tell me, how the fuck did she get the Pounders to take out Charlie Chops?'

'I don't know the ins and outs, but it looks like Charlie pinched a load of diamonds from them and Garrett arranged for them to be found. Now that he's dead, once we get you out of here, it leaves more opportunity for you.'

'Or Maynard. He'll be in there first, like a fucking vulture, picking out the bits he wants for himself.'

'He seems to be keeping his head down. Him and Garrett are right cosied up together. He's probably involved in the set-up somewhere along the line – that's why he's laying low now.'

'Probably. Thanks, Frank. You're right, that has cheered me up. Charlie Chops pushing up daisies… at least that's one face out of the way. Do me a favour. Do a bit more digging, see what else you can find out. If the Pounders got rid of Charlie and Maynard is involved, with the right information perhaps we can orchestrate them killing off Maynard too.'

'I don't know, Mickey. If I start asking around too much, I might cause suspicion, especially as Maynard's business ain't on my beat. I think you should concentrate on one thing at a time. Get rid of Georgina Garrett first. She's your biggest rival.'

Mickey rested his head back on his pillow and closed his eyes. Hatred filled his heart as he pictured George Garrett, the woman who'd looked and acted like a bloke. It was bad enough she'd humiliated him years ago when she'd punched him to the ground, but they'd been younger then. Now, as an adult, she'd taken it further but had gone too far. He couldn't work out how she'd done it, but he held her responsible for the bullet in his spine. Because of her, Mickey knew he had to somehow accept that he would never walk again and he inwardly seethed.

One day soon he'd see that bloody Georgina Garrett got her comeuppance.

22

It was the morning of Georgina's wedding and she was feeling surprisingly calm. She'd given specific instructions for no fuss but that hadn't stopped Dulcie from baking a celebratory cake, or Molly from turning up with rice to throw.

Georgina checked her reflection in her bedroom mirror, happy with what she saw. Mary next door had arranged for her daughter, Aileen, to call in to do Georgina's hair and make-up. The last time Aileen had given her a makeover, it had transformed her from George to Georgina and that transformation had led to her meeting Lash.

Her stomach flipped at the thought of him. In less than two hours' time, she'd be his wife. But was she doing the right thing? Was it a mistake to marry Lash? Or were her doubts just pre-wedding nerves?

Georgina drew in a deep breath and sat on the edge of her bed. If she wanted to change her mind, it wasn't too late. But she loved him. He drove her crazy and at times she felt like she could throttle him, but she knew she wanted to spend the rest of her life with him.

A light tap on the door distracted her and she called, 'Come in.'

The door opened and her father walked in, bleary-eyed but not yet paralytic drunk. His dishevelled clothes bore days-old stains and with his un-brushed hair, and a long scar running across his face, he looked a frightful sight.

'You look beautiful, my girl,' he said and his eyes began to well up when he added, 'just like your mother on the day I married her.'

'Thanks, Dad,' Georgina said. It was nice that he'd remained sober this morning, though she could smell the stale beer on his breath from the previous night.

'She would have been very proud of you. You're a beautiful young woman and clever too, just like she was.'

Georgina looked at her mother's wedding ring. She had no memory of the woman, nor any idea of what she looked like. 'I wish I'd known my mum. And I wish you wouldn't drink like you do, Dad.'

Jack took her hand. 'I know, sweetheart. Your mother always said I couldn't handle me booze. I'm sorry. I've let you down, haven't I?'

'Yes, Dad, you have. I've needed you but you've had your head stuck in a bottle. Please, come back to me. I miss you, Dad,' Georgina answered.

'Answer me one thing. If I was sober and here for you, would you still be marrying Lash?'

Georgina had asked herself the same question many times. 'Yes, I love him, Dad. But I'd be a lot happier if I knew you were here to look after Gran.'

'I've been a mess since that time when I saw you beaten up, lying there, battered and broken. I thought I was gonna lose you, like I lost your mother. It's no excuse, I know. I've got to pull me socks up, and I promise you, my girl, I will.'

'Really? Are you really going to stop drinking? Because if you don't, Lash is going to lock you up until your blood is clean. Please, Dad, don't make us do that to you.'

'Oh, Georgina, what an 'orrible situation I've put you in! I'm gonna try my best – no more booze from now on, but if I slip up you make sure that new husband of yours does whatever he has to do, and with my blessing.'

'I'll give you a chance to get yourself straight. If not, I'll hand you over to Lash.'

'Fair enough. It sounds like your man is downstairs and no doubt he'll be wanting to see you. Have a special day, sweetheart. I hope your Lash realises what a very lucky man he is.'

'I'm sure he does. Thanks, Dad.'

The door closed behind him and moments later, Lash walked in. Georgina had never seen him looking so smart and as his dark eyes roamed over her, she could feel her heart pounding faster.

'I thank the fate that brought to me the most beautiful woman on Earth. I love you, Georgina... Mrs Hearn.'

'Ah, about that,' Georgina said uncomfortably. 'I haven't had a chance to speak to you about it yet, but the last name thing...'

'What about it?' Lash asked.

'I'll take your name on paper, but I still want to be known as Georgina Garrett. It's purely for business purposes, you understand, don't you, Lash?'

She saw his jaw clench and his eyes turned from loving to cold.

'No, Georgina, I don't understand. Are you ashamed to have me as your husband?'

'Don't be daft, of course I'm not!'

'Are you ashamed to be married to a gypsy?'

'No, not at all.'

'So tell me what's so bad about using the name you will take when we are married. MY NAME!'

'Please, Lash, don't be angry. It's just that I've spent a while building the Garrett name and it means something. I realise the business isn't important to you, but it is to me. I'd love to have your support instead of you fighting me on this.'

'Are you mad, woman? How can you expect anything else but anger from me? I'm a man, a proud man and you make me feel like shit,' Lash seethed through gritted teeth.

'It's only a name! I'll still be your wife.'

'I'm not so sure about that,' Lash said and turned his back.

Georgina thought he was going to walk out and grabbed his arm and asked, 'Do you still want to marry me?'

Lash spun back round. 'Yes,' he hissed, 'but I don't know why! What do you think my family will say when they hear of this?'

'They don't have to know.'

'I won't lie to them,' Lash ground out.

'Well just don't mention it then.'

'Have you any idea how this makes me feel?'

'Well, I knew you wouldn't be happy.'

'Yet you continued to go along with what you want. You're selfish, Georgina, selfish and cruel.'

'You're the selfish one for making such a song and dance about a name!'

'A song and dance... Women *always* take their man's family name. But, no, not you. You have to be different.

Hearn isn't good enough for you. It doesn't match up to the mighty Georgina GARRETT! You treat *me* like the wife and I'm sick of it. I'm a man, Georgina, your man, and from now on, you'll do as I tell you to!'

'No, I won't. No man tells me what to do,' Georgina spat and spun around.

She felt Lash yank her back and thought he was going to passionately kiss her. After all, they frequently argued but it always finished in a breathless clinch. But instead, she felt a sharp sting across her cheek and saw a black look in Lash's eyes. He'd slapped her with the back of his hand and as the reality of what he'd done began to sink in, Georgina felt her own anger rising. She reacted instinctively and punched a powerful blow to his eye socket.

'Don't you ever hit me again,' she blazed at him. She paused then, waiting to gauge his reaction. If he was going to retaliate she was ready to dodge his fists.

Instead, his hand touched where she'd whacked him. Blood oozed from his brow bone and the corner of his eye was now swollen and blue. With a shake of his head and a grin he said, 'You're a hard bitch, but you're *my* hard bitch. I'm sorry. I've never raised my hand to a woman before and I never will again. You infuriate me, but in one hour you're going to be my wife. Shall we go, Mrs Georgina Garrett?'

'Miss,' she answered with a wry smile. 'Miss Georgina Garrett.'

Dulcie rolled her eyes to Molly as they heard the quarrelling couple upstairs.

'They're always at it,' she whispered. 'Then the next minute, they're back in love. It's a fiery relationship, that one. At least their marriage won't be boring.'

'Georgina needs a man who'll stand up to her,' Molly answered.

'Yes, and Lash does challenge her, though she always ends up getting her own way.'

They heard the bedroom door open and footsteps coming down the stairs. 'Here they come,' Dulcie said, excited to see her granddaughter. When Georgina walked into the room, Dulcie gasped, 'Oh, love, you look beautiful.'

Georgina's pale gold satin dress, cinched at the waist, hugged her hips and flared out at the bottom, stopping inches above her ankles. She'd told Dulcie that she'd instructed Mary not to add padding to the shoulders, stating that she was already broad enough. It had a high neck with lace detail and she had a matching flat hat worn to the side. Dulcie didn't think her outfit of choice was very traditional, but then her granddaughter was always breaking the rules when it came to tradition.

'I'm so happy for you,' Molly sniffed and dabbed at her watery eyes. 'You look a picture.'

Dulcie noticed Georgina's cheek was red and first thought the girl was blushing, but then realised the redness was only on the one side of her face. Lash walked in behind Georgina and Dulcie immediately saw his bruised and swollen eye. They'd clearly been fighting but by the looks of it, Georgina had been the victor. No alarm bells went off in Dulcie's head. She didn't feel the need to take her granddaughter to one side and advise her to walk away from Lash. She knew

Georgina could look after herself and if Lash was brave or stupid enough to hit her, then he should expect to get a bashing in return.

Varvara had been waiting outside but now walked into the room. Dulcie eyed the woman up and down and bit her tongue. For some reason, Varvara had cut her long blonde hair short and wore it greased back, like a man. She dressed in a grey suit – loose, men's trousers with matching jacket and white shirt. Yet she didn't appear masculine, not like when Georgina had dressed as a man. Varvara was as tall as Georgina, but her cheekbones were higher and more prominent. With her long, slender neck, she looked extremely elegant and strangely the men's attire somehow suited her.

'It is time,' Varvara said in her deep Russian husk.

'Wish me luck,' Georgina said to Dulcie.

'You don't need luck, you've got yourself a good man,' Dulcie answered and smiled warmly at Lash.

'But I think I may need it.' Lash laughed.

'Wait, let me go first,' Molly said and dashed from the room.

Dulcie knew the girl wanted to throw rice over the happy couple, though it was tradition to do it after the wedding, not before. But with strict instructions from Georgina that no fuss was to be made, nobody had been invited to the registry office.

Dulcie had been disappointed at first but she could understand Georgina's decision. After all, they'd only recently buried poor Ethel. It had broken Dulcie's heart to see that young and precious woman-child put in the ground.

It was unfair. Ethel had never hurt a soul and Dulcie had once again been reminded that the good die young. Just like her first husband, Georgina's grandfather. He'd have been chuffed to have seen Georgina looking such a picture today and would have been out in the street organising a knees-up no matter what. Nothing had kept that man from making sure everyone around him laughed until their bellies ached. She still missed him. Unlike Percy, her second husband, rotting in the barrel next to the coal bunker.

'They've gone, but there was a chap outside who gave her these,' Molly said, breaking into Dulcie's thoughts. 'Didn't she look stunning, Dul?'

Dulcie looked up to see Molly holding a large bouquet of flowers. 'Yes, she did. What have you got there?'

'There's a card. It says, *Congratulations Georgina, David* and there's a kiss.'

'Um, Lash wants to watch out for that David Maynard bloke. There's trouble brewing, I can feel it in my water.'

'What makes you think that?'

'He ain't mentioned Lash in his best wishes and let's face it, you couldn't blame the man for falling for Georgina.'

'No, if I was a bloke, I reckon I'd want to marry her too. She's very special.'

'Gifted, that's what I think. She's always got her face in the newspapers and the stuff she comes out with, it goes right over my head. The way she talks, I reckon she'd do a better job of running the country than them swines in parliament.'

'You ain't wrong there, Dul. I don't know what she's talking about sometimes so just sit there and nod me head. It's a good job that Lash can hold his own with her.'

'She gets her brains and pretty face from her mother's side, definitely not from my Jack.' Dulcie chuckled. 'And what's going on with that Varvara, dressing like a bloke?'

'It's fashionable, apparently.'

'Huh, well you can keep it. Put the kettle on, love, and pass me that bonny boy of yours for a cuddle with his aunty Dul.'

'I'll have a cuppa if there's one going,' Jack said as he walked in and sat on the sofa.

Dulcie was surprised to see her son sober for once and studied his sheepish expression.

'I'm gonna get me act together,' he told her when Molly left the room.

'About bloody time too,' Dulcie answered haughtily.

'I know, Mum. I'm sorry.'

'All right, Son. You've never been one for the drink for most of your life so I'll give you the benefit of the doubt, and I'm glad you're sorting yourself out.'

'I promised George I would.'

'Don't let her hear you call her George. She don't like it. It's Georgina now.'

'All right, I promised *Georgina* I wouldn't let her down, and I won't.'

'I'm glad to hear it. You need to keep busy though, Jack. Distract your mind from the beer. After you've had that cuppa, you can wallpaper this room for me. Everything you need is in the shed. I'll clear away me ornaments.'

'Leave it out, Mum, I feel right rough.'

'I couldn't give a shit how rough you feel. That's nothing to what you've put me and your daughter through this last year. You'll get this room decorated by the end of the week, and when you've finished that, you can make a start on the passageway. And don't you dare think about walking out that door. If you're serious about staying off the booze, you'll do as I say.'

Jack hung his head, obviously ashamed of himself. Good, thought Dulcie, and so he should be.

'There's tea in the pot,' Molly said when she came back into the room, 'but I'd better be off now. I don't like to leave me mum for too long.'

'How is she?' Dulcie asked.

'Not great. I think it'll help when we move away. There's too many memories of Ethel here.'

Dulcie could see Molly's eyes welling up again and quickly changed the subject. 'All right, love. You get off before Edward starts bawling for his lunch. I'll sweep up all that blinkin' rice that's probably over me nice white-chalked doorstep.'

'Sorry, Dulcie, but it's not every day that your best friend gets married.'

'Go on, bugger off,' Dulcie said with an affectionate smile as she handed Edward back to Molly.

The front door closed and Dulcie leaned back against it, sighing heavily. Georgina would be a married woman now. She and Lash would soon want a place of their own. At least that would mean Jack could have Georgina's bedroom and wouldn't have to sleep on the sofa any longer. The house would seem strange without her, but even if Georgina offered to take her with them, Dulcie knew she couldn't leave. Burying Percy in the backyard had sealed her fate.

She was trapped in the house with him. Just like marriage –
'til death us do part.

Varvara and Victor had been witnesses to the marriage of
Georgina and Lash.

Huh, Lash, Varvara thought, wanting to spit his name.
When the newlyweds had sealed their vows with a kiss,
Varvara had looked away. She couldn't stand to see
Georgina lavishing affection on the lowly gypsy. Of course,
she and Georgina could never be married, but it didn't
stop her from thinking that she could make Georgina so
much happier than Lash ever could. After all, Varvara
believed Lash was nothing more than a contemptuous
man. He didn't understand Georgina, not in the way she
did. Lash didn't appreciate Georgina's strength or admire
her undeniable ingenuity. He didn't worship her. Varvara
did, and she knew she could give Georgina's body exquisite
pleasure. She doubted Lash would know how to please a
woman. In her experience, few men did.

As they descended the steps from the registry office,
Victor walked ahead. He crossed a small road to where
they'd left the car and opened the back door. Georgina had
her arm linked through her new husband's and Varvara felt
disgusted at hearing them whispering and giggling with
each other. She clenched her jaw and stared ahead, just as a
black car sped around the corner. Intuitively, Varvara sensed
trouble and tensed.

The car screeched to a halt. The window was already
down and Varvara saw the car held four young men. As

Victor ran towards them the man in the front seat shouted, 'Congratulations, Miss Garrett.'

He had something in his hand. Varvara couldn't see what it was, but he threw it towards Georgina. It could be explosives, and keeping to her promise of her life for Georgina's, Varvara leapt in front of it. She felt the package hit her shoulder and closed her eyes, expecting her head to be blown off. But instead, she retched at the disgusting smell of dog's muck and heard the mocking laughter of the men as they drove off.

Victor was poised with his gun aimed at the car.

'Put it away in public,' Georgina instructed him and then turned to Varvara. 'Dirty bastards,' she hissed, as she wrinkled her nose at the disgusting smell of the dog's faeces now smeared on Varvara's jacket.

'Are you all right?' Lash asked Georgina.

'Yes, I'm fine. But look at the state of Varvara. That shit was meant for me.'

Victor was now standing in front of them. 'That was Charlie's crew.'

'I know exactly who it was and we've been expecting something like this,' Georgina answered and looked at Varvara knowingly.

'I thought the Pounders killed off Charlie's men?' Lash asked.

'They did, but that lot are lower down the food chain. They're chancing their luck but they won't get away with it.'

Victor handed Varvara a handkerchief and she tried not to heave as she wiped the dog's mess off her clothes.

SAM MICHAELS

'Varvara,' Georgina said, her voice grave, 'you know what to do. It's time to put our plan into action.'

Varvara smiled wickedly at her boss. When she and Georgina had discussed the possibility of retaliation from Charlie Chops' gang, the strategy they'd come up with had left Varvara secretly hoping the gang would do something. And now they'd played straight into her hands.

'Yes, Miss Garrett,' she answered, 'I know *exactly* what to do.'

23

A week later, Benjamin nervously placed the lid on his pen and coughed to clear his throat. He'd been dreading breaking the news to Georgina. She'd been in such a good mood since she'd married Lash and he feared he was about to change it. 'Erm, Miss Garrett,' he said quietly.

Georgina looked up from her desk.

'We... we need to talk.'

'Spit it out then.'

'I've had this, erm, notification to quit from the landlord's solicitor. The landlord has passed away and his family are requesting the vacant possession of Queenstown Road. They would like to continue with the rentals of the other properties and are happy for the business to act as the collection agent.'

Georgina nodded her head and he noticed she was twisting the small gold band she wore on her little finger.

'How long?'

'Six weeks.'

'I see. And there's not enough capital in the business to invest in purchasing our own property?'

'Considering the monies required to settle with Mrs Wilcox, no, we haven't. If you still want to buy her out at the cost you've suggested it will leave you with very little capital.'

'It's important Molly receives a more than fair price for her share of the business so that's not open for discussion. Do you have any suggestions?'

'I'm afraid not. Every aspect of the business is running in profit, but it will take you more than six weeks to accumulate enough to purchase a sizeable property in this area.'

'Right, get back to their solicitor and tell him we will be vacating when I see fit and make it clear that this is not open for negotiation. Or... we could leave in four weeks.'

'But how?' Benjamin asked.

'I'll sell The Penthouse Club.'

Benjamin looked at her, appalled at the idea. He loved managing the place; it was his life.

'Just kidding, don't look so worried,' Georgina said, adding, 'but I have got a plan. In the meantime, as I said, get back to the solicitor and tell him I'll move when I'm ready. If he'd like to discuss the matter any further, arrange for him to come in.'

So, Georgina has a plan, Benjamin thought. He had no doubt about the woman's abilities but wished she would share more with him. He only ever found out about things after the event. He understood it was for his own protection but Benjamin had got a taste for danger and he liked it.

The door flew open and Victor burst in looking unusually agitated. 'The Portland Pounders are pulling up outside,' he said with urgency.

Georgina spun around in her chair and glanced out of the window behind her. 'Shit,' she mumbled. 'What the hell do they want?'

Benjamin could feel that the atmosphere had instantly become tense. Be careful what you wish for, he thought, as his heart raced. Yes, he'd discovered he liked a bit of danger in his life, but the Portland Pounders' reputation terrified him. Their thump on the front door left Benjamin quaking.

'Go, Benjamin, leave out of the back door,' Georgina told him.

He wanted to. He wanted to flee the room and save his life but fear rooted him to the spot and rendered him unable to speak.

Georgina didn't have time to repeat herself and before he knew it, Victor had opened the front door. Kevin Kelly, the Pounders' boss, walked in followed by his entourage of what Benjamin would describe as unpleasant-looking thugs.

'Miss Garrett, I'm pleased to finally meet you,' Kevin Kelly said and sat down without invitation.

'Likewise, Mr Kelly,' Georgina answered, as charming and composed as ever. 'You and your men are a long way from home. Can I offer you a drink?'

'No, that won't be necessary,' Kevin answered.

Benjamin tried to keep his head down and hoped he wouldn't be noticeable in the corner. He peeped over the top of his round-rimmed glasses at the man who owned the most frightening name in England. Kevin Kelly didn't look scary. He was a surprisingly short man and older than Benjamin had imagined. Then Kevin removed his black trilby hat, revealing his thick, white hair, which was neatly combed around his weathered face. He reminded Benjamin of an old sailor he'd once known. Stocky, with no neck and an etched face that had seen a thousand worlds.

'What brings you to Battersea?' Georgina asked.

'You do, Miss Garrett. I hear your man is a fighter?'

'Lash, my husband?'

'Yes. He's got quite a name for himself in the ring.'

'He was in the ring when I first saw him,' Georgina said, smiling.

Benjamin was impressed with how calm she seemed. No nerves showed in her voice or her body language. The same couldn't be said for Victor. The giant man was looking anxiously around the room from one brute to another and Benjamin knew his hand was ready to grab his gun if needed.

'I'm sure he impressed you. I want a fight set up with my champ. He's undefeated and needs a challenge.'

'I'm sorry, Mr Kelly, but Lash has retired from fighting now.'

Benjamin's eyes widened. He doubted Kevin Kelly was the sort of man who was told *no*.

'I don't think so, Miss Garrett. He can come out of retirement for this fight.'

'He won't. He doesn't fight anymore.'

Kevin Kelly drummed his fingers on his knees. 'He will, once you understand the stakes.'

'Then please explain them to me.'

'If your man wins, I'll wipe out what's left of Charlie's gang. I know your girls have already got rid of one of them, but I'll do the rest of the dirty work for you. And, of course, you'll keep the purse from the fight, which will be substantial.'

This was news to Benjamin. He'd seen that Varvara and Georgina had been up to something but hadn't known they'd been killing off Charlie's men. As usual, Benjamin was the last to know.

'And if your man wins?' Georgina asked.

'You give me back the diamonds that you swapped with the paste ones.'

Benjamin gulped. He couldn't see how Georgina could get herself out of this, other than to agree with Kevin Kelly's terms.

'I won't insult your intelligence and deny any involvement but I don't have your diamonds.'

'That's not my problem, it's yours. I want my diamonds back, but I like a bit of fair sport too. Look, Miss Garrett, I don't want to hurt you. You're fucking good at what you do and it's nice to see a pretty face in that seat for a change. Play along with me, there's a good girl.'

'I want to change the stakes,' Georgina answered confidently.

'Let's hear your offer then.'

'I don't need you to get rid of Charlie's idiots. I'm more than capable of sorting them out myself. When my man wins I want the purse, and the stones plus the two large diamonds that were in the pouch with the paste ones.'

'How do you know the police haven't still got them? They're not likely to hand me back stolen jewels,' Kevin said and guffawed.

Georgina ignored Kevin's rebuke and repeated, 'The purse and the diamonds and my man will fight.'

Kevin spat in his stumpy hand. 'Deal,' he said, and offered it to her.

'Deal,' Georgina repeated but turned her nose up at shaking Kevin's hand, which appeared to amuse the man.

'The last Friday of the month. The fight will be in Liverpool. I'll send the arrangements. Good day, Miss Garrett.'

'Good day to you, Mr Kelly,' Georgina said and rose to her feet.

Shortly after, through the window, they saw the Pounders' car speed away and it felt as if the walls of the room breathed a sigh of relief.

'Shit, shit, shit,' Georgina spat. 'Kevin Kelly's diamonds will buy us more than one house but what if Lash loses? David Maynard is never going to agree to give me his diamonds and I can't steal them from him.'

'Lash will have to win, Miss Garrett. I, erm, I think all our lives will depend on it.'

Later that evening, Varvara adjusted her dark brown wig. 'This bloody thing is making my scalp itch,' she told her sister, Dina.

'It is better that than being recognised,' Dina replied flatly, speaking in Russian.

They were on their way to one of Charlie Chops' seedier clubs on the pretence of looking for work.

'This is it,' Varvara said as the cab pulled up outside. 'Be careful, Dina,' she whispered as they climbed out.

She'd easily talked her sister into this. Too easily, in fact. But is seemed Dina had no feelings left. Years of sexual abuse since they were children had destroyed the young woman. Her emotions were dead. Just as Varvara's had once been until Georgina had relit a fire. Now, for Dina, there was only hate left in her heart for men. That was why she'd readily agreed to help Varvara get rid of Miss Garrett's adversaries, relishing in the task of killing them.

They walked towards the club but were quickly stopped at the door. 'Oi, you two. Where do you fink you're going? Sling ya fucking hook. You ain't touting for business in here.'

'We would like to see the manager,' Varvara said.

'Well he don't wanna see you so fuck off,' the man growled, then muttered, 'Slags.'

'We are here to work for him. We are good, no?' Varvara purred and pushed her breasts up against the man.

'Gerroff me, fucking whores. I wouldn't touch any of you with a barge pole. Go on, inside. Ask for Nuts.'

Varvara quickly pulled Dina into the dark room and squinted as her eyes adjusted to the low lights and smoky atmosphere. She saw a woman, topless except for a string of fake pearls draped over her chest, and another, with just a bra and no knickers, both walking around carrying drinks on a tray. At the end of the bar, another woman writhed her semi-naked body on an older man sat on a stool, and on the small stage, a man slapped a dancer's backside and laughed with his friends.

'This place is disgusting,' Dina said quietly.

Varvara saw a face she recognised. He'd been the one who'd thrown the dog's muck at her. He turned around to speak to the barman and Varvara marched towards him. She tapped his shoulder and he spun to face her.

'Men and whores only are allowed in here,' he said, then reached his hand up her beaded dress and grabbed her bare vagina. 'You ain't a man so you must be a whore,' he sneered.

'Yes, and we are very good at what we do. I am looking for Nuts.'

'You've found him.'

'Good. I am Tattia and this is my friend, Anna. We would like to work under your protection. We will make good money for you.'

'I couldn't care a less what your names are. Do you work together? Two tarts for the price of one?'

'If you like. Perhaps we can show you what we can do?' Varvara said teasingly and rubbed her hand over his groin. When he didn't protest, she leaned in closer and purred in his ear, 'You like, we both fuck you?'

Nuts eyes darted around. 'Come on, with me,' he said eagerly and led them through a dark curtain and into a small room. From there he opened another door to a room lit by a gas lantern and furnished with a table, a chair and a bookshelf, stacked high with illegally brewed bottles of gin. Varvara's nose twitched at the smell of damp in the windowless room and she glanced over her shoulder at Dina. Her sister looked back at her with a blank expression. Even murder left Dina numb.

Nuts stood in front of the table. 'You first,' he told Dina. 'Take your clothes off. I like to see what I'm getting.'

'Slow down. Let us do the work for you,' Varvara said huskily and ran her tongue around Nut's neck and to his ear. Here she nuzzled on his lobe as she undid his trousers and Dina pulled them to his ankles.

RIVALS

'Lie back on the table,' Varvara instructed. 'Relax and let me show you the incredible things I can do with my mouth.'

Nuts was keen to oblige and scrambled onto the table. He laid back with his hands behind his head and his legs dangling over the edge. Varvara began with popping her breasts over the top of her dress and rubbing her nipples gently over his lips. At the same time, Dina pulled Nuts' legs apart and stood in between them and began to skilfully manipulate his manhood.

'You are liking this, no?' Varvara asked.

'Oh, yeah, I'm liking it all right,' Nuts answered and closed his eyes.

Varvara, satisfied that her victim had let his guard down, held her thumb up to Dina. It was the signal. The sign to tell her to act now. With one hand still massaging Nuts' penis, Dina used her other to pull out a razor blade hidden in the waistband of her skirt. Then, Varvara moved to stand at the top of Nuts' head and sensually massaged his scalp, gently pulling his head back to expose the man's neck. In one swift move, Dina swiped the razor blade across his throat, cutting him deeply.

Blood spurted up the walls and over Dina's dress. There was no scream. No call for help. And as the blood flow subsided, they heard a soft gurgling noise as the crimson liquid seeped from the long gash across Nuts' neck. He put his hands over the wound but it did nothing to stem the bleeding and Varvara watched as his blood oozed through his fingers and pooled on the table.

'He is dying. Good work, sister,' she told Dina, and fished in her pocket for a note. Then she leaned over Nuts and drawled, 'I do not like it when dog's mess is thrown at me.'

SAM MICHAELS

A bubbling noise emerged from Nuts' throat though no words came. But she saw a glint of recognition in his eyes and felt avenged. She placed the note across his now very limp penis.

'What does it say?' Dina asked.

'It is from Miss Garrett, sending her regards,' Varvara answered proudly.

'We can do better. You see that lamp – we could set the place on fire.'

'No, Dina, we have completed our work. Let's go,' Varvara said. 'And keep your head down. You have a lot of blood on you.'

As they hurried back through the club and out onto the night streets, Varvara worried about her sister. She'd have happily razed the club to the ground with no regard for anyone who may have been injured or killed in the fire. There were many women working in there – women like them. Whores, forced to earn a living by men using and degrading them. Dina had shown no compassion for those women. No thought for their safety.

Varvara had already realised that she and Dina's harsh and cruel upbringing had damaged her sister, but until tonight she hadn't known how deep the damage had been. It was bad – really bad. It seemed there was nothing left of Dina but a cold, empty shell and Varvara pitied her.

As they lay in Georgina's single bed, she ran her fingers through the soft dark hair on Lash's chest. 'So, you're happy to fight him?' she asked.

'I've always wanted to fight him but haven't had the money to get close enough. He's big stakes. I've never had a promoter or manager. I'm just a gypsy bare-knuckle fighter and if you want to be in the ring with him, you have to have the cash to put in.'

'Good. It's all arranged. But are you positive you can beat him?'

'I'm sure of it, Georgina. Feel this,' Lash said and took her hand and placed it flat on his chest. 'Can you feel that? That's my heart beating and pumping the blood around my body. You've just made it pump harder. I feel alive again. I was made for fighting and I've missed it.'

'Oh, Lash, I know you're confident you can win but I hate the thought of anyone throwing punches at you.'

'Don't worry, my beautiful wife, he won't get many punches in.'

'I hope not. I'm really not sure about this but, well, it's not like I have a lot of choice.'

'What do you mean?'

'Nothing. I don't mean anything,' Georgina quickly answered, realising she'd said too much.

'Are you keeping something from me?'

'No,' Georgina lied.

Lash tucked his finger under her chin and pulled her face up to look in her eyes. 'Tell me the truth, Georgina,' he said.

She felt herself crumble under his scrutiny and told him the whole story, about how the forthcoming boxing match had really come to be.

'I should have known you hadn't set this up just to please me.'

'To be fair, Lash, I wouldn't have known the first thing about arranging a fight for you. But when Kevin Kelly suggested it, I knew you'd jump at the opportunity, though I'm not going to lie and say I'm thrilled about the idea of you in the ring again.'

'I can see why you're so keen for me to win.'

'It's not just about the diamonds. I don't want to see you hurt.'

'And you don't want your reputation hurt either,' Lash said and threw back the bed covers.

'This isn't about me,' Georgina protested.

'Yes it is. Everything's always about you. I can imagine how humiliated you'd be if I was to lose the fight. You're worried I'll show you up.'

'Maybe, but you've told me you're going to win.'

'Yes, I am,' Lash replied angrily, 'but for me, Georgina, not for you. I'm going to win this fight so I can claw back a bit of my pride.'

'Good. You win and we'll both be happy then,' Georgina said cheekily and knelt up to place her arms around Lash who was now sitting on the edge of the bed.

'You don't half push your luck, woman.'

'I know, but get back into bed. It's cold without you.'

Lash lay back down and pulled the covers over them both. 'It won't happen, but just say I lose this fight. What will be the consequences?'

Georgina closed her eyes and tried to blot out the truth. If Lash lost the fight, she'd be expected to give back the diamonds that David Maynard had stolen from the Pounders. That was never going to happen. Lash *had* to win. Kevin Kelly wasn't known for showing any mercy to anyone who crossed him. If Lash lost and she couldn't produce the diamonds, she'd be the next one to be finished off by the bullets of the Portland Pounders. The thought terrified her and she squeezed her eyes shut.

'Hey, what's wrong?' Lash asked.

'Just win. Please, just make sure you win this fight.'

24

The next evening, Georgina marched into The Penthouse Club with Victor and Johnny Dymond at her side. Lash had waited outside, citing how uncomfortable the club made him feel. This suited Georgina. She'd received word from what was left of Charlie's gang that they wanted to meet with her, and on their suggestion, they would be arriving at 7 p.m., just before the club opened.

'Hello, Miss G,' Ivy chirped from behind the bar, clearly pleased to see Georgina. 'What's your poison?'

'Nothing for me, thanks, Ivy. I don't want to drink the profits. You're looking lovely – this work obviously suits you,' Georgina commented as she took in Ivy's immaculate but heavily made-up face and rather flamboyant dress, adorned with peacock feathers, mirrored beads and gold chain tassels.

'This,' Ivy said and did a quick turn, 'is all thanks to me friends in here. They love dressing me up and doing my face.'

Georgina smiled warmly at the young woman. It was nice to see her happy and playing dressing-up games, something Ivy had probably never had an opportunity to do as a child.

She was still very young and the customers might be treating her like a doll, but it was obviously done with affection.

A man walked towards them and Georgina had to take a double look before she realised it was Benjamin. She'd never seen him with powder and rouge on his face and he seemed to be carrying himself differently too.

He greeted her with a theatrical air, waving his arms as he said, 'Miss Garrett, delighted to see you here. Ivy, champagne, chop chop, dear.'

He minced towards a small round table where Georgina had once sat, cutting the deal to buy the place. She followed him, astounded at this new persona she was seeing and wondered if this was the *real* Benjamin and not the awkward and shy accountant who had a desk next to hers.

Ivy placed a bottle of champagne in a tall, silver ice bucket on a stand and two glasses on the table. 'Are you here to see the act tonight?' she asked.

'Yes, something like that,' Georgina answered. 'Listen, Ivy. I'd like you to go out back and do a stock check on the alcohol. Make sure it takes you at least an hour.'

'Ah, right. Something's going down tonight, ain't it?'

'Just do as you're told, Ivy.'

'No way! If there's gonna be a big bust-up, I want to see it.'

'IVY!' Georgina took a deep breath and continued, 'It's for your own protection. Just stay out of the way.'

'But...'

'No buts.'

Ivy pouted like a sulking child. 'Enjoy your champagne,' she said moodily as she sloped off.

'I hope you're paying for this,' Georgina said to Benjamin as he poured them both a glass.

'Of course. Though you do know that as your accountant, I could easily fiddle the books.'

'Yes, and you do know that as your boss I could easily blow your brains out.'

'Touché,' Benjamin said with a smile and clinked his glass to hers.

Georgina checked the time. Charlie's men should arrive in fifteen minutes. She felt sure they'd come with their caps in their hands and beg for a truce but she couldn't be sure. There was always the possibility that they'd try and barge in with all guns blazing or even throw some explosives in like she'd once done to Battersea police station. But she had the Barker twins on the outside door with Lash and five other blokes lining the corridors. All eyes would be on Charlie's gang but still, anything could happen.

Exactly on time, the door opened and Ned informed Victor of the gang's arrival. There were three of them, hardly heavy-handed, and the Barker twins had already frisked them. Victor showed them in and Johnny stood by Georgina's side.

'Miss Garrett. Thank you for agreeing to meet us. I'm Fred, this is Pearly and Len.'

Georgina remained seated and glanced up at Johnny.

'They call him Pearly on account of his teeth... he ain't got none,' Johnny told her.

She looked the three men up and down. They were young, barely out of short trousers and she could tell they were extremely anxious. 'What do you want?' she asked them bluntly.

Fred looked from one of his blokes to the other then answered, 'We don't want nuffink, Miss Garrett. We're sorry about what happened on your wedding day. We'll stay out of your way and you won't get no trouble from us.'

'I see. You're asking me to leave you alone?'

'Yes. Please.'

'And what's in it for me?'

'Anything you want. If we've got it, you can have it.'

'I don't want your shitty little clubs. I know you rent the premises and from what I've heard, that's about all you've got left. So, I'll ask again... what's in it for me?'

'I can give you some information. Valuable information,' Fred offered. 'I was gonna tell you about it anyway.'

'If that's all you've got, you'd better give it to me then, but keep in mind that if I wanted to I could beat the information out of you.'

'Do you mind if I sit down?'

'Yes, I do. Just tell me what you know.'

'Fair enough... It's that copper. The one who works for you.'

'Cunningham... What about him?'

'He's Mickey's cousin and they're as thick as thieves.'

Georgina tried not to look either surprised or impressed by the information imparted and exchanged a look with Johnny. 'Mickey who took over the Wilcox business from Billy?'

'Yeah, him.'

'How do I know you're telling me the truth?'

'Tell her, Pearly, tell Miss Garrett what you told me,' Fred encouraged.

Pearly swallowed hard before he spoke. 'It's true, Miss Garrett, I swear. My dad works for the electric board, converting houses from gas lighting. He come home from work the other night and asked me if I'd heard of you. When I said yes, he told me that he was at this house where there was a geezer in one of them chairs with wheels. Said his name was Mickey. He said this copper called in to visit and he heard the copper telling Mickey stuff about you. He said he reckoned the copper was right bent and from what he heard, you'd better watch your back 'cos Mickey is out to get you.'

'Bit of a coincidence, isn't it? I mean, what's the chances of your dad working in Mickey's house and hearing all this? Sounds to me like this could be a bit of a fairy tale?'

'No, Miss Garrett, it's all true, honest. My old man was listening out 'cos he's got a lot to hide from the Old Bill. He's always nicking stuff from the houses he works in so when the copper turned up my dad nearly shit himself. He was right chuffed when he heard them talking about you instead of collaring him!'

'If this is true, why didn't you just sit back and allow Mickey and Cunningham to get me?'

Fred spoke now. "Cos Ted is my brother, and he was Charlie's driver. It was Cunningham who stopped Ted on Battersea Bridge that night. Before Ted legged it down to Bristol, he told me Cunningham was spitting venom about you. Mind you, so was Ted, but he said Cunningham wasn't gonna stop with you. If he had his way, all of London would be under Cunningham's control. And I know Mickey always had big ideas too. Right pair, them two. Ted reckons Cunningham's got a screw loose and warned me to stay out of his way.'

'So you want me to sort Cunningham because you lot don't have the balls to do the job yourselves. Fine.'

'Are we all square now, Miss Garrett?' Fred asked.

'For now. But I know where to find you if I want you for anything. Keep your mouths shut about this. You can go now.'

Victor led them back out and Johnny pulled out a seat opposite Georgina.

'Dirty, filthy, scheming cunt!' Johnny sneered as he sat down.

'I never liked Cunningham but I didn't see this coming.'

'How are we going to deal with him?' Johnny asked.

'I'm not sure yet. I'll have to think about it. We'll need to be careful. I don't want to feel the force of the Met on my back.'

'Yeah, and I tell you what, Miss Garrett... If Cunningham believes he's got the power to take over London, it shows he's a complete nutter and nutters scare the fucking life out of me. They're unpredictable.'

'Don't worry, Johnny. If you get scared, Victor will hold your hand,' Georgina said and laughed.

'You can take the piss all you like, but we've got to get on top of this before he thinks about making a move.'

'Oh, rest assured, Johnny. I'm going to be all over this like a nasty rash.'

Mickey lay in the darkness of his bedroom staring at the shadows cast by the moon shining through the window. He knew it would be pointless to call again, but even so, he yelled his brother's name. No-one came. No-one answered.

He could hear a faint murmuring from downstairs. His aged mother and his useless brother talking, no doubt about him. Sitting there together, laughing. Making cruel jibes about his inability to walk. And there was nothing Mickey could do about it.

'For fuck's sake,' he screeched, aware that he'd defecated himself again. The smell turned his stomach but he couldn't help himself. Not only had the bullet in his spine left him without the use of his legs, he was also incontinent.

Using the side of his fist, Mickey repeatedly thudded the wall next to his bed. He knew they could hear him downstairs. Yet they chose to ignore him. He hadn't moved from the bed for two days and nights now. They'd left him to rot on his urine-sodden mattress, lying in his own filth. 'I'll never forgive them for this,' he cursed.

Mickey had been home from the hospital for over a week and at first, after some initial adjustments, they'd coped well. He'd been made comfortable on the sofa, visitors had called in and between his mother and brother, they'd cared well for him. His mother had fetched and carried meals, drinks and cleaned up any accidents, while his brother had helped to move him, even carrying Mickey up the stairs to bed at night and back down in the morning. But for the last couple of nights the bedroom door had been closed and he'd been left with just a jug of water and a box of biscuits.

'I fucking hate you!' he screamed. So much for family, he thought, feeling neglected by his. Granted, he'd had a go at his mother for undercooking his eggs and had told his brother he was thick, but that didn't warrant this treatment.

Mickey stared at the ceiling and the flaking paint over a damp patch in the corner. He thought about pushing himself off the bed and dragging himself to the top of the stairs but he knew it was too much of a risk. The doctors had warned him, no sudden movements. If the bullet in his spine was dislodged, it could kill him. He had to be gentle with himself so throwing himself out of bed wasn't an option.

He shivered. Although he had no feeling from the waist down, he knew his legs were cold. He guessed they were probably covered in sores too. 'MOTHER,' he shouted again, 'I'm sorry.'

Eventually he heard footsteps coming up the stairs. At last, someone was going to see to him. But then his heart sunk as he heard his mother's bedroom door close and the sound of mattress springs as she climbed into her bed. How could they be so cruel? He hated being reliant on them and now wished he'd gone into an institution instead. Though from the horror stories he'd heard, he doubted he'd have been treated any better.

Mickey closed his eyes. Maybe it would be different in the morning. Frank had said he'd pop in to see him. Surely they wouldn't let Frank witness the conditions they'd left him in? Yes, tomorrow would be different. Frank would be appalled if he knew what was going on. Mickey would tell him. He'd tell Frank everything. His cousin and good friend would see to it that he got the care he deserved. And once Mickey had his strength back, he'd make sure his mother and brother paid for this. They could rot in fucking hell and keep Georgina Garrett company.

Mickey's eyes shot open and he looked towards the bedroom door when he heard it creak as it opened. He saw the silhouette of his brother approaching him. 'About fucking time,' Mickey snapped. 'Get me out of this shit.'

'Here's your medicine. Mother said you can do without it but I thought you might want it,' his brother said and left a bottle on the table by the side of the bed.

'Yeah, I do. My back is killing me.'

His brother backed away, obviously disgusted by the stench. 'Night, then,' he said as he opened the door again.

'No... wait... come back. You can't leave me like this!' Mickey shouted, but the door closed. 'You fucking bastards, the pair of ya!'

Exhausted by pain and worn out with frustration, Mickey picked up the bottle. He only had about half a glass of water left but thought it was probably enough to down most of the pills in the bottle. That should kill him. He wasn't sure how, but he'd heard people had died from overdosing on medicine. Death would be an escape for him, a way out of the misery. It had to be better than this.

Mickey tipped a few pills into the palm of his hand and stared at the small, white tablets. Would these be the last thing he'd ever see? No, he thought, they wouldn't and in anger, he threw them across the room.

'I ain't fucking dying, you bastards,' he muttered. 'I'm gonna live and make sure the fucking lot of you pay for what you've done to me.'

25

The last Friday of the month had come round quickly. Lash had been training hard and convinced Georgina he was ready for the fight. They sat in the back of the car with Johnny in the front and Victor driving, heading for Liverpool. Varvara had been left in Battersea to look after the fort and Georgina inwardly smiled. Varvara had willingly stepped up to the mark and dressed elegantly in her masculine-style trouser suits, which Georgina thought looked quite the part.

'My family will be in Battersea by Sunday. My pa will be a proud man and there'll be celebrations like you've never seen before,' Lash said to Georgina.

'Because you're going to win this fight?'

'And because I have a beautiful new wife.'

'Are we invited to the party, Lash? I love a good knees-up,' Johnny said.

'Of course. You haven't seen a good knees-up 'til you've been to a gypsy celebration.'

'Great, but let's stay focused for now, eh? We're not out on a Beano,' Georgina said. Her stomach churned with nerves and she felt giddy.

'Are you all right?' Lash asked. 'You look very pale.'

Georgina nodded, too afraid to open her mouth for fear of vomit spewing from it.

'You're not, are you?' Lash pressed.

'I feel sick,' Georgina managed to answer quietly. 'Shush, don't make a fuss.'

'How long have you been feeling like this?'

'Just this morning. It's this bloody fight, it's getting to me.'

Georgina watched a smile spread across Lash's face. 'What's that look for?' she asked him.

Lash leaned in to her and whispered in her ear, 'I thought for a minute that you might be with child, Georgina.'

She gasped and stared back at him in disbelief. 'No... not yet. I'm not ready for that yet.'

'Soon though, eh?'

'What's that?' Johnny asked.

'I was just telling Georgina that I'm looking forward to being a—' Lash started to say.

But Georgina quickly cut in, 'Champion. Lash will be the official undefeated champion.'

She saw the hurt look in Lash's eyes and squeezed his hand as she whispered, 'No talk of babies in front of the men.'

This seemed to placate Lash and the rest of the journey passed quietly, which pleased Georgina as it gave her time to think. Pregnancy and childbirth hadn't been on her agenda yet. She knew Lash wanted a big family but she hadn't considered that he'd want to start so soon. Her mind was a whirl with questions, none of which she could answer. If she fell pregnant, could she continue in her position with the business? Would she be putting an unborn child at risk? Would she be a good mother? Could she love a child in the way Molly loved Edward? Did she even want a baby? She churned the questions over and with no answers, her mind once again focused on the enormity of the outcome of the impending fight. Before she knew it, they'd arrived in Liverpool.

As the car weaved its way through the bustling docks, she stared out of the window at the impressive Liver building that overlooked the wharf. The place reminded her a little of London – imposing buildings of rich architecture contrasting with dilapidated and damp-looking dwellings. The sudden sound of the car horn made her jump.

Victor leaned out of the window and shouted, 'Get out the fucking way,' and waved his hand to encourage a group of young lads to step to one side.

It was a busy area. Ships lined the docks and all around them men were grafting, carrying huge sacks of merchandise on their shoulders. She saw many children begging and quite a few women touting for business. Then as they came to the end of the quay, she spotted Kevin Kelly's car parked with several others outside an isolated building.

It was quieter up here, away from the large merchants' buildings and the unloading bays. Georgina could see why Kevin had chosen to live and work from here. There was a tranquillity close to the water's edge and the building offered privacy.

'We're here,' she said gravely.

As Victor pulled up outside, two of Kevin's men casually held their guns towards them. It seemed to be the natural way they greeted visitors. Then she saw Kevin appear in the large doorway, a cigarette in one hand and a glass in the other. She couldn't hear what he said but his henchmen put their guns away.

Lash took Georgina's hand and helped her out of the car. She straightened her elegant but simple purple dress, pulled her fur stole around her shoulders and clutching her handbag, she sauntered towards the head of the Pounders.

'Miss Garrett, I trust you had a good journey?'

'Yes, thank you, Mr Kelly.'

'Please, come in. There's refreshments prepared and a couple of rooms available for your use. After all, we want to ensure our fighter here is well rested and prepared for tonight's bout. Lash, pleased to meet you,' Kevin said and put his cigarette in his mouth to extend a hand to him.

Georgina followed Kevin into the building and found herself impressed by the tasteful décor.

'Designed by my third wife,' Kevin told her as her eyes flitted around the panelled walls and gilded furniture. 'But now my fourth wife wants to change it all. Women, eh, no offence.'

'None taken,' Georgina answered as they entered the main reception room and then her opinion of the décor changed.

A long table stretched through the middle with heavy dark wood and burgundy chairs. A luxurious buffet was spread across crisp white table linen under an overbearing chandelier. The food looked fancy but didn't appeal to Georgina as she was still feeling queasy. Her eyes went from the table to a huge oil painting over the marble fireplace and there she saw a life-size portrait of Kevin Kelly standing alongside a racehorse.

'The wife commissioned it,' Kevin said, almost sounding embarrassed.

'It's very flattering,' Georgina lied, thinking it was ridiculously ostentatious.

'The trouble is, I treat my wives like queens so they've done the place up like a fucking palace. Every time I get a new wife, she wants to outdo the last one. Mabel's just finished this room. As you can see, her taste is... unique.'

Georgina glanced around the room at the Italian-style statues, the stuffed animals that looked as if they were coming out of the walls and the two red velvet and gold chairs next to the fireplace, which she could only describe as thrones.

'I drew the line at having the ceiling painted like the Sistine Chapel.'

Georgina smiled at Kevin. He didn't seem quite as intimidating when he spoke about his wives. She'd have liked to meet his latest one and Kevin appeared to read her mind.

'Mabel will be out later to see the fight. She's looking forward to meeting you. Anyway, I'll leave you to rest after your drive here. Help yourself to the spread and Michael here will show you your rooms. I'll be back in a couple of hours.' Kevin swaggered towards the door, puffing on his cigarette and leaving a trail of smoke behind him. Then he turned back to Georgina. 'By the way, I assume you have the diamonds with you?'

'No. Why would I? My man isn't going to lose.'

'We'll see about that. And when he does, you'd better be ready to produce.'

There it was, a gentle threat. Georgina had been wondering for how long he'd keep up the nice guy act. As it turned out, not for very long!

SAM MICHAELS

Kevin left and Georgina quickly pulled out a heavy chair from under the table and flopped down. Her legs felt shaky. She knew it was fear. Lash rested his hand on her shoulder.

'Don't worry, I won't let you down,' he said quietly.

She patted his hand and tried to swallow but her mouth felt dry. So much rested on the fight tonight – her reputation, money and their lives.

Mickey sat in Frank's small back garden and though the sun was shining, he had a blanket over his legs. Frank had acquired the wooden chair with wheels for him. The wheels were rickety but it made his life a bit easier. Mickey couldn't manoeuvre himself but Frank was able to push him.

'Do you want a cup of tea?' Frank's wife called from the back door.

'No,' Mickey answered, unable to bring himself to be polite to the woman.

He'd heard her last night, going on to Frank again about him staying with them. She didn't want Mickey in the house and resented caring for him. Frank had told her to shut up but she'd kept on and on and on. What was it she'd called him? Oh yes, Mickey remembered her words – a useless shitting piss bucket cripple who should sit outside the station and beg for his keep. She hadn't minced her words or hidden her contempt for him.

Mickey ground his teeth as anger simmered. It wasn't his fault he was reliant on them. He hadn't put the bullet in his spine. He couldn't force his mother and brother to look after him. He hated being in this situation, clearly unwanted and an obvious burden. Still, Frank's missus never went

306

short and as far as Mickey was concerned, she had fuck all else to do so why not make her graft for a change.

The warmth of the sun's rays on Mickey's cheeks disappeared as it slipped behind a grey cloud. There'd only be a few more weeks left of summer. Autumn followed, then Christmas would be soon on them. It would be different this year. He wouldn't sit at the same table as his mother or brother. In fact, he hoped they choked on turkey bones.

'I'm going shopping,' Frank's wife called from the kitchen.

Mickey went to shout back to tell her to bring him inside, but she'd already gone. 'Fuck it,' he mumbled as the temperature dropped and the sky darkened. He desperately tried to turn the wheels of the chair but they wouldn't budge. 'You've done this on purpose, you fucking bitch,' he screeched as he felt raindrops on his cheeks.

He took the blanket from his legs and wrapped it around his head and shoulders. But following a huge clap of thunder, the skies opened and heavy rain began to pour. The blanket was soon wet through and Mickey was left shivering and soaked.

As his teeth chattered, a dark mood descended on him. This was no way to live and Mickey couldn't see it ever getting better. He wished the bullet had killed him instead of leaving him incapacitated. He couldn't continue like this. Yes, Frank had big plans for them both, but Mickey knew, in reality, he couldn't do it, not in this condition. 'I might as well be dead,' he said solemnly, and his mind was made up.

Now that he'd made his decision, it felt as though a weight had been lifted off his shoulders and for the first time in a long while, Mickey smiled. He was ready to die.

But he didn't plan on going alone. He'd fulfil his last wish – to take Georgina Garrett with him to her death.

'Sitting there suits you,' Benjamin said, 'but don't get used to it.'

Varvara placed her hands on Georgina's desk and leaned back in the seat. It felt good to be in her boss's shoes and finally, she could command respect. 'Don't worry, Mr Harel. I have no illusions of being in charge. But yes, this is better for me not to be a whore, yes?'

'Yes, erm, no, what?' Benjamin said and pushed his glasses up his nose, looking confused. 'Varvara, how long have you lived in England?'

'All of my life. I have never visited the mother land.'

'So why do you speak with such a strong Russian accent?'

'It was forbidden to speak English in my home and I received no schooling. So this is how I sound. Many men think it is sexy. You think it is sexy, Mr Harel?' she teased. It amused her to see him looking flummoxed.

Benjamin cleared his throat. 'I, erm, think it's very exotic.'

'Pew, you queer men. You are very funny but I prefer exotic, or strong. To sound strong like Miss Garrett would be good, no?'

'Erm, yes, I think. You do sound strong, Varvara, and you certainly look strong. Like an Amazon warrior woman.'

'What is this amazing warrior woman?'

'Amazon. It's a river in a jungle.'

'You think I am like a Zulu?' Varvara asked, surprised at his opinion of her.

'No, a Zulu is from Africa.'

'I think the Zulu is from the jungle.'

'Completely different continents. Look, it doesn't matter. What I was trying to say is you look impressive… and capable. I'd feel safe if I knew you was committed to me like you are to Miss Garrett.'

This pleased Varvara and she grinned at Benjamin. It was the only time she could remember offering a genuine smile to a man. 'You know, before I went to live with Dina's family, I was the daughter of a Russian baker and he made the best bread in Battersea.'

The door flew open and Gwyneth, the prostitute who'd replaced Varvara, burst in looking flush-faced and breathless.

'Knock next time and wait to be told to enter. What do you want?' Varvara asked sternly. She was sure Gwyneth wouldn't have so rudely intruded if Miss Garrett had been present.

'I've got a customer upstairs who said he ain't gonna pay me.'

'Why is he still here? Is he waiting to be beaten?'

'No,' Gwyneth squealed in her high-pitched voice, 'I managed to shackle him to me bed post and took the money from his pocket.'

'So, what is the problem?'

'I'm scared he's gonna go for me when I let him go, ain't I.'

'Of course. Come,' Varvara said and marched from the office and upstairs. She thrust open the bedroom door and saw a podgy man in a vest and baggy trousers, handcuffed to the bed and looking rather annoyed. Varvara spotted a cane on the floor by the side of the bed and picked it up, then swiftly lashed it across the man's face.

The thrash took him by surprise and he looked at Varvara with wide eyes. 'Gwyneth will release you now and you will leave. You are not welcome here again,' she said and rifled through his pockets. 'For my expenses,' she said and took his remaining money.

The man didn't argue and once freed, hurriedly gathered the rest of his clothes before running out of the door. They heard him stumble down the stairs and Varvara watched from the window as he scuttled up the street.

'Back to work,' she told Gwyneth and returned to the office.

Benjamin looked at her with raised eyebrows and remarked, 'He left in rather a hurry.'

'I think because he valued his life,' Varvara answered.

'There, I told you. You are strong and capable. That chap obviously thought so too. Miss Garrett will be pleased with your work.'

Varvara hoped so.

'But I'm afraid we have a problem developing. I've just taken a telephone call. It's Cyril, the old man at the bike shop. He's been taking bets on the fight tonight, big wagers that he's not even sure he can cover. He's been offering better odds than the Maynards and now he's heard that Maynard's blokes have got wind of it.'

'Miss Garrett specifically told him not to accept any bets regarding the fight. He is supposed to send punters to Maynard's men, especially the big spenders. He shouldn't be accepting large bets for anything. What is that silly old man playing at?'

'I don't know but you'd better get down there quick and sort it out.'

'OK, but maybe Mr Maynard will send his men here?'

'Oh, shit. I hadn't thought of that. Stay here, just in case.'

Varvara could hear the fear in Benjamin's voice and guessed he didn't want to be alone to deal with them. 'Fine. Any suggestions what I should tell them?'

'No, but I suppose wait and see what they have to say.'

Varvara leaned her head back and closed her eyes as she thought, what would Miss Garrett do?

'No! I will deal with this now,' she said and picked up the telephone.

'What are you doing?' Benjamin asked and she sensed the panic in his voice.

'I'm going to speak to David Maynard. That is how Miss Garrett would deal with this.'

'I don't think that's a good idea, Varvara. It's one thing for Miss Garrett to call him, but I don't think it would be the correct protocol for *you* to ring him.'

'Why not? Because I am just a whore?'

'No, Varvara. Because you are *not* the boss. Only bosses speak to bosses in this world.'

Varvara replaced the receiver. Perhaps Benjamin was right. But Cyril had now left them in a vulnerable position. David Maynard would know Georgina was in Liverpool. The bicycle shop and Cyril could be in imminent danger, as were she and Benjamin. She was very aware that friendship between gangsters meant nothing if one thought the other was double-crossing them. 'Mr Harel, please contact the

Barker twins and instruct them to guard the bike shop. Have Ned escort Cyril here. Tell him to bring all the betting slips and the money. I will give it to Mr Maynard and any winning bets that are over the odds, we will pay the difference.'

'But that could be a small fortune! We have no idea what odds Cyril has given out or to how many people. It's a huge risk, Varvara.'

'It is better to pay money than be shot, no?'

'I, erm, suppose so but I don't think Miss Garrett will be pleased.'

'No, I don't think she will, but this is Cyril's fault. We are just cleaning up his mess.'

Benjamin nodded and got on the telephone whilst Varvara hoped it wouldn't come down to any blood being spilt. Yet she'd been around people like David Maynard long enough to know that money was worth more to men like him than a life was.

An hour later, with Cyril and Ned tucked away in the back room, Varvara saw a dark car pull up outside. 'Here we go,' she told Benjamin and waited at her desk as Gwyneth showed David Maynard into the office. His driver waited in the car. She thought this was a healthy sign.

Varvara rose to her feet to greet the man but he didn't look pleased to be there. She was immediately struck by how young he looked, and though she didn't like men, she acknowledged his good looks. 'Good day, Mr Maynard. I am Varvara, pleased to meet you,' she said. She thought the fear in her voice showed and she wasn't nearly as composed as Miss Garrett would be. It was one thing to play boss, but now realised she was out of her depth.

'So, Miss Garrett has left a Russian tart in charge. Well she's either original or very misguided.'

'I know why you are here and can I firstly apologise for the inconvenience and assure you that Miss Garrett will be furious when she returns and discovers the terrible mistake Cyril has made.'

'As I thought, you lot are going to deny knowing anything about what your man was up to. You were hoping you'd get away with it and cash in. How unfortunate for you that I stumbled on your little scheme.'

'Honestly, I can assure you, Mr Maynard, we were as much in the dark about Cyril's activities as you were. In fact, you probably knew about it before we did.'

'Honestly... did a tart just say to me, *honestly*? Don't make me laugh. Actually, I've been thinking on my way over here and I don't reckon this is Miss Garrett's style. I wouldn't be surprised if you lot hatched this without her knowing to make a quick buck the minute her back is turned? When the cat's away, the mice will play. Is that it, eh? Did you think you could get one over on her *and* me?'

'No, Mr Maynard, no! I would protect Miss Garrett with my own life. I'd never deceive her. Never!'

'Well, she talks with some passion, what about you, Jew boy?'

'I, erm, err...'

'I want to know what you're proposing to do about it? And it had better be good because I don't want to leave a bloody mess in Miss Garrett's office.'

'Actually, we have all the bets and monies here... for you. And we will pay out the difference on the winnings that were offered higher than your odds.'

'I don't think so. I'll take the bets but you will be paying out every penny of all the wins, not just the difference. Cheeky fuckers, but it was a nice try.'

'But... but we won't have the money from the losing bets to cover the pay-outs.'

'Your lookout, not mine. Unless you'd like to do it another way but I don't suppose either of you want your faces rearranged?'

'No, Mr Maynard. Thank you, I will accept your generous offer.'

'And what are you going to do about this Cyril bloke? The one you say stitched you up? I mean, if it was one of my blokes there'd be no question about getting rid of him... for good.'

'Yes, Mr Maynard, I'll see to it.'

'Fair enough. I'm sure Miss Garrett will be happy with the way you've handled things in her absence. You can tell her from me that if she's got a problem with any of this, to come and see me.'

Varvara glanced across at Benjamin as David Maynard collected up the bets and left without bidding them goodbye.

'Phew,' Varvara said and steadied herself on Georgina's desk. 'I thought for a moment that he was going to kill us.'

'Yes, me too. But what about Cyril? Maynard expects us to get rid of him.'

'Then it will be done.'

'You can't... How?'

'Shoot him.'

'NO!'

'Why?'

'Because, err...err...'

'Everyone who works for Miss Garrett must know their place,' Varvara interrupted. 'Cyril must die. I will see to it.'

'Wait... please, Varvara... what would Miss Garrett do? She's a compassionate woman. I'm sure she'd give Cyril another chance.'

'No, I do not think so. Do you have a silencer on your gun?'

'I don't have a gun. You're not going to kill him here?'

'Yes, it is convenient. We will need another layer of wet concrete for the cellar.'

'No, Varvara. I'm having nothing to do with this.'

'Go, then. You have not the stomach.'

Benjamin pulled on his jacket and picked up his briefcase. 'You're making a terrible mistake,' he said as he walked out of the door. 'And Miss Garrett won't thank you for this.'

'I think she will,' Varvara called after him. 'I think she'll thank me very much.'

26

Georgina sat ringside in the crowded hall. This was billed as the biggest fight anyone had seen in a very long time and men had turned out in their droves, jostling for a better viewing position.

Georgina's heart pounded so loudly she was sure it could be heard over the cacophony of men's voices. Then she spotted Mabel, Kevin Kelly's wife, edging her way between the ring and the seating area, heading in her direction. Georgina could tell from the way she was dressed that it had to be Mabel. Her clothes looked very much like the reception room in Kevin's house – over the top and distasteful, though the height of fashion. From the cut of her long gown, with billowing sleeves and a large neck bow, Georgina could tell the dress was imported from New York and hadn't been knocked up on the sewing machine from a Simplicity pattern. Unlike her own. Mary next door did a great job of creating suitable work dresses for her, but the woman was limited in skills and her clothes lacked detail.

'Miss Garrett, I've been really looking forward to meeting you. I've heard so much about you. My goodness, you really are as beautiful as they say. Oh, I'm Mrs Kelly, you can call me Mabel. Shall I call you Georgina? After all, we're friends now. You must be so nervous about this fight. He's your husband, isn't he? I hear he's a gypsy. That must be exciting. I've never met a gypsy before. Will I meet your husband after the fight? Do you think he will win? Of course, I'll be cheering him on but I don't think Kevin will like me to. Oh my, listen to me babbling on; whatever must you think of me? Not to worry, Kevin's always telling me I talk too much.'

'Yes, you do,' Kevin said as he came to stand beside his wife.

Georgina was glad to see him. His presence had at least momentarily shut up Mabel.

'Miss Garrett, you've met my wife then?'

'Yes, good evening, Mr Kelly.'

'I hope your man is prepared for a pasting. Mine is in peak condition. But whatever the outcome, it will be a fair fight. Look at this crowd, a good earner too, for the winner.'

'Quite,' Georgina answered, feeling sick to her stomach.

'You don't look too happy. I'm surprised. I heard fighting is right up your street.'

'It is, Mr Kelly, but not when it's my husband in the ring.'

'Ah, don't worry. He's a hard bloke, one of the best, which is why I wanted him to fight my man. He can take a few good punches and it won't kill him. But, hey, don't you go jumping in that ring with your handbag swinging, will you?' Kevin said and chuckled.

'There's no fear of that happening,' Georgina answered. 'Lash is more than capable of fighting his own battles.'

'Come on, Mabel, we best take our seats before the fight starts. Good luck, Miss Garrett and may the best man win.'

Georgina watched as he walked away, shaking men's hands as he went and clearly lapping up the adoration for him in the room. Then the referee climbed through the ropes and Georgina looked around for Lash. She'd seen him minutes earlier and could still taste his kiss on her lips. She'd gone over it a thousand times in her mind and still couldn't believe she'd allowed them to get into this position.

She saw Lash coming through the crowds and inadvertently jumped to her feet. A few men applauded him but, as expected, most booed. Lash locked eyes with her as he climbed into the ring and she mouthed the words, 'I love you.'

Then the opposition appeared and the crowd broke into rapturous cheers. Kevin looked across to her and she saw the confidence in his eyes. He was so sure his man would win but she prayed he'd underestimated Lash.

The bell rang and both boxers met in the middle of the floor. Lash threw the first punch and missed. He threw another but missed again. A third, fourth and then a fifth, none of them connecting. Georgina twisted her mother's wedding ring. She knew boxing. She understood the moves and the tactics. This man was trying to wear Lash down. He was coaxing Lash to do all the work, hoping Lash would tire. The crowd jeered at every punch Lash attempted to land and Georgina saw Kevin Kelly smirk.

The bell rang and both boxers retreated to their corners. 'Tell Lash to conserve his energy. Tell him to step back, let him come to him,' Georgina told Johnny and pushed him to his feet. 'Go on, tell him,' she urged but it was too late and the bell rang again.

This time, Lash came out fiercer than before and as a quick left jab missed, his right upper cut caught the man's jaw. He jabbed him again with his left twice and then a right to the side of his head. The man dropped to his knees and the referee began to count. At three, he got back on his feet and charged at Lash. Lash did well defending himself but as he backed away, Georgina shouted, 'NO,' when she saw he was trapped against the ropes.

Two hard knocks sent Lash's head flicking sideways but he suddenly came back and punched his opponent across the ring. After several blows to the head, the undefeated champion crouched down and held his fists over his face. The referee pulled Lash away and the champ came back at him, but Lash unleashed a tremendous amount of energy that knocked the man to the floor. Again, the referee began to count and Georgina willed him to stay down. But he slowly climbed to his feet again and then the bell rang for the end of round two.

By round six, Georgina thought they were more or less equally matched but she could see Lash was losing momentum. She'd noticed Kevin elbow Mabel in the ribs when she'd talked of supporting Lash, and now the woman sat quietly, her face grim. Her eyes fell on Kevin. He didn't appear concerned and he smiled snidely at her.

Georgina turned to look back at the ring. The noise from the crowd was almost deafening as Lash pummelled his opponent's face. Somehow, the man managed to stay on his feet and was only saved by the bell.

Johnny was waiting in Lash's corner and when round seven began, he came back to sit beside Georgina and told her, 'Lash said he's got this. That bloke is going down in this round.'

Georgina nodded. She hoped with every part of her body and soul that Lash was right. She saw her husband swing a punch. It was a good one and connected with the man's eye socket, but he punched back and then she saw blood shoot out from Lash's mouth as his body turned sideways and followed his head towards the floor. He landed with his back to her. She couldn't see how badly injured he was and she jumped to her feet again. Johnny grabbed her arm. 'It's all right, he'll get back up.'

Georgina took her seat and willed her husband to move. The referee had started counting. 'Come on, Lash, come on,' she urged.

He was on all fours now and she could see he seemed dizzy, yet somehow he pulled himself up on the ropes. She prayed for the bell but it didn't come. Instead, Lash's opponent punched him again and this time Georgina could see her husband was unconscious before his face hit the floor. But something wasn't right. She knew Lash could take harder hits than the punch she'd seen thrown at him. It didn't make sense that he'd be out cold. Unless Lash's opponent was playing dirty and he had something in his glove.

There was no time to think about that now. Her husband was lying motionless. She once again jumped to her feet and ran towards the ropes. Johnny tugged her back and then she heard the referee declare Lash out. It was over. Lash had lost but right now that didn't matter. She had to be sure he wasn't badly hurt. Crowds suddenly filled the ring. The champion had been lifted onto shoulders and was being paraded as everyone cheered. She couldn't see Lash and felt herself being shoved and pushed. Johnny wrapped his arm over her shoulder and pulled her out of the throng.

'Come on, I saw them stretcher him out. He'll be in the back getting seen to,' he said and led her through a door.

Georgina glanced over her shoulder. Victor was right behind them. Kevin Kelly was nowhere to be seen.

'Where is he? Where's Lash?' Johnny asked two men guarding a closed door.

They didn't answer.

Victor came from behind and pushed one of them against the wall and held him by his throat. Johnny asked again.

Georgina heard a voice from behind and spun round to see Kevin Kelly stood with several armed men.

'Your husband is receiving the medical attention he requires, Miss Garrett.'

'I want to see him,' she demanded.

'That won't be possible until you give me the diamonds, as agreed.'

'I said I'd give you the diamonds if Lash lost. And he wouldn't have if you hadn't cheated!'

'I don't know what you mean, Miss Garrett.'

'Come off it. Lash would have won but your man had something in his gloves.'

'Yeah, his fists and you can't prove otherwise. Now, where are the diamonds?'

'I don't have them with me.'

'When you do, you can have your husband back.'

'Nothing was agreed about you keeping him from me.'

'Emm, we didn't cover the finer details, did we?' Kevin said and paused to take a long draw on his cigarette. 'I'll be looking after Lash for the foreseeable, and once you have given me the diamonds, I'll give you back your husband. A fair exchange.'

'You can't do that!'

'I can and I am. It's obvious you haven't got them with you, so I'll give you three days, Miss Garrett. You have three days and if I don't have the diamonds in my hand by then, Lash will be swimming in the Mersey with a lump of concrete attached to him. I hope he's a better swimmer than he is a boxer,' Kevin said and laughed. 'Have a safe journey home,' he added and walked away.

Georgina went to chase after him but Johnny and Victor both grabbed her.

'No, Miss Garrett, you can't. He'll kill you and then Lash. You've got to do it his way.'

'Yeah, well, we'll see about that,' she spat, but had no idea how she was going to get her husband back in one piece.

Dulcie tutted to herself, disappointed that her son hadn't stuck to his promise to Georgina and had again succumbed to the perils of the booze. But at least he'd come home full of apologies.

'It's the last time, Mum, I swear. I promise I won't drink again. I need the karzy,' he said as he stumbled towards the door. ''Ere, Mum, I've heard there's a load of tenement blocks being built near the park and they've got privies on the balcony. Fancy that.'

'Yeah, fancy that, indeed. And as for you not drinking, I'll believe it when I see it,' Dulcie snapped. 'Get yourself some bread and dripping. You need something to soak it up.'

Jack came back from the toilet but she could see he hadn't taken her advice about the food.

'I told you to make yourself something to eat.'

'I ain't hungry.'

'I don't suppose you are. You're too bloated with beer. Gawd help me when that girl moves out.'

Jack belched loudly and flopped back on the sofa. 'Georgina moving out?' he asked.

'She's a married woman, Jack, and her small bedroom ain't no good for the two of them. It'll only be a matter of time and she'll be in her own place.'

'My George, all grown up,' Jack said and hiccupped.

'She ain't your George. She hates being called that.'

'She'll always be my little girl.'

'Yes, she will and it's about bleedin' time you started behaving like a good father instead of an old drunk.'

'It was one mistake, Mum. I told you, I won't drink again.'

'I've heard it all before, Jack. And I'm warning you... once Georgina has left home, I won't be so tolerant with your behaviour. You either get yourself sober or get out of my house. I wouldn't have let me husband come home in your state so I certainly ain't gonna put up with it from you.'

Jack's eyebrows rose as his head bobbed. 'I never knew my dad but you put up with it from Percy. He was always drunk.'

'But that's where you're wrong, Jack. I never put up with it from Percy.'

'Come off it, Mum, he spent the last years of his life pissed.'

'Yes, and I got rid of him when I'd had enough.'

'What you on about? Percy went missing.'

'No, he didn't. I know exactly where he is.'

'You're joking? Why ain't you said nothing before? Where is he?'

Jack's interest was piqued and he seemed to have sobered up. Dulcie wished now that she'd kept her big mouth shut because she knew her son wouldn't let it go. But she couldn't tell him the truth. Percy had been the only father Jack had known and though he'd been drunk in his later years, before the onset of the alcoholism, he'd been a good stepdad.

'Take no notice of me, Son. I just always suspected Percy had gone off and shacked up with another woman somewhere. I doubt he's even alive now. Probably drunk himself into an early grave. And if you ain't careful, you'll do the same.'

'Leave off, Mum. I told you I won't drink again so stop bloody nagging.'

Good, her back-tracking about Percy had worked. And anyway, Jack was probably too inebriated to even remember the conversation.

'Try sticking to your word this time. Lash's family are gonna be in Battersea this weekend and Georgina wants us to meet them all. But look at the state of you. You're a bleedin' disgrace and should be ashamed of yourself. I raised you better than this, Jack. Sort yourself out, please, Son.'

'For Christ's sake, no wonder Percy fucked off! You could chew the hind legs orf a donkey.'

'How dare you speak to me like that! Let me tell you something. Georgina's gonna come home and ask me how you've been. If I tell her you've been pissing all your money up the wall again, she's already said she won't give you any more. How do you like that, eh? You'd have to get off your slovenly arse and earn your own keep.'

'I can graft, better than most of the blokes round here.'

'I know you can, Jack. You've always been a good grafter and provided well for us. That's why it's hard to stomach seeing you like this. Sissy wouldn't have liked it.'

Jack dropped his head and Dulcie knew that mentioning his dead wife would hit a raw nerve.

'I miss her, Mum.'

'I'm sure you do. I still miss your father. That never goes away. But you promised Sissy that you'd look after Georgina. Just because she's got herself a husband now, it doesn't mean she doesn't need her dad.'

'You're right. I really mean it this time – no more booze.'

'Good. We'll keep this incident between ourselves but I ain't giving you any more chances. I'm going up to bed before you start snoring on the sofa. Night, Son.'

'Night and thanks, Mum. I needed that reminder.'

Dulcie pushed herself up and slowly climbed the stairs. She knew in her heart that Jack was a good man. He'd just got himself lost after seeing Georgina nearly die. At the time, it'd been hard on them all but Jack had taken it really badly. Bloody men, thought Dulcie. They were weak, all of them.

As she pulled back her covers and climbed into bed, she chuckled to herself. Her granddaughter was strong – stronger than any man she knew. Lash had taken on a whole world of trouble when he married her but he knew what he was getting himself into and went ahead regardless.

Dulcie closed her eyes and hoped Lash had won his fight tonight. She couldn't imagine the stick he'd receive from Georgina if he lost. The poor bloke. She smiled. As Georgina's husband, he had a lot to live up to and Gawd help him if he let her down.

27

Benjamin watched anxiously as Georgina paced the office floor. It was Saturday morning and she'd called an emergency meeting with him, Victor, Johnny and Varvara. He'd never seen her like this before, almost out of control, and it worried him.

'I say we should take Mr Kelly and put his body in the cellar with Cyril. The cementing hasn't been done yet. It would save having to relay the floor twice.'

Georgina stopped pacing and glared at Varvara. 'This isn't a joke. My husband's life is at risk here. Is that the best you can come up with? And as for killing Cyril, I'll deal with that one later. Right now, I need helpful, doable and constructive ideas.'

'But I wasn't joking, Miss Garrett.'

'Then unless you can come up with something that might actually work, I suggest you keep your fucking mouth shut!'

Varvara looked hurt, like a young child who'd had her lollipop taken from her. Benjamin swallowed hard. He didn't have any ideas, and even if he did, he'd be too nervous to say anything. The mood Georgina was in, she would likely bite his head off.

'Have you considered talking to Mr Maynard about the diamonds? Perhaps he'd sell them to you?' Victor suggested.

It sounded like a good idea but Benjamin knew there wasn't enough readily available cash to purchase several small diamonds.

'Thank you, Victor. It's nice to see that someone is *trying* to offer something positive. But no, that's out of the question. Unless I sold an asset, like the house in Clapham, we just don't have the money and anyway, there isn't time to sell anything.'

'You could ask Mr Kelly for an extension, to, you know, give you more time,' from Johnny.

'No. I won't have Lash held by the Pounders for any longer than need be. They could be doing anything to...' Georgina stopped and caught her breath.

It was clear she was trying to hold herself together and Benjamin felt so sad for her. He'd grown very fond of Georgina and her kind heart and quick tongue. He didn't understand how she'd managed to get herself ensnared in the Portland Pounders' web as she was normally far too clever to be trapped. But somehow it had happened and he could see her pain.

'What about you, Mr Harel. Any ideas?' Johnny asked.

All eyes were on Benjamin and he could feel himself getting clammy. 'I, err, erm...'

'Let's just fucking kill them all,' Varvara said under her breath, but they all heard her.

Georgina stormed towards the woman and slapped her across the cheek.

'I told you to keep your fucking mouth shut. I can't think clearly with you coming out with crap.'

'I'm sorry, Miss Garrett. I just want to help.'

'You can help by clearing off and getting out of my sight.'

'But…'

'PISS OFF!' Georgina screamed.

Varvara sloped quietly out of the office. Benjamin had little sympathy for her. He'd warned her not to kill Cyril and told her Miss Garrett wouldn't be happy. But Varvara hadn't listened and gone ahead regardless. Thankfully, she'd murdered him execution style and the man hadn't died a prolonged and torturous death. But, as he'd suspected, Georgina had been furious with her and Varvara was yet to discover how she'd be dealt with.

'Well, Benjamin. Any input from you?' Georgina asked.

'You should speak to Lash's family,' he suggested.

Georgina looked at him as though she was staring straight through him. He liked this response. She appeared to be deep in thought, which meant she was mulling the idea over and he was pleased she hadn't jumped down his throat.

After a while, she spoke. 'Yes, I should. Very good, Benjamin, very good.'

Benjamin pushed his glasses up his nose and wanted to smile but didn't. It wasn't an appropriate time to feel pleased with himself.

'That ain't 'alf bad, Mr Harel,' Johnny said.

'Victor, drive me there now. There's no time to waste,' Georgina said and grabbed her handbag before leaving.

Benjamin glanced out of the window as she sped off with Johnny and Victor. The door opened again and Varvara came in.

'What are they doing?' she asked.

'They've gone to speak to Lash's family.'

'And this will be good, no?'

'Yes… I think it is,' Benjamin answered and hoped it was.

Varvara went to turn away but the telephone trilled on Georgina's desk. 'Should I answer it?' she asked.

Benjamin nodded uncertainly and waited tensely.

'Good morning, Mr Maynard,' Varvara said and looked across to Benjamin.

He was relieved it wasn't Kevin Kelly but he didn't trust Varvara to say the right thing. 'Give it here,' he mouthed urgently at her as he dashed towards Georgina's desk.

'Just one moment, Mr Maynard, I will pass the receiver to Mr Harel.'

Benjamin could see his hand shaking as he took the mouthpiece from Varvara. 'Hello, Mr Maynard, this is Benjamin Harel,' he said, trying to keep his voice steady.

The line was crackly but he could hear the anger in David Maynard's voice. 'Tell Miss Garrett she is to come and see me by the end of the day.'

'Yes, Mr Maynard, I'll be sure to pass…'

The line went dead before Benjamin had finished his sentence.

'What did he want?' Varvara asked.

'Miss Garrett.'

'I think she is more concerned with other matters for now.'

'Yes,' Benjamin replied and sat back at his own desk. He began to pack away his pens and papers and, though he hadn't been working long for Miss Garrett, he had enjoyed his time immensely. He hoped he wasn't reading too much into it, but after that telephone conversation, he feared his time with Miss Garrett may all be coming to an abrupt end. Not only did Georgina have the Portland Pounders to contend with, it also sounded like she'd made an enemy of David Maynard.

Molly let herself into Dulcie's house, hoping there'd be good news about Lash.

'I don't know what's going on, love,' Dulcie told her. 'She went to the office this morning and I haven't heard anything since.'

'Oh, blimey, Dulcie, it's a terrible worry. I've heard such nasty things about them Pounders.'

'I know. There won't be any negotiating with them. It'll be the diamonds in return for Lash and if she don't provide them with what they want, Lash will be coming home in a coffin.'

'Is there any way she can get the gems?'

'No. She's adamant David won't help.'

'Has she asked him?'

'She won't. Mind you, I don't think she's had any sleep. They drove through the night to get back and she went out again at the crack of dawn. I just hope she's keeping a calm head on her shoulders and thinking clearly.'

'Why won't she be up front with David, considering what's at risk?'

'If you think about it, it was David who got her into this position in the first place. She set up Charlie Chops to get knocked off by the Pounders as part of the deal with David in exchange for Victor and his car. The Pounders heard the set-up was her doing so put two and two together and come up with six. They're assuming it was her who stole their diamonds and she ain't told them otherwise 'cos she can't drop David in the shit. This is payback. She's lucky they offered her the fight instead of killing her.'

'I still don't see why she can't ask David for help?'

'If she does, she'll lose face with him and her reputation would be destroyed. Once that happens, she'll lose control of the business. And anyhow, he doesn't seem the charitable type, so why would he hand over a small fortune? If anything, Georgina said she wouldn't be surprised if David would be glad to see Lash out of the picture.'

'Why?'

''Cos he wants her for himself.'

'So, even if she said stuff it to the business and went cap in hand to David, she doesn't think he'd help?'

'No. I'm afraid she's dug herself into a bloody big hole.'

'I wish there was something I could do to help. Mum's keeping an eye on Edward for me and Oppo said he'd be straight round after work, but what can we do?'

'Not much. Just be here for her, I suppose, and pray it don't go tits up.'

They heard a car pull up outside and Molly jumped up to look out of the window. 'It's Georgina,' she told Dulcie who was sat wringing her hands.

Georgina walked into the room looking fraught.

'What's happening, love?' Dulcie asked.

'I've been to see Lash's parents and told them everything.'

'They must be upset?'

'Yes, of course they are,' Georgina snapped, then took a deep breath and added, 'I'm sorry.'

'It's all right. Have you worked out what you're going to do?'

'Lash's dad told me to come home and sit tight. They would sort it and bring Lash home to me.'

'Do they know how dangerous the Pounders are?' Molly asked.

'Yes, but they said I must leave it to them.'

'What are they going to do?' Dulcie asked.

'I'm not entirely sure. Several family members were involved in the conversation and they were talking in their own language. I didn't understand most of it but Lash's mother told me the Pounders would be cursed and Lash would be safe.'

'What did she mean by that?' Molly questioned, unsure if curses even worked.

'I don't really know but I trust them. I don't have any other choice.'

'I think you've done the right thing, love. It's what Lash would have wanted you to do,' Dulcie said.

'Maybe. But this is all my fault. Ethel is dead and now Lash could be too.'

'Ethel's death wasn't your fault, Georgina,' Molly said softly.

'She's right, you should listen to Molly. And Lash's family will do everything in their power to get him back.'

'I know the saying about live by the sword and die by it, but it should be me, not Lash or Ethel.'

Before either woman could reply to Georgina, they heard a tap on the front door and Varvara's voice. When she walked into the room, Molly noticed Georgina look at Varvara scathingly and wondered what the Russian woman had done to annoy her friend.

'What do you want?' Georgina asked coldly.

'I have a message... from Mr Maynard. He said you are to see him before the end of the day.'

'Go back to the office.'

The door closed behind Varvara and Georgina moaned, 'This is all I need.'

'What do you think he wants?' Molly asked.

'I don't know. There was some trouble with Cyril taking bets yesterday. It could be something to do with that.'

Dulcie guffawed. 'He's a cheeky bugger, that Cyril. Did you pass on my regards to him?'

'Yes, Gran. But he's dead now.'

'Eh? Cyril, dead? When did that happen?' Dulcie asked.

'Yesterday. Varvara took it upon herself to dish out punishment. Before you say anything, I'll sort it but first I need to get Lash home.'

'Oh dear, I can imagine how Cyril's wife must be feeling.'

'Yes, me too but I've made sure she's getting a good pay-out. Trouble is, I can't give her his body to bury, not with a bullet in his head.'

Molly tried to block out the last of the conversation between Dulcie and Georgina. She found the subject matter far too upsetting and the way they casually discussed corpses unnerved her.

'I'd better get over to David Maynard before he pops a blood vessel and then I'm going to join Lash's family up to Liverpool.'

'But they told you to sit tight and they'd bring Lash to you,' Dulcie reminded Georgina.

'Yes, I know, Gran, but I can't sit here twiddling me thumbs. I need to do this.'

'I don't think you should,' Molly offered. 'Let them do it their way.'

Dulcie spoke again, 'You don't like not being in control, ain't that right, love?'

'I just want to make sure they get Lash.'

'They've said they will, so do as you've been told. I know it goes against the grain for you, but they'll have their own way of doing things and won't thank you for interfering.'

'I get that, Gran, but I'm only planning on tagging along.'

'No, Georgina. I'm putting my foot down now. You'll do as you've been told... for once.'

Molly's heart began to race as she waited for an explosive response from Georgina but her friend just nodded instead. It had been a long time since she'd seen Georgina so meek. She'd dropped her tough persona and Molly saw tears begin to well in her violet eyes. It was rare for her to cry. Molly could only recall one occasion and that had been after Georgina had been abused in a police station. Even then, her tears had been short-lived and quickly replaced with anger.

Molly went to her friend and pulled her close. As she wrapped her arms around Georgina, she felt her body stiffen. 'It'll be all right. They'll bring him home,' she said soothingly.

Georgina stepped back. 'Thanks,' she replied to Molly, her face hard again. 'But I don't need tea and sympathy yet. Lash is not dead. I know he's not dead. It sounds stupid but I'd *know* if he was. I'd feel it.'

Dulcie sat on the edge of her chair. 'Good girl. No need for weeping. Let the gypsies get on with doing their business and you concentrate on sorting out your own. Get yourself orf to that Maynard fella and see what he wants. Then, when you've done that, you can deal with that bloody Russian thing. Don't you let her get away with killing Cyril. He didn't deserve it.'

Georgina drew in a deep breath and held her head high. 'You're right, I've got work to do and Lash will be home soon.'

Georgina left and Molly flopped back onto the sofa, deep in thought. She hoped Jane would be well enough to leave hospital soon. As soon as Jane was released, Molly planned on leaving. She was glad she'd stayed until now, to be here when her friend needed her, but she didn't want to stay a minute longer than she had to. She loved Georgina but not the Wilcox business and her friend was too deeply entrenched in it now. Her dear sister, Ethel, had lost her young life and now Lash's was in danger. Who next? thought Molly.

She had to get away from this world of crooks, murderers and madmen. It was the only way she could protect her son.

'What do you think then?' Frank asked as he drained the last of his whisky.

'I ain't sure I'm ready,' Mickey replied.

They were sat in Frank's front room enjoying a late Sunday afternoon tipple with full stomachs after a roast dinner.

'We can't keep holding back, Mickey. She's going from strength to strength. From what I've heard, her gypo husband is in a bit of bother with the Portland Pounders. I don't know if it's related, but the gypsies arrived on Friday night and now they've buggered off again. I've never known them to set off so quickly. Something's going down, I'm sure of it. But you know what that lot are like. They don't trust us coppers. We can't get close.'

'He lost the fight then?'

'Yes. That's why I reckon we should act now. She's distracted. It's perfect timing.'

Mickey took a large swig of his drink. Him and Frank had always planned on expanding the Wilcox business, swallowing up David Maynard's and then working their way North, but Georgina Garrett had come along and stopped them in their tracks. Since then, Frank had kept close to her, sure that one day he and Mickey would get the opportunity to claim back what was already theirs. And now Frank seemed convinced that the time was right.

Mickey wasn't so sure. He wasn't bothered about the business. He couldn't care a less about taking over the Maynards. He just wanted out of this life and to take Georgina with him. But he knew he couldn't do it alone so went along with Frank's plans, for now. 'Have you managed to convince any of the blokes to come on side?'

'Knuckles is keen. He's not happy working for Maynard and wants to be back in Battersea. He's dropping by next week. I think he wants to see with his own eyes that you're alive and kicking.'

'Alive, yes but kicking is stretching it a bit.'

'And Stephen. He walked out when Garrett took over. Said he'd never work for a woman. He's been doing a bit of work here and there to get by but he can't wait to join us. He laughed when I told him. Apparently he predicted this and told her so. When he left, he warned her she wouldn't last and he'd soon have his job back.'

'Huh, he weren't wrong,' Mickey said, faking a chuckle.

'Willy West won't go nowhere near, not after what that Russian tart did to him. But he said his son is up for it. He hates the bitch and reckons he could get his two brothers on board too.'

'That's a good start, Frank. But we'll need a lot more manpower.'

'I'm working on it but we've got enough for a takeover and then once we're back in the seat, the rest of the men will follow. They're not going to have any loyalty to a *woman* boss. I think they've got more self-respect than to answer to a tart.'

'Even Johnny Dymond?'

'No, he's gone soft in the head, but fuck him, Mickey. He can die with the bitch.'

Frank took their glasses into the kitchen and came back with them refilled. 'Cheers, to us. I'll get the blokes together and we'll put our plans into action. Two weeks, I think. Two weeks and then you'll be sat back at *your* desk and the world, as they say, will be our oyster.'

'Yeah, cheers,' Mickey said and raised his glass but he'd never liked oysters. He'd seen Billy Wilcox eat them once and thought they looked like giant bogies. No, oysters weren't for him and neither was the Wilcox business. Not anymore. His dreams had been shattered along with his spine and now the only thought that gave him any pleasure was his own death. And Georgina Garrett's.

As Frank chatted on about how they'd execute the takeover, Mickey's mind wandered to his own plans.

Knuckles was coming to see him. That was perfect. He knew the man was stupid and easily manipulated. Frank didn't realise but he'd just given Mickey everything he needed on a plate.

He smiled as he pictured the scene of his own death in his head and killing Georgina Garrett would be the last thing he'd ever do.

Later that evening, Georgina arrived home, exhausted. She'd managed to catch a couple of hours' sleep in the back of the car on the return from Liverpool, but it had been punctured with images of Lash being beaten. Since then she'd been on the go all day and the thought of going to bed alone tonight terrified her.

'Hello, love. How did it go?' her gran asked.

'Actually, David was very sympathetic. He appreciated me taking it on the chin and not bringing his name into it.'

'I should think so to! Did he offer you the diamonds?'

'No. He said he would have sold them to me if he had them but they've already been shifted.'

'That's convenient for him. So he gets off scot-free with robbing the Pounders and quids in whilst you're left to deal with them.'

'Yep, that's pretty much it.'

'Do you believe he's sold them?'

'I dunno, Gran. Possibly. I doubt it though. I can't see him getting rid of them so quickly, not while they're hot. There's too much interest in them. I don't think anyone would touch them yet, not even Ezzy.'

'You've been a long time, what kept you?'

'He insisted on taking me for dinner. He said I looked like I needed it. To be honest, Gran, I hadn't even thought about food.'

'No, I don't suppose you had, but you've got to look after yourself.'

Georgina nodded, her mind void of any thought for herself.

'Molly and Oppo waited but I told them to get off home. They said they'd call back in tomorrow.'

'And what about my dad? Please don't tell me he's in the pub.'

'No, love. He's... he's gawn orf with Lash's family.'

'What?'

'He wanted to help. He's done the right thing and it's about time he started behaving like your father again.'

Georgina dropped onto the sofa, surprised but also appreciative of her dad's intervention. She understood that she couldn't have gone with the family. It was difficult enough to be a woman in charge in her world, but impossible in Lash's. Her dad riding alongside them was the next best thing.

'Why don't you try and get some rest, love?'

Georgina wanted to. She really did, but was put off by the thought of what she'd see when she closed her eyes. 'I'll just sit here, Gran,' she answered and watched the hands of the clock slowly turn.

It was going to be a long night. Georgina's eyes felt heavy and the hand of the clock had hardly moved. She was vaguely aware of her gran putting a blanket over her.

'Rest now, child,' she heard her gran say over the imagined cries of Lash, and she finally drifted off into a restless sleep.

28

Benjamin was surprised when Georgina had decided to go ahead with the usual Monday morning meeting with all the men. Johnny had offered to cancel for her but she insisted on business as usual. So, as the men began to arrive, Benjamin warned Varvara to expect some flak. Cyril had been a popular old man and Benjamin guessed word had already spread that she'd killed him. They wouldn't be happy about it and he thought they might even demand retribution from Georgina.

Benjamin looked up from his desk. The office had filled and he could feel the tense atmosphere. Some of the men were looking daggers at Varvara but she didn't seem concerned as she stood behind Georgina's desk, looking disdainfully back at them.

'I'll keep this brief today. You all know the situation with the Portland Pounders. Rest assured the matter is in hand and Lash will be returning to us today. Any questions?'

No-one spoke. Benjamin thought they were probably all glad they hadn't been roped in to help. No-one would want to willingly deal with the Pounders, especially working against them.

'Right, next on the agenda. The Maynards have a large shipment of silk coming in. Most of it will be unloaded on Commercial Street, not our patch, but there's plenty available so if you've got any buyers in the dress or scarf making industry, put in an order with Mr Harel. Obviously it's cheap 'cos it's nicked so be careful who you speak to. Moving on, I've heard Wayne is back and heading up the Vauxhall mob. So far, he's kept himself to himself but I expect he'll soon be pushing the boundaries. I want any sightings of him or his lot in Battersea reported straight back to me.

'And lastly, someone turned over the post office cart near the Latchmere baths. The police don't have any leads. I want to know who did this! Find them and bring them in. And when you're looking for them, put out a reminder that no jobs over the limit are to be done without my permission. You all know the limit and I want it known that it's only breached if I give it the go-ahead. And I take a cut. That's it, we're done.'

'What about Cyril?' one of the Barker twins asked and the other added, 'Ain't you gonna mention him?'

'Yeah, that fucking tart done him in,' Ned shouted.

Benjamin could see the men were agitated and hoped Georgina could calm them.

'Cyril broke the rules and cost the business a lot of money,' she said.

'Come off it, Miss Garrett. He's always taken dodgy bets, everyone knows it.'

'Yes, and I let him get away with it, but he got greedy and went too far.'

Benjamin couldn't see who shouted next but he heard a man call from the back, 'That don't warrant that fucking whore murdering him!'

'Are you gonna let her get away with it?' Ned asked.

'She needs stringing up,' the Barker twins said in unison.

'Do you lot think you're running the show now?' Georgina snapped and glared at them.

'No, Miss Garrett, but what she did ain't right,' Ned answered.

'I'm dealing with it, and how is none of your business. So I suggest you keep your mouths shut and your opinions to yourselves. Got it?'

Benjamin inwardly cringed. He didn't think Georgina was handling the edgy situation well but it wasn't any wonder considering she had the worry of Lash on her mind.

'It don't look like you're dealing with it. Look at her, stood there with that smug fucking look on her face,' Ned said.

Then her father's friend spoke. 'And where's old Cyril? In the cellar with Mr Wilcox? He should have had a proper burial.'

'If any of you think you can do a better job than me, come and have a go. Fill your boots. Anyone?'

The men looked at one another and then her father's friend spoke again. 'No, Miss Garrett. We weren't sure about you at first but you're all right, you are. We ain't never been so well off and you're fair, which is more than can be said for Billy or Mickey. But 'cos you're fair, we don't understand why you're letting that Russian bit get away with what she did. That's all. We just wanna know when you're gonna deal with it.'

Georgina hung her head and when she looked back up, her face had softened. 'I realise I haven't been here long but have I ever let you down?'

A unanimous, 'No,' echoed through the room.

'And I won't this time. I give you my word. Now, bugger off back to work. I've got more important things to be doing than stood here listening to you whinging bastards.'

This time, Benjamin saw a glimmer of a smile on her face and the men responded favourably. She'd won them over but she still had to be seen to punish Varvara and Benjamin pondered what action she'd take. He'd come to learn that in this criminal environment, life was cheap and could be taken away with a single thoughtless bullet. Varvara may look smug now but Benjamin thought she may die with that look forever frozen on her face.

Varvara had stood her ground and hadn't shown any regret for her actions. As far as she was concerned, Cyril had wronged Miss Garrett and she'd seen to his punishment. Even Mr Maynard had implied that Cyril should die. Admittedly, Georgina hadn't seemed pleased but Varvara assumed her angst was due to Lash being held by the Liverpool gang.

This information had pleased Varvara. She didn't like to see Georgina suffering but if the Portland Pounders killed Lash, she felt sure Georgina would get over it. After all, he was only a man. There were plenty more of them available to Georgina, many better than Lash and more suited to her boss's stature. Georgina may not realise it yet but Varvara thought she'd be better rid of her contemptible husband.

The office emptied and Varvara offered to fetch coffee. Miss Garrett ignored her. This hurt Varvara. Couldn't the woman see that she'd done what was needed? She'd killed the old man for *her*. She'd do anything for Georgina, anything at all. But now Varvara felt she was being repaid with disapproval. She hadn't wanted thanks or gratitude. Just acknowledgement. But it seemed Miss Garrett's disapproval was going to be extended to a punishment, if only to keep the rest of the disgusting men quiet. It wasn't fair but if her boss felt she deserved to be punished, then Varvara would readily accept whatever was thrown at her. At the end of the day, it couldn't be any worse than what Billy Wilcox had done to her when he'd cut off her finger. Yes, Miss Garrett was strong but Varvara didn't believe she was cruel.

Just then, Victor showed in PC Cunningham. Ha, Varvara thought, if anyone looked smug, it was him, flicking off a piece of fluff from his immaculate uniform and pulling out a chair as though he owned the place.

'Good day, Miss Garrett. I trust you are well?'

Varvara couldn't see Georgina's face but she imagined it would be adorned with a smile that didn't reach her beautiful eyes.

'I hear you've had a bit of bother with the Pounders?' he continued.

'It's in hand,' Georgina answered.

'The gypsies have gone to get back one of their own, have they?'

'As I said, it's in hand.'

'You won't be requiring my assistance then?'

'No, well, not on that matter but there is something I'd like to discuss with you.'

'Fire away,' PC Cunningham said and then laughed to himself. 'That's probably the wrong thing to say to you, isn't it?'

God, Varvara found him maddening. He wasn't funny and asked so many questions. But she was interested to hear what Georgina wanted to discuss with him.

'I have a very reliable source who's informed me that a hitman from Portsmouth is in the area and I'm his target. I'm not sure who he's working for, yet, but I've had eyes on him.'

'It's always a risk in your line of work. There'll always be someone wanting to have a pop at you. You know who this hitman is?'

'Yes. Oliver Reading. He's unlike any hitman I've ever heard of. This man's got class. He's been seen at the opera and partaking in tea at the Doncaster. My sources tell me that he's worked in America with the Mafia, and I won't, but I could name at least one very well-known target he's hit. I don't know why he's taken on the job to kill the likes of me, but he has.'

'And you have no idea who's hired him?'

'None. But it's someone with money who wants me out of the picture. It's not confirmed but word has it that I'm just the start of his campaign. Someone out there has got big ideas. Someone wants to take over all of London.'

This seemed to pique PC Cunningham's interest and he shifted to the edge of his chair and placed his helmet on Georgina's desk. 'I don't like the sound of this, Miss Garrett. It's going to lead to trouble.'

'I know, but if *I* arrange for him to be taken out of the picture, another hitman will be sent. You know how it works.'

'Yes, yes, I do. I can see we have a major problem on our hands. I mean, we don't want overly ambitious men upsetting the apple cart, do we?'

'No, we don't, PC Cunningham. Which is why I've come up with a possible solution that will keep my name out of it and, at the same time, find out who is behind this and give you the arrest of the century.'

'Go on, I'm all ears.'

'As I said, I've had eyes on him. I know where he's staying and his every move. He appears to be enjoying what London has to offer but he'll be making his move on me soon. He uses various aliases, even calling himself a Right Honourable, Sir, or Lord. To be fair, he's believable.'

'Lord, you say. Huh, I wouldn't be taken in by that.'

'I'm sure you wouldn't. You can take it as a fact that he keeps a record of each of his hits – names, places and times. I'm told he even has the bullet casings. We've seen him guarding a leather briefcase and he takes it with him everywhere. Inside is where you'll find your evidence.'

'You expect me to arrest him?'

'Of course. And then you can question him and get the name of who's hired him. He'll be leaving the Doncaster this evening and taking a taxi cab to dine alone at Simpson's in the Strand. It would be easy to intercept the taxi and make your outstanding arrest. You'd be killing two birds with one stone. I get him out of my hair and you'll undoubtedly receive a promotion and probably a commendation.'

All of this was news to Varvara and she was most disappointed that Miss Garrett hadn't shared it with her. After all, she was tasked with protecting the woman's life!

'I'm not sure, Miss Garrett. This isn't even in my area.'

'Oh, come on, PC Cunningham. Surely you're not going to let this opportunity pass you? You've been handed on a plate all the information you need, it would be a doddle – and think of the accolade.'

'Yes, it does sound straightforward enough. But if this Oliver Reading is as good as you say he is, wouldn't I be putting myself at risk?'

'Our observations show that he doesn't carry a gun. Well, not until he's on the job. You'd be arresting an unarmed man carrying evidence of multiple and worldwide murders. The only problem you'll have to contend with is getting him to reveal his true identity as he's bound to try and fob you off with some fancy title he's using. Look, if you ain't got the balls to see this through, then I'll speak to another of my connections in the Met and they can take all the credit.'

'Hang on, slow down. I didn't say I wouldn't do it.'

'So, you will?'

'Yes, but give me all the details again.'

Varvara listened as Miss Garrett confirmed the plan. She couldn't understand why Georgina would trust the stupid policeman to carry out such important work. Lives were at risk here – Georgina's life. And Varvara felt she was far more capable of ensuring the demise of Oliver Reading than PC Cunningham was. But she'd already antagonised her boss and though she desperately wanted to visit the Doncaster hotel and slit the throat of this man, she thought better of it and knew she had to toe the line. Miss Garrett sounded confident that she had the situation in hand and Varvara wasn't prepared to risk losing her job. She couldn't bear to be apart from Georgina – ever.

Molly was in a world of her own as she dried the breakfast dishes and flinched when she heard a hammering on the front door. Her mother was still in bed. Fear coursed through her veins as her mind raced with images of what monster was behind the door. She felt so alone and though Molly had never liked Knuckles, she now wished he was still in the house to protect her.

The knocking became louder and faster, which matched Molly's heartbeat. She quietly placed the plate and towel on the side, opened a drawer and picked up a large carving knife. Then, as she tried to hold back tears and with her hand shaking, she tiptoed to the hallway.

Again, there was furious knocking but then Molly heard a girl's voice calling, 'Molly... Molly... It's me, Colleen... Are you in there?'

She was so relieved to hear Colleen's Irish twang but then another fear struck her. Colleen was one of Mary's daughters, Dulcie's neighbour, and Georgina had been paying the girl to sit with her gran.

She rushed to open the door and was filled with dread when she saw Colleen's panicked and flushed face.

'Come quick, Molly, it's Dulcie. Me ma is with her but she's not good.'

'I'll be straight there. Just give me a minute to call Georgina,' Molly answered and went to the telephone.

When Georgina answered she gabbled out what she knew and told her to come home. She then grabbed Edward to put him in his pram and ran behind Colleen towards Dulcie's house.

When they arrived, Mary was stood in the street doorway, her expression grim.

'Is she... is she...' Molly tried to ask but couldn't speak the word.

'Yes, pet, she's gone. She's resting now and I hope she made her peace with the Lord.'

'It wasn't my fault,' Colleen began to cry. Her red hair streaked across her face and her green eyes pleaded with Molly. 'Please tell Georgina it wasn't my fault.'

'It's all right. Tell me what happened?' Molly said. The reality hadn't yet hit her and she felt as if she was functioning mechanically.

'No... no, I can't go in there!' Colleen screamed.

'Shush, it's all right, you don't have to,' Molly soothed, crouching down in front of the girl to gently hold her shoulders. 'You can tell me here.'

'She made me do some reading. She said if I wasn't going to school then I was to learn me three r's with her. I was sat on the floor by her legs and reading her the newspaper. I thought she'd fallen asleep. She looked like she was sleeping,' Colleen said and began bawling again.

'It's all right, you didn't do anything wrong at all and I promise to tell Georgina what a good girl you've been,' Molly said and stood up. She looked at Mary and asked, 'Do you want to take her indoors to yours?'

'No, I'll stay here. Colleen, get yourself inside and look after the bairns. Finish patching the bedroom floor for me,' then Mary turned back to Molly. 'The damn floorboards have rotted through but nothing that some stiff cardboard won't mend. Are you coming in, Molly?'

Molly gulped. She didn't want to. She'd seen her father's dead body but hadn't felt anything. This was different. This was Dulcie and she loved the woman like she'd been her own gran.

'It's not so scary, Molly. You can see the peace on her face. She died quietly, with no pain or disease and knowing she was loved. What a beautiful way for a soul to leave this world. Come, say goodbye.'

Mary helped Molly in with the pram. She left Edward in the hallway and tensed as Mary opened the front room door.

'Go on, pet, see for yourself.'

Molly slowly walked in with her eyes fixated on the armchair where Dulcie sat. Colleen was right, she did look as if she was sound asleep. A lump caught in her throat. She half expected Dulcie to open her eyes and say hello. To offer her a slice of cake. Or to tell her off. The woman had a fierce tongue and had scolded Molly on many occasions when she'd deserved it.

Molly moved closer and summoning up all her courage, she knelt down and took Dulcie's cold hand in her own. It felt strange. She could tell the woman wasn't there and hoped she was somewhere in heaven with Ethel. 'Oh, Dulcie,' she cried, 'Rest in peace, dear lady. Look out for my Ethel up there. Tell her how much I miss her and that I'll always love her.'

Tears rolled down Molly's cheeks now and as she placed Dulcie's hand back on the armchair, she thought about Georgina. This was going to break her heart. Dulcie was the matriarch of their small family and the only mother Georgina had ever really known. She wondered how her friend would deal with it. Grief could do strange things to people. She'd seen what it had done to Jane and now her own mother wasn't herself. And this was the last thing Georgina needed right now. With Lash held captive, she had enough to be dealing with. Georgina's shoulders were broad but Molly wondered how much more she could take before she tipped over the edge.

'No... wait... please,' Mary pleaded as she tried to stop Georgina on the doorstep.

Georgina could tell by the woman's sympathetic eyes that she was about to walk in on something devastating. She pushed open the front room door and burst in. Her gran was sleeping in her chair and Molly was knelt at her side, her face wet with tears.

'I'm so sorry, Georgina,' Molly whispered, 'she's passed away.'

Georgina couldn't bring her legs to work. She wanted to move closer to her gran but felt fixed to the spot. 'No... she can't be... you haven't checked properly...' she uttered.

'I'm afraid she is. She died peacefully in her sleep.'

'No, Molly, no... she's a deep sleeper, you know what she's like. I'll get her a blanket, her legs will be cold.'

Georgina spun on her heels and ran up the stairs. There, she grabbed a cover from her gran's bed, but suddenly gasped as an overwhelming pain felt as if it was cracking open her chest. Her throat constricted. She stepped back to lower herself onto the bed and pulled the blanket up to her face. It smelt of her gran. A comforting aroma, warm and safe. 'Oh, gran, please be sleeping. You can't die... you can't leave me...' she sobbed.

'There you are,' Mary said as she came into the room. 'I've made you a cup of tea with lots of sugar.'

Georgina looked up at her life-long neighbour. 'Is it true, Mary? Is me gran really dead?'

'Yes, pet, I'm sorry to say she is.'

Georgina grabbed at her chest and leant forward. 'It hurts so much, I don't think I can breathe,' she moaned as she tried to catch her breath.

'That'll be the shock and the pain of grief. Let it out, pet, let it all out. Tears will help to heal you.'

'No... I can't cry... I won't. My gran wouldn't want me to.'

'Yes she would. She wouldn't want you bottling up all your pain and making yourself ill, now, would she? No, she'd tell you to have a bloody good cry and then to get on with it. No moping. No being unhappy. You know what she was like.'

'Yes, I do. That's exactly what she would have said,' Georgina answered with affection.

'There you go. Come on downstairs now.'

'No... not yet. Just give me a few moments.'

Her neighbour gave Georgina's shoulder a quick rub and then pulled the door closed behind her as she left. Georgina stared at it, confused. She wasn't sure how she was supposed to feel or what she had to do next. Her father! Oh, God, he was going to come home to this! He'd only just sobered himself up and this could send him into the bottle again. But she couldn't think about that for now. Her dear, beloved gran, was sitting in a chair but she was dead and it seemed undignified. She should be in a bed. Georgina looked behind her at her gran's puffed-up pillows. This is where she should be, she thought, and left the blanket where she'd found it before walking out.

The front room door was open and as Georgina came downstairs, she could see her gran's legs. She felt that same pain in her chest again and the feeling of her throat tightening. Mary came into the hallway.

'Are you all right, pet? You don't look very well.'

'I... I'm fine.'

'You can't hold your pain in, and that's what's troubling you. You're fighting yourself, Georgina. You don't have to be strong at a time like this.'

'I know, thank you, Mary. Is Colleen all right? It must have been awful for her.'

'Aye, she's fine. It's you I'm worried about.'

Georgina took in a deep breath and pushed her shoulders back. 'I'm taking my gran to her bed.'

'No, Georgina, leave her be. I've called the doctor and he'll arrange for the funeral home to collect her.'

'How dare you!' Georgina snapped. 'My gran's not going anywhere... she's staying here... do you hear me?'

'I'm... I'm... sorry, pet... I was only trying to help.'

Georgina, stood halfway down the stairs and croaked, 'Sorry, Mary, and thank you for taking things in hand, but I would still like to take my gran to her bed. If you'll excuse me,' she said, and stepped past her.

In the front room, Georgina froze again. She couldn't bring herself to get any closer to her gran. Then she felt Molly's arm over her shoulder.

'Come on, give your gran a kiss goodbye. I think she'd like that.' Molly's voice was gentle as she tried to urge Georgina towards Dulcie.

'I can't... I can't do it. I can't say goodbye to her,' Georgina replied, emphatically shaking her head. 'I wish Lash was here.'

'I know you do. Why don't you go and sit in the kitchen?'

'No, I won't leave me gran alone.'

'I'll sit with her,' Mary said. 'She won't be alone.'

Georgina allowed Molly to lead her through to the kitchen. She felt guilty that she couldn't face her gran in death and yearned to feel the comfort of Lash's strong arms. 'Can you tell Victor to come in, please?'

Moments later, Victor stood in the kitchen doorway. He looked uncomfortable with the situation, and a man of few words, he offered Georgina a sympathetic smile.

'I need you to wait outside for my father. I expect he'll be back from Liverpool today. Don't allow him to come in to the house until I've spoken to him.'

Victor left and she was grateful that he didn't say much. Then Molly came back into the kitchen. 'I've called Benjamin and told him you won't be back in the office for a few days.'

'So much for The Maids of Battersea. We ain't as strong as we used to be, what with Jane in hospital, your mother hating me, and now my gran...' Georgina felt the consuming pain in her chest again and her throat tightening. She let out a small gasp. That gasp led to a long groan and that groan changed to a sob. She didn't recognise the noise that came from inside her but she knew it was her grief. She was vaguely aware of Molly fussing but she was wailing now, allowing her pain to flood out. 'I can't believe she's gone,' she cried and hung her head in her hands as tears streamed down her face. Her mind spun. She'd never hear her gran's reassuring voice or get a ticking off from her again. It didn't seem right. Dulcie wasn't old. She had bad bones but that was all. She shouldn't be dead and to leave so suddenly without a chance for Georgina to say goodbye ripped at her insides.

After a while her tears dried and her chest stopped hurting. She felt she could finally breathe again. Mary had been wise. She'd told her to let it out. She had, yet it hadn't taken away her sorrow. And the way she felt at the moment, she couldn't imagine this feeling of heartbreak ever leaving her.

29

The following morning, Georgina sat on the edge of her bed and twisted her mother's wedding ring. Her tears had dried but she'd spent most of the night crying. Thankfully, her dad had proved himself to be stronger than she thought he would be and had so far avoided turning to the bottle for solace.

He tapped lightly on her door.

'Come in,' she called.

Jack stuck his head round the door. 'The kettle's on if you fancy a cuppa,' he said.

'Thanks, Dad, I'll be down in a minute.'

He smiled lovingly at her before pulling the door closed again.

Georgina ran her fingers across her neatly made bed. She missed Lash and craved his love. It had been awful sleeping without him again, especially when she'd needed his comfort. But his family had taken him with them, promising to bring him home when he was recovered. Her father had spared her the details of how badly Lash had been hurt by the Pounders but she could tell it was awful.

And now she had no way of contacting him. She could only hope his family would return him soon.

Georgina made her way down to the kitchen and sat at the table. Her dad poured her a cup of hot tea and sat next to her. She looked down into her cup. The tea looked weak, almost transparent.

'I think I need more practice at brewing a decent cuppa,' Jack said.

Georgina half-heartedly smiled at him. She could feel her emotions bubbling to the surface again and tried to quell them.

'I expect you're missing Lash?' her dad asked.

'Yes,' she answered, unable to speak for fear of her pain overflowing again.

'He'll be back, love. And when he is, don't you go giving him a hard time for going off with his family. I know you.'

'I won't, Dad.'

'He didn't want to go. But, well, to tell you the truth, he wasn't in much of a fit state to argue with them. They'll take good care of him. It's their way, Georgina.'

'I know.'

'Cor, they're something else, they really are! You should have seen the way they went charging in. I don't suppose the docks have ever seen anything like it. Thirty-odd blokes on horseback must have been a sight to behold. It gave me a real sense of pride to be a part of it. You've married into something big, my girl. When you married Lash, you married his family too. You'll never be alone. Just you remember that.'

Georgina placed her hand gently on her stomach. There was no child in there yet but when the time came, her baby would be their blood. Lash's family's blood. She lived in a dangerous world and it gave her some reassurance to know that her child would always be protected, even if she wasn't around.

'Dad... about Gran's funeral...' Georgina began to say but was interrupted by a knock on the door.

'I'll get it,' Jack said as he scraped his seat back.

Moments later, Varvara stood awkwardly in the kitchen doorway.

'I'll leave you two to have a chat,' her dad said and closed the door.

'What do you want?' Georgina asked, her tone sharp. She still had to deal with the woman for murdering Cyril.

'I wanted to offer my condolences.'

'I see. Well you've done that now so you can leave.'

'But, Miss Garrett, please, allow me to perform my duties, especially at this sensitive time for you.'

'Varvara, just piss off. I know you mean well but I've got Victor here. What you did to Cyril was unacceptable and you will be dealt with... just not now.'

'I do not regret punishing Cyril for the error of his ways. But I understand that I must accept whatever punishment you see as fit.'

'Good. Now get out of my sight. With Lash away, I want you taking care of the brothels.'

'Yes, Miss Garrett, I will do that.'

'And, Varvara... DO NOT kill anyone.'

'Yes, Miss Garrett.'

'Go on then. You can go now.'

'Yes. Thank you, Miss Garrett,' Varvara answered and slowly turned to leave.

Georgina had the feeling that there was more the woman wanted to say and was grateful when she quietly left.

Her dad came back into the kitchen. 'Everything all right, love?'

'Yes, just business,' she answered. She knew her father didn't approve of brothels and thought he'd be horrified at some aspects of her work. Her gran had understood and supported everything she'd done. But Dulcie was gone now. And though her father had said she'd never be alone, Georgina felt lonely... and afraid. Just like she had when she'd been abused in the police station cell. That same feeling of dread. Of wanting the pain to stop and go away.

'Tell me what happened with Kevin Kelly.'

'I told ya, we went riding in and got Lash back.'

'Yes, but how? Did Kevin just hand him over, or what?'

'No, love, not quite. It took a bit of negotiating but you won't be hearing from the Pounders again.'

'Dad, you're not very good at this. I want to know all the details, everything.'

'Huh, you sound just like your gran. You women love a bit of gossip.'

'Tell me then.'

'Well, like I said, we went charging through the docks. All you could hear was the sound of the horses' hooves pounding the concrete. Like thunder. It drowned out the noise of the police bells. Men jumped into the water to get out the way. Sacks of flour went flying and women were running. We weren't stopping for nothing or no-one. Once we got to Kelly's place, it was surrounded. About forty-odd men with rifles and pistols stood between us and him. He was waiting on his doorstep, holding a glass in his hand like he didn't have a care in the world.'

'Yeah, I can picture him, the horrible git.'

'Next thing I know, half a dozen cop cars and horses have pulled up but Kelly waved his hand and they buggered off. He's got some clout up there. I don't mind telling you that I was worried at this point. I had no idea what was gonna happen next but we were outnumbered and the coppers were waiting at the far end of the dock for us.'

'Were Lash's lot armed?'

'Yeah, up to the hilt. Kelly's men were aiming at us and we were aiming back. I was thinking to meself, I hope no-one pulls a trigger. It would have been a bloodbath. Anyway, Kelly knocked back his drink and said he knew why we was there, then offered Lash's dad a drink. He refused it and demanded back his son. Kelly laughed, said he wanted his diamonds first and wasn't handing Lash over until he got them. Lash's dad jumped off his horse and stormed up to Kelly. I thought Kelly's men were gonna shoot him but Kelly told 'em to let him pass. I couldn't hear what was being said but I saw Kelly laugh in his face at first. Next thing I know, I looked behind and saw more men arriving, loads of them. They were marching towards the house carrying sticks and crowbars, all sorts of weapons. I nearly shit meself until the bloke on the horse next to me told me the Manchester side of the clan had arrived. He said the Irish lot would be coming soon too. Lash's dad gestured and three more blokes got off their horses and then I saw Lash being dragged out of the house by a couple of Kelly's men. The gypsies picked Lash up and his dad walked away. We rode off, back the way we'd come, past the coppers and out of Liverpool.'

'Do you know what Lash's dad and Kelly discussed?'

'Yeah, he told me later. He said he made it clear to Kelly that if Lash wasn't brought to him, every bleedin' gypsy from all four corners of the world would descend on Liverpool and rip him from limb to limb. I don't think Kelly believed him 'til he saw reinforcements turn up.'

'How do you know I won't be hearing from the Pounders again?'

'Because it was made clear that if Kelly or any of his men ever step foot in Battersea or if there was any retribution, Kelly would be killed.'

'He's not the sort of bloke to be put off by threats.'

'Georgina, you had to be there to believe it. I've never seen anything like it and I don't suppose Kelly has. I'm telling ya, that man knows his card is marked and now he's seen how many men he'd be up against, he ain't gonna risk taking on Lash's family. That means you and all. *You're* his family too. You're safe from Kelly.'

'So, apart from Lash, no-one was hurt?'

'Nope, thank Gawd. It would have been all-out war, not that I would have reckoned much on any of Kelly's blokes surviving. But it's over with now. Done. You've just got to sit tight and wait for your husband to come home.'

Georgina sighed with relief. She didn't whole-heartedly believe that it was the last she'd hear from Kevin Kelly, though it did sound like the man had been intimidated. At least for now, she had one less rival to deal with.

Mickey watched as Frank paced the room in anger.

'The bitch, she set me up,' he fumed.

'Why though? I don't get it,' Mickey asked, trying to fathom why Georgina would have Frank attempt to arrest Archibald Compton-Stapleford, a Lord to the Treasury of King George V's government. If it hadn't been so humiliating for Frank, Mickey would have seen the funny side.

'She's made me a laughing stock. My sergeant has already dragged me across the coals but the Met hasn't finished with me yet.'

'Will you lose your job over it?'

'I don't know, quite possibly. She's stitched me right up, good and proper.'

'She needs you on her side. I still don't get it. Why would she do it?' Mickey asked again.

'Christ knows. I've been racking my brains all morning. Maybe she's rumbled me, you know, found out me and you are family.'

'It's the only thing that makes any sense,' Mickey mused.

'I tell you, I've never been so embarrassed in my life. My name's a fucking joke in the station now. Fancy dragging in a top politician and accusing him of being an international hitman! When I couldn't find the so-called evidence in his briefcase, I took him in and demanded his bag be pulled apart at the seams. I'm fucking stupid... The official-looking papers he was carrying didn't even register with me. I was so focused on what I thought I'd find. Needless to say, Compton-Stapleford was none too pleased with his treatment. Fucking hell, Mickey, she's done me up like a kipper.'

'Can't you just ride it out? It'll pass and this time next week it'll be forgotten.'

'No. No, Mickey. This won't be forgotten. This will stick with my name for the rest of my years in the force. That's if I've even got a job this time next week,' Frank said and sat on the sofa. 'We're going to have to put our plans into action sooner than anticipated.'

'But I ain't ready, Frank.'

'You'll have to be. Garrett needs taking down before she gets any more powerful. Knuckles will be here in a minute. I've got to go back to the station so it'll be down to you to convince him. Tell him everything, Mickey. He'll jump on board, I'm sure of it.'

Mickey nodded. Yes, he had no doubt that Knuckles would want to be part of the Wilcox business if Georgina was out of the way. But Mickey had different plans now. He was still set on shooting Georgina but he had two bullets in his gun – one for her and the second one for his own head.

'I'll see you later. I'd better get back and face the music,' Frank said as he stood up and placed his policeman's helmet on his head.

'Yeah, see ya later and good luck.'

'I'm going to need more than luck to get me out of this. But thanks.'

The door closed behind Frank and Mickey sighed. He thought his cousin would be all right. After all, he had an exemplary police record and though he'd made a ridiculous error of judgement, it was a simple mistake and no-one had been harmed. At least, he hoped Frank's career would be secure because without the Wilcox business, Frank was going to need his job. And Mickey knew that Frank would never attempt to run the business alone, without him. But Mickey just couldn't face continuing his life as a cripple. Neither could he admit to Frank how he felt. He knew if he did, Frank would try to talk him out of his decision; but Mickey didn't want to change his mind.

A knock on the front door snapped him from his thoughts and Frank's wife showed Knuckles in.

'Hello, mate, good to see you,' Knuckles said as he fervently shook Mickey's hand.

His grip was so tight that Mickey felt his fingers were being crushed. 'Yeah, you too, Knuckles,' he replied.

'Soon as Frank told me what you and him have got in mind, I jacked it in with Maynard. I can't wait to see that Garrett slag get what's coming to her. I knew she wouldn't last long.'

'Well, you know me, Knuckles. This chair ain't gonna hold me back.'

'Yeah, good on ya. Frank said you'd fill me in on what we're gonna do.'

'That's right. But we've got a feeling that she's got wind of this so we've got to get on with it. You sure you're up for this?'

'Too right, I am. It ain't on, is it, Mickey? A woman running Billy's business. Fuck me, he'd be turning in his grave. And to top it all, he couldn't stand her. We have to get rid of her. It's the right thing to do.'

'Yeah, it is. And we're the right people to do it,' Mickey said and told Knuckles all about his and Frank's plans.

'Love it,' Knuckles said once Mickey had finished minutes later. 'So what do you need from me?'

'You've got a good relationship with Fanny Mipple. I need you to go to the house and get her grandson. Bring the baby here.'

'But she ain't going to hand over the baby to me. And what about Frank's missus?'

'Don't worry about her. She'll be about all day tomorrow. As for getting the child… gain her trust then take him.'

'I dunno, Mickey, Fanny's all right, I don't want to hurt her.'

'You don't have to. Just be nice to her then have it away on your toes when she ain't looking.'

'You ain't going to hurt the baby are you? That's Billy's baby.'

'I know that, Knuckles. No, of course I won't hurt him but it'll get Garrett here. You'll leave them this note. It's got instructions, see, saying how Georgina has to come alone or Edward will die. If we want her dead, we've got to get her away from Victor and that Russian whore.'

'I get it. That's fucking clever, Mickey. Then once you've killed her off, can I take the baby back to Fanny? She'll be fucking pissed off with me for taking Edward but she won't be sorry to see Miss Garrett gone.'

'Yeah, and it's just as Billy would have wanted,' Mickey answered though he really couldn't care less what happened to Edward.

'All right. Tomorrow at eleven, I'll give Fanny this letter and bring Edward here. Then we wait. Is that right?'

'That's right, Knuckles. We wait for Garrett to turn up and then I'll shoot her. Right between the fucking eyes.'

30

'Are you sure you don't mind looking after Edward?' Molly asked her mother as she pulled her coat on.

'I'm sure, though why you want to help the Garretts with Dulcie's funeral arrangements is beyond me. This family's seen enough of death just lately.'

'Because regardless of what you think about Georgina, she's still my best friend and she needs me.'

'That woman doesn't need anyone. She's nothing but a heartless cow.'

'Please, Mum, stop harping on about her. I'll be back as soon as I can.'

'Don't rush. I enjoy having my grandson for company.'

Molly pulled the door closed behind her and set off for Dulcie's house. She passed her old place where she'd been brought up. It hadn't changed and a new family were living in there now. She felt sorry for them as she remembered the freezing cold winters with no glass in the window and the long trek to the shared privy used by countless neighbours. She'd had a tough upbringing in dire poverty and with a father who mercilessly beat her mother. It felt like life had come on a long way since those sorry days and Molly could understand why her mother had become bitter. Just when things were on the up, Ethel's life had been snubbed out in the cruellest fashion.

She was soon outside Dulcie's and let herself in. 'It's me,' she called and found Georgina sat at the table in the kitchen.

'Hello, Molly, there's tea in the pot, but my dad made it and it's like cat's pee.'

Molly studied her friend's face. She could see Georgina had shed many tears but there was something different about her, though she couldn't put her finger on what. Resilience, maybe?

'I'm all right, thanks, I've just had one. How are you today?'

'Not bad, actually.'

'Good. Where's your dad?'

'He didn't say but I think he's gone to talk to the people about gran's funeral plan. You know what she was like about her penny plan. She paid into it for as long as I can remember so there should be a reasonable pay-out.'

'Has he... erm...'

'He hasn't had a drink.'

'Aw, that's great news.'

'Yeah, he's done well. Is Edward with your mum?'

'Yes. Keeps her mind off things.'

'How's Charlotte been?'

'The same little madam she always is,' Molly answered and rolled her eyes. 'I don't suppose you've heard anything from Lash?'

'No. And I won't. But he won't stay away for any longer than he has to. By the way, I've heard from the hospital and Jane's treatment is going well. The doctor said there's been significant improvement and she could be home in the next month.'

'That's good news. Is she allowed visitors yet?'

'Yes, but she's requested no-one sees her in there.'

'I can't say I blame her. Oppo will be pleased that Jane will be home soon. He's itching to get his farm idea off the ground. You'd think he'd be sick to the back teeth of vegetables after working in the greengrocers all his life but he's keen to start growing our own and making a living from it.'

'Good on him. And are you sure it's what you really want?'

'I think so. I know I have to get away from here, for Edward's sake. But Battersea is all I've ever known and... I'll miss you.'

'I'll miss you too. I can't imagine you as a farmer's wife but I think it'll suit you.'

'I hope so.'

Georgina drained the last of her tea and pulled a face. 'Yuk, that was cold. Anyway, I'm glad you're here because I need to start sorting my gran's things. Do you mind helping me?'

'That's why I'm here, to help. Whatever you want. Are you sure you're ready to do this? It doesn't have to be done today.'

'Yes. Yes, it does. I'm going to move into my gran's room and then my dad can have my room. It makes sense and it's what me gran would have told me to do.'

'Dulcie was a very practical woman.'

'Exactly. It's stupid me and Lash being cooped up in a small bed and my dad on the sofa. It's been years since he's had his own bed and room, bless him. I don't suppose there's any mad rush for me and Lash to find our own home now.'

'Sounds sensible. If you're sure you can face this, let's get started.'

Both women pushed their chairs back and then they heard the telephone trill. 'Bloody thing,' Georgina moaned. 'I wish I'd listened to me gran now and didn't have it installed here. It's probably Benjamin. There's only him and you that know the number.'

'And my mum,' Molly answered.

Georgina went to the hallway and answered the call. Molly could hear the one-sided conversation and flew into the hallway after her friend.

'Yes... yes, Fanny. We'll be straight there,' Georgina said and replaced the receiver.

Molly panicked as soon as she saw the look on Georgina's face. 'What's happened? Is it Edward?'

'We need to go, quickly,' Georgina answered and told Victor, 'Take me to Jane's house.'

'Tell me what's going on, Georgina. What's wrong with Edward?' Molly asked again as she ran from the house behind Georgina and jumped into the car.

'It'll be all right, Molly.'

'What will? Please tell me what my mum said,' Molly pleaded now and could feel tears pricking her eyes.

'I don't know exactly what's happened but your mum said Knuckles has got Edward.'

Molly gasped and felt her pulse racing. 'Knuckles? Where has he taken him? Why has Knuckles got Edward?'

'I don't know yet. Please, try and stay calm. Knuckles would never do anything to harm Edward.'

'You don't know that! Shit, shit, shit! I don't understand. Oh, my baby. My Edward. What's going on?'

Moments later, the car screeched to a stop outside Jane's house. Molly was out of the car first and through the front door, followed by Georgina then Victor. They found Fanny, on her knees, in the middle of the front room wailing and clutching a piece of paper to her chest.

'Where's Edward?' Molly asked frantically.

'He took him... I turned me back for a minute and he was gone... I trusted him. I trusted Knuckles. How could he do this to me?' Fanny cried.

'Who took him? Knuckles?' Georgina asked.

'Yes... look,' Fanny answered and held out the piece of paper.

Molly snatched it from her mother's hand and quickly read it, before crying in anguish, 'It says they're going to kill Edward.'

Georgina took the note from her and Molly felt she was in some sort of a daze. Her mother was still on the floor and bawling. Georgina was pacing. The colour had drained from Victor's face. And now the room began to spin. The next thing Molly became aware of was arms supporting her and she was led to the sofa. 'Edward...'

'Don't worry, Molly. I'll get him back safely. I promise,' Georgina said.

Her mother sprung to her feet and then began shouting in a high-pitched grating voice. 'You can't promise that! How dare you give Molly false hope. You promised Ethel would come home safely. Where is she, eh? Where's Ethel? She's dead... because of you.'

Georgina looked hurt as she looked from Fanny to Molly. 'I know that. I'm sorry. But I *will* bring Edward home.'

Molly hung her head. Her hands were clasped on her lap and she watched as tears fell from her eyes onto them.

Then her mother began talking scathingly again, aiming all her hatred at Georgina. 'Molly should have left when she wanted to, but she stayed because of *you*. And look what's happened now! I swear, Georgina, if anything happens to that baby, I'll kill you myself.'

'MUM! Please, you're not helping,' Molly cried. She then looked into Georgina's eyes. 'Bring my baby back to me. Do whatever you have to do but please, bring him home.'

'I will,' Georgina answered and Molly knew that her friend would do everything in her power to keep Edward from harm.

Varvara couldn't bear to be away from Georgina and had remained hidden from view outside her house. It had upset Varvara to see her boss grieving over Dulcie and it had cut even deeper when Miss Garrett had coldly dismissed her. Varvara longed to hold Georgina close and soothe her broken heart but she knew it wasn't possible. And with Lash away, there was no-one else to offer the woman comfort. The very least she could do was protect her, as she'd vowed to. Granted, Miss Garrett had Victor but Varvara didn't believe he'd truly give his life for her, not in the way Varvara knew she would willingly do.

SAM MICHAELS

Dulcie's front door flew open and Varvara covertly watched as Georgina, Molly and Victor jumped into the car and drove off at speed. She immediately sensed that something wasn't right and her heart began to pound. Impulsively, she gave chase, dashing along the road but she couldn't keep up with the speeding car and it turned a corner, out of sight.

Varvara carried on running, her teeth and fists clenched tight, and tried to think where they could be going. Queenstown Road, maybe? But Molly hadn't visited the premises since the day Varvara had seen her there with Billy Wilcox. No, she didn't think they'd be on their way there or to Livingstone Road. As she followed in the car's path and turned the corner, a few streets further down she spotted it outside Jane's house. Of course, that made sense. They'd be taking Molly home but why the rush? The ashen looks she'd seen on their faces indicated that something was dreadfully wrong.

Now breathless, Varvara stood on the other side of the road and watched the house. She was aware of a few strange looks from the local women but she was used to it now. These weren't the type of ladies who wore anything other than their washed-out ragged dresses and aprons. Unlike her, in a sleek trouser suit and high-buttoned white shirt. Varvara knew her look made her stand out, but she was proud of herself. Her clothes were the height of ladies' fashion but with a masculine touch. Coupled with her tall frame, she knew she looked strong and though the women of this street might stare, none dared to challenge her.

Varvara looked anxiously on, waiting for any sign of what was wrong. It felt like hours but just minutes later, the door opened again and Georgina emerged with Victor.

She saw them having words and then Georgina hurried off along the street alone, leaving Victor looking perplexed standing by the side of the car.

Varvara ran across the street. 'Where is Miss Garrett going?' she demanded to know.

'Knuckles has taken Edward. She's gone to get him back.'

'Why aren't you with her?'

'Mickey left Miss Garrett instructions to come alone or they'd kill the baby.'

'No… no, Victor. We must be with her.'

'She ordered me to wait here for her and look after Mrs Wilcox.'

'She cannot go alone. They will murder her. Where has she gone?'

'Varvara, if anything happens to the baby because you turn up there, Miss Garrett will go mad.'

'Tell me where she has gone,' Varvara demanded again, then softened her voice as she'd seen Georgina do on many occasions when winning her own way with men. 'Please, Victor. I will be very discreet but I have to help her. She will be walking into an ambush.'

'God, I shouldn't tell you – just don't let on that it came from me. Here's where to go,' Victor said and gave Varvara directions.

As she turned to walk away, Victor added, 'Don't let them kill her and be careful.'

Varvara had no intention of letting anyone kill Georgina and raced through the streets. She knew she wasn't far behind Georgina and hoped she wasn't too late.

When she found the house, Varvara thought it looked much nicer than where Georgina and Molly lived. This couldn't be Mickey's address, surely? But according to Victor, she was in the correct place. Her mind raced. Should she kick the door down and burst in? Knock and see what happened? Smash the window, cause a distraction? It was hard to know what was going on behind the clean net curtains and she wasn't sure what to do for the best. But she knew, the longer she hung around outside dithering, the more time it gave them to hurt Georgina.

Varvara felt under the back of her jacket. The small handgun that Miss Garrett had given her was tucked into the waistband of her trousers. She'd executed Cyril with the same gun. That had been easy. The man had whimpered and begged but she'd used one clean shot to his head. This was a very different situation. She'd never fired the gun at a moving target and hoped her aim would be good. After all, Georgina's life depended on it.

Without further hesitation, Varvara pulled out the gun and marched towards the front door. She hammered loudly and at the window to the side; she saw the net curtains move. Moments later the door opened just a crack and Varvara found herself looking down the barrel of a pistol. She couldn't see who was holding it but judging by the size of the hand, she assumed it was Knuckles.

'Drop your gun,' he growled, 'or I'll shoot you where you're standing.'

Yes, it was Knuckles. She recognised his voice. Varvara slowly crouched down and placed the gun on the floor in front of her. 'I am unarmed,' she said.

Knuckles pulled the door open a little wider and looked outside to make sure that she was alone. 'Right, you can stand up again now.'

In that moment, Varvara grabbed the gun, cocked the hammer and she reached out to fire. She heard a terrific bang. Knuckles had pulled his trigger first but she shot back. The door swung open and she saw him fall backwards as blood spread across his shirt. She'd hit him, somewhere near his heart.

Varvara ran past Knuckles and shouted Miss Garrett's name. She dashed through the first door and then stopped at the shocking sight. Mickey was holding the baby, a wicked leer on his face and a large knife in his hand. She saw a gun by his side too. Georgina was on the other side of the room, sitting grim-faced on a wooden stool.

'Don't move, Varvara.' Georgina said her words slowly. 'He'll cut the baby's throat.'

Varvara tried to think fast. If her aim was good and if she moved quickly, could she shoot Mickey before he had a chance to slice at the baby? No, she doubted it.

'Varvara, I wasn't expecting to see you here. I'm guessing one of those shots we heard has killed Knuckles?'

Varvara nodded, hardly daring to breathe.

'The great, useless lump,' Mickey said, as if he was talking about an old armchair. 'So it's just us now. Right, well, I can see how this will work. Varvara... slide your gun into the middle of the room, slowly... very slowly. And let me just remind you, one move out of either of you, and you can watch baby Edward bleed to death.'

Varvara looked at Georgina who quickly nodded. Then, as instructed, she pushed the gun across the paisley-patterned rug.

'Good. Now, Miss Garrett. Pick up the gun. Take your time. Don't give me any reason to hurt this child.'

Georgina did as she was told.

'Good. Now, Varvara, walk around the outside of the room and stand in the far corner over there,' Mickey said and pointed to the other side of the room.

Varvara kept her back to the wall and edged around until she was in position.

'You're doing as you're told, and it's about time too. Your pathetic game of playing boss is over, Georgina. It's time for the big boys to take control now.'

'Don't make me laugh,' she said scathingly. 'You're nothing, Mickey, and Billy Wilcox knew it too. Look at your face, burnt and scarred by Billy. And just because you gave him a bit of backchat. He left his mark on you to warn others. Branded you, like a cow. Yet you continued to lick his arse. *That's* pathetic, not me.'

'Shut up! You don't know what you're talking about.'

'Don't I? Do you know what we call you? Mickey the Matchstick. Yes, that's right... we've had a right laugh about you.'

'I'm warning you... shut your fucking mouth or I swear, I'll kill this baby right now.'

'What's wrong, Mickey? Don't you like hearing the truth?'

Varvara couldn't believe Miss Garrett was goading him. All the while Mickey had a knife to the baby's throat, he had the upper hand. It was typical of Georgina, Varvara thought, she wouldn't go down quietly.

'I've had enough of this. You can say your goodbyes to each other.'

Varvara wasn't sure how Mickey planned on taking them out at the same time but while Georgina had a gun, there was still hope.

'I don't want another word out of you. Georgina, point that gun at your Russian tart and shoot her. Don't disappoint me. You know what will happen to this baby if you do.'

Varvara now realised how Mickey planned on killing them both. She looked into Georgina's beautiful eyes and saw the hopelessness of the situation. She could see her boss didn't want to kill her, but understood there was no choice. Resigned to the fact it would be her life or Edward's, Varvara nodded her head.

Georgina stood with the gun outstretched and Varvara heard the click of it being prepared to fire. She knew it would be better to close her eyes but couldn't pull them away from Georgina's. She wanted Georgina's face to be the last thing she ever saw.

'I'm waiting,' Mickey said, mocking them.

'I can't... I can't do it,' Georgina said in a whisper.

'Fine, don't. But you can watch the baby die instead.'

'No,' Varvara screamed. 'Kill me, Miss Garrett. DO IT!'

Seconds later there was a deafening noise that reverberated off the four walls and Varvara fell to the floor. She didn't feel like she'd been shot, more like someone had punched her breast. As she stared up at the ceiling she thought she could hear the baby crying but her ears were ringing, muting all other sound. Her hand reached up and she felt a dampness on her chest. She looked at her palm. It was red with her own blood. Georgina had shot her but she was still breathing. Only just, but she wasn't dead yet. She crooked her head and tried to lift it off the floor, but then another loud noise pierced the ringing in her ears. She wasn't sure if this was a part of dying or if another shot had been fired. Then she saw Georgina on the floor. Had Mickey killed her?

Varvara's head slumped back down and she struggled to pull air into her lungs. This was it. It was over. She coughed. It hurt. She could taste blood in her mouth. She closed her eyes and pictured Georgina smiling at her. She tried to reach out her hand to touch Georgina but she was too far away. As her life ebbed away and her blood seeped onto the varnished floorboards, Varvara knew it was over. Mickey, had won and Varvara hoped he'd spare the life of the baby.

Georgina heard a third gunshot and opened her eyes. She looked across to Mickey. There wasn't much left of the side of his head. She saw Edward on the floor, kicking his legs out as he bawled. The loud noises must have terrified him. She glanced around the room. There was nobody else there, so who had shot Mickey? Were they still in the house?

Her head was pounding but she pushed herself up. The bullet had grazed her temple and she'd bashed her head when she'd fallen. She reached for the stool and stumbled as she climbed to her feet. Her nose twitched at the smell of acetone in the room. The aroma of the cordite hung in her nostrils.

Feeling dazed, Georgina touched her sore and bleeding head where the bullet had scraped and tried to pull herself together. Whoever had shot Mickey could gun her down at any moment. She staggered over to the baby and dropped to her knees to examine him. Relief washed over her at the absence of any obvious injuries. Then, still fearing that someone would burst into the room and shoot her, she gathered Edward in her arms.

'Shush, little one, it's all right,' she whispered in his ear as she climbed back on her feet. That's when she noticed the framed photograph on the mantel. PC Frank Cunningham, smiling on his wedding day. They were in a policeman's house and dead bodies littered the floor. She had to get out and fast but how had this happened? She saw Mickey's gun was lying on the floor by the side of his chair and briefly closed her eyes as she tried to recall the events of the last few minutes.

He'd aimed his gun at her and fired. She clearly remembered that. Then the other shot. The one that had blown Mickey's head apart. Where had that come from? She hadn't fired it and she was sure Varvara hadn't. Could Mickey have blown out his own brains? It was the only answer that made any sense.

Georgina held Edward close to her chest and hurried across the room to where Varvara was lying in a pool of her own blood. It had been a horrendous decision, Varvara or the baby, but Edward had to come first. She'd aimed the shot to one side, hoping she wouldn't hit any vital organs, and when Varvara suddenly spluttered Georgina dropped to her knees beside her. It had worked. Varvara was alive. 'I'm going to get help, Varvara. Please, hold on... you'll be fine.'

Varvara's eyes slowly opened and fluttered before she focused on Georgina.

'Did you hear me, Varvara? I'm going to make sure you get out of here.'

'No, it's too late,' Varvara whispered, her voice weak.

'Hang on, Varvara, please... Fight. Live.'

'I'm sorry,' she whispered and coughed again. More blood trickled from her mouth.

Georgina could see the agony in Varvara's face. 'Please don't give up,' she begged but knew it was too late.

'Miss Garrett...'

Georgina lowered her head to Varvara's face so she could hear her dying words. She felt Varvara clench her hand a little tighter.

Then Varvara husked, 'I love you. I've always loved you.'

Georgina quickly sat upright, shocked. She had no idea that Varvara had feelings for her. She looked down into her watery eyes. 'I know,' she lied as a tear slipped down her cheek. 'And I thank you for loving me. No-one could have asked for a sweeter love,' she said, and leaned back down to gently kiss Varvara's cheek.

She felt her hand go limp in her own and Varvara's head rolled to one side. She was gone but at least Georgina had been able to offer some small amount of comfort in her last moments. 'You were a courageous woman, Varvara. Thank you. Rest in peace, dear lady,' she said softly.

As Edward's crying intensified, Georgina heard the distinctive sound of police bells drawing closer. She had to think quickly. The law was speeding towards her and if they found her here, it would look as though she'd committed mass murder. She glanced out of the window. A crowd had gathered outside. Georgina made a run for the back door and slipped out, hoping that none of the neighbours would spot her.

With Edward pulled in to her chest, she was soon near the familiar streets of home and satisfied that she was in the clear. 'Your mum is going to be pleased to see you,' she cooed in Edward's ear.

When Georgina saw Victor running towards them, she felt the urge to burst out crying but held herself together. It wouldn't do for the men to see her in tears. She had to keep up her tough image but really, she could feel herself crumbling inside. Varvara was dead, but thankfully she'd saved Edward. If she hadn't she knew she'd never have been able to forgive herself – and neither would Molly.

31

Two days later, Molly still wouldn't allow Edward out of her sight. It was the day of Dulcie's funeral and though her child was fretful, she had every intention of taking him to the church.

'Have you noticed Edward seems very quiet?' Molly asked her mum.

Fanny turned round from the kitchen sink, her hands covered in suds and wiped her forearm across her brow. 'Yes, but he's probably traumatised, the poor mite.'

'Yes, probably, but thank goodness he's too young to remember any of it. Anyway, where's Ivy? I thought she was coming with us today.'

'She is. She's gone over to see Georgina. She's like a bloody whirlwind, that girl. Don't sit still for a minute. No wonder she's so skinny.'

Molly smiled. Yes, Ivy certainly had an abundance of energy and a charm about her that lit up the room. 'I've grown quite fond of her.'

'Me too,' Fanny said. 'I'll miss her when we move on. Talking of which, I hope this episode with Edward has brought you to your senses.'

'What do you mean?' Molly asked.

'Well, please don't tell me you're still going to wait for Jane to get out of hospital?'

'She'll be home soon,' Molly answered defensively and wished her mum would drop the subject.

'I'm home now,' Jane said.

Molly threw her head round at the sound of Jane's voice and saw her standing in the kitchen doorway. She looked well and her face and blonde hair were immaculately styled.

'Jane! How... what... Oh, my goodness, you're home!' Molly gushed, delighted to see the woman.

'Yes, you're not seeing things. Any tea in the pot? I'm parched.'

'Of course, sit down and make yourself at home,' Fanny said with a small laugh.

'Why didn't you tell us you was coming back today? We would have arranged something nice for you,' Molly said.

Jane placed her small suitcase on the floor against the wall and pulled out a chair to sit down before she spoke. 'I wasn't sure myself, not until this morning. Then I made my mind up, discharged myself and called for a taxi cab. Oh, by the way, he's outside. I, erm, don't have any money on me.'

'It's fine. Mum, take some from my purse and pay him, please.'

Fanny dried her hands and went outside.

'You discharged yourself. Is that wise? I mean, are you well enough?'

'Yes, Molly, I'm perfectly well now. You see, Sally came to see me last week and it made me realise how much my girls need me. I know they've been fine with my sister, but I'm fully recovered now and don't intend on ever leaving them again. I've arranged for them to come home, just as soon as I've settled in.'

'That's lovely, Jane. I'm sure they would have missed you. Probably just as well they're not here today as it's Dulcie's funeral.'

'Dulcie's dead?'

'Yes, I'm afraid so. She passed away peacefully in her sleep.'

'Oh, poor Georgina! How's she taken it?'

'Better than I expected. But you never know with her. It might all just be a brave face. I'm sorry you haven't come home to better news.'

'Well, whilst I've been cocooned in the hospital, life goes on. I suppose I've quite a lot of catching up to do?'

'Yes, I'll tell you this quickly but please don't mention it in front of Mum, but Ethel has died too. She was killed.'

'Molly, I'm so sorry,' Jane said.

'Shush, here she comes,' Molly whispered urgently.

'Fanny, be a dear and take this case upstairs for me.'

'Does Georgina know you're home?' Molly asked.

'Probably. I should imagine the doctors have called her. Now, let me have a look at my gorgeous grandson,' Jane said as she reached out her arms towards him.

Molly flinched and held him closer. But then reminded herself that Jane was better and passed the baby over, though she didn't feel comfortable doing so.

'It's all right, Molly. I know what you must be thinking. I wasn't myself, I can see that now. But, it's amazing what a bit of rest can do.'

Molly relaxed a little. Jane did seem to be fine and she hoped it would last.

'So, I gather you have plans to move out now that I'm home?'

'Too right and not a day too soon,' Fanny said when she came back into the kitchen.

'Yes. We're moving out of Battersea, to the country in Kent. Oppo wants to buy a small farm. It'll be lovely for Edward to grow up in clean air.'

'Oppo?' Jane asked.

'Yes, we're, erm, going to get married.'

'Oh! I didn't see that coming. Congratulations.'

'Thank you. Do you feel up to coming to the funeral today?'

'Yes, of course. I've had my run-ins with Dulcie in the past but I've always had the greatest respect for her. She'll be sorely missed. I'd better go upstairs and get changed into something more suitable.'

'Can you just give me a minute to clear your bedroom? I've been sleeping in there but I'll bunk in with me mum for now.'

'Great,' Fanny remarked. 'You're such a bleedin' fidget.'

'By the sound of it, it won't be for long, Fanny, and just think of the room you'll have when you move to the country. You must be looking forward to it.'

'Can't bloody wait,' Fanny said.

'I hope I'll be receiving plenty of invites to come and visit. I wouldn't want to miss out on seeing this little chap growing up.'

'You don't need an invite, Jane. You'd be more than welcome any time you'd like,' Molly said though she secretly hoped it wouldn't be too often. She had nothing against Jane but seeing her again reminded her of Billy and all the carnage he'd caused. 'If you'll excuse me, I'll get your room ready now.'

SAM MICHAELS

Molly took Edward back and went upstairs where she sat on the edge of Jane's bed and sighed deeply. Everything was changing and it felt like life was moving too fast for her to keep up. With Jane home, there was no reason for her not to move away and she wanted to. For Edward's sake. But the thought terrified her. What if she wasn't happy living in the countryside? Was she sure she really loved Oppo? She liked him. She always had. But was it enough to marry him? Or was she just latching on to him because he offered her a way out of Battersea for the safety of Edward?

She'd mulled over the questions in her head night after night. When she was away from Oppo, the doubts crept in and niggled her. But they soon vanished and were replaced with butterflies in her stomach whenever she saw him. Is that how love was? She wasn't sure.

Edward gurgled and she gazed down at his cute button nose and wisps of fine hair. This was a love she was sure of. All-consuming and unconditional. Nothing compared to it. But with Oppo, she remained to be convinced.

Georgina stood at her gran's graveside and felt her father slip his hand into hers.

'Time to go, sweetheart,' he said as the mourners began to disperse.

'Just give me a minute, please, Dad.'

'I'll be waiting in the car.'

'And take Victor with you. I need a few moments alone.'

Jack walked off quietly and Georgina looked all around. She was finally alone. It felt like she hadn't had a moment to herself and she had something important to tell her gran.

'I don't know if I ever told you, Gran, but I love you.' The tears she'd held in all through the service began to slip out now and she wished she hadn't mistakenly left her clutch bag in the car. It held her gun but also her handkerchief. She wiped her wet cheek with the back of her hand, then continued, 'Who'd have thought it, eh? Me, running the Wilcox business. I don't know if I could have done it without you. You made me what I am today and to be honest, Gran, without you, I'm terrified! I hope you'll be watching over me. Anyway, I wanted you to know how much I'll miss you.'

'Very fucking touching.'

Georgina spun on her heel and saw PC Cunningham stood just a couple of feet behind her and he was mockingly applauding her.

'What are you doing here?' she asked as she dashed away her tears.

'I'd like to say I've come to pay my respects to your grandmother but I'd be lying. I hope she rots in fucking hell.'

'You bastard,' Georgina said scathingly and stepped towards him with her fists clenched.

Frank pulled out a gun and held it pointed at her. 'Whoa. Slow down, Miss Garrett. You don't want to be striking an officer of the law. You'd end up in very deep trouble... or dead.'

Georgina looked over Frank's shoulder but the car with Victor and her father was obscured from view by a large bush.

'That's right. It's just me and you,' he said, 'and your dead gran.'

'What do you want, Cunningham?'

'Your fucking head served up on a platter like John the Baptist.'

'Go on, take it,' Georgina coaxed and took another step forward.

'I intend to and do you know why?'

'I'm pretty sure it's got something to do with your cousin's brains splattered up the wall in your sitting room. Bet your wife was pleased to be cleaning up the mess. Did his blood stain the rug?'

'You're not normal. No woman could do the things you do. You're disgusting and I pity your husband.'

'Save your pity for Mickey. He took his own life. Shot himself in the head.'

Frank looked shocked. 'No, he wouldn't do that. You're a lying bitch.'

'Am I? Why would I lie? If he hadn't killed himself, I would have done it for him. So I've no reason to fib about it. Your cousin led you a right merry dance. He let you think the two of you had big ambitions yet all the while, he knew exactly what he was going to do. See, Frank, you're not that clever, are you? And I've heard your colleagues at the station are still laughing about the fiasco with Compton-Stapleford. I've got to be honest, Frank, I never really believed you'd try and arrest him. Clearly, I should have known how ridiculously bloody thick you are, and you proved it.'

This appeared to rile Frank. His face turned bright red and he looked at her with hatred. But before he could pull the trigger, Georgina leapt forward and knocked Frank's arm heavily with her own. This sent the gun flying from Frank's hand and it landed several feet away.

'Now it's just you and me,' she said.

Frank spat on the ground before swinging his arm to throw a punch. Georgina dodged his fist but he quickly threw another. Again, he missed and she could see he was infuriated now. His arms were flailing as he uncontrollably vented his anger at her. Each time he swung at her, she expertly moved and he missed. Eventually, spent, his arms fell to his sides and he gasped for breath.

'I should have shot you in the back,' he said in between breaths.

'Yes, if you wanted to kill me, that's what you should have done. But you can't, can you? That's why you needed Mickey. You ain't got it in you to kill cold-blooded and you know it. You thought you'd be the brains and Mickey would do the dirty work. Turns out you ain't got the brains either.'

Frank looked down at the grass, deflated. She'd succeeded in humiliating him.

'Are you finished? Only, my dad's waiting to go home.'

'For now. But you'll be in that grave with your grandmother soon enough, mark my words.'

'Only if you can find someone to do it for you. Good luck,' she said flippantly and walked past him.

Georgina picked up the gun and considered turning it on Frank. But killing a copper was risky, especially in a public place in broad daylight. No, she wasn't prepared to swing on the end of a rope for the life of PC Cunningham. He wasn't worth it, so she marched towards the car and resisted the temptation to look over her shoulder. Her nonchalance would show him that he was nothing to her.

But then she felt a force in her back that sent her stumbling forwards and she saw the ground rushing up towards her.

Frank had pushed her and now she found herself lying face down in the grass. She'd dropped the gun and saw it was just inches from her grasp. As she reached for it, Frank's large boots kicked it away. She rolled to her side and was about to get up when Frank kicked her hard in the stomach. Georgina cried out in pain, and though winded, she tried again to climb to her feet. Frank hit her again, with the butt of his truncheon this time. The strength of the blow went deep and she screamed out in agony and doubled over, clutching her aching guts.

'I hope you're damaged good and proper. I hope your stomach falls out of you and you're left barren. We could do without any more Garretts on the streets,' Frank growled with spite and she saw him turn his back and walk off.

Georgina tried to catch her breath but the pain was intense. She managed to crawl along the grass until she was in sight of the car.

'Help,' she called weakly but there was no way they would hear her. Then she saw her father running towards her with Victor just behind. They'd seen her, thank goodness, but Cunningham had gone. She'd get him. In her own time, she'd get him all right.

32

It had been three weeks since Georgina's gran had been buried and Benjamin hoped the surprise party he'd planned for her birthday would lift her spirits. She'd understandably been down in the dumps and he wanted to see her beautiful smile again. The beating she'd taken from Cunningham had put her out of action for a couple of days but she'd quickly returned to work. Benjamin admired his boss. Nothing slowed her down and, though she lacked formal education, he found her to be more intelligent than any of his peers. But he also feared her and tonight he prayed she wouldn't be annoyed at him for being a part of this surprise.

Down in The Penthouse Club, he was adding the finishing touches and unbeknown to his boss, he had the ultimate gift ready and waiting for her.

'Ivy, have you double-checked there's enough champagne?' he asked as he walked behind the bar.

'Yes, Mr Harel, now stop flapping. Everything is shipshape and ready for Miss G.'

'Good girl. And you're sure she doesn't suspect anything?'

'I think she's been too sad lately to notice much at all. This is just what she needs.'

'Oh, Ivy, I do hope so. What if she doesn't like it? I'm getting so nervous.'

'It's too late for any nerves. Your first guests have arrived.'

Benjamin looked to where Ivy had indicated and saw the two Mrs Wilcoxes arrive along with Oppo. He rushed to meet them and was surprised to notice Molly Wilcox had brought the baby with her.

'Hello, Benjamin. I know we're a bit early but we thought we'd come down and see if you needed any help,' Jane Wilcox said as her eyes flitted round the club. 'It looks wonderful, you've done a fabulous job.'

'Thank you. I think everything is in hand. The band is just setting up. Please, make yourselves comfortable and Ivy will fetch you drinks. Mrs Mipple isn't with you?'

'No, my mum decided to stay at home. She wasn't in the mood for a party,' Molly answered.

'I can't wait to see Georgina's face when she walks in. I think this was a brilliant idea, Benjamin. Just what she needs.'

'Thank you, though I can't take all the credit, but I do hope you're right.'

'Don't look so worried,' Jane said. 'Molly's right. This is just what Georgina needs to drag her out of the doldrums and wait until she sees her big finale! If that doesn't put a smile back on her face, then nothing will.'

'Well, everything is all lined up and ready to go. If you'll excuse me, there's more guests arriving,' Benjamin said and bowed before dashing off to greet Mr Maynard and his entourage.

'Mr Harel, your invite was a pleasant surprise.'

'Thank you for coming. I know Miss Garrett and yourself have a special relationship. It wouldn't have been a surprise party without *all* of her friends attending.'

'I noticed you have extra security on the door but I've left a couple of my men there too. Just in case. And they're out of sight. Georgina won't suspect a thing.'

'Thank you. Please, take a table. Ivy will see to you.'

David Maynard was closely followed by Mary and her husband, Dulcie's next-door neighbours. Benjamin thought the woman looked very out of place but had clearly made an effort to look nice though her long dress looked like something she'd bought during Victoria's reign on the throne. She appeared to be quite intimidated by her surroundings so he immediately sent a bottle of bubbly to her table and hoped a few glasses would help her relax.

Jack arrived next but quickly declined the offer of champagne.

'No, thanks, Benjamin. I'd like to keep a clear head to see my girl enjoying her birthday. It was good of you to arrange this. I've never thrown a party for her. It's not been a day I've felt like celebrating before, you know, on account of Georgina's mum dying on this day. But that was a long time ago now. Did you know Georgina was born on the day war was declared?'

'Yes, Mr Garrett, and given Miss Garrett's character, I think it's very apt.'

'Yeah, you're not wrong there,' Jack replied with a small chuckle.

The club soon filled with an array of people who worked for and with Miss Garrett. As Benjamin looked around, he realised she had very few real friends yet everyone in the room held her in high regard. She'd destroyed many enemies on her journey to become the most revered woman in their part of London and had also gained the affection of those she'd helped. It wasn't something that Georgina made a big deal of, but Benjamin knew she'd assisted lots of the downtrodden women of Battersea and their gratitude was clear to see, especially amongst the battered women who'd been helped by The Maids of Battersea.

Johnny Dymond came through the doors, his face flushed. 'She's pulling up outside,' he told Benjamin who quickly took to the stage.

'Please, can we have absolute silence. She's here,' he said and could feel the excitement buzzing through the room like an electric current.

The lights were dimmed and everyone remained quiet. They waited. Any moment now, Georgina Garrett would walk through the doors. A last-minute fear ran through Benjamin's mind. He hoped being taken by surprise wouldn't cause her to pull out her pistol and fire!

Georgina didn't mind working on her birthday. After all, she didn't feel she had much to celebrate. Her gran was dead and Lash was still away with his family. Hardly cause for jubilation.

Victor pulled up outside The Penthouse Club. Benjamin had requested for her to come down tonight as they'd had a very unpleasant character causing problems. Georgina was looking forward to dealing with the man and wouldn't mind if she'd have to exert a bit of a heavy hand to get rid of him.

She climbed out of the car, acknowledged the doormen and made her way down to the club but noticed she couldn't hear the usual sound of muffled music and laughter floating up the stairs. 'What's the time, Victor?' she asked, wondering if it was earlier than she'd thought.

'Eight, on the dot, Miss Garrett.'

'It seems terribly quiet so why has Mr Harel got an extra man on the door? Is he expecting trouble that he hasn't told me about?'

'Not that I know of,' Victor answered.

'Stop,' Georgina told him.

They were halfway down the flight of stairs.

'Turn around and look at me.'

Victor did as he was told.

'I'm going to ask you again. Am I going to find trouble behind those doors?'

'No, Miss Garrett. Not that I know of.'

Georgina's eyes narrowed. 'You're lying to me, Victor. I can see you squirming,' she said as she reached inside her clutch bag and felt the cold metal of the gun as her fingers wrapped around it.

'No. No, Miss Garrett. I promise you, there's no trouble here.'

'Something's going on. I can feel it. And I know you. You're hiding something from me.'

'I'm not, please, Miss Garrett, you have to believe me.'

Victor never spoke much but she could tell by the way he was avoiding eye contact with her that he was keeping something from her. And one thing she'd learnt – she couldn't trust anyone.

SAM MICHAELS

Georgina pulled out her gun and pointed it at Victor. 'Put your hands above your head… slowly,' she said.

Victor took a deep breath and followed her instructions.

'No funny business. I don't want to use this, but you know I will if I have to. So, are you going to tell me what's going on?'

She saw Victor gulp. She knew it! There was something! Was he leading her into an ambush? And were Benjamin and Ivy held hostage or worse?

'You'd better tell me, or else,' she threatened.

'Shit. I'm not supposed to talk. Mr Harel and Johnny will be right pissed off with me.'

'Benjamin is involved?' Georgina asked, shocked. She'd have never thought he'd turn on her.

'Yes, it was his idea. Him and Johnny actually. They've arranged a birthday party for you. It's supposed to be a surprise.'

'Are you kidding me?'

'No. That's why it's so quiet. All your friends and family are waiting for you.'

A smile began to spread across Georgina's face. She could see Victor was telling her the truth yet here she was, waving a gun at him. 'I'm so sorry,' she said as she put it away.

'Don't let on that I told you,' Victor asked.

'No, I won't. I'll act surprised. Shit, Victor, sorry.'

'It's all right. I suppose I should be pleased that I got you this far before you became suspicious. Can we go in now?'

'Yes, and thank you. Hang on, let me put on my best astonished face. How's this?' Georgina asked and looked at Victor with her mouth agape.

'It'll pass muster,' he answered and led her down the rest of the stairs.

He opened the door and as they walked in, the lights went up and Georgina was met with an array of voices shouting, 'Surprise,' and paper party streamers floated through the air towards her. She glanced around and pretended to be amazed.

'Happy birthday, Miss Garrett,' Benjamin beamed as he handed her a glass of champagne, though she noticed he was shaking.

'Thank you. Did you do all this?'

'Erm, some of it.'

'It's wonderful. Thank you,' she told him and hoped she'd put his fears at rest.

Her father hugged her and Georgina was pleased to see he was sober. Her eyes roamed the club, noting all the familiar faces. It was a shame her gran's was missing but Georgina felt sure she was there somewhere in spirit.

'You invited David Maynard?' she whispered to Benjamin.

'Was that a mistake?'

'No, not at all. I'm just surprised he came.'

'Georgina, happy birthday. This is from me and Oppo,' Molly said and handed her a wrapped box.

'Thank you. I can't believe you kept this a secret from me. To tell you the truth, I thought everyone had forgotten my birthday.'

'It wasn't easy and as if we'd forget. Come and say hello to Jane. She's busy trying to calm Edward down. I think the loud noise when we all shouted surprise has startled him.'

It probably had, Georgina thought. It wasn't that long ago when the poor baby had been petrified by the noise of gunfire. Georgina had been concerned that his ears may have been affected but so far, he hadn't shown any signs of lasting damage.

'I'll be over in a minute,' she told Molly. 'I just have to say hello to David.'

It took her several minutes to cross the room. Everyone wanted to give her their best wishes but eventually, she stood at David's table and he rose to his feet.

'This is for the birthday girl,' he said and handed her a gift.

'Thank you but you shouldn't have,' she replied and smiled at him.

'Open it, then.'

Georgina looked into his eyes and felt herself caught there again. Embarrassed, she quickly pulled her own away, worried that someone may recognise the attraction between them. She pulled at the white ribbon around the small velvet box and opened the lid, then gasped.

'Oh, David, this is too much,' she said as the sapphire earrings twinkled in the lights.

'Shut up, you silly cow, and try them on.'

'I can't. They're stunning but I can't accept them.'

'Come now, Georgina, you wouldn't want to hurt my feelings?'

'No, of course not.'

'Here, let me help you,' David said and pulled back her hair on one side. 'There you go, clip it on.'

Georgina felt his hand had gently brushed her cheek and found herself fighting against feelings she didn't want to emerge. She loved Lash. This, whatever it was with David

Maynard, wasn't right. She clipped one earring on and then the other.

'Beautiful,' David said as he studied her. 'But not as beautiful as you. They match your eyes.'

'Thank you. Have you, erm… er, have you got enough drinks?' she asked, stumbling over her words.

'Yes, we've been well looked after. Are you joining me?'

Benjamin appeared at her side and had found his Penthouse Club persona again, the one so different from the Benjamin in the office. 'Sorry to interrupt, but can I steal Miss Garrett away? We have a very special birthday treat for her.'

Georgina had never been so glad of an interruption. 'I'm in demand tonight.' She smiled at David. 'What's a girl to do?'

'Bring her back to me,' David told Benjamin.

Georgina felt Benjamin's hand under her arm and he led her towards the end of the bar. 'Sit here, and close your eyes. I'll tell you when to open them.'

'Oh, you're giving out the orders to me now, are you?' she said jokingly.

'Yes, and for once, do as you're told,' then he shouted, 'Drum roll, please.'

Georgina sat on the tall bar stool and closed her eyes. She expected he'd be bringing out a birthday cake and she wouldn't have been surprised if one of Benjamin's acts had jumped out of it.

'You can open your eyes now.'

Georgina blinked. There was no cake. No candles. She jumped down from the stool and felt tears begin to prick her eyes. 'Lash…' she said and fell into his open arms.

His lips were on hers and she could feel herself melting into him. 'I've missed you,' he husked into her ear.

'I've missed you too,' she whispered back. 'I can't believe you're in the club. I know you hate it.'

'I do, but I guessed you'd never expect me to be here so I asked Benjamin to arrange this party for you.'

A round of applause echoed round the room and she realised everyone was watching them. She pulled away from him and stood at his side with his arm around her waist. 'This has been the best birthday, ever. Thank you,' she shouted.

Glasses were raised and Ivy appeared with the cake Georgina had expected. As she blew out the candles, she noticed David slip out of the doors.

The cake sliced, toasts done and glasses refilled, Georgina couldn't wait to get Lash alone and dragged him past the stage and into the small dressing room. Here, he pushed her against the dressing table and cupped her face as he passionately kissed her. His hands roamed down her neck, over her breasts and then stopped on her stomach.

'I want to put a child in here,' he said and kissed her again.

Georgina now reached up to his face and held it in her hands as she looked into his dark eyes. 'Not yet, sorry, Lash,' she said and shook her head.

'When?'

'One day.'

'When you're ready. I'm sorry I wasn't here for you when your gran passed away.'

'It's all right. It wasn't your fault. My dad explained everything. Your family had to take you, I understand.'

'I should have been stronger, Georgina. You needed me. I'm so ashamed I left you alone to deal with it.'

'It's fine. I'm fine. Like I said, my dad explained everything.'

'I would have won that fight. They cheated.'

'I know. He had something in his glove.'

'Yes, he did. But you'll never have any trouble from the Portland Pounders again. They've had the pleasure of running into my family and not even Kevin Kelly is mad enough to bring my lot down on him again.'

'My dad said it was very impressive. I wish I'd been there.'

'I'm glad you wasn't.'

'Where did your family take you?'

'To Ireland. I've brought you back something. In that bag, over there.'

Georgina walked over to a brown pigskin bag in the corner of the room and crouched down to pull it open. 'Oh, my goodness,' she exclaimed as she peered at the wads of notes inside. 'Where did you get this much money from?'

'It doesn't matter where it came from. It's yours. Do whatever you want with it.'

'But, Lash, there's a small fortune here.'

'I know. It doesn't make up for leaving you alone all this time but it's good to feel like a man and bring home the bacon.'

Georgina stood up and turned to Lash. 'I'm the one who should be apologising, not you. I've been awful to you. I'm sorry for how I've made you feel.'

'You did what you had to do. I was under no false pretence when I took you for my wife. I'm proud of you and what you've achieved. You're like no other woman,

Georgina, and I wouldn't want to change you. But you have to let me be a man sometimes. Your husband.'

'I know and I will. Please tell me how you got your hands on this much cash.'

'Ha, a typical woman, you have to know everything.'

'Please, Lash, stop teasing me.'

'I robbed the National bank in Ireland. Just a small village branch. It was easy. The manager and his wife and children lived on the premises. No-one was hurt. Just the threat of violence was enough for the manager to open the safe. I'm clean away, Georgina.'

'Shit, Lash! Robbing banks! That's madness.'

'I know, but it was easy.'

'Well, what's done is done and to be honest, we need the money.'

'Is business not going well?'

'It's doing all right but I need money to buy a property. We have to leave Queenstown Road and I don't want to rent again. This is perfect timing. With this, I've got enough to pay Molly off and to buy a large house. Oh, Lash, I love you,' Georgina said and stepped back across the room and flung her arms around his neck.

'Do you want to stay at this party? I was thinking we could get away early and...' he said as he nuzzled her ear. Then stopped suddenly. 'These are new earrings. A gift?'

Georgina felt herself burning red. 'Yes. For my birthday. From David.'

'They're a very expensive gift from an associate.'

'Well, he's either a generous man or he's being flash.'

'Or he's trying to impress you. I bet he'll be gutted to hear I'm back.'

'Maybe,' Georgina answered, and recalled the disappointed expression on David's face as he'd left the club when he'd seen Lash.

Lash pulled her closer. 'I can't blame the man for wanting you for himself. But you're mine,' he said and kissed her again. 'I want to make love to you, Georgina. Would you like that?'

'Yes... yes, please,' she answered. 'And I can leave this party early. I'd much rather be naked with you.'

'You may not want a baby yet but we can have fun practising to make one,' he told her before kissing her again.

As Lash's tongue probed her mouth, she tried to dismiss the memory of Frank Cunningham kicking her stomach and his wishes for her to remain forever childless. She'd heard he'd lost his job but he hadn't yet paid for attacking her. And she couldn't tell Lash what had happened. She wanted her own retribution and she planned on getting it.

'Yes,' she answered Lash and rested her head on his shoulder. 'We can have lots and lots of practice.'

Georgina Garrett was at the top of her game. It had been hard work of late. A never-ending cycle of fighting for those she loved and battling for what she wanted. Now, with her husband home, her father sober, Molly content and Jane recovered, life at last felt good. Her gran had died but that was out of Georgina's control. She'd always miss Dulcie, but finally there was some peace and Georgina allowed herself to feel a glimmer of happiness. For now.

About the Author

SAM MICHAELS lives in Spain with her family and a plethora of animals. Having been writing for years, *Rivals* is her second novel.

Hello from Aria

We hope you enjoyed this book! If you did let us know,
we'd love to hear from you.

We are Aria, a dynamic digital-first fiction imprint from
award-winning independent publishers Head of Zeus.
At heart, we're committed to publishing fantastic
commercial fiction – from romance and sagas to crime,
thrillers and historical fiction. Visit us online and discover
a community of like-minded fiction fans!

We're also on the look out for tomorrow's superstar
authors. So, if you're a budding writer looking for
a publisher, we'd love to hear from you.
You can submit your book online at ariafiction.com/
we-want-read-your-book

You can find us at:
Email: aria@headofzeus.com
Website: www.ariafiction.com
Submissions: www.ariafiction.com/
we-want-read-your-book

[f] @ariafiction
[y] @Aria_Fiction
[o] @ariafiction